LIGHTNING

Also by
Dean R. Koontz

WATCHERS

STRANGERS

PHANTOMS

WHISPERS

THE VISION

NIGHT CHILLS

LIGHTNING

Dean R. Koontz

G. P. PUTNAM'S SONS
New York

G. P. Putnam's Sons
Publishers Since 1838
200 Madison Avenue
New York, NY 10016

Published simultaneously in Canada

Library of Congress Cataloging-in-Publication Data

Koontz, Dean R. (Dean Ray), date.
Lightning / Dean R. Koontz.
p. cm.
ISBN 0-399-13319-4
I. Title.
PS3561.O55L5 1988 87-21649
813'.54—dc19 CIP

Printed in the United States of America
6 7 8 9 10

To Greg and Joan Benford.
Sometimes I think that you're
the most interesting people
we know. Then I always take
two aspirin and lie down.
But the thought persists.

The wailing of the newborn infant
is mingled with the dirge for the dead.

—LUCRETIUS

I'm not afraid to die.
I just don't want to be there when it happens.

—WOODY ALLEN

Roller coaster:
1) a small gravity railroad . . . with steep inclines
that produce sudden, speedy plunges
for thrill-seeking passengers.

—THE RANDOM HOUSE DICTIONARY

Part One

LAURA

Being deeply loved by someone
gives you strength;
while loving someone deeply
gives you courage.

—LAO TZU

One

A CANDLE IN THE WIND

·1·

A storm struck on the night Laura Shane was born, and there was a strangeness about the weather that people would remember for years.

Wednesday, January 12, 1955, was frigid, gray, and somber. At twilight thick, fluffy snowflakes spiraled out of the low sky, and the people of Denver huddled in expectation of a Rocky Mountain blizzard. By ten o'clock that night, a bitterly cold gale blew in from the west, howling out of the mountain passes and shrieking down those rugged, wooded slopes. The snowflakes grew smaller, until they were as fine as sand, and they sounded as abrasive as sand, too, when the wind blew them across the windows of Dr. Paul Markwell's book-lined study.

Markwell slumped in the chair behind his desk, drinking Scotch to keep warm. The persistent chill that troubled him was not caused by a winter draft but by an internal frigidity of the mind and heart.

In the four years since his only child, Lenny, had died of polio, Markwell's drinking had gotten steadily worse. Now, though on call for emergencies at County Medical, he picked up the bottle and poured more Chivas Regal.

In the enlightened year of 1955, children were being inoculated with Dr. Jonas Salk's vaccine, and the day was near when no child would be paralyzed or die from poliomyelitis. But Lenny had been afflicted in 1951, a year before Salk tested the vaccine. The boy's respiratory muscles had been paralyzed, too, and the case had been complicated by bronchopneumonia. Lenny never had a chance.

From the mountains to the west, a low rumble echoed across the winter night, but at first Markwell thought nothing of it. He was so involved with his own enduring, bile-black grief that sometimes he was only subliminally aware of events that transpired around him.

A photograph of Lenny stood on his desk. Even after four years he was tortured by his son's smiling face. He should have put the photo away but instead left it in view because unceasing self-flagellation was his method of attempting to atone for his guilt.

None of Paul Markwell's colleagues were aware of his drinking problem. He never appeared to be drunk. The errors he made in the treatment of some patients had resulted in complications that might have arisen naturally and were not attributed to malpractice. But *he* knew that he had blundered, and self-loathing only induced him to drink more.

The rumbling came again. This time he recognized the thunder, but he still did not wonder about it.

The phone rang. The Scotch had left him numb and slow to react, so he did not pick up the receiver until the third ring. "Hello?"

"Dr. Markwell? Henry Yamatta." Yamatta, an intern at County Medical, sounded nervous. "One of your patients, Janet Shane, was just brought in by her husband. She's in labor. Fact is, they were delayed by the storm, so she was well along when they got here."

Markwell drank Scotch while he listened. Then, pleased to hear that his voice was not slurred, he asked, "She still in first stage?"

"Yes, but her labor pains are intense and unusually protracted for this point in the process. There's blood-tinged vaginal mucus—"

"That's to be expected."

Impatiently Yamatta said, "No, no. This isn't ordinary show."

Show, or blood-tainted vaginal mucus, was a reliable sign that labor was impending. However Yamatta had said Mrs. Shane was already well into labor. Markwell had blundered by suggesting that the intern was reporting ordinary show.

Yamatta said, "Not enough blood for hemorrhage, but something's wrong. Uterine inertia, obstruction of the pelvis, systemic disease—"

"I'd have noticed any physiological irregularity that would've made pregnancy dangerous," Markwell said sharply. But he knew that he might *not* have noticed . . . if he had been drunk. "Dr. Carlson's on duty tonight. If something goes wrong before I get there, he—"

"We've just had four accident victims brought in, two in bad shape. Carlson's hands are full. We need you, Dr. Markwell."

"I'm on my way. Twenty minutes."

Markwell hung up, finished his Scotch, and took a peppermint lozenge from his pocket. Since becoming a heavy drinker, he always carried mints. As he unwrapped the lozenge and popped it into his mouth, he left the study and went along the hall to the foyer closet.

He was drunk, and he was going to deliver a baby, and maybe he was going to botch it, which would mean the end of his career, the destruction of his reputation, but he did not care. In fact he anticipated that catastrophe with a perverse longing.

He was pulling on his overcoat when a peal of thunder rocked the night. The house reverberated with it.

He frowned and looked at the window beside the front door. Fine, dry snow swirled against the glass, briefly hung suspended as the wind held its breath, then swirled again. On a couple of other occasions over the years, he had heard thunder in a snowstorm, though always at the beginning, always soft and far away, nothing as menacing as this.

Lightning flashed, then again. Falling snow flickered queerly in the inconstant light, and the window was briefly transformed into a mirror in which Markwell saw his own haunted face. The subsequent crash of thunder was the loudest yet.

He opened the door and peered curiously at the turbulent night. The hard-driving wind hurled snow under the porch roof, drifting it against the front wall of the house. A fresh, two- or three-inch white mantle covered the lawn, and the windward boughs of the pine trees were flocked as well.

Lightning flared bright enough to sting Markwell's eyes. The thunderclap was so tremendous that it seemed to come not only from the sky but from the ground, too, as if heaven and earth were splitting open, announcing Armageddon. Two extended, overlapping, brilliant bolts seared the darkness. On all sides eerie silhouettes leaped, writhed, throbbed. The shadows of porch railings, balusters, trees, barren shrubs, and streetlamps were so weirdly distorted by every flash that Markwell's familiar world acquired the characteristics of a Surrealistic painting: the unearthly light illuminated common objects in such a way as to give them mutant forms, altering them disturbingly.

Disoriented by the blazing sky, thunder, wind, and billowing white curtains of the storm, Markwell abruptly *felt* drunk for the first time that night. He wondered how much of the bizarre electrical phenomenon was real and how much was alcohol-induced hallucination. He edged cautiously across the slippery porch to the head of the steps that led to the snow-covered front walk, and he leaned against a porch post, craning his head out to look up at the light-shattered heavens.

A chain of thunderbolts made the front lawn and street appear to jump repeatedly as if that scene were a length of motion picture film stuttering in a jammed projector. All color was burned out of the night, leaving only the dazzling white of the lightning, the starless sky, the sparkling white of snow, and ink-black shuddering shadows.

As he stared in awe and fear at the freakish celestial display, another jagged crack opened in the heavens. The earth-seeking tip of the hot bolt touched an iron streetlamp only sixty feet away, and Markwell cried out in fear. At the moment of contact the night became incandescent, and the glass panes in the lamp exploded. The clap of thunder vibrated in Markwell's teeth; the porch floor rattled. The cold air instantly reeked of ozone and hot iron.

Silence, stillness, and darkness returned.

Markwell had swallowed the peppermint.

Astonished neighbors appeared on their porches along the street. Or perhaps they were present throughout the tumult, and perhaps he saw them only when the comparative calm of an ordinary blizzard was restored. A few trudged through the snow to have a closer look at the stricken streetlamp, the iron crown of which appeared half melted. They called to one another and to Markwell, but he did not respond.

He had not been sobered by the terrifying exhibition. Afraid that neighbors would detect his drunkenness, he turned away from the porch steps and went into the house.

Besides, he had no time to chat about the weather. He had a pregnant woman to treat, a baby to deliver.

Striving to regain control of himself, he took a wool scarf from the foyer closet, wound it around his neck, and crossed the ends over his chest. His hands were trembling, and his fingers were slightly stiff, but he managed to button his overcoat. Fighting dizziness, he pulled on a pair of galoshes.

He was gripped by the conviction that the incongruous lightning had some special meaning for him. A sign, an omen. Nonsense. Just the whiskey confusing him. Yet the feeling remained as he went into the garage, put up the door, and backed the car into the driveway, the chain-wrapped winter tires crunching and clinking softly in the snow.

As he shifted the car into park, intending to get out and close the garage, someone rapped hard on the window beside him. Startled, Markwell turned his head and saw a man bending down and peering at him through the glass.

The stranger was approximately thirty-five. His features were bold, well-formed. Even through the partly fogged window he was a striking man. He was wearing a navy peacoat with the collar turned up. In the arctic air his nostrils smoked, and when he spoke, the words were dressed in pale puffs of breath. "Dr. Markwell?"

Markwell rolled down the window. "Yes?"

"Dr. Paul Markwell?"

"Yes, yes. Didn't I just say so? But I've no office hours here tonight, and I'm on my way to see a patient at the hospital."

The stranger had unusually blue eyes that conjured in Markwell the image of a clear winter sky reflected in the millimeter-thin ice of a just-freezing pond. They were arresting, quite beautiful, but he knew at once that they were also the eyes of a dangerous man.

Before Markwell could throw the car into gear and reverse toward the street where help might be found, the man in the peacoat thrust a pistol through the open window. "Don't do anything stupid."

When the muzzle pressed into the tender flesh under his chin, the physician realized with some surprise that he did not want to die. He had long nursed the idea that he was ready to embrace death. Yet now, instead of welcoming the realization of his will to live, he was guilt-stricken. To embrace life seemed a betrayal of the son with whom he could be joined only in death.

"Kill the headlights, Doctor. Good. Now switch off the engine."

Markwell withdrew the key from the ignition. "Who are you?"

"That's not important."

"It is to me. What do you want? What're you going to do to me?"

"Cooperate, and you won't be hurt. But try to get away, and I'll blow your damn head off, then empty the gun into your dead body just for the hell of it." His voice was soft, inaptly pleasant, but full of conviction. "Give me the keys."

Markwell passed them through the open window.

"Now come out of there."

Slowly sobering, Markwell got out of the car. The vicious wind bit his face. He had to squint to keep the fine snow out of his eyes.

"Before you close the door, roll up the window." The stranger crowded him, allowing no avenue of escape. "Okay, very good. Now, Doctor, walk with me to the garage."

"This is crazy. What—"

"Move."

The stranger stayed at Markwell's side, holding him by the left arm. If someone was watching from a neighboring house or from the street, the gloom and falling snow would conceal the gun.

In the garage, at the stranger's direction, Markwell pulled the big door shut. The cold, unoiled hinges squealed.

"If you want money—"

"Shut up and get in the house."

"Listen, a patient of mine is in labor at the county—"

"If you don't shut up, I'll use the butt of this pistol to smash every tooth in your head, and you won't be *able* to talk."

Markwell believed him. Six feet tall, about a hundred and eighty pounds, the man was Markwell's size but was intimidating. His blond hair was frosted with melting snow, and as the droplets trickled down his brow and temples, he appeared to be as devoid of humanity as an ice statue at a winter carnival. Markwell had no doubt that in a physical confrontation the stranger in the peacoat would win handily against most adversaries, especially against one middle-aged, out-of-shape, drunken physician.

Bob Shane felt claustrophobic in the cramped maternity-ward lounge provided for expectant fathers. The room had a low acoustic-tile ceiling, drab green walls, and a single window rimed with frost. The air was too warm. The six chairs and two end tables were too much furniture for the narrow space. He had an urge to push through the double swinging doors into the corridor, race to the other end of the hospital, cross the main public lounge, and break out into the cold night, where there was no stink of antiseptics or illness.

He remained in the maternity lounge, however, to be near to Janet if she needed him. Something was wrong. Labor was supposed to be painful but not as agonizing as the brutal, extended contractions that Janet had endured for so long. The physicians would not admit that serious complications had arisen, but their concern was apparent.

Bob understood the source of his claustrophobia. He was not actually afraid that the walls were closing in. What was closing in was death, perhaps that of his wife or of his unborn child—or both.

The swinging doors opened inward, and Dr. Yamatta entered.

As he rose from his chair, Bob bumped the end table, scattering half a dozen magazines across the floor. "How is she, Doc?"

"No worse." Yamatta was a short, slender man with a kind face and large, sad eyes. "Dr. Markwell will be here shortly."

"You're not delaying her treatment until he arrives, are you?"

"No, no, of course not. She's getting good care. I just thought you'd be relieved to know that your own doctor is on his way."

"Oh. Well, yeah . . . thank you. Listen, can I see her, Doc?"

"Not yet," Yamatta said.

"When?"

"When she's . . . in less distress."

"What kind of answer's that? When will she *be* in less distress? When the hell will she come out of this?" He instantly regretted the outburst. "I . . . I'm sorry, Doc. It's just . . . I'm afraid."

"I know. I know."

An inside door connected Markwell's garage to the house. They crossed the kitchen and followed the first-floor hallway, switching on lights as they went. Clumps of melting snow fell off their boots.

The gunman looked into the dining room, living room, study, medical office, and the patients' waiting room, then said, "Upstairs."

In the master bedroom the stranger snapped on one of the lamps. He moved a straight-backed, needlepoint chair away from the vanity and stood it in the middle of the room.

"Doctor, please take off your gloves, coat, and scarf."

Markwell obeyed, dropping the garments on the floor, and at the gunman's direction he sat in the chair.

The stranger put the pistol on the dresser and produced a coiled length of sturdy rope from one pocket. He reached beneath his coat and withdrew a short, wide-bladed knife that was evidently kept in a sheath attached to his belt. He cut the rope into pieces with which, no doubt, to bind Markwell to the chair.

The doctor stared at the pistol on the dresser, calculating his chances of reaching the weapon before the gunman could get it. Then he met the stranger's winter-blue eyes and realized that his scheming was as transparent to his adversary as a child's simple cunning was apparent to an adult.

The blond man smiled as if to say, Go ahead, go for it.

Paul Markwell wanted to live. He remained docile and compliant, as the intruder tied him, hand and foot, to the needlepoint chair.

Making the knots tight but not painfully so, the stranger seemed oddly concerned about his captive. "I don't want to have to gag you. You're drunk, and with a rag jammed in your mouth, you might vomit, choke to death. So to some extent I'm going to trust you. But if you cry out for help at any time, I'll kill you on the spot. Understand?"

"Yes."

When the gunman spoke more than a few words, he revealed a vague accent, so mild that Markwell could not place it. He clipped the ends of some words, and occasionally his pronunciation had a guttural note that was barely perceptible.

The stranger sat on the edge of the bed and put one hand on the telephone. "What's the number of the county hospital?"

Markwell blinked. "Why?"

"Damn it, I asked you the number. If you won't give it to me, I'd rather beat it out of you than look it up in the directory."

Chastened, Markwell gave him the number.

"Who's on duty there tonight?"

"Dr. Carlson. Herb Carlson."

"Is he a good man?"

"What do you mean?"

"Is he a better doctor than you—or is he a lush too?"

"I'm not a lush. I have—"

"You're an irresponsible, self-pitying, alcoholic wreck, and you know it. Answer my question, Doctor. Is Carlson reliable?"

Markwell's sudden nausea resulted only partly from overindulgence in Scotch; the other cause was revulsion at the truth of what the intruder had said. "Yeah, Herb Carlson's good. A very good doctor."

"Who's the supervising nurse tonight?"

Markwell had to ponder that for a moment. "Ella Hanlow, I think. I'm not sure. If it isn't Ella, it's Virginia Keene."

The stranger called the county hospital and said he was speaking on behalf of Dr. Paul Markwell. He asked for Ella Hanlow.

A blast of wind slammed into the house, rattling a loose window, whistling in the eaves, and Markwell was reminded of the storm. As he watched the fast-falling snow at the window, he felt another gust of disorientation blow through him. The night was so eventful—the lightning, the inexplicable intruder—that suddenly it did not seem real. He pulled at the ropes that bound him to the chair, certain that they were fragments of a whiskey dream and would dissolve like gossamer, but they held him fast, and the effort made him dizzy again.

At the phone the stranger said, "Nurse Hanlow? Dr. Markwell won't be able to come to the hospital tonight. One of his patients there, Janet Shane, is having a difficult labor. Hmmmm? Yes, of course. He wants Dr. Carlson to handle the delivery. No, no, I'm afraid he can't possibly make it. No, not the weather. He's drunk. That's right. He'd be a danger to the patient. No . . . he's so drunk, there's no point putting him on the line. Sorry. He's been drinking a lot lately, trying to cover it, but tonight he's worse than usual. Hmmmm? I'm a neighbor. Okay. Thank you, Nurse Hanlow. Good-bye."

Markwell was angry but also surprisingly relieved to have his secret revealed. "You bastard, you've ruined me."

"No, Doctor. You've ruined yourself. Self-hatred is destroying your career. And it drove your wife away from you. The marriage was already troubled, sure, but it might've been saved if Lenny had lived, and it might even have been saved after he died if you hadn't withdrawn into yourself so completely."

Markwell was astonished. "How the hell do you know what it was like with me and Anna? And how do you know about Lenny? I've never met you before. How can you know anything about me?"

Ignoring the questions, the stranger piled two pillows against the padded headboard of the bed. He swung his wet, dirty, booted feet onto the covers and stretched out. "No matter how you feel about it, losing your son wasn't your fault. You're just a physician, not a miracle worker. But losing Anna *was* your fault. And what you've become—an extreme danger to your patients—that's your fault too."

Markwell started to object, then sighed and let his head drop forward until his chin was on his chest.

"You know what your trouble is, Doctor?"

"I suppose you'll tell me."

"Your trouble is you never had to struggle for anything, never knew adversity. Your father was well-to-do, so you got everything you wanted, went to the finest schools. And though you were successful in your practice, you never needed the money—you had your inheritance. So when Lenny got polio, you didn't know how to deal with adversity because you'd never had any practice. You hadn't been *inoculated,* so you had no resistance, and you got a bad case of despair."

Lifting his head, blinking until his vision cleared, Markwell said, "I can't figure this."

"Through all this suffering, you've learned something, Markwell, and if you'll sober up long enough to think straight, you might get back on track. You've still got a slim chance to redeem yourself."

"Maybe I don't want to redeem myself."

"I'm afraid that could be true. I think you're scared to die, but I don't know if you have the guts to go on living."

The doctor's breath was sour with stale peppermint and whiskey. His mouth was dry, and his tongue swollen. He longed for a drink.

He halfheartedly tested the ropes that bound his hands to the chair. Finally, disgusted by the self-pitying whine in his own voice but unable to regain his dignity, he said, "What do you want from me?"

"I want to prevent you from going to the hospital tonight. I want to be damn sure you don't deliver Janet Shane's baby. You've become a butcher, a potential killer, and you have to be stopped this time."

Markwell licked his dry lips. "I still don't know who you are."

"And you never will, Doctor. You never will."

Bob Shane had never been so scared. He repressed his tears, for he had the superstitious feeling that revealing his fear so openly would tempt the fates and insure Janet's and the baby's deaths.

He leaned forward in the waiting-room chair, bowed his head, and prayed silently: Lord, Janet could've done better than me. She's so pretty, and I'm as homely as a rag rug. I'm just a grocer, and my corner store isn't ever going to turn big profits, but she loves me. Lord, she's good, honest, humble . . . she doesn't deserve to die. Maybe You want to take her 'cause she's already good enough for heaven. But *I'm* not good enough yet, and I need her to help me be a better man.

One of the lounge doors opened.

Bob looked up.

Doctors Carlson and Yamatta entered in their hospital greens.

The sight of them frightened Bob, and he rose slowly from his chair.

Yamatta's eyes were sadder than ever.

Dr. Carlson was a tall, portly man who managed to look dignified even in his baggy hospital uniform. "Mr. Shane . . . I'm sorry. I'm so sorry, but your wife died in childbirth."

Bob stood rock-still, as if the dreadful news had transformed his flesh to stone. He heard only part of what Carlson said:

". . . major uterine obstruction . . . one of those women not really designed to have children. She should never have gotten pregnant. I'm sorry . . . so sorry . . . everything we could . . . massive hemorrhaging . . . but the baby . . ."

The word "baby" broke Bob's paralysis. He took a halting step toward Carlson. "What did you say about the baby?"

"It's a girl," Carlson said. "A healthy little girl."

Bob had thought everything was lost. Now he stared at Carlson, cautiously hopeful that a part of Janet had not died and that he was not, after all, entirely alone in the world. "Really? A girl?"

"Yes," Carlson said. "She's an exceptionally beautiful baby. Born with a full head of dark brown hair."

Looking at Yamatta, Bob said, "My baby lived."

"Yes," Yamatta said. His poignant smile flickered briefly. "And you've got Dr. Carlson to thank. I'm afraid Mrs. Shane never had a chance. In less experienced hands the baby might've been lost too."

Bob turned to Carlson, still afraid to believe. "The . . . the baby lived, and that's something to be thankful for, anyway, isn't it?"

The physicians stood in awkward silence. Then Yamatta put one hand on Bob Shane's shoulder, perhaps sensing that the contact would comfort him.

Though Bob was five inches taller and forty pounds heavier than the diminutive doctor, he leaned against Yamatta. Overcome with grief he wept, and Yamatta held him.

The stranger stayed with Markwell for another hour, though he spoke no more and would respond to none of Markwell's questions. He lay on the bed, staring at the ceiling, so intent on his thoughts that he seldom moved.

As the doctor sobered, a throbbing headache began to torment him. As usual his hangover was an excuse for even greater self-pity than that which had driven him to drink.

Eventually the intruder looked at his wristwatch. "Eleven-thirty. I'll be going now." He got off the bed, came to the chair, and again drew the knife from beneath his coat.

Markwell tensed.

"I'm going to saw part way through your ropes, Doctor. If you struggle with them for half an hour or so, you'll be able to free yourself. Which gives me time enough to get out of here."

As the man stooped behind the chair and set to work, Markwell expected to feel the blade slip between his ribs.

But in less than a minute the stranger put the knife away and went to the bedroom door. "You do have a chance to redeem yourself, Doctor. I think you're too weak to do it, but I hope I'm wrong."

Then he walked out.

For ten minutes, as Markwell struggled to free himself, he heard occasional noises downstairs. Evidently the intruder was searching for valuables. Although he had seemed mysterious, perhaps he was nothing but a burglar with a singularly odd modus operandi.

Markwell finally broke loose at twenty-five past midnight. His wrists were severely abraded, bleeding.

Though he had not heard a sound from the first floor in half an hour, he took his pistol from the nightstand drawer and descended the stairs with caution. He went to his office in the professional wing, where he expected to find drugs missing from his medical supplies; neither of the two tall, white cabinets had been touched.

He hurried into his study, convinced that the flimsy wall safe had been opened. The safe was unbreached.

Baffled, turning to leave, he saw empty whiskey, gin, tequila, and vodka bottles piled in the bar sink. The intruder had paused only to locate the liquor supply and pour it down the drain.

A note was taped to the bar mirror. The intruder had printed his message in neat block letters:

> IF YOU DON'T STOP DRINKING, IF YOU DON'T LEARN TO ACCEPT LENNY'S DEATH, YOU WILL PUT A GUN IN YOUR MOUTH AND BLOW YOUR BRAINS OUT WITHIN ONE YEAR. THIS IS NOT A PREDICTION. THIS IS A FACT.

Clutching the note and the gun, Markwell looked around the empty room, as if the stranger was still there, unseen, a ghost that could choose at will between visibility and invisibility. "Who are you?" he demanded. "Who the *hell* are you?"

Only the wind at the window answered him, and its mournful moan had no meaning that he could discern.

At eleven o'clock the next morning, after an early meeting with the funeral director regarding Janet's body, Bob Shane returned to the county hospital to see his newborn daughter. After he donned a cotton gown, a cap, and a surgical mask, and after thoroughly scrubbing his hands under a nurse's direction, he was permitted into the nursery, where he gently lifted Laura from her cradle.

Nine other newborns shared the room. All of them were cute in one way or another, but Bob did not believe he was unduly prejudiced in his judgment that Laura Jean was the cutest of the crop. Although the popular image of an angel required blue eyes and blond hair, and though Laura had brown eyes and hair, she was nevertheless angelic in appearance. During the ten minutes that he held her, she did not cry; she blinked, squinted, rolled her eyes, yawned. She looked pensive, too, as if perhaps she knew that she was motherless and that she and her father had only each other in a cold, difficult world.

A viewing window, through which relatives could see the newborns, filled one wall. Five people were gathered at the glass. Four were smiling, pointing, and making funny faces to entertain the babies.

The fifth was a blond man wearing a navy peacoat and standing with his hands in his pockets. He did not smile or point or make faces. He was staring at Laura.

After a few minutes during which the stranger's gaze did not shift from the child, Bob became concerned. The guy was good looking and clean-cut, but there was a hardness in his face, too, and some quality that could not be put into words but that made Bob think this was a man who had seen and done terrible things.

He began to remember sensational tabloid stories of kidnappers, babies being sold on the black market. He told himself that he was paranoid, imagining a danger where none existed because, having lost Janet, he was now worried about losing his daughter as well. But the longer the blond man studied Laura, the more uneasy Bob became.

As if sensing that uneasiness, the man looked up. They stared at each other. The stranger's blue eyes were unusually bright, intense. Bob's fear deepened. He held his daughter closer, as if the stranger might smash through the nursery window to seize her. He considered calling one of the creche nurses and suggesting that she speak to the man, make inquiries about him.

Then the stranger smiled. His was a broad, warm, genuine smile that transformed his face. In an instant he no longer looked sinister but friendly. He winked at Bob and mouthed one word through the thick glass: "Beautiful."

Bob relaxed, smiled, realized his smile could not be seen behind his mask, and nodded a thank you.

The stranger looked once more at Laura, winked at Bob again, and walked away from the window.

Later, after Bob Shane had gone home for the day, a tall man in dark clothing approached the creche window. His name was Kokoschka. He studied the infants; then his field of vision shifted, and he became aware of his colorless reflection in the polished glass. He had a broad, flat face with sharp-edged features, lips so thin and hard that they seemed to be made of horn. A two-inch dueling scar marked his left cheek. His dark eyes had no depth, as if they were painted ceramic spheres, much like the cold eyes of a shark cruising in shadowy ocean trenches. He was amused to realize how starkly his face contrasted to the innocent visages of the cradled babies beyond the window; he smiled, a rare expression for him, which imparted no warmth to his face but actually made him appear more threatening.

He looked beyond his reflection again. He had no trouble finding Laura Shane among the swaddled infants, for the surname of each child was printed on a card and affixed to the back of his or her cradle.

Why is there such interest in you, Laura? he wondered. Why is your life so important? Why all this energy expended to see that you are brought safely into the world? Should I kill you now and put an end to the traitor's scheme?

He'd be able to murder her without compunction. He had killed children before, though none quite so young as this. No crime was too terrible if it furthered the cause to which he had devoted his life.

The babe was sleeping. Now and then her mouth worked, and her tiny face briefly wrinkled, as perhaps she dreamed of the womb with regret and longing.

At last he decided not to kill her. Not yet.

"I can always eliminate you later, little one," he murmured. "When I understand what part you play in the traitor's plans, *then* I can kill you."

Kokoschka walked away from the window. He knew he would not see the girl again for more than eight years.

·2·

In southern California rain falls rarely in the spring, summer, and autumn. The true rainy season usually begins in December and ends in March. But on Saturday the second of April, 1963, the sky was overcast, and humidity was high. Holding open the front door of his small, neighborhood grocery in Santa Ana, Bob Shane decided that the prospects were good for one last big downpour of the season.

The ficus trees in the yard of the house across the street and the date palm on the corner were motionless in the dead air and seemed to droop as if with the weight of the oncoming storm.

By the cash register, the radio was turned low. The Beach Boys were singing their new hit "Surfin' U.S.A." Considering the weather, their tune was as appropriate as "White Christmas" sung in July.

Bob looked at his watch: three-fifteen.

There'll be rain by three-thirty, he thought, and a lot of it.

Business had been good during the morning, but the afternoon had been slow. At the moment no shoppers were in the store.

The family-owned grocery faced new, deadly competition from convenience-store chains like 7-Eleven. He was planning to shift to a deli-style operation, offering more fresh foods, but was delaying as long as possible because a deli required considerably more work.

If the oncoming storm was bad he would have few customers the rest of the day. He might close early and take Laura to a movie.

Turning from the door, he said, "Better get the boat, doll."

Laura was kneeling at the head of the first aisle, across from the cash register, absorbed in her work. Bob had carried four cartons of canned soup from the stockroom, then Laura had taken over. She was only eight years old, but she was a reliable kid, and she liked to help out around the store. After stamping the correct price on each of the cans, she stacked them on the shelves, remembering to cycle the merchandise, putting the new soup behind the old.

She looked up reluctantly. "Boat? What boat?"

"Upstairs in the apartment. The boat in the closet. From the look of the sky, we're going to need it to get around later today."

"Silly," she said. "We don't have a boat in the closet."

He walked behind the checkout counter. "Nice little blue boat."

"Yeah? In a closet? Which closet?"

He began to clip packages of Slim Jims to the metal display rack beside the snack pack crackers. "The library closet, of course."

"We don't have a library."

"We don't? Oh. Well, now that you mention it, the boat isn't in the library. It's in the closet in the toad's room."

She giggled. "What toad?"

"Why, you mean to tell me that you don't know about the toad?"

Grinning, she shook her head.

"As of today we are renting a room to a fine, upstanding toad from England. A gentleman toad who's here on the queen's business."

Lightning flared and thunder rumbled through the April sky. On the radio, static crackled through The Cascades' "Rhythm of the Rain."

Laura paid no attention to the storm. She was not frightened of things that scared most kids. She was so self-confident and self-contained that sometimes she seemed to be an old lady masquerading as a child. "Why would the queen let a toad handle her business?"

"Toads are excellent businessmen," he said, opening one of the Slim Jims and taking a bite. Since Janet's death, since moving to California to start over, he had put on fifty pounds. He had never been a handsome man. Now at thirty-eight he was pleasantly round, with little chance of turning a woman's head. He was not a great success, either; no one got rich operating a corner grocery. But he didn't care. He had Laura, and he was a good father, and she loved him with all her heart, as he loved her, so what the rest of the world might think of him was of no consequence. "Yes, toads are excellent businessmen indeed. And this toad's family has served the crown for hundreds of years. In fact he's been knighted. Sir Thomas Toad."

Lightning crackled brighter than before. The thunder was louder as well.

Having finished stocking the soup shelves, Laura rose from her knees and wiped her hands on the white apron that she was wearing over T-shirt and jeans. She was lovely; with her thick, brown hair and large, brown eyes, she bore more than a passing resemblance to her mother. "And how much rent is Sir Thomas Toad paying?"

"Six pence a week."

"Is he in the room next to mine?"

"Yes, the room with the boat in the closet."

She giggled again. "Well, he better not snore."

"He said the same of you."

A battered, rusted Buick pulled up in front of the store, and as the driver's door opened, a third thunderbolt blasted a hole in the darkening sky. The day was filled with molten light that appeared to flow liquidly along the street outside, sprayed lavalike over the parked Buick and the passing cars. The accompanying thunder shook the building from roof to foundation, as though the stormy heavens were reflected in the land below, precipitating an earthquake.

"Wow!" Laura said, moving fearlessly toward the windows.

Though no rain had fallen yet, wind suddenly swept in from the west, harrying leaves and litter before it.

The man who got out of the decrepit, blue Buick was looking at the sky in astonishment.

Bolt after bolt of lightning pierced the clouds, seared the air, cast their blazing images in windows and automobile chrome, and with each flash came thunder that struck the day with god-size fists.

The lightning spooked Bob. When he called to Laura—"Honey, get away from the windows"—she rushed behind the counter and let him put an arm around her, probably more for his comfort than hers.

The man from the Buick hurried into the store. Looking out at the fulminous sky, he said, "You see that, man? Whew!"

The thunder faded; silence returned.

Rain fell. Fat droplets at first struck the windows without much force then came in blinding torrents that blurred the world beyond the small shop.

The customer turned and smiled. "Some show, huh?"

Bob started to respond but fell silent when he took a closer look at the man, sensing trouble as a deer might sense a stalking wolf. The guy was wearing scuffed engineer boots, dirty jeans, and a stained windbreaker half zipped over a soiled white T-shirt. His windblown hair was oily, and his face was shaded with beard stubble. He had bloodshot, fevered eyes. A junkie. Approaching the counter, he drew a revolver from his windbreaker, and the gun was no surprise.

"Gimme what's in the register, asshole."

"Sure."

"Make it quick."

"Just take it easy."

The junkie licked his pale, cracked lips. "Don't hold out on me, asshole."

"Okay, okay, sure. You got it," Bob said, trying to push Laura behind him with one hand.

"Leave the girl so I can see her! I want to *see* her. Now, right now, get her the fuck out from behind you!"

"Okay, just cool off."

The guy was strung out as taut as a dead man's grin, and his entire body vibrated visibly. "Right where I can see her. And don't you reach for nothin' but the cash register, don't you go reachin' for no gun, or I'll blow your fuckin' head off."

"I don't have a gun," Bob assured him. He glanced at the rain-washed windows, hoping that no other customers would arrive while the holdup was in progress. The junkie seemed so unstable that he might shoot anyone who walked through the door.

Laura tried to ease behind her father, but the junkie said, "Hey, don't move!"

Bob said, "She's only eight—"

"She's a bitch, they're all fuckin' bitches no matter how big or little." His shrill voice cracked repeatedly. He sounded even more frightened than Bob was, which scared Bob more than anything else.

Though he was focused intently on the junkie and the revolver, Bob was also crazily aware that the radio was playing Skeeter Davis singing "The End of the World," which struck him as uncomfortably prophetic. With the excusable superstition of a man being held at gunpoint, he wished fervently that the song would conclude before it magically precipitated the end of his and Laura's world.

"Here's the money, here's all of it, take it."

Scooping the cash off the counter and stuffing it into a pocket of his dirty windbreaker, the man said, "You got a storeroom in back?"

"Why?"

With one arm the junkie angrily swept the Slim Jims, Life Savers, crackers, and chewing gum off the counter onto the floor. He thrust the gun at Bob. "You got a storeroom, asshole, I know you do. We're gonna go back there in the storeroom."

Bob's mouth was suddenly dry. "Listen, take the money and go. You got what you want. Just go. Please."

Grinning, more confident now that he had the money, emboldened by Bob's fear but still visibly trembling, the gunman said, "Don't worry, I ain't gonna kill no one. I'm a lover not a killer. All I want's a piece of that little bitch, and then I'm out of here."

Bob cursed himself for not having a gun. Laura was clinging to him, trusting in him, but he could do nothing to save her. On the way to the storeroom, he'd lunge at the junkie, try to grab the revolver. He was overweight, out of shape. Unable to move fast enough, he would be shot in the gut and left to die on the floor, while the filthy bastard took Laura into the back room and raped her.

"Move," the junkie said impatiently. *"Now!"*

A gun fired, Laura screamed, and Bob pulled her tight against him, sheltering her, but it was the junkie who had been shot. The bullet struck his left temple, blowing out part of his skull, and he went down hard atop the Slim Jims and crackers and chewing gum that he had knocked off the counter, dead so instantaneously that he did not even reflexively pull the trigger of his own revolver.

Stunned, Bob looked to his right and saw a tall, blond man with a pistol. Evidently he had entered the building through the rear service door and had crept silently through the storage room. Upon entering the grocery he had shot the junkie without warning. As he stared at the dead body, he looked cool, dispassionate, as if he were an experienced executioner.

"Thank God," Bob said, "police."

"I'm not the police." The man wore gray slacks, a white shirt, and a dark gray jacket under which a shoulder holster was visible.

Bob was confused, wondering if their rescuer was *another* thief about to take over where the junkie had been violently interrupted.

The stranger looked up from the corpse. His eyes were pure blue, intense, and direct.

Bob was sure that he had seen the guy before, but he could not remember where or when.

The stranger looked at Laura. "You all right, sweetheart?"

"Yes," she said, but she clung to her father.

The pungent odor of urine rose from the dead man, for he had lost control of his bladder at the moment of death.

The stranger crossed the room, stepping around the corpse, and engaged the dead-bolt lock on the front door. He pulled down the shade. He looked worriedly at the big display windows over which flowed a continuous film of rain, distorting the stormy afternoon beyond. "No way to cover those, I guess. We'll just have to hope nobody comes along and looks in."

"What're you going to do to us?" Bob asked.

"Me? Nothing. I'm not like that creep. I don't want anything from you. I just locked the door so we could work out the story you're going to have to tell the police. We have to get it straight before anyone walks in here and sees the body."

"Why do I need a story?"

Stooping beside the corpse, the stranger took a set of car keys and the wad of money from the pockets of the bloodstained windbreaker. Rising again, he said, "Okay, what you have to tell them is that there were *two* gunmen. This one wanted Laura, but the other was sickened by the idea of raping a little girl, and he just wanted to get out. So they argued, it got nasty, the other one shot this bastard and skipped with the money. Can you make that sound right?"

Bob was reluctant to believe that he and Laura had been spared. With one arm he held his daughter tightly against him. "I . . . I don't understand. You weren't really with him. You're not in trouble for killing him—after all, he was going to kill us. So why don't we just tell them the truth?"

Stepping to the end of the checkout counter, returning the money to Bob, the man said, "And what is the truth?"

"Well . . . you happened along and saw the robbery in progress—"

"I didn't just *happen* along, Bob. I've been watching over you and Laura." Slipping his pistol into his shoulder holster, the man looked down at Laura. She stared at him wide-eyed. He smiled and whispered, "Guardian angel."

Not believing in guardian angels, Bob said, "Watching over us? From where, how long, why?"

In a voice colored by urgency and by a vague, unplaceable accent that Bob heard for the first time, the stranger said, "Can't tell you that." He glanced at the rain-washed windows. "And I can't afford to be questioned by police. So you've got to get this story straight."

Bob said, "Where do I know you from?"

"You don't know me."

"But I'm sure I've seen you before."

"You haven't. You don't need to know. Now for God's sake, hide that money and leave the register empty; it'll seem odd if the second man left without what he came for. I'll take his Buick, abandon it in a few blocks, so you can give the cops a description of it. Give them a description of me, too. It won't matter."

Thunder rumbled outside, but it was low and distant, not like the explosions with which the storm had begun.

The humid air thickened as the slower-spreading, coppery scent of blood mixed with the stench of urine.

Queasy, leaning on the counter but still holding Laura at his side, Bob said, "Why can't I just tell them how you interrupted the robbery, shot the guy, and didn't want publicity, so you left?"

Impatient, the stranger raised his voice. "An armed man just happens to stroll by while the robbery's in progress and decides to be a hero? The cops won't believe a cockeyed story like that."

"That's what happened—"

"But they won't buy it! Listen, they'll start thinking maybe *you* shot the junkie. Since you don't own a gun, at least not according to public record, they'll wonder if maybe it was an illegal weapon and if you disposed of it after you shot this guy, then cooked up a crazy story about some Lone Ranger type walking in and saving your ass."

"I'm a respectable businessman with a good reputation."

In the stranger's eyes a peculiar sadness arose, a haunted look. "Bob, you're a nice man . . . but you're a little naive sometimes."

"What're you—"

The stranger held up a hand to silence him. "In a crunch a man's reputation never counts for as much as it ought to. Most people are good-hearted and willing to give a man the benefit of the doubt, but the poisonous few are eager to see others brought down, ruined." His voice had fallen to a whisper, and although he continued to look at Bob, he seemed to be seeing other places, other people. "Envy, Bob. Envy eats them alive. If you had money, they'd envy you that. But since you don't, they envy you for having such a good, bright, loving daughter. They envy you for just being a happy man. They envy you for *not* envying them. One of the greatest sorrows of human existence is that some people aren't happy merely to be alive but find their happiness only in the misery of others."

The charge of naiveté was one that Bob could not refute, and he knew the stranger spoke the truth. He shivered.

After a moment of silence, the man's haunted expression gave way to a look of urgency again. "And when the cops decide you're lying about the Lone Ranger who saved you, then they'll begin to wonder if maybe the junkie wasn't here to rob you at all, if maybe you knew him, had a falling out with him over something, even *planned* his murder and tried to make it look like a robbery. That's how cops think, Bob. Even if they can't pin this on you, they'll try so hard that they'll make a mess of your life. Do you want to put Laura through that?"

"No."

"Then do it my way."

Bob nodded. "I will. Your way. But who the hell are you?"

"That doesn't matter. We don't have time for it anyway." He stepped behind the counter and stooped in front of Laura, face to face with her. "Did you understand what I told your father? If the police ask you what happened—"

"You were with that man," she said, pointing in the general direction of the corpse.

"That's right."

"You were his friend," she said, "but then you started arguing about me, though I'm not sure why, 'cause I didn't do anything—"

"It doesn't matter why, honey," the stranger said.

Laura nodded. "And the next thing you shot him and ran out with all our money and drove away, and I was very scared."

The man looked up at Bob. "Eight years old, huh?"

"She's a smart girl."

"But it'd still be best if the cops didn't question her much."

"I won't let them."

"If they do," Laura said, "I'll just cry and cry till they stop."

The stranger smiled. He stared at Laura so lovingly that he made Bob uneasy. His manner was not that of the pervert who had wanted to take her into the storeroom; his expression was tender, affectionate. He touched her cheek. Astonishingly, tears shimmered in his eyes. He blinked, stood. "Bob, put that money away. Remember, *I* left with it."

Bob realized the wad of cash was still in his hand. He jammed it into his pants pocket, and his loose apron concealed the bulge.

The stranger unlocked the door and put up the shade. "Take care of her, Bob. She's special." Then he dashed into the rain, letting the door stand open behind him, and got into the Buick. The tires squealed as he pulled out of the parking lot.

The radio was on, but Bob heard it for the first time since "The End of the World" had been playing, before the junkie had been shot. Now Shelley Fabares was singing "Johnny Angel."

Suddenly he heard the rain again, not just as a dull background hiss and patter but really *heard* it, beating furiously on the windows and on the roof of the apartment above. In spite of the wind rushing through the open door, the stink of blood and urine was abruptly far worse than it had been a moment ago, and just as precipitously, as if coming out of a trance of terror and regaining his full senses, he realized how close his precious Laura had come to dying. He scooped her into his arms, lifted her off the floor, and held her, repeating her name, smoothing her hair. He buried his face against her neck and smelled the sweet freshness of her skin, felt the pulse of the artery in her throat, and thanked God that she was alive.

"I love you, Laura."

"I love you, too, Daddy. I love you because of Sir Tommy Toad and a million other reasons. But we've got to call the police now."

"Yes, of course," he said, reluctantly putting her down.

His eyes were full of tears. He was so unnerved that he could not recall where the telephone was.

Laura had already taken the handset off the hook. She held it out to him. "Or I can call them, Daddy. The number's right here on the phone. Do you want me to call them?"

"No. I'll do it, baby." Blinking back tears, he took the phone from her and sat on the old wooden stool behind the cash register.

She put one hand on his arm, as if she knew he needed her touch. Janet had been emotionally strong. But Laura's strength and self-possession were unusual for her age, and Bob Shane was not sure where they came from. Maybe being motherless made her self-reliant.

"Daddy?" Laura said, tapping the phone with one finger. "The police, remember?"

"Oh, yeah," he said. Trying not to gag on the odor of death that permeated the store, he dialed the police emergency number.

Kokoschka sat in a car across the street from Bob Shane's small grocery, thoughtfully fingering the scar on his cheek.

The rain had stopped. The police had gone. Neon shop signs and lampposts lit at nightfall, but the macadam streets glistened darkly in spite of that illumination, as if the pavement absorbed the light instead of reflecting it.

Kokoschka had arrived in the neighborhood simultaneously with Stefan, the blond and blue-eyed traitor. He had heard the shooting, had seen Stefan flee in the dead man's car, had joined the crowd of onlookers when the police arrived, and had learned most of the details of what had happened in the store.

He had, of course, seen through Bob Shane's preposterous story about Stefan having been merely a second thief. Stefan was not their assailant but their self-appointed guardian, and he had no doubt lied to cover his true identity.

Laura had been saved again.

But why?

Kokoschka tried to imagine what part the girl could possibly play in the traitor's plans, but he was stumped. He knew nothing would be gained by interrogating the girl, for she was too young to have been told anything useful. The reason for her rescue would be as much a mystery to her as it was to Kokoschka.

He was sure that her father knew nothing, either. The girl was obviously the one who interested Stefan, not the father, so Bob Shane would not have been made privy to Stefan's origins or intentions.

Finally Kokoschka drove several blocks to a restaurant, had dinner, then returned to the grocery well after nightfall. He parked on the side street, in the shadows under the expansive fronds of a date palm. The store was dark, but lights shone at the windows of the second-floor apartment.

From a deep pocket of his raincoat, he withdrew a revolver. It was a snub-nosed Colt Agent .38, compact but powerful. Kokoschka admired well-designed and well-made weapons, and he especially liked the feel of this gun in his hand: this was Death himself imprisoned in steel.

Kokoschka could cut the Shanes' phone wires, quietly force entry, kill the girl and her father, and slip away before police responded to the shots. He had a talent and affinity for that kind of work.

But if he killed them without knowing *why* he was killing them, without understanding what role they played in Stefan's schemes, he might later discover that eliminating them was a mistake. He had to know Stefan's purpose before acting.

Reluctantly he put the revolver in his pocket.

·3·

In the windless night, rain fell straight down on the city, as if every droplet was enormously heavy. It drummed noisily on the roof and windshield of the small, black car.

At one o'clock in the morning on that Tuesday in late March, the rainswept streets, flooded at some intersections, were generally deserted but for military vehicles. Stefan chose an indirect route to the institute to avoid known inspection stations, but he was afraid of encountering an impromptu checkpoint. His papers were in order, and his security clearance exempted him from the new curfew. Nevertheless he preferred not to come under the scrutiny of military police. He could not afford to have the car searched, for the suitcase on the back seat contained copper wire, detonators, and plastic explosives not legally in his possession.

Because his breath fogged the windshield, because rain obscured the eerily dark city, because the car's wipers were worn, and because the hooded headlights illuminated a limited field of vision, he almost missed the narrow, cobblestone street that led behind the institute. He braked, turned the wheel sharply. The sedan took the corner with a shudder and a squeal of tires, sliding slightly on the slick cobbles.

He parked in darkness near the rear entrance, got out of the car, and took the suitcase from the back seat. The institute was a drab, four-story brick building with heavily barred windows. An air of menace hung about the place, though it did not look as if it harbored secrets that would radically change the world. The metal door had concealed hinges and was painted black. He pushed the button, heard the buzzer ring inside, and waited nervously for a response.

He was wearing rubber boots and a trenchcoat with the collar turned up, but he had neither a hat nor an umbrella. The cold rain pasted his hair to his skull and drizzled down the nape of his neck.

Shivering, he looked at a slit window that was set in the wall beside the door. It was six inches wide, a foot high, with glass that was mirrored from outside, transparent from inside.

He patiently listened to the rain beating on the car, splashing in puddles, and gurgling in a nearby downspout. With a cold sizzle it struck the leaves of plane trees at the curb.

A light came on above the door. It was in a cone-shaped shade, the yellow glow tightly contained and directed straight down on him.

Stefan smiled at the mirrored observation window, at the guard he could not see.

The light went out, the lock bolts clattered open, and the door swung inward. He knew the guard: Viktor something, a stout, fiftyish man with close-cropped gray hair and steel-rimmed spectacles, who was more pleasant-tempered than he looked and was in fact a mother hen who worried about the health of friends and acquaintances.

"Sir, what are you doing out at this hour, in this downpour?"

"Couldn't sleep."

"Dreadful weather. Come in, in! You'll catch cold for sure."

"Kept worrying about work I'd left undone, so I thought I might as well come in and *do* it."

"You'll work yourself into an early grave, sir. Truly you will."

As Stefan stepped into the antechamber and watched the guard close the door, he searched his memory for a scrap of knowledge about Viktor's personal life. "From the look of you, I guess your wife still makes those incredible noodle dishes you've told me about."

Turning from the door, Viktor laughed softly, patted his belly. "I swear, she's employed by the devil to lead me into sin, primarily gluttony. What's that, sir, a suitcase? Are you moving in?"

Wiping rain from his face with one hand, Stefan said, "Research data. Took it home weeks ago, been working on it evenings."

"Have you no private life at all?"

"I get twenty minutes for myself every second Thursday."

Viktor clucked his tongue disapprovingly. He stepped to the desk that occupied a third of the floor space in the small room, picked up the phone, and called the other night guard, who was stationed in a similar antechamber at the front entrance to the institute. When anyone was let in after hours, the admitting guard always alerted his colleague at the other end of the building, in part to avoid false alarms and perhaps the accidental shooting of an innocent visitor.

Dripping rain on the worn carpet runner, fishing a set of keys from his trenchcoat pocket, Stefan went to the inner door. Like the outer portal, it was made of steel with concealed hinges. However, it could be unlocked only with two keys turned in tandem—one belonging to an authorized employee, the other carried by the guard on duty. The work being conducted at the institute was so extraordinary and secret that even the night watchmen could not be trusted to have access to the labs and file rooms.

Viktor put down the phone. "How long are you staying, sir?"

"A couple of hours. Is anyone else working tonight?"

"No. You're the only martyr. And no one truly appreciates martyrs, sir. You'll work yourself to death, I swear, and for what? Who'll care?"

"Eliot wrote: 'Saints and martyrs rule from the tomb.' "

"Eliot? He a poet or something?"

"T. S. Eliot, a poet, yes."

" 'Saints and martyrs rule from the tomb'? I don't know about this fellow. Doesn't sound like an *approved* poet. Sounds subversive." Viktor laughed warmly, apparently amused by the ridiculous notion that his hard-working friend could be a traitor.

Together they opened the inner door.

Stefan lugged the suitcase of explosives into the institute's ground-floor hallway, where he switched on the lights.

"If you're going to make a habit of working in the middle of the night," Viktor said, "I'll bring you one of my wife's cakes to give you energy."

"Thank you, Viktor, but I hope not to make a habit of this."

The guard closed the metal door. The lock bolt clanked shut automatically.

Alone in the hallway Stefan thought, not for the first time, that he was fortunate in his appearance: blond, strong-featured, blue-eyed. His looks partly explained why he could brazenly carry explosives into the institute without expecting to be searched. Nothing about him was dark, sly, or suspect; he was the ideal, angelic when he smiled, and his devotion to country would never be questioned by men like Viktor, men whose blind obedience to the state and whose beery, sentimental patriotism prevented them from thinking clearly about a lot of things. A lot of things.

He rode the elevator to the third floor and went directly to his office where he turned on a brass, gooseneck lamp. After removing his rubber boots and trenchcoat, he selected a manila folder from the file cabinet and arranged its contents across the desk to create a convincing impression that work was underway. In the unlikely event that another staff member decided to put in an appearance in the heart of the night, as much as possible must be done to allay suspicion.

Carrying the suitcase and a flashlight that he had taken from an inner pocket of his trenchcoat, he climbed the stairs past the fourth floor and ascended all the way to the attic. The flashlight revealed huge timbers from which a few misdriven nails bristled here and there. Though the attic had a rough wood floor, it was not used for storage and was empty of all but a film of gray dust and spiderwebs. The space under the highly pitched slate roof was sufficient to allow him to stand erect along the center of the building, though he would have to drop to his hands and knees when he worked closer to the eaves.

With the roof only inches away, the steady roar of the rain was as thunderous as the flight of an endless fleet of bombers crossing low overhead. That image came to mind perhaps because he believed that exactly such ruination would be the inevitable fate of his city.

He opened the suitcase. Working with the speed and confidence of a demolitions expert, he placed the bricks of plastic explosives and shaped each charge to direct the power of the explosion downward and inward. The blast must not merely blow the roof off but pulverize the middle floors and bring the heavy roof slates and timbers crashing down through the debris to cause further destruction. He secreted the plastique among the rafters and in the corners of the long room, even pried up a couple of floorboards and left explosives under them.

Outside, the storm briefly abated. But soon more ominous peals of thunder rolled across the night, and the rain returned, falling harder than before. The long-delayed wind arrived, too, keening along the gutters and moaning under the eaves; its strange, hollow voice seemed simultaneously to threaten and mourn the city.

Chilled by the unheated attic air, he conducted his delicate work with increasingly tremulous hands. Though shivering, he broke out in a sweat.

He inserted a detonator in every charge and strung wire from all the charges to the northwest corner of the attic. He braided them to a single copper line and dropped it down a ventilation chase that went all the way to the basement.

The charges and wire were as well concealed as possible and would not be spotted by someone who merely opened the attic door for a quick look. But on closer inspection or if the space was needed for storage, the wires and molded plastique surely would be noticed.

He needed twenty-four hours during which no one would go into the attic. That wasn't much to ask, considering that he was the only one who had visited the institute's garret in months.

Tomorrow night he would return with a second suitcase and plant charges in the basement. Crushing the building between simultaneous explosions above and below was the only way to be certain of reducing it—and its contents—to splinters, gravel, and twisted scraps. After the blast and accompanying fire, no files must remain to rekindle the dangerous research now conducted there.

The great quantity of explosives, although carefully placed and shaped, would damage structures on all sides of the institute, and he was afraid that other people, some of them no doubt innocent, would be killed in the blast. Those deaths could not be avoided. He dared not use less plastique, for if every file and every duplicate of every file throughout the institute were not utterly destroyed, the project might be quickly relaunched. And this was a project that must be brought to an end swiftly, for the hope of all mankind hinged on its destruction. If innocent people perished, he would just have to live with the guilt.

In two hours, at a few minutes past three o'clock, he finished his work in the attic.

He returned to his office on the third floor and sat for a while behind his desk. He did not want to leave until his sweat-soaked hair had dried and he had stopped trembling, for Viktor might notice.

He closed his eyes. In his mind he summoned Laura's face. He could always calm himself with thoughts of her. The mere fact of her existence brought him peace and greater courage.

·4·

Bob Shane's friends did not want Laura to attend her father's funeral. They believed that a twelve-year-old girl ought to be spared such a grim ordeal. She insisted, however, and when she wanted anything as badly as she wanted to say one last goodbye to her father, no one could thwart her.

That Thursday, July 24, 1967, was the worst day of her life, even more distressing than the preceding Tuesday when her father had died. Some of the anesthetizing shock had worn off, and Laura no longer felt numb; her emotions were closer to the surface and less easily controlled. She was beginning to realize fully how much she had lost.

She chose a dark blue dress because she did not own a black one. She wore black shoes and dark blue socks, and she worried about the socks because they made her feel childish, frivolous. Having never worn nylons, however, she didn't think it a good idea to don them for the first time at the funeral. She expected her father to look down from heaven during the service, and she intended to be just the way he remembered her. If he saw her in nylons, a changeling striving awkwardly to be grown up, he might be embarrassed for her.

At the funeral home she sat in the front row between Cora Lance, who owned a beauty shop half a block from Shane's Grocery, and Anita Passadopolis, who had done charity work with Bob at St. Andrew's Presbyterian Church. Both were in their late fifties, grandmotherly types who touched Laura reassuringly and watched her with concern.

They did not need to worry about her. She would not cry, become hysterical, or tear out her hair. She understood death. Everyone had to die. People died, dogs died, cats died, birds died, flowers died. Even the ancient redwood trees died sooner or later, though they lived twenty or thirty times longer than a person, which didn't seem right. On the other hand, living a thousand years as a tree would be a lot duller than living just forty-two years as a happy human being. Her father had been forty-two when his heart failed—bang, a sudden attack—which was too young. But that was the way of the world, and crying about it was pointless. Laura prided herself on her sensibleness.

Besides, death was not the end of a person. Death was actually only the beginning. Another and better life followed. She knew that must be true because her father had told her so, and her father never lied. Her father was the most truthful man, and kind, and sweet.

As the minister approached the lectern to the left of the casket, Cora Lance leaned close to Laura. "Are you okay, dear?"

"Yes. I'm fine," she said, but she did not look at Cora. She dared not meet anyone's eyes, so she studied inanimate things with great interest.

This was the first funeral home she had ever entered, and she did not like it. The burgundy carpet was ridiculously thick. The drapes and upholstered chairs were burgundy, too, with only minimal gold trim, and the lamps had burgundy shades, so all the rooms appeared to have been decorated by an obsessed interior designer with a burgundy fetish.

Fetish was a new word for her. She used it too much, just as she always overused a new word, but in this case it was appropriate.

Last month, when she'd first heard the lovely word "sequestered," meaning "secluded or isolated," she had used it at every opportunity, until her father had begun to tease her with silly variations: "Hey, how's my little sequestrian this morning?" he would say, or "Potato chips are a high turnover item, so we'll shift them into the first aisle, closer to the register, 'cause the corner they're in now is sort of sequesteriacious." He enjoyed making her giggle, as with his tales of Sir Tommy Toad, a British amphibian he had invented when she was eight years old and whose comic biography he embellished nearly every day. In some ways her father had been more of a child than she was, and she had loved him for that.

Her lower lip trembled. She bit it. Hard. If she cried, she'd be doubting what her father had always told her about the next life, the better life. By crying she would be pronouncing him dead, dead for once and all, forever, *finito*.

She longed to be sequestered in her room above the grocery, in bed, the covers pulled over her head. That idea was so appealing, she figured she could easily develop a fetish for sequestering herself.

From the funeral home they went to the cemetery.

The graveyard had no headstones. The plots were marked by bronze plaques on marble bases set flush with the ground. The rolling green lawns, shaded by huge Indian laurels and smaller magnolias, might have been mistaken for a park, a place to play games and run and laugh—if not for the open grave over which Bob Shane's casket was suspended.

Last night she'd awakened twice to the sound of distant thunder, and though half asleep she had thought she'd seen lightning flickering at the windows, but if unseasonal storms had passed through during the darkness, there was no sign of them now. The day was blue, cloudless.

Laura stood between Cora and Anita, who touched her and murmured reassurances, but she was not comforted by anything they did or said. The bleak chill in her deepened with each word of the minister's final prayer, until she felt as if she were standing unclothed in an arctic winter instead of in the shade of a tree on a hot, windless July morning.

The funeral director activated the motorized sling on which the casket was suspended. Bob Shane's body was lowered into the earth.

Unable to watch the slow descent of the casket, having difficulty drawing breath, Laura turned away, slipped out from under the caring hands of her two honorary grandmothers, and took a few steps across the cemetery. She was as cold as marble; she needed to escape the shade. She stopped as soon as she reached sunlight, which felt warm on her skin but which failed to relieve her chills.

She stared down the long, gentle hill for perhaps a minute before she saw the man standing at the far end of the cemetery in shadows at the edge of a large grove of laurels. He was wearing light tan slacks and a white shirt that appeared faintly luminous in that gloom, as if he were a ghost who had forsaken his usual night haunts for daylight. He was watching her and the other mourners around Bob Shane's grave near the top of the slope. At that distance Laura could not see his face clearly, but she could discern that he was tall and strong and blond—and disturbingly familiar.

The observer intrigued her, though she did not know why. As if spellbound, she descended the hill, stepping between and across the graves. The nearer she drew to the blond, the more familiar he looked. At first he did not react to her approach, but she knew he was studying her intently; she could feel the weight of his gaze.

Cora and Anita called to her, but she ignored them. Seized by an inexplicable excitement, she walked faster, now only a hundred feet from the stranger.

The man retreated into the false twilight among the trees.

Afraid that he would slip away before she had gotten a good look at him—yet not certain why seeing him more clearly was so important—Laura ran. The soles of her new black shoes were slippery, and several times she nearly fell. At the place where he had been standing, the grass was tramped flat, so he was no ghost.

Laura saw a flicker of movement among the trees, the spectral white of his shirt. She hurried after him. Only sparse, pale grass grew under the laurels, beyond the reach of the sun. However, surface roots and treacherous shadows sprouted everywhere. She stumbled, grabbed the trunk of a tree to avoid a bad fall, regained her balance, looked up—and discovered that the man had vanished.

The grove was comprised of perhaps a hundred trees. The branches were densely interlaced, allowing sunlight through only in thin golden threads, as if the fabric of the sky had begun unraveling into the woods. She hurried forward, squinting at the darkness. Half a dozen times she thought she saw him, but it was always phantom movement, a trick of light or of her own mind. When a breeze sprang up, she was certain she heard his furtive footsteps in the masking rustle of the leaves, but when she pursued the crisp sound, its source eluded her.

After a couple of minutes she came out of the trees to a road that served another section of the sprawling cemetery. Cars were parked along the verge, sparkling in the brightness, and a hundred yards away was a group of mourners at another graveside service.

Laura stood at the edge of the lane, breathing hard, wondering where the man in the white shirt had gone and why she had been compelled to chase him.

The blazing sun, the cessation of the short-lived breeze, and the return of perfect silence to the cemetery made her uneasy. The sun seemed to pass through her as if she were transparent, and she was strangely light, almost weightless, and mildly dizzy too: She felt as if she were in a dream, floating an inch above an unreal landscape.

I'm going to pass out, she thought.

She put one hand against the front fender of a parked car and gritted her teeth, struggling to hold on to consciousness.

Though she was only twelve she did not often think or act like a child, and she never *felt* like a child—not until that moment in the cemetery when suddenly she felt very young, weak, and helpless.

A tan Ford came slowly along the road, slowing even further as it drew near her. Behind the wheel was the man in the white shirt.

The moment she saw him, she knew why he'd seemed familiar. Four years ago. The robbery. Her guardian angel. Although she had been just eight years old at the time, she would never forget his face.

He brought the Ford almost to a halt and drifted by her slowly, scrutinizing her as he passed. They were just a few feet apart.

Through the open window of his car, every detail of his handsome face was as clear as on that terrible day when she had first seen him in the store. His eyes were as brilliantly blue and riveting as she had remembered. When their gazes locked, she shuddered.

He said nothing, did not smile, but studied her intently, as if trying to fix every detail of her appearance in his mind. He stared at her the way a man might stare at a tall glass of cool water after crossing a desert. His silence and unwavering gaze frightened Laura but also filled her with an inexplicable sense of security.

The car was rolling past her. She shouted, "Wait!"

She pushed away from the car against which she had been leaning, dashed toward the tan Ford. The stranger accelerated and sped out of the graveyard, leaving her alone in the sun until a moment later she heard a man speak behind her, "Laura?"

When she turned she could not see him at first. He called her name again, softly, and she spotted him fifteen feet away at the edge of the trees, standing in the purple shadows under an Indian laurel. He wore black slacks, a black shirt, and seemed out of place in this summer day.

Curious, perplexed, wondering if somehow this man was connected with her guardian angel, Laura started forward. She closed to within two steps of the new stranger before she realized that the disharmony between him and the bright, warm summer day was not solely a result of his black clothing; wintry darkness was an integral part of the man himself; a coldness seemed to come from within him, as if he had been born to dwell in polar regions or in the high caves of ice-bound mountains.

She stopped less than five feet from him.

He said no more but stared at her intently, with a look that seemed as much puzzlement as anything.

She saw a scar on his left cheek.

"Why you?" the wintry man asked, and he took a step forward, reaching for her.

Laura stumbled backward, suddenly too scared to cry out.

From the middle of the copse of trees, Cora Lance called, "Laura? Are you all right, Laura?"

The stranger reacted to the nearness of Cora's voice, turned, and moved away through the laurels, his black-clad body disappearing quickly in the shadows, as if he had not been a real man at all but a bit of darkness briefly come to life.

Five days after the funeral, on Tuesday the twenty-ninth of July, Laura was back in her own room above the grocery store for the first time in a week. She was packing and saying goodbye to the place that had been home to her for as long as she could recall.

Pausing to rest, she sat on the edge of the rumpled bed, trying to remember how secure and happy she had been in that room only days ago. A hundred paperback books, mostly dog and horse stories, were shelved in one corner. Fifty miniature dogs and cats—glass, brass, procelain, pewter—filled the shelves above the headboard of her bed.

She had no pets, for the health code prohibited animals in an apartment above a grocery. Some day she hoped to have a dog, perhaps even a horse. But more importantly she might be a veterinarian when she grew up, a healer of sick and injured animals.

Her father had said she could be anything: a vet, a lawyer, a movie star, anything. "You can be a moose herder if you want, or a ballerina on a pogo stick. Nothing can stop you."

Laura smiled, remembering how her father had imitated a ballerina on a pogo stick. But she also remembered he was gone, and a dreadful emptiness opened in her.

She cleaned out the closet, carefully folded her clothes, and filled two large suitcases. She had a steamer trunk as well, into which she packed her favorite books, a few games, a teddy bear.

Cora and Tom Lance were taking an inventory of the contents of the rest of the small apartment and of the grocery store downstairs. Laura was going to stay with them, though she was not yet clear as to whether the arrangement was permanent or temporary.

Made nervous and fretful by thoughts of her uncertain future, Laura returned to her packing. She pulled open the drawer in the nearest of the two nightstands and froze at the sight of the elfin boots, tiny umbrella, and four-inch-long neck scarf that her father had acquired as proof that Sir Tommy Toad indeed rented quarters from them.

He had persuaded one of his friends, a skilled leatherworker, to make the boots, which were wide and shaped to accommodate webbed feet. He had obtained the umbrella from a shop that sold miniatures, and he had made the green-plaid scarf himself, laboriously fashioning fringe for the ends of it. On her ninth birthday, when she came home from school, the boots and umbrella were standing against the wall just inside the apartment door, and the scrap of scarf was hung carefully on the coatrack. "Sssshh," her father whispered dramatically. "Sir Tommy has just returned from an arduous trip to Ecuador on the queen's business—she owns a diamond farm there, you know—and he's exhausted. I'm sure he'll sleep for *days*. However, he told me to wish you a very happy birthday, and he left a gift in the yard out back." The gift had been a new Schwinn bicycle.

Now, staring at the three items in the nightstand drawer, Laura realized that her father had not died alone. With him had gone Sir Tommy Toad, the many other characters he had created, and the silly but wonderful fantasies with which he'd entertained her. The webbed-foot boots, the tiny umbrella, and the little scarf looked so sweet and pathetic; she could almost believe that Sir Tommy, in fact, had been real and that he was now gone to a better world of his own. A low, miserable groan escaped her. She fell onto the bed and buried her face in the pillows, muffling her agonized sobs, and for the first time since her father's death she finally let her grief overwhelm her.

She did not want to live without him, yet she must not only live but prosper because every day of her life would be a testament to him. Even as young as she was, she understood that by living well and being a good person, she would make it possible for her father to go on living in some small way through her.

But facing the future with optimism and finding happiness was going to be hard. She now knew that life was frighteningly subject to tragedy and change, blue and warm one moment, cold and stormy the next, so you never knew when a bolt of lightning might strike someone you cared about. Nothing lasts forever. Life is a candle in the wind. That was a hard lesson for a girl her age, and it made her feel old, very old, ancient.

When the flood of warm tears abated, she did not take long to collect herself, for she did not want the Lances to discover that she had been crying. If the world was hard and cruel and unpredictable, then it did not seem wise to show the slightest weakness.

She carefully wrapped the webbed-foot boots, umbrella, and little scarf in tissue paper. She tucked them away in the steamer trunk.

When she had disposed of the contents of both nightstands, she went to her desk to clean that out as well, and on the felt blotter she found a folded sheet of tablet paper with a message for her in clear, elegant, almost machine-neat handwriting.

Dear Laura,

Some things are meant to be, and no one can prevent them. Not even your special guardian. Be content with the knowledge that your father loved you with all his heart in a way that few people are ever lucky enough to be loved. Though you think now that you will never be happy again, you are wrong. In time happiness will come to you. This is not an empty promise. This is a fact.

The note was unsigned, but she knew who must have written it: the man who had been at the cemetery, who had studied her from the passing car, who years ago saved her and her father from being shot. No one else could call himself her special guardian. A tremor swept through her not because she was afraid but because the strangeness and the mystery of her guardian filled her with curiosity and wonder.

She hurried to the bedroom window and pushed aside the sheer curtain that hung between the drapes, certain that she would see him standing in the street, watching the store, but he was not there.

The man in dark clothing was not there, either, but she had not expected to see him. She had half convinced herself that the other stranger was unrelated to her guardian, that he had been in the cemetery for some other reason. He had known her name . . . but perhaps he had heard Cora calling her earlier, from the top of the graveyard hill. She was able to put him out of her mind because she did not *want* him to be part of her life, not as she so desperately wanted to have a special guardian.

She read the message again.

Although she did not understand who the blond man was or why he had taken an interest in her, Laura was reassured by the note he had left. Understanding wasn't always necessary, as long as you *believed.*

·5·

The following night, after he had planted explosives in the attic of the institute, Stefan returned with the same suitcase, claiming he had insomnia again. Anticipating the post-midnight visit, Viktor had brought half of one of his wife's cakes as a gift.

Stefan nibbled at the cake while he shaped and placed the plastic explosives. The enormous basement was divided into two rooms, and unlike the attic it was used daily by employees. He would have to conceal the charges and wires with considerable care.

The first chamber contained research files and a pair of long, oak worktables. The file cabinets were six feet tall and stood in banks along two of the walls. He was able to place the explosives atop the cabinets, tucking them toward the back, against the walls, where not even the tallest man on the staff could see them.

He strung the wires behind the cabinets, though he was forced to drill a small hole in the partition between halves of the cellar in order to continue that detonation line into the next chamber. He managed to put the hole in an inconspicuous place, and the wires were visible only for a couple of inches on either side of the partition.

The second room was used for storage of office and lab supplies and to cage the score of animals—several hamsters, a few white rats, two dogs, one energetic monkey in a big cage with three bars to swing on—that had participated in (and survived) the institute's early experiments. Though the animals were of no more use, they were kept in order to learn if over the long term they developed unforeseen medical problems that could be related to their singular adventures.

Stefan molded powerful charges of plastique into hollow spaces toward the back of the stacked supplies and brought all of the wires to the screened ventilation chase down which he had dropped the attic wires the previous night, and as he worked, he felt the animals watching with unusual intensity, as if they knew they had less than twenty-four hours to live. His cheeks flushed with guilt, which strangely he had failed to feel when contemplating the deaths of the men who worked in the institute, perhaps because the animals were innocent and the men were not.

By four o'clock in the morning, Stefan had finished both the job in the basement and the work he had to do in his office on the third floor. Before leaving the institute, he went to the main lab on the ground floor and for a minute stared at the gate.

The gate.

The scores of dials and gauges and graphs in the gate's support machinery all glowed softly orange, yellow, or green, for the power to it was never turned off. The thing was cylindrical, twelve feet long and eight feet in diameter, barely visible in the dim light; its stainless-steel outer skin gleamed with faint reflections of the spots of light in the machinery that lined three of the room's walls.

He had used the gate scores of times, but he was still in awe of it—not so much because it was an astonishing scientific breakthrough but because its potential for evil was unlimited. It was not a gate to hell, but in the hands of the wrong men, it might as well have been just that. And it was indeed in the hands of the wrong men.

After thanking Viktor for the cake and claiming to have eaten all that he had been given—though in fact he fed the larger part of it to the animals—Stefan drove back to his apartment.

For the second night in a row, a storm raged. Rain slashed out of the northwest. Water foamed out of downspouts into nearby drains, drizzled off roofs, puddled in the streets, and overflowed gutters, and because the city was almost entirely dark, the pools and streams looked more like oil than water. Only a few military personnel were out, and they all wore dark slickers that made them look as if they were creatures from an old Gothic novel by Bram Stoker.

Stefan took a direct route home, making no effort to skirt the known police inspection stations. His papers were in order; his exemption from curfew was current; and he was no longer transporting illegally obtained explosives.

In his apartment he set the alarm on the large bedside clock and fell almost immediately to sleep. He desperately needed his rest because, in the afternoon to come, there would be two arduous journeys and much killing. If he was not fully alert, he might find himself on the wrong end of a bullet.

His dreams were of Laura, which he interpreted as a good omen.

Two

THE ENDURING FLAME

·1·

Laura Shane was swept from her twelfth through her seventeenth years as if she were a tumbleweed blown across the California deserts, coming to rest briefly here and there in becalmed moments, torn loose and sent rolling again as soon as the wind gusted.

She had no relatives, and she could not stay with her father's best friends, the Lances. Tom was sixty-two, and Cora was fifty-seven, and though married thirty-five years, they had no children. The prospect of raising a young girl daunted them.

Laura understood and bore no grudge against them. On the day in August when she left the Lance house in the company of a woman from the Orange County Child Welfare Agency, Laura kissed both Cora and Tom and assured them that she would be fine. Riding away in the social worker's car, she waved gaily, hoping they felt absolved.

Absolved. That word was a recent acquisition. Absolved: freed from the consequences of one's actions; to set free or release from some duty, obligation, or responsibility. She wished that she could grant herself absolution from the obligation to make her way in the world without the guidance of a loving father, absolution from the responsibility to live and carry on his memory.

From the Lances' house she was conveyed to a child shelter—the McIlroy Home—an old, rambling, twenty-seven-room Victorian mansion built by a produce magnate in the days of Orange County's agricultural glory. Later it had been converted to a dormitory where children in public custody were housed temporarily between foster homes.

That institution was unlike any she had read about in fiction. For one thing, it lacked kindly nuns in flowing black habits.

And there was Willy Sheener.

Laura first noticed him shortly after arriving at the home, while a social worker, Mrs. Bowmaine, was showing her to the room she would share with—she had been told—the Ackerson twins and a girl named Tammy. Sheener was sweeping a tile-floored hallway with a pushbroom.

He was strong, wiry, pale, freckled, about thirty, with hair the color of a new copper penny and green eyes. He smiled and whistled softly while he worked. "How're you this morning, Mrs. Bowmaine?"

"Right as rain, Willy." She clearly liked Sheener. "This is Laura Shane, a new girl. Laura, this is Mr. Sheener."

Sheener stared at Laura with a creepy intensity. When he managed to speak, the words were thick, "Uhhh . . . welcome to McIlroy."

Following the social worker, Laura glanced back at Sheener. With no one but Laura to see, he lowered one hand to his crotch and lazily massaged himself.

Laura did not look at him again.

Later, as she was unpacking her meager belongings, trying to make her quarter of the third-floor bedroom more like home, she turned and saw Sheener in the doorway. She was alone, for the other kids were at play in the backyard or the game room. His smile was different from the one with which he'd favored Mrs. Bowmaine: predatory, cold. Light from one of the two small windows fell across the doorway and met his eyes at such an angle as to make them appear silver instead of green, like the cataract-filmed eyes of a dead man.

Laura tried to speak but could not. She edged backward until she came up against the wall beside her bed.

He stood with his arms at his sides, motionless, hands fisted.

The McIlroy Home was not air conditioned. The bedroom windows were open, but the place was tropically hot. Yet Laura had not been sweating until she turned and saw Sheener. Now her T-shirt was damp.

Outside, children at play shouted and laughed. They were nearby, but they sounded far away.

The hard, rhythmic rasp of Sheener's breathing seemed to grow louder, gradually drowning out the voices of the children.

For a long time neither of them moved or spoke. Then abruptly he turned and walked away.

Weak-kneed, sweat-soaked, Laura moved to her bed and sat on the edge of it. The mushy mattress sagged, and the springs creaked.

As her thudding heartbeat deaccelerated, she surveyed the gray-walled room and despaired of her circumstances. In the four corners were narrow, iron-framed beds with tattered chenille spreads and lumpy pillows. Each bed had a battered, Formica-topped nightstand, and on each was a metal reading lamp. The scarred dresser had eight drawers, two of which were hers. There were two closets, and she was allotted half of one. The ancient curtains were faded, stained; they hung limp and greasy from rust-spotted rods. The entire house was moldering and haunted; the air had a vaguely unpleasant odor; and Willy Sheener roamed the rooms and halls as if he were a malevolent spirit waiting for the full moon and the blood games attendant thereon.

That night after dinner the Ackerson twins closed the door to the room and encouraged Laura to join them on the threadbare maroon carpet where they could sit in a circle and share secrets.

Their other roomie—a strange, quiet, frail blonde named Tammy—had no interest in joining them. Propped up by pillows, she sat in bed and read a book, nibbling her nails continuously, mouselike.

Laura liked Thelma and Ruth Ackerson immediately. Having just turned twelve, they were only months younger than Laura and were wise for their age. They had been orphaned when they were nine and had lived at the shelter for almost three years. Finding adoptive parents for children their age was difficult, especially for twins who were determined not to be split up.

Not pretty girls, they were astonishingly identical in their plainness: lusterless brown hair, myopic brown eyes, broad faces, blunt chins, wide mouths. Although lacking in good looks, they were abundantly intelligent, energetic, and good-natured.

Ruth was wearing blue pajamas with dark green piping on the cuffs and collar, blue slippers; her hair was tied in a ponytail. Thelma wore raspberry-red pajamas and furry yellow slippers, each with two buttons painted to represent eyes, and her hair was unfettered.

With darkfall the insufferable heat of the day had passed. They were less than ten miles from the Pacific, so the night breezes made comfortable sleep possible. Now, with the windows open, currents of mild air stirred the aged curtains and circulated through the room.

"Summer's a bore here," Ruth told Laura as they sat in a circle on the floor. "We're not allowed off the property, and it's just not big enough. And in the summer all the do-gooders are busy with their own vacations, their own trips to the beach, so they forget about us."

"Christmas is great, though," Thelma said.

"All of November and December are great," Ruth said.

"Yeah," Thelma said. "Holidays are fine because the do-gooders start feeling guilty about having so much when we poor, drab, homeless waifs have to wear newspaper coats, cardboard shoes, and eat last year's gruel. So they send us baskets of goodies, take us on shopping sprees and to the movies, though never the *good* movies."

"Oh, I like some of them," Ruth said.

"The kind of movies where no one ever, ever gets blown up. And *never* any feelies. They'll never take us to a movie in which some guy puts his hand on a girl's boob. Family films. Dull, dull, dull."

"You'll have to forgive my sister," Ruth told Laura. "She thinks she's on the trembling edge of puberty—"

"I *am* on the trembling edge of puberty! I feel my sap rising!" Thelma said, thrusting one thin arm into the air above her head.

Ruth said, "The lack of parental guidance has taken a toll on her, I'm afraid. She hasn't adapted well to being an orphan."

"You'll have to forgive *my* sister," Thelma said. "She's decided to skip puberty and go directly from childhood to senility."

Laura said, "What about Willy Sheener?"

The Ackerson twins glanced knowingly at each other and spoke with such synchronization that not a fraction of a second was lost between their statements: "Oh, a disturbed man," Ruth said, and Thelma said, "He's scum," and Ruth said, "He needs therapy," and Thelma said, "No, what he needs is a hit over the head with a baseball bat maybe a dozen times, maybe two dozen, then locked away for the rest of his life."

Laura told them about encountering Sheener in her doorway.

"He didn't say anything?" Ruth asked. "That's creepy. Usually he says 'You're a very pretty little girl' or—"

"—he offers you candy." Thelma grimaced. "Can you *imagine?* Candy? How trite! It's as if he learned to be a scumbag by reading those booklets the police hand out to warn kids about perverts."

"No candy," Laura said, shivering as she remembered Sheener's sun-silvered eyes and heavy, rhythmic breathing.

Thelma leaned forward, lowering her voice to a stage whisper. "Sounds like the White Eel was tongue-tied, too hot even to *think* of his usual lines. Maybe he has a special lech for you, Laura."

"White Eel?"

"That's Sheener," Ruth said. "Or just the Eel for short."

"Pale and slick as he is," Thelma said, "the name fits. I'll bet the Eel has a special lech for you. I mean, kid, you *are* a knockout."

"Not me," Laura said.

"Are you kidding?" Ruth said. "That dark hair, those big eyes."

Laura blushed and started to protest, and Thelma said, "Listen, Shane, the Dazzling Ackerson Duo—Ruth and moi—cannot abide false modesty any more than we can tolerate bragging. We're straight-from-the-shoulder types. We know what *our* strengths are, and we're proud of them. God knows, neither of us will win the Miss America contest, but we're intelligent, very intelligent, and we're not reluctant to admit to brains. And *you* are gorgeous, so stop being coy."

"My sister is sometimes too blunt and too colorful in the way she expresses herself," Ruth said apologetically.

"And *my* sister," Thelma told Laura, "is trying out for the part of Melanie in *Gone With the Wind*." She put on a thick Southern accent and spoke with exaggerated sympathy: "Oh, Scarlett doesn't mean any harm. Scarlett's a lovely girl, really she is. Rhett is so lovely at heart, too, and even the Yankees are lovely, even those who sacked Tara, burned our crops, and made boots out of the skin of our babies."

Laura began to giggle halfway through Thelma's performance.

"So drop the modest maiden act, Shane! You're gorgeous."

"Okay, okay. I know I'm . . . pretty."

"Kiddo, when the White Eel saw you, a fuse blew in his brain."

"Yes," Ruth agreed, "you stunned him. That's why he couldn't even think to reach in his pocket for the candy he always carries."

"Candy!" Thelma said. "Little bags of M&Ms, Tootsie Rolls!"

"Laura, be real careful," Ruth warned. "He's a sick man—"

"He's a geek!" Thelma said. "A sewer rat!"

From the far corner of the room, Tammy said softly, "He's not as bad as you say."

The blond girl was so quiet, so thin and colorless, so adept at fading into the background that Laura had forgotten her. Now she saw that Tammy had put her book aside and was sitting up in bed; she had drawn her bony knees against her chest and wrapped her arms around her legs. She was ten, two years younger than her roommates, small for her age. In a white nightgown and socks Tammy looked more like an apparition than like a real person.

"He wouldn't hurt anyone," Tammy said hesitantly, tremulously, as though stating her opinion about Sheener—about anything, anyone—was like walking on a tightrope without a net.

"He *would* hurt someone if he could get away with it," Ruth said.

"He's just . . ." Tammy bit her lip. "He's . . . lonely."

"No, honey," Thelma said, "he's not lonely. He's so much in love with himself that he'll never be lonely."

Tammy looked away from them. She got up, slipped her feet into floppy slippers, and mumbled, "Almost bedtime." She took her toiletry kit from her nightstand and shuffled out of the room, closing the door behind her, heading for one of the baths at the end of the hall.

"She takes the candy," Ruth explained.

An icy wave of revulsion washed through Laura. "Ah, no."

"Yes," Thelma said. "Not because she wants the candy. She's . . . messed up. She needs the kind of approval she gets from the Eel."

"But why?" Laura asked.

Ruth and Thelma exchanged another of their looks, through which they seemed to debate an issue and reach a decision in a second or two, without words. Sighing, Ruth said, "Well, see, Tammy needs that kind of approval because . . . her father taught her to need it."

Laura was jolted. "Her own *father*?"

"Not all the kids at McIlroy are orphans," Thelma said. "Some are here because their parents committed crimes and went to jail. And others were abused by their folks physically or . . . sexually."

The freshening air coming through the open windows was probably only a degree or two colder than when they had sat down in a circle on the floor, but it seemed to Laura like a chilly late-autumn wind that had mysteriously leaped the months and infiltrated the August night.

Laura said, "But Tammy doesn't really *like* it?"

"No, I don't think she does," Ruth said. "But she's—"

"—compelled," Thelma said, "can't help herself. Twisted."

They were all silent, thinking the unthinkable, and finally Laura said, "Strange and . . . so sad. Can't we stop it? Can't we tell

Mrs. Bowmaine or one of the other social workers about Sheener?"

"It wouldn't do any good," Thelma said. "The Eel would deny it, and *Tammy* would deny it, too, and we don't have any proof."

"But if she's not the only kid he's abused, one of the others—"

Ruth shook her head. "Most have gone to foster homes, adoptive parents, or back to their own families. Those two or three still here . . . well, they're either like Tammy, or they're just scared to death of the Eel, too scared ever to rat on him."

"Besides," Thelma said, "the adults don't want to know, don't want to deal with it. Bad publicity for the home. And it makes them look stupid to have this going on under their noses. Besides, who can believe children?" Thelma imitated Mrs. Bowmaine, catching the note of phoniness so perfectly that Laura recognized it at once: "Oh, my dear, they're horrible, lying little creatures. Noisy, rambunctious, bothersome little beasts, capable of destroying Mr. Sheener's fine reputation for the fun of it. If only they could be drugged, hung on wall hooks, and fed intravenously, how much more efficient that system would be, my dear—and really so much better for them, too."

"Then the Eel would be cleared," Ruth said, "and he'd come back to work, and he'd find ways to make us pay for speaking against him. It happened that way before with another perv who used to work here, a guy we called Ferret Fogel. Poor Denny Jenkins . . ."

"Denny ratted on Ferret Fogel; he told Bowmaine the Ferret molested him and two other boys. Fogel was suspended. But the two other boys wouldn't support Denny's story. They were afraid of the Ferret . . . but they also had this sick need for his approval. When Bowmaine and her staff interrogated Denny—"

"They hammered at him," Ruth said angrily, "with trick questions, trying to trip him up. He got confused, contradicted himself, so they said he was making it all up."

"And Fogel came back to work," Thelma said.

"He bided his time," Ruth said, "and then he found ways to make Denny miserable. He tormented the boy relentlessly until one day . . . Denny just started screaming and couldn't stop. The doctor had to give him a shot, and then they took him away. Emotionally disturbed, they said." She was on the brink of tears. "We never saw him again."

Thelma put one hand on her sister's shoulder. To Laura, she said,

"Ruth was fond of Denny. He was a nice boy. Small, shy, sweet . . . he never had a chance. That's why you've got to be tough with the White Eel. You can't let him see that you're afraid of him. If he tries anything, scream. And kick him in the crotch."

Tammy returned from the bathroom. She did not look at them but stepped out of her slippers and got under the covers.

Although Laura was repulsed by the thought of Tammy submitting to Sheener, she regarded the frail blonde with less disgust than sympathy. No sight could be more pitiful than that small, lonely, defeated girl lying on her narrow, sagging bed.

That night Laura dreamed of Sheener. He had his own human head, but his body was that of a white eel, and wherever Laura ran, Sheener slithered after her, wriggling under closed doors and other obstacles.

·2·

Sickened by what he'd just seen, Stefan returned from the institute's main lab to his third-floor office. He sat at his desk with his head in his hands, shaking with horror and anger and fear.

That red-haired bastard, Willy Sheener, was going to rape Laura repeatedly, beat her half to death, and leave her so traumatized that she would never recover. That was not just a possibility; it would come to pass if Stefan did not move to prevent it. He had *seen* the aftermath: Laura's bruised face, broken mouth. Her eyes had been the worst of it, so flat looking and half-dead, the eyes of a child who no longer had the capacity for joy or hope.

Cold rain tapped on the office windows, and that hollow sound seemed to reverberate within him, as if the terrible things he had seen had left him burnt out, an empty shell.

He had saved Laura from the junkie in her father's grocery, but here was another pedophile already. One of the things he had learned from the experiments in the institute was that reshaping fate was not always easy. Destiny struggled to reassert the pattern that was meant to be. Perhaps being molested and psychologically destroyed was such an immutable part of Laura's fate that Stefan could not prevent it from happening sooner or later. Perhaps he could not save her from Willy Sheener, or perhaps if he thwarted Sheener, *another* rapist would enter the girl's life. But he had to try.

Those half-dead, joyless eyes . . .

·3·

Seventy-six children resided at the McIlroy Home, all twelve or younger; upon turning thirteen, they were transferred to Caswell Hall in Anaheim. Since the oak-paneled dining hall would hold only forty, meals were served in two shifts. Laura was on the second shift, as were the Ackerson twins.

Standing in the cafeteria line between Thelma and Ruth on her first morning at the shelter, Laura saw that Willy Sheener was one of the four attendants serving from behind the counter. He monitored the milk supply and dispensed sweet rolls with a pair of tongs.

As Laura moved along the line, the Eel spent more time looking at her than at the kids he was serving.

"Don't let him intimidate you," Thelma whispered.

Laura tried to meet Sheener's gaze—and his challenge—boldly. But she was the one who always broke the staring match.

When she reached his station, he said, "Good morning, Laura," and put a sweet roll on her tray, a particular pastry he had saved for her. It was twice as large as the others, with more cherries and icing.

On Thursday, Laura's third full day at the shelter, she endured a how-are-we-adjusting meeting with Mrs. Bowmaine in the social worker's first-floor office. Etta Bowmaine was stout, with an unflattering wardrobe of flower-print dresses. She spoke in clichés and platitudes with that gushy insincerity that Thelma had imitated perfectly, and she asked a lot of questions to which she actually did not want honest answers. Laura lied about how happy she was at McIlroy, and the lies pleased Mrs. Bowmaine enormously.

Returning to her room on the third floor, Laura encountered the Eel on the north stairs. She turned at the second landing, and he was on the next flight, wiping the oak handrail with a rag. An unopened bottle of furniture polish stood on the step below him.

She froze, and her heart began to pound double time, for she knew he had been lying in wait for her. He'd have known about her summons to Mrs. Bowmaine's office and would have counted on her using the nearest stairs to return to her room.

They were alone. At any time another child or staff member might come along, but for the moment they were alone.

Her first impulse was to retreat and use the south stairs, but she remembered what Thelma had said about standing up to the Eel and about how his type preyed only on weaklings. She told herself that the best thing to do was walk past him without saying a word, but her feet seemed to have been nailed to the step; she could not move.

Looking down at her from half a flight up, the Eel smiled. It was a horrible smile: His skin was white, and his lips were colorless, but his crooked teeth were as yellow and mottled with brownish spots as the skin of a ripe banana. Under his unruly copper-red hair, his face resembled a clown's countenance—not the kind of clown you'd see in a circus but the kind you might run into on Halloween night, the kind that might carry a chainsaw instead of a seltzer bottle.

"You're a very pretty little girl, Laura."

She tried to tell him to go to hell. She couldn't speak.

"I'd like to be your friend," he said.

Somehow she found the strength to start up the steps toward him.

He smiled even more broadly, perhaps because he thought she was responding to his offer of friendship. He reached into a pocket of his khaki pants and withdrew a couple of Tootsie Rolls.

Laura recalled Thelma's comical assessment of the Eel's stupidly unimaginative gambits, and suddenly he did not look as scary to her as he had before. Offering Tootsie Rolls, leering at her, Sheener was a ridiculous figure, a caricature of evil, and she would have laughed at him if she had not known what he had done to Tammy and other girls. Though she could not quite laugh, the Eel's ludicrous appearance and manner gave her the courage to move swiftly around him.

When he realized she was not going to take the candy or respond to his offer of friendship, he put a hand on her shoulder to stop her.

She angrily took hold of his hand and threw it off. "Don't you ever touch me, you geek."

She hurried up the stairs, struggling against a desire to run. If she ran he would know that her fear of him had not been entirely banished. He must see absolutely no weakness in her, for weakness would encourage him to continue harassing her.

By the time she was only two steps from the next landing, she allowed herself to hope that she had won, that her toughness had impressed him. Then she heard the unmistakable sound of a zipper. Behind her, in a loud whisper he said, "Hey, Laura, look at this.

Look at what I have for you." There was a demented, hateful tone in his voice. "Look, look at what's in my hand now, Laura."

She did not glance back.

She reached the landing and started up the next flight, thinking: There's no reason to run; you don't *dare* run, don't run, don't run.

From one flight below, the Eel said, "Look at the big Tootsie Roll I have in my hand now, Laura. It's lots bigger than those others."

On the third floor Laura hurried directly to the bathroom where she vigorously scrubbed her hands. She felt filthy after taking hold of Sheener's hand in order to remove it from her shoulder.

Later, when she and the Ackerson twins convened their nightly powwow on the floor of their room, Thelma howled with laughter when she heard about the Eel wanting Laura to look at his "big Tootsie Roll." She said, "He's priceless, isn't he? Where do you think he gets these lines of his? Does Doubleday publish the *Perverts' Book of Classic Come-ons* or something?"

"The point is," Ruth said worriedly, "he wasn't turned off when Laura stood up to him. I don't think he's going to give up on her as quickly as he gives up on other girls who resist him."

That night Laura had difficulty sleeping. She thought about her special guardian, and she wondered if he would appear as miraculously as before and if he would deal with Willy Sheener. Somehow she didn't think she could count on him this time.

During the following ten days, as August waned, the Eel shadowed Laura as reliably as the moon shadowed the earth. When she and the Ackerson twins went to the game room to play cards or Monopoly, Sheener arrived within ten minutes and set to work ostensibly washing windows or polishing furniture or repairing a drapery rod, though in fact his attention was primarily focused on Laura. If the girls sought refuge in a corner of the playground behind the mansion, either to talk or play a game of their own devising, Sheener entered the yard shortly thereafter, having suddenly found shrubbery that had to be pruned or fertilized. And although the third floor was for girls only, it was open to male staff members for the purpose of maintenance between ten in the morning and four in the afternoon on weekdays, so Laura could not escape to her room during those hours with any degree of safety.

Worse than the Eel's diligence was the frightening rate at which his dark passion for her grew, a sick need revealed by the steadily increasing intensity of his gaze and the sour sweat that burst from him when he was in the same room with her for more than a few minutes.

Laura, Ruth, and Thelma tried to convince themselves that the threat from the Eel lessened with every day he did not act, that his hesitation revealed his awareness of Laura as unsuitable prey. At heart they knew they were hoping to slay the dragon with a wish, but they were unable to face the full extent of the danger till a Saturday afternoon late in August, when they returned to their room and found Tammy destroying Laura's book collection in a fit of twisted jealousy.

The library of fifty paperbacks—her favorite books, which she had brought with her from the apartment above the grocery—were kept under Laura's bed. Tammy had brought them out into the middle of the room and in a hateful frenzy had ripped apart two-thirds of them.

Laura was too shocked to act, but Ruth and Thelma pulled the girl away from the books and restrained her.

Because those were her favorite books, because her father bought them for her and they were therefore a link to him, but most of all because she owned so little, Laura was pained by the destruction. Her possessions were so meager, of no value, but she suddenly realized that they formed ramparts against the worst cruelties of life.

Tammy lost interest in the books now that the true object of her rage stood before her. "I hate you, I hate you!" Her pale, drawn face was alive for the first time since Laura had known her, flushed and contorted with emotion. The bruiselike circles around her eyes hadn't vanished, but they no longer made her appear weak or broken; instead she looked wild, savage. "I hate you, Laura, I hate you!"

"Tammy, honey," Thelma said, struggling to hold on to the girl, "Laura's never done anything to you."

Breathing hard but no longer thrashing to break free of Ruth and Thelma, Tammy shrieked at Laura: "You're all he talks about, he isn't interested in me any more, just you, he can't stop talking about you, I hate you, why did you have to come here, I hate you!"

No one had to ask her to whom she was referring. The Eel.

"He doesn't want me any more, nobody wants me now, he only wants me so I can help him get to you. Laura, Laura, Laura. He wants me to trick you into a place where he can get you alone, where it'll be safe for him, but I won't do it, I won't! 'Cause then what would I have once he's got you? Nothing." Her face was a furious red. Worse than her rage was the awful desperation that lay behind it.

Laura ran out of the room, down the long hall into the lavatory. Sick with disgust and fear, she fell to her knees on the cracked yellow tiles before one of the toilets and threw up. Once her stomach was purged she went to one of the sinks, rinsed her mouth repeatedly, then splashed cold water on her face. When she raised her head and looked in the mirror, the tears came at last.

It was not her own loneliness or fear that brought her to tears. She was crying for Tammy. The world was an unthinkably mean place if it would allow a ten-year-old girl's life to be devalued to such an extent that the only words of approval she ever heard from an adult were those spoken by the demented man who abused her, that the only possession in which she could take pride was the underdeveloped sexual aspect of her own thin, prepubescent body.

Laura realized that Tammy's situation was infinitely worse than her own. Even stripped of her books, Laura had good memories of a loving, kind, gentle father, which Tammy did not. If what few things she owned were taken from her, Laura would still be whole of mind, but Tammy was psychologically damaged, perhaps beyond repair.

·4·

Sheener lived in a bungalow on a quiet street in Santa Ana. It was one of those neighborhoods built after World War II: small, neat houses with interesting architectural details. In this summer of 1963, the various types of ficus trees had reached maturity, spreading their limbs protectively over the homes; Sheener's place was further cloaked by overgrown shrubbery—azaleas, eugenias, and red-flowering hibiscus.

Near midnight, using a plastic loid, Stefan popped the lock on the back door and let himself into the house. As he inspected the bungalow, he boldly turned on lights and did not bother to draw the drapes at the windows.

The kitchen was immaculate. The blue Formica counters glistened. The chrome handles on the appliances, the faucet in the sink, and the metal frames of the kitchen chairs all gleamed, unmarred by a single fingerprint.

He opened the refrigerator, not sure what he expected to find there. Perhaps an indication of Willy Sheener's abnormal psychology; a former victim of his molestations, murdered and frozen to preserve the memories of twisted passion? Nothing that dramatic. However, the man's fetish for neatness was obvious: All the food was stored in matching Tupperware containers.

Otherwise, the only thing odd about the contents of both the refrigerator and cupboards was the preponderance of sweets: ice cream, cookies, cakes, candies, pies, doughnuts, even animal crackers. There were a great many novelty foods, too, like Spaghetti-Os and cans of vegetable soup in which the noodles were shaped like popular cartoon characters. Sheener's larder looked as if it had been stocked by a child with a checkbook but no adult supervision.

Stefan moved deeper into the house.

·5·

The confrontation over the shredded books was sufficient to drain what little spirit Tammy possessed. She said no more about Sheener and seemed no longer to harbor any animosity toward Laura. Retreating further into herself day by day, she averted her eyes from everyone, hung her head lower; her voice grew softer.

Laura wasn't sure which was less tolerable—the constant threat posed by the White Eel or watching Tammy's already wispy personality fading further as she slid toward a state hardly more active than catatonia. But on Thursday, August 30, those two burdens were lifted unexpectedly from Laura's shoulders when she learned that she would be transferred to a foster home in Costa Mesa the following day, Friday.

However, she regretted leaving the Ackersons. Though she'd known them only a few weeks, friendships forged in extremity solidified faster and felt more enduring than those made in more ordinary times.

That night, as the three of them sat on the floor of their room, Thelma said, "Shane, if you wind up with a good family, a happy home, just settle down snug and *enjoy*. If you're in a good place, forget us, make new friends, get on with your life. *But* the legendary Ackerson sisters—Ruth and moi—have been through the foster-family mill, three bad ones, so let me assure you that if you wind up in a *rotten* place, you don't have to stay there."

Ruth said, "Just weep a lot and let everyone know how unhappy you are. If you can't weep, pretend to."

"Sulk," Thelma advised. "Be clumsy. Accidentally break a dish each time you've got to wash them. Make a nuisance of yourself."

Laura was surprised. "You did all that to get back into McIlroy?"

"That and more," Ruth said.

"But didn't you feel terrible—breaking their things?

"It was harder for Ruth than me," Thelma said. "I've got the devil in me, while Ruth is the reincarnation of an obscure, treacly, fourteenth-century nun whose name we've not yet ascertained."

Within one day Laura knew she did not want to remain in the care of the Teagel family, but she tried to make it work because at first she thought their company was preferable to returning to McIlroy.

Real life was just a misty backdrop to Flora Teagel, for whom only crossword puzzles were of interest. She spent days and evenings at the table in her yellow kitchen, wrapped in a cardigan regardless of the weather, working through books of crossword puzzles one after another with a dedication both astonishing and idiotic.

She usually spoke to Laura only to give her lists of chores and to seek help with knotty crossword clues. As Laura stood at the sink, washing dishes, Flora might say, "What's a seven-letter word for cat?"

Laura's answer was always the same: "I don't know."

" 'I don't know, I don't know, I don't know,' " Mrs. Teagel mocked. "You don't seem to know anything, girl. Aren't you paying attention in school? Don't you care about language, about words?"

Laura, of course, was *fascinated* with words. To her, words were things of beauty, each like a magical powder or potion that could be combined with other words to create powerful spells. But to Flora Teagel, words were game chips needed to fill blank puzzle squares, annoyingly elusive clusters of letters that frustrated her.

Flora's husband, Mike, was a squat, baby-faced truck driver. He spent evenings in an armchair, poring over the *National Enquirer* and its clones, absorbing useless facts from dubious stories about alien contact and devil-worshiping movie stars. His taste for what he called "exotic news" would have been harmless if he'd been as self-absorbed as his wife, but he often popped in on Laura when she was doing chores or in those rare moments when she was given time for homework, and he insisted on reading aloud the more bizarre articles.

She thought these stories were stupid, illogical, pointless, but she could not tell him so. She had learned that he would not be offended if she said his newspapers were rubbish. Instead he'd regard her pityingly; then with maddening patience, with an infuriating know-it-all manner found only in the overeducated and totally ignorant, he would proceed to explain how the world worked. At length. Repeatedly. "Laura, you've got a lot to learn. The big shots who run things in Washington, *they* know about the aliens and the secrets of Atlantis . . ."

As different as Flora was from Mike, they shared one belief: that the purpose of sheltering a foster child was to obtain a free servant. Laura was expected to clean, do laundry, iron clothes, and cook.

Their own daughter—Hazel, an only child—was two years older than Laura and thoroughly spoiled. Hazel never cooked, washed dishes, did laundry, or cleaned house. Though she was just fourteen, she had perfectly manicured, painted fingernails and toenails. If you had deducted from her age the number of hours she had spent primping in front of a mirror, she would have been only five years old.

"On laundry day," she explained on Laura's first day in the Teagel house, "you must press *my* clothes first. And always be sure that you hang them in my closet arranged according to color."

I've read this book and seen this movie, Laura thought. Gad, I've got the lead in *Cinderella!*

"I'm going to be a major movie star or a model," Hazel said. "So my face, hands, and body are my future. I've got to protect them."

When Mrs. Ince—the wire-thin, whippet-faced child-welfare worker assigned to the case—paid a scheduled visit to the Teagel house on Saturday morning, September 16, Laura intended to demand to be returned to McIlroy Home. The threat posed by Willy Sheener had come to seem less of a problem than everyday life with the Teagels.

Mrs. Ince arrived on schedule to find Flora washing the first dishes she had washed in two weeks. Laura was sitting at the kitchen table, apparently working a crossword puzzle that in fact had been shoved into her hands only when the doorbell had rung.

In that portion of the visit devoted to a private interview with Laura in her bedroom, Mrs. Ince refused to believe what she was told about Laura's load of housework. "But dear, Mr. and Mrs. Teagel are exemplary foster parents. You don't look to me as if you've been worked to the bone. You've even gained a few pounds."

"I didn't accuse them of starving me," Laura said. "But I never have time for schoolwork. I go to bed every night exhausted—"

"Besides," Mrs. Ince interrupted, "foster parents are expected not merely to house children but to *raise* them, which means teaching manners and deportment, instilling good values and good work habits."

Mrs. Ince was hopeless.

Laura resorted to the Ackersons' plan for shedding an unwanted foster family. She began to clean haphazardly. When she was done with the dishes, they were spotted and streaked. She ironed wrinkles *into* Hazel's clothes.

Because the destruction of most of her book collection had taught her a profound respect for property, Laura could not break dishes or anything else that belonged to the Teagels, but for that part of the Ackerson Plan she substituted scorn and disrespect. Working a puzzle, Flora asked for a six-letter word meaning "a species of ox," and Laura said, "Teagel." When Mike began to recount a flying-saucer story he had read in the *Enquirer,* she interrupted to spin a tale about mutated mole men living secretly in the local supermarket. To Hazel, Laura suggested that her big break in show business might best be achieved by applying to serve as Ernest Borgnine's stand-in: "You're a dead-ringer for him, Hazel. They've *got* to hire you!"

Her scorn led swiftly to a spanking. With his big, calloused hands Mike had no need of a paddle. He thumped her across the bottom, but she bit her lip and refused to give him the satisfaction of her tears. Watching from the kitchen doorway, Flora said, "Mike, that's enough. Don't mark her." He quit reluctantly only when his wife entered the room and stayed his hand.

That night Laura had difficulty sleeping. For the first time she had employed her love of words, the power of language, to achieve a desired effect, and the Teagels' reactions were proof that she could use words well. Even more exciting was the half-formed thought, still too new to be fully understood, that she might possess the ability not only to defend herself with words but to earn her way in the world with them, perhaps even as an author of the kind of books she so much enjoyed. With her father she'd talked of being a doctor, ballerina, veterinarian, but that had been just talk. None of those dreams had filled her with as much excitement as the prospect of being a writer.

The next morning, when she went down to the kitchen and found the three Teagels at breakfast, she said, "Hey, Mike, I've just discovered there's an intelligent squid from Mars living in the toilet tank."

"What *is* this?" Mike demanded.

Laura smiled and said, "Exotic news."

Two days later Laura was returned to McIlroy Home.

·6·

Willy Sheener's living room and den were furnished as if an ordinary man lived there. Stefan was not sure what he had expected. Evidence of dementia, perhaps, but not this neat, orderly home.

One of the bedrooms was empty, and the other was decidedly odd. The only bed was a narrow mattress on the floor. The pillowcases and sheets were for a child's room, emblazoned with the colorful, antic figures of cartoon rabbits. The nightstand and dresser were scaled to a child's dimensions, pale blue, with stenciled animals on the sides and drawers: giraffes, rabbits, squirrels. Sheener owned a collection of Little Golden Books, as well, and other children's picture books, stuffed animals, and toys suitable for a six- or seven-year-old.

At first Stefan thought that room was designed for the seduction of neighborhood children, that Sheener was unstable enough to seek out prey even on his home ground, where the risk was greatest. But there was no other bed in the house, and the closet and dresser drawers were filled with a man's clothing. On the walls were a dozen framed photos of the same red-headed boy, some as an infant, some when he was seven or eight, and the face was identifiably that of a younger Sheener. Gradually Stefan realized the decor was for Willy Sheener's benefit alone. The creep slept here. At bedtime Sheener evidently retreated into a fantasy of childhood, no doubt finding a desperately needed peace in his eerie, nightly regression.

Standing in the middle of that strange room, Stefan felt both saddened and repelled. It seemed that Sheener molested children not solely or even primarily for the sexual thrill of it but to absorb their youth, to become young again like them; through perversion he seemed to be trying to descend not into moral squalor so much as into a lost innocence. He was equally pathetic and despicable, inadequate to the challenges of adult life but nonetheless dangerous for his inadequacies.

Stefan shivered.

•7•

Her bed in the Ackerson twins' room was now occupied by another kid. Laura was assigned to a small, two-bed room at the north end of the third floor near the stairs. Her bunkmate was nine-year-old Eloise Fischer, who had pigtails, freckles, and a demeanor too serious for a child. "I'm going to be an accountant when I grow up," she told Laura. "I like numbers a lot. You can add up a column of numbers and get the same answer every time. There're no surprises with numbers; they're not at all like people." Eloise's parents had been convicted of drug dealing and sent to prison, and she was in McIlroy while the court decided which relative would be given custody of her.

As soon as Laura had unpacked, she hurried to the Ackersons' room. Bursting in on them, she cried, "I is free, I is free!"

Tammy and the new girl looked at her blankly, but Ruth and Thelma ran to her and hugged her, and it was like coming home to real family.

"Your foster family didn't like you?" Ruth asked.

Thelma said, "Ah ha! You used the Ackerson Plan."

"No, I killed them all while they slept."

"That'll work," Thelma agreed.

The new girl, Rebecca Bogner, was about eleven. She and the Ackersons obviously were not sympatico. Listening to Laura and the twins, Rebecca kept saying "you're weird" and "too weird" and "jeez, what weirdos," with such an air of superiority and disdain that she poisoned the atmosphere as effectively as a nuclear detonation.

Laura and the twins went outside to a corner of the playground where they could share five weeks of news without Rebecca's snotty commentary. It was early October, and the days were still warm, though at a quarter till five the air was cooling. They wore jackets and sat on the lower branches of the jungle gym, which was abandoned now that the younger children were washing up for the early dinner.

They had not been in the yard five minutes before Willy Sheener arrived with an electric shrub trimmer. He set to work on a eugenia hedge about thirty feet from them, but his attention was on Laura.

At dinner the Eel was at his serving station on the cafeteria line, passing out cartons of milk and pieces of cherry pie. He had saved the largest slice for Laura.

On Monday she entered a new school where the other kids already had four weeks to make friends. Ruth and Thelma were in a couple of her classes, which made it easier to adjust, but she was reminded that the primary condition of an orphan's life was instability.

Tuesday afternoon, when Laura returned from school, Mrs. Bowmaine stopped her in the hall. "Laura, may I see you in my office?"

Mrs. Bowmaine was wearing a purple floral-pattern dress that clashed with the rose and peach floral patterns of her office drapes and wallpaper. Laura sat in a rose-patterned chair. Mrs. Bowmaine stood at her desk, intending to deal with Laura quickly and move on to other tasks. Mrs. Bowmaine was a bustler, a busy-busy type.

"Eloise Fischer left our charge today," Mrs. Bowmaine said.

"Who got custody?" Laura asked. "She liked her grandmother."

"It was her grandmother," Mrs. Bowmaine confirmed.

Good for Eloise. Laura hoped the pigtailed, freckled, future accountant would find something to trust besides cold numbers.

"Now you've no roommate," Mrs. Bowmaine said briskly, "and we've no vacant bed elsewhere, so you can't just move in with—"

"May I make a suggestion?"

Mrs. Bowmaine frowned with impatience and consulted her watch.

Laura said quickly, "Ruth and Thelma are my best friends, and their roomies are Tammy Hinsen and Rebecca Bogner. But I don't think Tammy and Rebecca get along well with Ruth and Thelma, so—"

"We want you children to learn how to live with people different from you. Bunking with girls you already like won't build character. Anyway, the point is, I can't make new arrangements until tomorrow; I'm busy today. So I want to know if I can trust you to spend the night alone in your current room."

"Trust me?" Laura asked in confusion.

"Tell me the truth, young lady. Can I trust you alone tonight?"

Laura could not figure what trouble the social worker anticipated from a child left alone for one night. Perhaps she expected Laura to barricade herself in the room so effectively that police would have to blast the door, disable her with tear gas, and drag her out in chains.

Laura was as insulted as she was confused. "Sure, I'll be okay. I'm not a baby. I'll be fine."

"Well . . . all right. You'll sleep by yourself tonight, but we'll make other arrangements tomorrow."

After leaving Mrs. Bowmaine's colorful office for the drab hallways, climbing the stairs to the third floor, Laura suddenly thought: *the White Eel!* Sheener would know she was going to be alone tonight. He knew everything that went on at McIlroy, and he had keys, so he could return in the night. Her room was next to the north stairs, so he could slip out of the stairwell into her room, overpower her in seconds. He'd club her or drug her, stuff her in a burlap sack, take her away, lock her in a cellar, and no one would know what had happened to her.

She turned at the second-floor landing, descended the stairs two at a time, and rushed back toward Mrs. Bowmaine's office, but when she turned the corner into the front hall, she nearly collided with the Eel. He had a mop and a wringer-equipped bucket on wheels, which was filled with water reeking of pine-scented cleanser.

He grinned at her. Maybe it was only her imagination, but she was certain that he already knew she would be alone that night.

She should have stepped by him, gone to Mrs. Bowmaine, and begged for a change in the night's sleeping arrangements. She could not make accusations about Sheener, or she would wind up like Denny Jenkins—disbelieved by the staff, tormented relentlessly by her nemesis—but she could have found an acceptable excuse for her change of mind.

She also considered rushing at him, shoving him into his bucket, knocking him on his butt, and telling him that she was tougher than him, that he had better not mess with her. But he was different from the Teagels. Mike, Flora, and Hazel were small-minded, obnoxious, ignorant, but comparatively sane. The Eel was insane, and there was no way of knowing how he would react to being knocked flat.

As she hesitated, his crooked, yellow grin widened.

A flush touched his pale cheeks, and Laura realized it might be a flush of desire, which made her nauseous.

She walked away, dared not run until she had climbed the stairs and was out of his sight. Then she sprinted for the Ackersons' room.

"You'll sleep here tonight," Ruth said.

"Of course," Thelma said, "you'll have to stay in your room until they finish the bed check, then sneak down here."

From her corner where she was sitting in bed doing math homework, Rebecca Bogner said, "We've only got four beds."

"I'll sleep on the floor," Laura said.

"This is against the rules," Rebecca said.

Thelma made a fist and glowered at her.

"Okay, all right," Rebecca agreed. "I never said *I* didn't want her to stay. I just pointed out that it's against the rules."

Laura expected Tammy to object, but the girl lay on her back in bed, atop the covers, staring at the ceiling, apparently lost in her own thoughts and uninterested in their plans.

In the oak-paneled dining room, over an inedible dinner of pork chops, gluey mashed potatoes, and leathery green beans—and under the watchful eyes of the Eel—Thelma said, "As for why Bowmaine wanted to know if she could trust you alone . . . she's afraid you'll try suicide."

Laura was incredulous.

"Kids have done it here," Ruth said sadly. "Which is why they stuff at least two of us into even very small rooms. Being alone too much . . . that's one of the things that seems to trigger the impulse."

Thelma said, "They won't let Ruth and me share one of the small rooms because, since we're identical twins, they think we're really like *one* person. They think they'd no sooner close the door on us than we'd hang ourselves."

"That's ridiculous," Laura said.

"Of course it's ridiculous," Thelma agreed. "Hanging isn't flamboyant enough. The amazing Ackerson sisters—Ruth and moi—have a flair for the dramatic. We'd commit hari-kiri with stolen kitchen knives, or if we could get hold of a chainsaw. . . ."

Throughout the room conversations were conducted in moderate voices, for adult monitors patrolled the dining hall. The third-floor Resident Advisor, Miss Keist, passed behind the table where Laura sat with the Ackersons, and Thelma whispered, "Gestapo."

When Miss Keist passed, Ruth said, "Mrs. Bowmaine means well, but she just isn't good at what she does. If she took time to learn what kind of person you are, Laura, she'd never worry about you committing suicide. You're a survivor."

As she pushed her inedible food around her plate, Thelma said,

"Tammy Hinsen was once caught in the bathroom with a packet of razor blades, trying to get up the nerve to slash her wrists."

Laura was suddenly impressed by the mix of humor and tragedy, absurdity and bleak realism, that formed the peculiar pattern of their lives at McIlroy. One moment they were bantering amusingly with one another; a moment later they were discussing the suicidal tendencies of girls they knew. She realized that such an insight was beyond her years, and as soon as she returned to her room, she would write it down in the notebook of observations she had recently begun to keep.

Ruth had managed to choke down the food on her plate. She said, "A month after the razor-blade incident, they held a surprise search of our rooms, looking for dangerous objects. They found Tammy had a can of lighter fluid and matches. She'd intended to go into the showers, cover herself with lighter fluid, and set herself on fire."

"Oh, God." Laura thought of the thin, blond girl with the ashen complexion and the sooty rings around her eyes, and it seemed that her plan to immolate herself was only a desire to speed up the slow fire that for a long time had been consuming her from within.

"They sent her away two months for intense therapy," Ruth said.

"When she came back," Thelma said, "the adults talked about how much better she was, but she seemed the same to Ruth and me."

Ten minutes after Miss Keist's nightly room check, Laura left her bed. The deserted, third-floor hall was lit only by three safety lamps. Dressed in pajamas, carrying a pillow and blanket, she hurried barefoot to the Ackersons' room.

Only Ruth's bedside lamp was aglow. She whispered, "Laura, you sleep on my bed. I've made a place for myself on the floor."

"Well, unmake it and get back in your bed," Laura said.

She folded her blanket several times to make a pad on the floor, near the foot of Ruth's bed, and she lay on it with her pillow.

From her own bed Rebecca Bogner said, "We're all going to get in trouble over this."

"What're you afraid they'll do to us?" Thelma asked. "Stake us in the backyard, smear us with honey, and leave us for the ants?"

Tammy was sleeping or pretending to sleep.

Ruth turned out her light, and they settled down in darkness.

The door flew open, and the overhead light snapped on. Dressed in a red robe, scowling fiercely, Miss Keist entered the room. "So! Laura, what're you doing here?"

Rebecca Bogner groaned. "I *told* you we'd get in trouble."

"Come back to your room right this minute, young lady."

The swiftness with which Miss Keist appeared was suspicious, and Laura looked at Tammy Hinsen. The blonde was no longer feigning sleep. She was leaning on one elbow, smiling thinly. Evidently she had decided to assist the Eel in his quest for Laura, perhaps with the hope of regaining her status as his favorite.

Miss Keist escorted Laura to her room. Laura got into bed, and Miss Keist stared at her for a moment. "It's warm. I'll open the window." Returning to the bed, she studied Laura thoughtfully. "Is there anything you want to tell me? Is anything wrong?"

Laura considered telling her about the Eel. But what if Miss Keist waited to catch the Eel as he crept into her room, and what if he didn't show? Laura would never be able to accuse the Eel again because she'd have a *history* of accusing him; no one would take her seriously. Then even if Sheener raped her, he'd get away with it.

"No, nothing's wrong," she said.

Miss Keist said, "Thelma's too sure of herself for a girl her age, full of false sophistication. If you're foolish enough to break the rules again just to have an all-night gabfest, develop some friends worth taking the risk for."

"Yes, ma'am," Laura said just to get rid of her, sorry that she had even considered responding to the woman's moment of concern.

After Miss Keist left, Laura did not get out of bed and flee. She lay in darkness, certain there would be another bed check in half an hour. Surely the Eel would not slither around until midnight, and it was only ten, so between Miss Keist's next visit and the Eel's arrival, she'd have plenty of time to get to a safe place.

Far, far away in the night, thunder grumbled. She sat up in bed. Her guardian! She threw back the covers and ran to the window. She saw no lightning. The distant rumble faded. Perhaps it had not been thunder after all. She waited ten minutes or more, but nothing else happened. Disappointed, she returned to bed.

Shortly after ten-thirty the doorknob creaked. Laura closed her eyes, let her mouth fall open, and feigned sleep.

Someone stepped quietly across the room, stood beside the bed.

Laura breathed slowly, evenly, deeply, but her heart was racing.

It was Sheener. She *knew* it was him. Oh, God, she had forgotten he was insane, that he was unpredictable, and now he was here earlier than she'd expected, and he was preparing the hypodermic.

He'd jam her into a burlap sack and carry her away as if he was a brain-damaged Santa Claus come to steal children rather than leave gifts.

The clock ticked. The cool breeze rustled the curtains.

At last the person beside the bed retreated. The door closed.

It had been Miss Keist, after all.

Trembling violently, Laura got out of bed and pulled on her robe. She folded the blanket over her arm and left the room without slippers because she would make less noise if she was barefoot.

She could not return to the Ackersons' room. Instead she went to the north stairs, cautiously opened the door, and stepped onto the dimly lit landing. She listened for the sound of the Eel's footsteps below. She descended warily, expecting to encounter Sheener, but she reached the ground floor safely.

Shivering as the cool tile floor imparted its chill to her bare feet, she took refuge in the game room. She didn't turn on the lights but relied on the ghostly glow of the streetlamps that penetrated the windows and silvered the edges of the furniture. She eased past chairs and game tables, bedding down on her folded blanket behind the sofa.

She dozed fitfully, waking repeatedly from nightmares. The old mansion was filled with stealthy sounds in the night: the creaking of floorboards overhead, the hollow popping of ancient plumbing.

·8·

Stefan turned out all the lights and waited in the bedroom that was furnished for a child. At three-thirty in the morning, he heard Sheener returning. Stefan moved silently behind the bedroom door. A few minutes later Willy Sheener entered, switched on the light, and started toward the mattress. He made a queer sound as he crossed the room, partly a sigh and partly the whimper of an animal escaping from a hostile world into its burrow.

Stefan closed the door, and Sheener spun around at the sound of movement, shocked that his nest had been invaded. "Who . . . who are you? What the hell are you doing here?"

From a Chevy parked in the shadows across the street, Kokoschka watched Stefan depart Willy Sheener's house. He waited ten minutes, got out of the car, walked around to the back of the bungalow, found the door ajar, and cautiously went inside.

He located Sheener in a child's bedroom, battered and bloody and still. The air reeked of urine, for the man had lost control of his bladder.

Someday, Kokoschka thought with grim determination and a thrill of sadism, I'm going to hurt Stefan even worse than this. Him and that damned girl. As soon as I understand what part she plays in his plans and why he's jumping across decades to reshape her life, I'll put both of them through the kind of pain that no one knows this side of hell.

He left Sheener's house. In the backyard he stared up at the star-spattered sky for a moment, then returned to the institute.

·9·

Shortly after dawn, before the first of the shelter's residents had arisen but when Laura felt the danger from Sheener had passed, she left her bed in the game room and returned to the third floor. Everything in her room was as she had left it. There was no sign that she'd had an intruder during the night.

Exhausted, bleary-eyed, she wondered if she had given the Eel too much credit for boldness and daring. She felt somewhat foolish.

She made her bed—a housekeeping chore every McIlroy child was expected to perform—and when she lifted her pillow she was paralyzed by the sight of what lay under it. A single Tootsie Roll.

That day the White Eel did not come to work. He had been awake all night preparing to abduct Laura and no doubt needed his sleep.

"How does a man like that sleep at all?" Ruth wondered as they gathered in a corner of McIlroy's playground after school. "I mean, doesn't his conscience keep him awake?"

"Ruthie," Thelma said, "he doesn't have a conscience."

"Everyone does, even the worst of us. That's how God made us."

"Shane," Thelma said, "prepare to assist me in an exorcism. Our Ruth is once again possessed by the moronic spirit of Gidget."

In an uncharacteristic stroke of compassion, Mrs. Bowmaine moved Tammy and Rebecca to another room and allowed Laura to bunk with Ruth and Thelma. For the time being the fourth bed was vacant.

"It'll be Paul McCartney's bed," Thelma said, as she and Ruth helped Laura settle in. "Anytime the Beatles are in town, Paul can come use it. And *I'll* use Paul!"

"Sometimes," Ruth said, "you're embarrassing."

"Hey, I'm only expressing healthy sexual desire."

"Thelma, you're only twelve!" Ruth said exasperatedly.

"Thirteen's next. Going to have my first period any day now. We'll wake up one morning, and there'll be so much blood this place will look like there's been a massacre."

"Thelma!"

Sheener did not come to work on Thursday, either. His days off that week were Friday and Saturday, so by Saturday evening, Laura and the twins speculated excitedly that the Eel would never show up again, that he had been run down by a truck or had contracted beriberi.

But at Sunday morning breakfast, Sheener was at the buffet. He had two black eyes, a bandaged right ear, a swollen upper lip, a six-inch scrape along his left jaw, and he was missing two front teeth.

"Maybe he *was* hit by a truck," Ruth whispered as they moved forward in the cafeteria line.

Other kids were commenting on Sheener's injuries, and some were giggling. But they either feared and despised him or scorned him, so none cared to speak to him directly about his condition.

Laura, Ruth, and Thelma fell silent as they reached the buffet. The closer they drew to him, the more battered he appeared. His black eyes were not new but a few days old, yet the flesh was still horribly discolored and puffy; initially both eyes must have been nearly swollen shut. His split lip looked raw. Where his face was not bruised or abraded, his usually milk-pale skin was gray. Under his mop of frizzy, copper-red hair, he was a ludicrous figure--a circus clown who had taken a pratfall down a set of stairs without knowing how to land properly and avoid injury.

He did not look up at any of the kids as he served them but kept his eyes on the milk and breakfast pastries. He seemed to tense when Laura came before him, but he did not raise his eyes.

At their table Laura and the twins arranged their chairs so they could watch the Eel, a turn of events they would not have contemplated an hour ago. But he was now less fearful than intriguing. Instead of avoiding him, they spent the day following him on his chores, trying to be casual about it, as if they just happened to wind up in the same places he did, watching him surreptitiously. Gradually it became clear that he was aware of Laura but was avoiding even glancing at her. He looked at other kids, paused in the game room to speak softly to Tammy Hinsen on one occasion, but seemed as loath to meet Laura's eyes as he would have been to stick his fingers in an electric socket.

By late morning Ruth said, "Laura, he's afraid of you."

"Damned if he isn't," Thelma said. "Was it *you* who beat him up, Shane? Have you been hiding the fact that you're a karate expert?"

"It *is* strange, isn't it? Why's he afraid of me?"

But she knew. Her special guardian. Though she had thought she would have to deal with Sheener herself, her guardian had come through again, warning Sheener to stay away from her.

She was not sure why she was reluctant to share the story of her mysterious protector with the Ackersons. They were her best friends. She trusted them. Yet intuitively she felt that the secret of her guardian was meant to remain a secret, that what little she knew of him was sacred knowledge, and that she had no right to prattle on about him to other people, reducing sacred knowledge to mere gossip.

During the following two weeks the Eel's bruises faded, and the bandage came off his ear to reveal angry red stitches where that flap of flesh nearly had been torn off. He continued to keep his distance from Laura. When he served her in the dining hall, he no longer saved the best dessert for her, and he continued to refuse to meet her eyes.

Occasionally, however, she caught him glaring at her from across a room. Each time he quickly turned away, but in his fiery green eyes she now saw something worse than his previous twisted hunger: rage. Obviously he blamed her for the beating he had suffered.

On Friday, October 27, she learned from Mrs. Bowmaine that she was going to be transferred to another foster home the following day. A couple in Newport Beach, Mr. and Mrs. Dockweiler, were new to the foster-child program and eager to have her.

"I'm sure this will be a more compatible arrangement," Mrs. Bowmaine said, standing at her desk in a blazing yellow floral-print dress that made her look like a sun-porch sofa. "The trouble you caused at the Teagels' better not be repeated with the Dockweilers."

That night in their room, Laura and the twins tried to put on brave faces and discuss the approaching separation in the equanimous spirit with which they had faced her departure for the Teagels'. But they were closer now than a month ago, so close that Ruth and Thelma had begun to speak of Laura as if she were their sister. Thelma even once had said, "The amazing Ackerson sisters—Ruth, Laura, and moi," and Laura had felt more wanted, more loved, more *alive* than at any time in the three months since her father died.

"I love you guys," Laura said.

Ruth said, "Oh, Laura," and burst into tears.

Thelma scowled. "You'll be back in no time. These Dockweilers will be horrid people. They'll make you sleep in the garage."

"I hope so," Laura said.

"They'll beat you with rubber hoses—"

"That would be good."

This time the lightning that struck her life was *good* lightning, or at least that was how it seemed at first.

The Dockweilers lived in a huge house in an expensive section of Newport Beach. Laura had her own bedroom with an ocean view. It was decorated in earth tones, mostly beige.

Showing her the room for the first time, Carl Dockweiler said, "We didn't know what your favorite colors were, so we left it like this, but we can repaint the whole thing, however you want it." He was fortyish, big as a bear, barrel-chested, with a broad, rubbery face that reminded her of John Wayne if John Wayne had been a bit amusing looking. "Maybe a girl your age wants a pink room."

"Oh, no, I like it just the way it is!" Laura said. Still in a state of shock over the sudden opulence into which she had been plunged, she moved to the window and looked out at the splendid view of Newport Harbor, where yachts bobbed on sun-spangled water.

Nina Dockweiler joined Laura and put one hand on her shoulder. She was lovely, with smoky coloring, dark hair, and violet eyes, a china doll of a woman. "Laura, the child-welfare file said you loved books, but we didn't know what kind of books, so we're going straight to the bookstore and buy whatever you'd like."

At Waldenbooks Laura chose five paperbacks, and the Dockweilers urged her to buy more, but she felt guilty about spending their money. Carl and Nina scouted the shelves, plucking off volumes and reading cover copy to her, adding them to her pile if she showed the slightest interest. At one point Carl was crawling on his hands and knees in the young-adult section, scanning titles on the bottom shelf—"Hey, here's one about a dog. You like animal stories? Here's a spy story!"—and he was such a comical sight that Laura giggled. By the time they left the store, they'd bought one hundred books, *bagsful* of books.

Their first dinner together was at a pizza parlor, where Nina exhibited a surprising talent for magic by plucking a pepperoni ring from behind Laura's ear, then making it vanish.

"That's amazing," Laura said. "Where'd you learn that?"

"I owned an interior design firm, but I had to give it up eight years ago. Health reasons. Too stressful. I wasn't used to sitting at home like a lump, so I did all the things I'd dreamed of when I was a businesswoman with no spare time. Like learning magic."

"Health reasons?" Laura said.

Security was a treacherous rug that people kept pulling out from under her, and now someone was getting ready to jerk the rug again.

Her fear must have been evident, for Carl Dockweiler said, "Don't worry. Nina was born with a bum heart, a structural defect, but she'll live as long as you or me if she avoids stress."

"Can't they operate?" Laura asked, putting down the slice of pizza she had just picked up, her appetite having suddenly fled.

"Cardiovascular surgery's advancing rapidly," Nina said. "In a couple years maybe. But, honey, it's nothing to worry about. I'll take care of myself, especially now I've got a daughter to spoil!"

"More than anything," Carl said, "we wanted kids, but couldn't have them. By the time we decided to adopt, we discovered Nina's heart condition, so then the adoption agencies wouldn't approve us."

"But we qualify as foster parents," Nina said, "so if you like living with us, you can stay forever, just as if you were adopted."

That night in her big bedroom with its view of the sea—now an almost scary, vast expanse of darkness—Laura told herself that she must not like the Dockweilers too much, that Nina's heart condition foreclosed any possibility of real security.

The following day, Sunday, they took her shopping for clothes and would have spent fortunes if she had not finally begged them to stop. With their Mercedes crammed full of her new clothes, they went to a Peter Sellers comedy, and after the movie they had dinner at a hamburger restaurant where the milkshakes were humongous.

Pouring catsup on her french fries, Laura said, "You guys are lucky that child-welfare sent me to you instead of some other kid."

Carl raised his eyebrows. "Oh?"

"Well, you're nice, *too* nice—and a lot more vulnerable than you realize. Any kid would see how vulnerable you really are, and a lot would take advantage of you. Mercilessly. But you can relax with me. I'll never take advantage of you or make you sorry you took me in."

They stared at her in amazement.

At last Carl looked at Nina. "They've tricked us. She's not twelve. They've palmed off a dwarf on us."

That night in bed, as she waited for sleep, Laura repeated her litany of self-protection: "Don't like them too much, don't like them too much . . ." But already she liked them enormously.

The Dockweilers sent her to a private academy where the teachers were more demanding than those in the public schools she had attended, but she relished the challenge and performed well. Slowly she made new friends. She missed Thelma and Ruth, but she took some comfort from knowing they would be pleased that she had found happiness.

She even began to think that she could have faith in the future and could dare to *be* happy. After all, she had a special guardian, didn't she? Perhaps even a guardian angel. Surely any girl blessed with a guardian angel was destined for love, happiness, and security.

But would a guardian angel actually shoot a man in the head? Beat another man to a bloody pulp? Never mind. She had a handsome guardian, angel or not, and foster parents who loved her, and she could not refuse happiness when it showered on her by the bucketful.

On Tuesday, December 5, Nina had her monthly appointment with her cardiologist, so no one was at home when Laura returned from school that afternoon. She let herself in with her key and put her textbooks on the Louis XIV table in the foyer near the foot of the stairs.

The enormous living room was decorated in shades of cream, peach, and pale green, which made it cozy in spite of its size. As she paused at the windows to enjoy the view, she thought of how much better it would be if Ruth and Thelma could enjoy it with her—and suddenly it seemed the most natural thing that they should be there.

Why not? Carl and Nina loved kids. They had enough love for a houseful of kids, for a thousand kids.

"Shane," she said aloud, "you're a genius."

She went to the kitchen and prepared a snack to take to her room. She poured a glass of milk, heated a chocolate croissant in the oven, and got an apple from the refrigerator, as she mulled over the ways in which she might broach the subject of the twins with the Dockweilers. The plan was such a natural that by the time she carried her snack to the swinging door that separated kitchen and dining room and pushed it open with her shoulder, she had been unable to think of a single approach that would fail.

The Eel was waiting in the dining room, and he grabbed her and slammed her up against the wall so hard that he knocked the wind out of her. The apple and chocolate croissant flew off the plate, the plate flew out of her hand, he knocked the glass of milk out of her other hand, and it struck the dining-room table, shattering noisily. He pulled her away from the wall but slammed her into it again, pain flashed down her back, her vision clouded, she knew she dared not black out, so she held on to consciousness, held on tenaciously though she was racked with pain, breathless, and half concussed.

Where was her guardian? Where?

Sheener shoved his face close to hers, and terror seemed to sharpen her senses, for she was acutely aware of every detail of his rage-wrenched countenance: the still red suture marks where his torn ear had been reattached to his head, the blackheads in the creases around his nose, the acne scars in his mealy skin. His green eyes were too strange to be human, as alien and fierce as those of a cat.

Her guardian would pull the Eel off her at any second now, pull him off her and kill him. Any second now.

"I got you," he said, his voice shrill, manic, "now you're mine, honey, and you're gonna tell me who that son of a bitch was, the one who beat on me, I'll blow his head off."

He was holding her by her upper arms, his fingers digging into her flesh. He lifted her off the floor, raised her to his eye level, and pinned her against the wall. Her feet dangled in the air.

"Who is the bastard?" He was so strong for his size. He lifted her away from the wall, slammed her against it again, keeping her at eye level. "Tell me, honey, or I'll tear *your* ear off."

Any second now. Any second.

Pain still throbbed through her back, but she was able to draw breath, although what she drew in was *his* breath, sour and nauseating.

"Answer me, honey."

She could die waiting for a guardian angel to intervene.

She kicked him in the crotch. It was a perfect shot. His legs were planted wide, and he was so unaccustomed to girls who fought back that he never saw it coming. His eyes widened—they actually looked like human eyes for an instant—and he made a low, strangled sound. His hands dropped away from her. Laura collapsed to the floor, and Sheener staggered backward, lost his balance, fell against the dining-room table, folded to his side on the Chinese carpet.

Nearly immobilized by pain, shock, and fear, Laura could not get to her feet. Rag legs. Limp. So crawl. She could crawl. Away from him. Frantically. Toward the dining-room archway. Hoping to be able to stand by the time she reached the living room. He grabbed her left ankle. She tried to kick loose. No good. Rag legs. Sheener held on. Cold fingers. Corpse-cold. He made a thin, shrieking sound. Weird. She put her hand in a milk-soaked patch of carpet. Saw the broken glass. The top of the tumbler had shattered. The heavy base was intact, crowned with sharp spears. Drops of milk clinging to it. Still winded, half paralyzed by pain, the Eel seized her other ankle. Hitched-twitched-dragged himself toward her. He was still shrieking. Like a bird. Going to throw himself on top of her. Pin her. She seized the broken glass. Cut her thumb. Didn't feel a thing. He let go of her ankles to grab at her thighs. She flipped-writhed onto her back. As if *she* were an eel. Thrust the jagged end of the broken tumbler at him, not intending to stab him, hoping only to ward him off. But he was heaving himself onto her, falling onto her, and the three glass points speared into his throat. He tried to pull away. Twisted the tumbler. The points broke off in his flesh. Choking, gagging, he nailed her to the floor with his body. Blood streamed from his nose. She squirmed. He clawed at her. His knee bore down hard on her hip. His mouth was at her throat. He bit her. Just nipped her skin. He'd get a bigger bite next time if she let him. She thrashed. Breath whistled and rattled in his ruined throat. She slithered free. He grabbed. She kicked. Her legs worked better now. The kick landed solidly. She crawled toward the living room. Gripped the frame of the dining-room archway. Pulled herself to her feet. Glanced back. The Eel was on his feet as well, a dining-room chair raised like a club. He swung it. She dodged. The chair hit the frame of the archway with a thunderous sound. She staggered into the living room, heading for the foyer, the door, escape. He threw the chair. It struck her shoulder. She went down. Rolled. Looked up. He towered over her, seized her left arm. Her strength faded. Darkness pulsed at the edges of her vision. He gripped her other arm. She was finished. Would have been finished, anyway, if the glass in his throat had not finally worked through one more artery. Blood suddenly *gushed* from his nose. He collapsed atop her, a great and terrible weight, dead.

She could not move, could barely breathe, and had to struggle to hold fast to consciousness. Above the eerie sound of her own strangled sobs, she heard a door open. Footsteps.

"Laura? I'm home." It was Nina's voice, light and cheery at first, then shrill with horror: "Laura? Oh, my God, *Laura!*"

Laura strove to push the dead man off her, but she was able to squirm only half free of the corpse, just far enough to see Nina standing in the foyer archway.

For a moment the woman was paralyzed by shock. She stared at her cream and peach and seafoam-green living room, the tasteful decor now liberally accented with crimson smears. Then her violet eyes returned to Laura, and she snapped out of her trance. "Laura, oh, dear God, Laura." She took three steps forward, halted abruptly, and bent over, hugging herself as if she had been hit in the stomach. She made an odd sound: "Uh, uh, uh, uh, uh." She tried to straighten up. Her face was contorted. She could not seem to stand erect, and finally she crumpled to the floor and made no sound at all.

It could not happen like this. This wasn't fair, damn it.

New strength, born of panic and of love for Nina, filled Laura. She wriggled free of Sheener and crawled quickly to her foster mother.

Nina was limp. Her beautiful eyes were open, sightless.

Laura put her bloody hand to Nina's neck, feeling for a pulse. She thought she found one. Weak, irregular, but a pulse.

She pulled a cushion off a chair and put it under Nina's head, then ran into the kitchen where the numbers of the police and fire departments were on the wall phone. Shakily, she reported Nina's heart attack and gave the fire department their address.

When she hung up, she knew everything was going to be all right because she had already lost one parent to a heart attack, her father, and it would be just too absurd to lose Nina the same way. Life had absurd moments, yes, but life *itself* wasn't absurd. Life was strange, difficult, miraculous, precious, tenuous, mysterious, but not flat-out absurd. So Nina would live because Nina dying made no sense.

Still scared and worried but feeling better, Laura hurried back to the living room and knelt beside her foster mother, held her.

Newport Beach had first-rate emergency services. The ambulance arrived no more than three or four minutes after Laura had called for it. The two paramedics were efficient and well equipped. Within just a few minutes, however, they pronounced Nina dead, and no doubt she had been dead from the moment she collapsed.

·10·

One week after Laura returned to McIlroy and eight days before Christmas, Mrs. Bowmaine reassigned Tammy Hinsen to the fourth bed in the Ackersons' room. In an unusual private session with Laura, Ruth, and Thelma, the social worker explained the reasoning behind that reassignment: "I know you say Tammy isn't happy with you girls, but she seems to get along better there than anywhere else. We've had her in several rooms, but the other children can't tolerate her. I don't know what it is about the child that makes her an outcast, but her other roommates usually end up using her as a punching bag."

Back in their room, before Tammy arrived, Thelma settled into a basic yoga position on the floor, legs folded in a pretzel form, heels against hips. She had become interested in yoga when the Beatles endorsed Eastern meditation, and she had said that when she finally met Paul McCartney (which was her indisputable destiny), "it would be nice if we have something in common, which we will if I can talk with some authority about this yoga crap."

Now, instead of meditating she said, "What would that cow have done if I'd said, 'Mrs. Bowmaine, the kids don't like Tammy because she let herself be diddled by the Eel, and she helped him target other vulnerable girls, so as far as they're concerned, she's the enemy.' What would Bovine Bowmaine have done when I laid *that* on her?"

"She'd have called you a lying scuz," Laura said, flopping down on her sway-backed bed.

"No doubt. Then she'd have eaten me for lunch. Do you believe the size of that woman? She gets bigger by the week. Anyone that big is dangerous, a ravenous omnivore capable of eating the nearest child, bones and all, as casually as she'd consume a pint of fudge ripple."

At the window, looking down at the playground behind the mansion, Ruth said, "It's not fair the way the other kids treat Tammy."

"Life isn't fair," Laura said.

"Life isn't a weenie roast, either," Thelma said. "Jeez, Shane, don't wax philosophical if you're going to be trite. You know we hate triteness here only slightly less than we hate turning on the radio and hearing Bobbie Gentry singing *Ode to Billy Joe.*"

When Tammy moved in an hour later, Laura was tense. She had killed Sheener, after all, and Tammy had been dependent on him. She expected Tammy to be bitter and angry, but in fact the girl greeted her only with a sincere, shy, and piercingly sad smile.

After Tammy had been with them two days, it became clear that she viewed the loss of the Eel's twisted affections with perverse regret but also with relief. The fiery temper she had revealed when she tore apart Laura's books was quenched. She was once again that drab, bony, washed-out girl who, on Laura's first day at McIlroy, had seemed more of an apparition than a real person, in danger of dissolving into smoky ectoplasm and, with the first good draft, dissipating entirely.

After the deaths of the Eel and Nina Dockweiler, Laura attended half-hour sessions with Dr. Boone, a psychotherapist, when he visited McIlroy every Tuesday and Saturday. Boone was unable to understand that Laura could absorb the shock of Willy Sheener's attack and Nina's tragic death without psychological damage. He was puzzled by her articulate discussions of her feelings and the adult vocabulary with which she expressed her adjustment to events in Newport Beach. Having been motherless, having lost her father, having endured many crises and much terror—but most of all, having benefited from her father's wondrous love—she was as resilient as a sponge, absorbing what life presented. However, though she could speak of Sheener with dispassion and of Nina with as much affection as sadness, the psychiatrist viewed her adjustment as merely apparent and not real.

"So you dream about Willy Sheener?" he asked as he sat beside her on the sofa in the small office reserved for him at McIlroy.

"I've only dreamed of him twice. Nightmares, of course. But all kids have nightmares."

"You dream about Nina, too. Are those nightmares?"

"Oh, no! Those are lovely dreams."

He looked surprised. "When you think of Nina, you feel sad?"

"Yes. But also . . . I remember the fun of shopping with her, trying on dresses and sweaters. I remember her smile and her laugh."

"And guilt? Do you feel guilty about what happened to Nina?"

"No. Maybe Nina wouldn't have died if I hadn't moved in with them and drawn Sheener after me, but I can't feel guilty about that. I tried hard to be a good foster daughter to them, and they were happy with me. What happened was that life dropped a big custard pie on us, and that's not my fault; you can never see the custard pies coming. It's not good slapstick if you see the pie coming."

"Custard pie?" he asked, perplexed. "You see life as slapstick comedy? Like the Three Stooges?"

"Partly."

"Life is just a joke then?"

"No. Life is serious *and* a joke at the same time."

"But how can that be?"

"If you don't know," she said, "maybe I should be the one asking the questions here."

She filled many pages of her current notebook with observations about Dr. Will Boone. Of her unknown guardian, however, she wrote nothing. She tried not to think of him, either. He had failed her. Laura had come to depend on him; his heroic efforts on her behalf had made her feel *special,* and feeling special had helped her cope since her father's death. Now she felt foolish for ever looking beyond herself for survival. She still had the note he had left on her desk after her father's funeral, but she no longer reread it. And day by day her guardian's previous efforts on her behalf seemed more like fantasies akin to those of Santa Claus, which must be outgrown.

On Christmas afternoon they returned to their room with the gifts they received from charities and do-gooders. They wound up in a sing-along of holiday songs, and both Laura and the twins were amazed when Tammy joined in. She sang in a low, tentative voice.

Over the next couple of weeks she nearly ceased biting her nails altogether. She was only slightly more outgoing than usual, but she seemed calmer, more content with herself than she had ever been.

"When there's no perv around to bother her," Thelma said, "maybe she gradually starts to feel clean again."

Friday, January 12, 1968, was Laura's thirteenth birthday, but she did not celebrate it. She could find no joy in the occasion.

On Monday, she was transferred from McIlroy to Caswell Hall, a shelter for older children in Anaheim, five miles away.

Ruth and Thelma helped her carry her belongings downstairs to the front foyer. Laura had never imagined that she would so intensely regret leaving McIlroy.

"We'll be coming in May," Thelma assured her. "We turn thirteen on May second, and then we're out of here. We'll be together again."

When the social worker from Caswell arrived, Laura was reluctant to go. But she went.

Caswell Hall was an old high school that had been converted to dormitories, recreational lounges, and offices for social workers. As a result the atmosphere was more institutional than at McIlroy.

Caswell was also more dangerous than McIlroy because the kids were older and because many were borderline juvenile delinquents. Marijuana and pills were available, and fights among the boys—and even among the girls—were not infrequent. Cliques formed, as they had at McIlroy, but at Caswell some of the cliques were perilously close in structure and function to street gangs. Thievery was common.

Within a few weeks Laura realized that there were two types of survivors in life: those, like her, who found the requisite strength in having once been loved with great intensity; and those who, having not been loved, learned to thrive on hatred, suspicion, and the meager rewards of revenge. They were at once scornful of the need for human feeling and envious of the capacity for it.

She lived with great caution at Caswell but never allowed fear to diminish her. The thugs were frightening but also pathetic and, in their posturing and rituals of violence, even funny. She found no one like the Ackersons with whom to share the black humor, so she filled her notebooks with it. In those neatly written monologues, she turned inward while she waited for the Ackersons to be thirteen; that was an intensely rich time of self-discovery and increasing understanding of the slapstick, tragic world into which she had been born.

On Saturday, March 30, she was in her room at Caswell, reading, when she heard one of her roomies—a whiny girl named Fran Wickert—talking to another girl in the hall, discussing a fire in which kids had been killed. Laura was eavesdropping with only half an ear until she heard the word "McIlroy."

A chill pierced her, freezing her heart, numbing her hands. She dropped the book and raced into the hallway, startling the girls. "When? When was this fire?"

"Yesterday," Fran said.

"How many were k-killed?"

"Not many, two kids I think, maybe only one, but I heard if you was there you could smell burnin' meat. Is that the grossest thing—"

Advancing on Fran, Laura said, "What were their names?"

"Hey, let me go."

"Tell me their names!"

"I don't know any names. Christ, what's the matter with you?"

Laura did not remember letting go of Fran, and she did not recall leaving the grounds of the shelter, but suddenly she found herself on Katella Avenue, blocks from Caswell Hall. Katella was a commercial street in that area, and in some places there was no sidewalk, so she ran on the shoulder of the road, heading east, with traffic whizzing by on her right side. Caswell was five miles from McIlroy, and she was not sure she knew the entire route, but trusting to instinct she ran until she was exhausted, then walked until she could run again.

The rational course would have been to go straight to one of the Caswell counselors and ask for the names of those kids killed in the fire at McIlroy. But Laura had the peculiar idea that the Ackerson twins' fate rested entirely upon her willingness to make the difficult trip to McIlroy to inquire about them, that if she asked about them by phone she would be told they were dead, that if instead she endured the physical punishment of the five-mile run, she'd find the Ackersons were safe. That was superstition, but she succumbed to it anyway.

Twilight descended. The late-March sky was filled with muddy-red and purple light, and the edges of the scattered clouds appeared to be aflame by the time Laura came within sight of the McIlroy Home. With relief she saw that the front of the old mansion was unmarked by fire.

Although she was soaked with sweat and shaking with exhaustion, though she had a throbbing headache, she did not slow when she saw the unscorched mansion but maintained her pace for the final block. She passed six kids in the ground-floor hallways and three more on the stairs, and two of them spoke to her by name. But she did not stop to ask them about the blaze. She had to *see*.

On the last flight of stairs she caught the scent of a fire's aftermath: the acrid, tarry stench of burnt things; the lingering, sour smell of smoke. When she went through the door at the top of the stairwell, she saw that the windows were open at each end of the third-floor hall and that electric fans had been set up in the middle of the corridor to blow the tainted air in both directions.

The Ackersons' room had a new, unpainted door frame and door, but the surrounding wall was scorched and smeared with black soot. A hand-printed sign warned of danger. Like all the doors in McIlroy, this one had no lock, so she ignored the sign and flung open the door and stepped across the threshold and saw what she had been so afraid of seeing: destruction.

The hall lights behind her and the purple glow of twilight at the windows did not adequately illuminate the room, but she saw that the remains of the furniture had been cleaned out; the place was empty but for the reeking ghost of the fire. The floor was blackened by soot and charred, though it looked structurally sound. The walls were smoke-damaged. The closet doors had been reduced to ashes but for a few burnt chunks of wood clinging to the hinges, which had partially melted. Both windows had blown out or been broken by those fleeing the flames; now those gaps were temporarily covered by sections of clear-plastic dropcloths stapled to the walls. Fortunately for the other kids at McIlroy, the fire had burned upward rather than outward, eating through the ceiling. She looked overhead into the mansion's attic where massive, blackened beams were dimly visible in the gloom. Apparently the flames had been stopped before they'd broken through to the roof, for she could not see the sky.

She was breathing laboriously, noisily, not only because of the exhausting trip from Caswell but because a vise of panic was squeezing her chest painfully, making it difficult to inhale. And every breath of the bitterly scented air brought the nauseating taste of carbon.

From that moment in her room at Caswell when she had heard of the fire at McIlroy, she had known the cause, though she had not wanted to admit to the knowledge. Tammy Hinsen once had been caught with a can of lighter fluid and matches with which she planned to set herself afire. On hearing of that intended self-immolation, Laura had known that Tammy had been serious about it because immolation seemed such a *right* form of suicide for her, an externalization of the inner fire that had been consuming her for years.

Please, God, she was alone in the room when she did it, please.

Gagging on the stink and taste of destruction, Laura turned away from the fire-blasted room and stepped into the third-floor corridor.

"Laura?"

She looked up and saw Rebecca Bogner. Laura's breath came

and went in wrenching inhalations, shuddering exhalations, but somehow she croaked their names: "Ruth . . . Thelma?"

Rebecca's bleak expression denied the possibility that the twins had escaped unharmed, but Laura repeated the precious names, and in her ragged voice she heard a pathetic, beseeching note.

"Down there," Rebecca said, pointing toward the north end of the hall. "The next to the last room on the left."

With a sudden rush of hope, Laura ran to the indicated room. Three beds were empty, but in the fourth, revealed by the light of a reading lamp, was a girl lying on her side, facing the wall.

"Ruth? Thelma?"

The girl on the bed slowly rose—one of the Ackersons, unharmed. She wore a drab, badly wrinkled, gray dress; her hair was in disarray; her face was puffy, her eyes moist with tears. She took a step toward Laura but stopped as if the effort of walking was too great.

Laura rushed to her, hugged her.

With her head on Laura's shoulder, face against Laura's neck, she spoke at last in a tortured voice. "Oh, I wish it'd been me, Shane. If it had to be one of us, why couldn't it have been me?"

Until the girl spoke, Laura had assumed that she was Ruth.

Refusing to accept that horror, Laura said, "Where's Ruthie?"

"Gone. Ruthie's gone. I thought you knew, my Ruthie's dead."

Laura felt as if something deep within her had torn. Her grief was so powerful that it precluded tears; she was stunned, numb.

For the longest time they just held each other. Twilight faded toward night. They moved to the bed and sat on the edge.

A couple of kids appeared at the door. They evidently shared the room with Thelma, but Laura waved them away.

Looking at the floor, Thelma said, "I woke up to this shrieking, such a horrible shrieking . . . and all this *light* so bright it hurt my eyes. And then I realized the room was on fire. *Tammy* was on fire. Blazing like a torch. Thrashing in her bed, blazing and shrieking . . ."

Laura put an arm around her and waited.

". . . the fire leaped off Tammy—*whoosh* up the wall, her bed was on fire, and fire was spreading across the floor, the rug was burning . . ."

Laura remembered how Tammy had sung with them on Christmas and had thereafter been calmer day by day, as if gradually finding inner peace. Now it was obvious that the peace she'd found had been based on the determination to end her torment.

"Tammy's bed was nearest the door, the door was on fire, so I broke the window over my bed. I called to Ruth, she . . . s-she said she was coming, there was smoke, I couldn't see, then Heather Dorning, who was bunking in your old bed, she came to the window, so I helped her get out, and the smoke was sucked out of the window, so the room cleared a little, which was when I saw Ruth was trying to throw her own blanket over Tammy to s-smother the flames, but that blanket had caught f-fire, too, and I saw Ruth . . . Ruth . . . Ruth on fire . . ."

Outside, the last purple light melted into darkness.

The shadows in the corners of the room deepened.

The lingering burnt odor seemed to grow stronger.

". . . and I would've gone to her, I would've gone, but just then the f-fire *exploded,* it was everywhere in the room, and the smoke was black and so thick, and I couldn't see Ruth any more or anything . . . then I heard sirens, loud and close, sirens, so I tried to tell myself they'd get there in time to help Ruth, which was a l-l-lie, a lie I told myself and wanted to believe, and . . . I left her there, Shane. Oh, God, I went out the window and left Ruthie on f-f-fire, burning . . ."

"You couldn't do anything else," Laura assured her.

"I left Ruthie burning."

"There was nothing you could do."

"I left Ruthie."

"There was no point in you dying too."

"I left Ruthie burning."

In May, after her thirteenth birthday, Thelma was transferred to Caswell and assigned to a room with Laura. The social workers agreed to that arrangement because Thelma was suffering from depression and was not responding to therapy. Maybe she would find the succor she needed in her friendship with Laura.

For months Laura despaired of reversing Thelma's decline. At night Thelma was plagued by dreams, and by day she stewed in self-recrimination. Eventually, time healed her, though her wounds never entirely closed. Her sense of humor gradually returned, and her wit became as sharp as ever, but there was a new melancholy in her.

They shared a room at Caswell Hall for five years, until they left the custody of the state and embarked on lives under no one's control but their own. They shared many laughs during those years. Life was good again but never the same as it had been before the fire.

·11·

In the main lab of the institute, the dominant object was the gate through which one could step into other ages. It was a huge, barrel-shaped device, twelve feet long and eight feet in diameter, of highly polished steel on the outside, lined with polished copper on the inside. It rested on copper blocks that held it eighteen inches off the floor. Thick electrical cables trailed from it, and within the barrel strange currents made the air shimmer as if it were water.

Kokoschka returned through time to the gate, materializing inside that enormous cylinder. He had made several trips that day, shadowing Stefan in far times and places, and at last he had learned why the traitor was obsessed with reshaping the life of Laura Shane. He hurried to the mouth of the gate and stepped down onto the lab floor, where two scientists and three of his own men were waiting for him.

"The girl has nothing to do with the bastard's plots against the government, nothing to do with his attempts to destroy the time-travel project," Kokoschka said. "She's an entirely separate matter, just a personal crusade of his."

"So now we know everything he's done and why," said one of the scientists, "and you can eliminate him."

"Yes," Kokoschka said, crossing the room to the main programming board. "Now that we've uncovered all the traitor's secrets, we can kill him."

As he sat down at the programming board, intending to reset the gate to deliver him to yet another time, where he could surprise the traitor, Kokoschka decided to kill Laura, too. It would be an easy job, something he could handle by himself, for he would have the element of surprise on his side; he preferred to work alone, anyway, whenever possible; he disliked sharing the pleasure. Laura Shane was no danger to the government or to its plans to reshape the future of the world, but he would kill her first and in front of Stefan, merely to break the traitor's heart before putting a bullet in it. Besides, Kokoschka liked to kill.

Three

A LIGHT IN THE DARK

·1·

On Laura Shane's twenty-second birthday, January 12, 1977, she received a toad in the mail. The box in which it came bore no return address, and no note was enclosed. She opened it at the desk by the window in the living room of her apartment, and the clear sunlight of the unusually warm winter day glimmered pleasingly on the charming little figurine. The toad was ceramic, two inches tall, standing on a ceramic lily pad, wearing a top hat and holding a cane.

Two weeks earlier the campus literary magazine had published "Amphibian Epics," a short story of hers about a girl whose father spun fanciful tales of an imaginary toad, Sir Tommy of England. Only she knew that the piece was as much fact as fiction, though someone apparently intuited at least something of the true importance that the story had for her, because the grinning toad in the top hat was packed with extraordinary care. It was carefully wrapped in a swatch of soft cotton cloth tied with red ribbon, then further wrapped in tissue paper, nestled in a plain white box in a bed of cotton balls, and that box was packed in a nest of shredded newspaper inside a still larger box. No one would go to such trouble to protect a five-dollar, novelty figurine unless the packing was meant to signify the sender's perception of the depth of her emotional involvement with the events of "Amphibian Epics."

To afford the rent, she shared her off-campus apartment in Irvine with two juniors at the university, Meg Falcone and Julie Ishimina, and at first she thought perhaps one of them had sent the toad. They seemed unlikely candidates, for Laura was not close to either of them. They were busy with studies and interests of their own; and they had lived with her only since the previous September. They claimed to have no knowledge of the toad, and their denials seemed sincere.

She wondered if Dr. Matlin, the faculty adviser to the literary magazine at UCI, might have sent the figurine. Since her sophomore year, when she had taken Matlin's course in creative writing, he had encouraged her to pursue her talent and polish her craftsmanship. He had been particularly fond of "Amphibian Epics," so maybe he had sent the toad to say "well done." But why no return address, no card? Why the secrecy? No, that was out of character for Harry Matlin.

She had a few casual friends at the university, but she was not truly close to anyone because she had little time to make and sustain deep friendships. Between her studies, her job, and her writing, she used up all the hours of the day not devoted to sleeping or eating. She could think of no one who would have gone out of his way to buy the toad, package it, and mail it anonymously.

A mystery.

The following day her first class was at eight o'clock and her last at two. She returned to her nine-year-old Chevy in the campus parking lot at a quarter till four, unlocked the door, got behind the wheel—and was startled to see another toad on the dashboard.

It was two inches high and four inches long. This one was also ceramic, emerald green, reclining with one arm bent and its head propped on its hand. It was smiling dreamily.

She was sure she had left the car locked, and in fact it had been locked when she returned from class. The enigmatic giver of toads had evidently gone to considerable trouble to open the Chevy without a key—a loid of some kind or a coathanger worked through the top of the window to the lock button—and leave the toad in a dramatic fashion.

Later she put the reclining toad on her nightstand where the top hat-and-cane fellow already stood. She spent the evening in bed, reading. From time to time her attention drifted away from the page to the ceramic figures.

The next morning when she left the apartment, she found a small box on her doorstep. Inside was another meticulously wrapped toad. It was cast in pewter, sitting upon a log, holding a banjo.

The mystery deepened.

In the summer she put in a full shift as a waitress at Hamburger Hamlet in Costa Mesa, but during the school year her course load was so heavy that she could work only three evenings a week. The Hamlet was an upscale hamburger restaurant providing good food for reasonable prices in a moderately plush ambience—crossbeam ceiling, lots of wood paneling, hugely comfortable armchairs—so the customers were usually happier than those in other places where she had waited tables.

Even if the atmosphere had been seedy and the customers surly, she would have kept the job; she needed the money. On her eighteenth birthday, four years ago, she learned that her father had established a trust fund, consisting of the assets liquidated upon his death, and that the trust could not be touched by the state to pay for her care at McIlroy Home and Caswell Hall. At that time the funds had become hers to spend, and she had applied them toward living and college expenses. Her father hadn't been rich; there was only twelve thousand dollars even after six years of accrued interest, not nearly enough for four years of rent, food, clothing, and tuition, so she depended upon her income as a waitress to make up the difference.

On Sunday evening, January 16, she was halfway through her shift at the Hamlet when the host escorted an older couple, about sixty, to one of the booths in Laura's station. They asked for two Michelobs while they studied the menu. A few minutes later, when she returned from the bar with the beers and two frosted mugs on a tray, she saw a ceramic toad on their table. She nearly dropped the tray in surprise. She looked at the man, at the woman, and they were grinning at her, but they weren't *saying* anything, so she said, "*You've* been giving me toads? But I don't even know you—do I?"

The man said, "Oh, you've gotten more of these, have you?"

"This is the fourth. You didn't bring this for me, did you? But it wasn't here a few minutes ago. Who put it on the table?"

He winked at his wife, and she said to Laura, "You've got a secret admirer, dear."

"Who?"

"Young fella was sitting at that table over there," the man said, pointing across the room to a station served by a waitress named Amy Heppleman. The table was now empty; the busboy had just finished clearing away the dirty dishes. "Soon as you left to get our beers, he comes over and asks if he can leave this here for you."

It was a Christmas toad in a Santa suit, without a beard, a sack of toys over its shoulder.

The woman said, "You don't really know who he is?"

"No. What'd he look like?"

"Tall," the man said. "Quite tall and husky. Brown hair."

"Brown eyes too," his wife said. "Soft-spoken."

Holding the toad, staring at it, Laura said, "There's something about this . . . something that makes me uneasy."

"Uneasy?" the woman said. "But it's just a young man who's smitten with you, dear."

"Is it?" she wondered.

Laura found Amy Heppleman at the salad preparation counter and sought a better description of the toad-giver.

"He had a mushroom omelet, whole-wheat toast, and a Coke," Amy said, using a pair of stainless-steel tongs to fill two bowls with salad greens. "Didn't you see him sitting there?"

"I didn't notice him, no."

"Biggish guy. Jeans. A blue-checkered shirt. His hair was cut too short, but he was kinda cute if you like the moose type. Didn't talk much. Seemed kinda shy."

"Did he pay with a credit card?"

"No. Cash."

"Damn," Laura said.

She took the Santa toad home and put it with the other figurines.

The following morning, Monday, as she left the apartment, she found yet another plain white box on the doorstep. She opened it reluctantly. It contained a clear glass toad.

When Laura returned from the UCI campus that same afternoon, Julie Ishimina was sitting at the dinette table, reading the daily paper and drinking a cup of coffee. "You got another one," she said, pointing to a box on the kitchen counter. "Came in the mail."

Laura tore open the elaborately wrapped package. The sixth toad was actually a pair of toads—salt and pepper shakers.

She put the shakers with the other figurines on her nightstand,

and for a long while she sat on the edge of her bed, frowning at that growing collection.

At five o'clock that afternoon she called Thelma Ackerson in Los Angeles and told her about the toads.

Lacking a trust fund of any size, Thelma had not even considered college, but as she said, that was no tragedy because she was not interested in academics. Upon completing high school, she had gone straight from Caswell Hall to Los Angeles, intent upon breaking into show business as a stand-up comic.

Nearly every night, from about six o'clock until two in the morning, she hung around the comedy clubs—the Improv, the Comedy Store, and all their imitators—angling for a six-minute, unpaid shot on the stage, making contacts (or hoping to make them), competing with a horde of young comics for the coveted exposure.

She worked days to pay the rent, moving from job to job, some of them decidedly peculiar. Among other things she had worn a chicken suit and sung songs and waited tables in a weird "theme" pizza parlor, and she'd been a picket-line stand-in for a few Writers Guild West members who were required by their union to participate in a strike action but who preferred to pay someone a hundred bucks a day to carry a placard for them and sign their names on the duty roster.

Though they lived just ninety minutes apart, Laura and Thelma got together only two or three times a year, usually just for a long lunch or dinner, because they led busy lives. But regardless of the time between visits, they were instantly comfortable with each other and quick to share their most intimate thoughts and experiences. "The McIlroy-Caswell bond," Thelma once said, "is stronger than being blood brothers, stronger than the Mafia covenant, stronger than the bond between Fred Flintstone and Barney Rubble, and those two are *close*."

Now, after she listened to Laura's story, Thelma said, "So what's your problem, Shane? Sounds to me like some big, shy hunk of a guy has a crush on you. Lots of women would swoon over this."

"Is that what it is, though? An innocent crush?"

"What else?"

"I don't know. But it . . . makes me uneasy."

"Uneasy? These toads are all cute little things, aren't they? None of them is a snarling toad? None of them is holding a bloody little butcher knife? Or a little ceramic chainsaw?"

"No."

"He hasn't sent you any *beheaded* toads, has he?"

"No, but—"

"Shane, the last few years have been calm, though of course you've had a pretty eventful life. It's understandable that you'd expect this guy to be Charles Manson's brother. But it's almost a sure bet he's just what he appears to be—a guy who admires you from afar, is maybe a little shy, and has a streak of romance in him about eighteen inches wide. How's your sex life?"

"I don't have any," Laura said.

"Why not? You're not a virgin. There was that guy last year—"

"Well, you know that didn't work out."

"Nobody since?"

"No. What do you think—I'm promiscuous?"

"Sheesh! Kiddo, two lovers in twenty-two years would not make you promiscuous even by the pope's definition. Unbend a little. Relax. Stop being a worrier. Flow with this, see where it goes. He might just turn out to be prince charming."

"Well . . . maybe I will. I guess you're right."

"But, Shane?"

"Yeah?"

"Just for luck, from now on you better carry a .357 Magnum."

"Very funny."

"Funny is my business."

During the following three days Laura received two more toads, and by Saturday morning, the twenty-second, she was equally confused, angry, and afraid. Surely no secret admirer would string the game out so long. Each new toad seemed to be mocking rather than honoring her. There was a quality of obsession in the giver's relentlessness.

She spent much of Friday night in a chair by the big living-room window, sitting in the dark. Through the half-open drapes, she had a view of the apartment building's covered veranda and the area in front of her own door. If he came during the night, she intended to confront him in the act. By three-thirty in the morning he had not arrived, and she dozed off. When she woke in the morning, no package was on the doorstep.

After she showered and ate a quick breakfast, she went down the outside stairs and around to the back of the building where she kept her car in the covered stall assigned to her. She intended to go to the library to do some research work, and it looked like a good day for being indoors. The winter sky was gray and low, and the air had a prestorm heaviness that filled her with foreboding—a feeling that intensified when she found another box on the dashboard of her locked Chevy. She wanted to scream in frustration.

Instead she sat behind the wheel and opened the package. The other figurines had been inexpensive, no more than ten or fifteen dollars each, some probably as cheap as three bucks, but the newest was an exquisite miniature porcelain that surely cost at least fifty dollars. However she was less interested in the toad than in the box in which it had come. It was not plain, as before, but imprinted with the name of a gift shop—Collectibles—in the South Coast Plaza shopping mall.

Laura drove directly to the mall, arrived fifteen minutes before Collectibles opened, waited on a bench in the promenade, and was first through the shop's door when it was unlocked. The store's owner and manager was a petite, gray-haired woman named Eugenia Farvor. "Yes, we handle this line," she said after listening to Laura's succinct explanation and examining the porcelain toad, "and in fact I sold it myself just yesterday to the young man."

"Do you know his name?"

"I'm sorry, no."

"What did he look like?"

"I remember him well because of his size. Very tall. Six five, I'd say. And very broad in the shoulders. He was quite well dressed. A gray pinstripe suit, blue and gray striped tie. I admired the suit, in fact, and he said it wasn't easy finding clothes to fit him."

"Did he pay cash?"

"Mmmmm . . . no, I believe he used a credit card."

"Would you still have the charge slip?"

"Oh, yes, we usually run a day or two behind in organizing them and transferring them to the master ticket for deposit." Mrs. Farvor led Laura past glass display cases filled with porcelains, Lalique and Waterford crystal, Wedgwood plates, Hummel figurines, and other expensive items, to the cramped office at the back of the store. Then she suddenly had second thoughts about sharing her customer's identity. "If his intentions are innocent, if he's just an admirer of yours—and I must say there seemed no harm in him; he seemed quite nice—then I'll be spoiling everything for him. He'll want to be revealing himself to you according to his own plan."

Laura tried hard to charm the woman and win her sympathy. She could not recall ever having spoken more eloquently or with such feeling; usually she was not as good at vocalizing her feelings as she was at putting them down in print. Genuine tears sprang to her assistance, surprising her even more than they did Eugenia Farvor.

From the MasterCard charge slip, she obtained his name—Daniel Packard—and his telephone number. She went directly from the gift shop to a public telephone in the mall and looked him up. There were two Daniel Packards in the book, but the one with that number lived on Newport Avenue in Tustin.

When she returned to the mall parking lot, a cold drizzle was falling. She turned up her coat collar, but she had neither a hat nor an umbrella. By the time she got to her car, her hair was wet, and she was chilled. She shivered all the way from Costa Mesa to North Tustin.

She figured there was a good chance he would be at home. If he was a student, he would not be in class on Saturday. If he worked an ordinary nine-to-five job, he would probably not be at the office, either. And the weather ruled out many of the usual weekend pastimes for outdoor-oriented southern Californians.

His address was an apartment complex of two-story, Spanish-style buildings, eight of them, in a garden setting. For a few minutes she hurried from building to building on winding walkways under dripping palms and coral trees, looking for his apartment. By the time she found it—a first-floor, end unit in the building farthest from the street—her hair was soaked. Her chill had deepened. Discomfort dulled her fear and sharpened her anger, so she rang his bell without hesitation.

He evidently did not peek through the fisheye security lens, for when he opened the door and saw her, he looked stunned. He was maybe five years older than she, and he was a big man indeed, fully six feet five, two hundred and forty pounds, all muscle. He was wearing jeans and a pale-blue T-shirt smeared with grease and spotted with another oily substance; his well-developed arms were formidable. His face was shadowed by beard stubble and smudged with more grease, and his hands were black.

Carefully staying back from the door, beyond his reach, Laura simply said, "Why?"

"Because . . ." He shifted from one foot to the other, almost too big for the doorway in which he stood. "Because . . ."

"I'm waiting."

He wiped one grease-covered hand through his close-cropped hair and seemed oblivious of the resultant mess. His eyes shifted away from her; he looked out at the rain-lashed courtyard as he spoke. "How . . . how'd you find out it was me?"

"That's not important. What's important is that I don't know you, I've never seen you before, and yet I've got a toad menagerie that you've sent me, you come around in the middle of the night to leave them on my doorstep, you break into my car to leave them on the dashboard, and it's been going on for *weeks,* so don't you think it's time I knew what this is all about?"

Still not looking at her, he flushed and said, "Well, sure, but I didn't . . . wasn't ready . . . didn't think the time was right."

"The time was right a week ago!"

"Ummmm."

"So tell me. *Why?*"

Looking down at his greasy hands, he said quietly, "Well, see . . ."

"Yes?"

"I love you."

She stared at him, incredulous. He finally looked at her. She said, "You *love* me? But you don't even *know* me. How can you love a person you've never met?"

He looked away from her, rubbed his filthy hand through his hair again, and shrugged. "I don't know, but there it is, and I . . . uh . . . well, ummmm, I have this feeling, see, this feeling that I've got to spend the rest of my life with you."

With cold rainwater trickling from her wet hair down the nape of her neck and along the curve of her spine, with her day at the library shot—how could she concentrate on research after this insane scene?—and with more than a little disappointment that her secret admirer had turned out to be this dirty, sweaty, inarticulate lummox, Laura said, "Listen, Mr. Packard, I don't want you sending me any more toads."

"Well, see, I really want to send them."

"But I don't want to receive them. And tomorrow I'll mail back the ones you've sent me. No, today. I'll mail them back today."

He met her eyes again, blinked in surprise, and said, "I thought you liked toads."

With growing anger, she said, "I *do* like toads. I love toads. I think toads are the cutest things in creation. Right now I even wish I *were* a toad, but I don't want *your* toads. Understand?"

"Ummmm."

"Don't harass me, Packard. Maybe some women surrender to your weird mix of heavy-handed romance and sweaty macho charm, but I'm not one of them, and I can protect myself, don't think I can't. I'm a lot tougher than I look, and I've dealt with worse than you."

She turned away from him, walked out from under the veranda into the rain, returned to her car, and drove back to Irvine. She shook all the way home, not only because she was wet and chilled but because she was in the grip of anger. The nerve of him!

At her apartment she undressed, bundled up in a quilted robe, and brewed a pot of coffee with which to ward off the chills.

She had just taken her first sip of coffee when the phone rang. She answered it in the kitchen. It was Packard.

Speaking so rapidly that he ran his sentences together in long gushes, he said, "Please don't hang up on me, you're right, I'm stupid about these things, an idiot, but give me just one minute to explain myself, I was fixing the dishwasher when you came, that's why I was such a mess, greasy and sweaty, had to pull it from under the counter myself, the landlord would have fixed it, but going through management takes a week, and I'm good with my hands, I can fix anything, it was a rainy day, nothing else to do, so why not fix it myself, I never figured you to show up. My name's Daniel Packard, but you know that already, I'm twenty-eight, I was in the army until '73, graduated from the University of California at Irvine with a degree in business just three years ago, work as a stockbroker now, but I take a couple night courses at the university, which is how I came across your story about the toad in the campus literary magazine, it was terrific, I loved it, a great story, really, so I went to the library and searched through back issues to find everything else you'd written, and I read it all, and a *lot* of it was good, damned good, not all of it, but a lot. I fell in love with you somewhere along the way, with the person I knew from her writing, because the writing was so beautiful and so real. One evening I was sitting there in the library reading one of your stories—they won't let anyone check out back issues of the literary magazine, they have them in binders, and you have to read them in the library—and this librarian was passing behind my chair, and she leaned over and asked if I liked the story, I said I did, and she said, 'Well, the author's right over there, if you want to tell her it's good,' and there you were just three tables away with a stack of books, doing research, scowling, making notes, and you were gorgeous. See, I knew you would be beautiful *inside* because your stories are beautiful, the sentiment in them is beautiful, but it never occurred to me that you'd be beautiful *outside,* too, and there was no way I could approach you because I've always been tongue-tied and stumble-footed around beautiful women, maybe because my mother was beautiful but cold and forbidding, so now maybe I think all beautiful women will reject me the way my mother did—a little half-baked analysis there—but it sure would've been a lot easier for me if you'd been ugly or at least plain looking. Because of your story I thought I'd use the toads, that whole secret admirer bit with the gifts, as a way to soften you up, and I planned to reveal myself after the third or fourth toad, I really did, but I kept delaying because I didn't want to be rejected, I guess, and I knew it was getting crazy, toad after toad after toad, but I just couldn't stop it and forget you, yet I wasn't able to face you, either, and that's it. I never meant you any harm, I sure didn't mean to upset you, can you forgive me, I hope you can."

He stopped at last, exhausted.

She said, "Well."

He said, "So will you go out with me?"

Surprised by her own response, she said, "Yes."

"Dinner and a movie?"

"All right."

"Tonight? Pick you up at six?"

"Okay."

After she hung up she stood for a while, staring at the phone. Finally she said aloud, "Shane, are you nuts?" Then she said, "But he told me my writing was 'so beautiful and so real.' "

She went into her bedroom and looked at the collection of toads on the nightstand. She said, "He's inarticulate and silent one time, a babbler the next. He could be a psycho killer, Shane." Then she said, "Yeah, he could be, but he's also a great literary critic."

Because he had suggested dinner and a movie, Laura dressed in a gray skirt, white blouse, and maroon sweater, but he showed up in a dark blue suit, white shirt with French cuffs, blue silk tie with tie chain, silk display handkerchief, and highly polished black wingtips, as if he were going to the season opener at the opera. He carried an umbrella and escorted her from her apartment to his car with one hand under her right arm, with such solemn concern that he seemed convinced that she would dissolve if touched by one drop of rain or shatter into a million pieces if she slipped and fell.

Considering the difference in their dress and the considerable difference in their size—at five-five, she was one foot shorter than he was; at a hundred fifteen pounds, she was less than half his weight—she felt almost as if she were going on a date with her father or an older brother. She was not a petite woman, but on his arm and under his umbrella she felt positively tiny.

He was uncommunicative again in the car, but he blamed it on the need to drive with special care in such rotten weather. They went to a small Italian restaurant in Costa Mesa, a place in which Laura had eaten a few good meals in the past. They sat down at their table and were given menus, but even before the waitress could ask if they would like a drink, Daniel said, "This is no good, this is all wrong, let's find another place."

Surprised, she said, "But why? This is fine. Their food's very good here."

"No, really, this is all wrong. No atmosphere, no style, I don't want you to think, ummmm," and now he was babbling as he'd done on the phone, blushing, "ummmm, well, anyway, this is no good, not right for our first date, I want this to be special," and he got up, "ummm, I think I know just the place, I'm sorry, Miss"—this to the startled young waitress—"I hope we haven't inconvenienced you," and he was pulling back Laura's chair, helping her up, "I know just the place, you'll like it, I've never eaten there but I've heard it's really good, excellent." Other customers were staring, so Laura stopped protesting. "It's close, too, just a couple of blocks from here."

They returned to his car, drove two blocks, and parked in front of an unpretentious-looking restaurant in a strip shopping center.

By now Laura knew him well enough to realize that his sense of courtliness required her to wait for him to come around and open her car door, but when he opened it she saw he was standing in a ten-inch-deep puddle. "Oh, your shoes!" she said.

"They'll dry out. Here, you hold the umbrella over yourself, and I'll lift you across the puddle."

Nonplussed, she allowed herself to be plucked from the car and carried over the puddle as if she weighed no more than a feather pillow. He put her down on higher pavement and, without the umbrella, he sloshed back to the car to close the door.

The French restaurant had less atmosphere than the Italian place. They were shown to a corner table too near the kitchen, and Daniel's saturated shoes squished and squeaked all the way across the room.

"You'll catch pneumonia," she worried when they were seated and had ordered two Dry Sacks on the rocks.

"Not me. I've got a good immune system. Never get sick. One time in Nam, during an action, I was cut off from my unit, spent a week on my own in the jungle, rained every minute, I was *shriveled* by the time I found my way back to friendly territory, but I never even got the sniffles."

As they sipped their drinks and studied the menu and ordered, he was more relaxed than Laura had yet seen him, and he actually proved to be a coherent, pleasant, even amusing conversationalist. But when the appetizers were served—salmon in dill sauce for her, scallops in pastry for him—it swiftly became clear that the food was terrible, even though the prices were twice those at the Italian place that they had left, and course by course, as his embarrassment grew, his ability to sustain his end of the conversation declined drastically. Laura proclaimed everything delicious and choked down every bite, but it was no use; he was not fooled.

The kitchen staff and the waiter were also slow. By the time Daniel had paid the check and escorted her back to the car—lifting her across the puddle again as if she were a little girl—they were half an hour late for the movie they had intended to see.

"That's all right," she said, "we can go in late and stay to see the first half hour of the next showing."

"No, no," he said. "That's a terrible way to see a movie. It'll ruin it for you. I wanted this night to be perfect."

"Relax," she said. "I'm having fun."

He looked at her with disbelief, and she smiled, and he smiled, too, but his smile was sick.

"If you don't want to go to the movie now," she said, "that's all right, too. Wherever you want to go, I'm game."

He nodded, started the car, and drove out to the street. They had gone a few miles before she realized that he was taking her home.

All the way from his car to her door, he apologized for what a lousy evening it had been, and she repeatedly assured him that she was not in the least disappointed with a moment of it. At her apartment, the instant she inserted her key in the door, he turned and fled down the stairs from the second-floor veranda, neither asking for a goodnight kiss nor giving her a chance to invite him in.

She stepped to the head of the stairs and watched him descend, and he was halfway down when a gust of wind turned his umbrella inside out. He fought with it the rest of the way, twice almost losing his balance. When he reached the walk below, he finally got the umbrella corrected—and the wind immediately turned it inside out again. In frustration he threw it into some nearby shrubbery, then looked up at Laura. He was soaked from head to toe by then, and in the pale light from a lamppost she could see that his suit hung on him shapelessly. He was a *huge* man, strong as two bulls, but he had been done in by little things—puddles, a gust of wind—and there was something quite funny about that. She knew she should not laugh, *dared* not laugh, but a laugh burst from her anyway.

"You're too damned beautiful, Laura Shane!" he shouted from the walk below. "God help me, you're just too beautiful." Then he hurried away through the night.

Feeling bad about laughing but unable to stop, she went into the apartment and changed into pajamas. It was only twenty till nine.

He was either a hopeless basket case or the sweetest man she had known since her father died.

At nine-thirty the phone rang. He said, "Will you ever go out with me again?"

"I thought you'd never call."

"You will?"

"Sure."

"Dinner and a movie?" he asked.

"Sounds good."

"We won't go back to that horrible French place. I'm sorry about that, I really am."

"I don't care where we go," she said, "but once we sit down in the restaurant, promise me we'll *stay* there."

"I'm a bonehead about some things. And like I said . . . I never have been able to cope around beautiful women."

"Your mother."

"That's right. Rejected me. Rejected my father. Never felt *any* warmth from that woman. Walked out on us when I was eleven."

"Must've hurt."

"You're more beautiful than she was, and you scare me to death."

"How flattering."

"Well, sorry, but I meant it to be. The thing is, beautiful as you are, you're not *half* as beautiful as your writing, and that scares me even more. Because what could a genius like you ever see in a guy like me—except maybe comic relief?"

"Just one question, Daniel."

"Danny."

"Just one question, Danny. What the hell kind of stockbroker are you? Any good at all?"

"I'm first-rate," he said with such genuine pride that she knew he was telling the truth. "My clients swear by me, and I've got a nice little portfolio of my own that's outperformed the market three years running. As a stock analyst, broker, and investment adviser, I never give the wind a chance to turn my umbrella inside out."

·2·

The afternoon following the placement of the explosives in the basement of the institute, Stefan took what he expected to be his next to last trip on the Lightning Road. It was an illicit jaunt to January 10, 1988, not on the official schedule and conducted without the knowledge of his colleagues.

Light snow was falling in the San Bernardino Mountains when he arrived, but he was dressed for the weather in rubber boots, leather gloves, and navy peacoat. He took cover under a dense copse of pines, intending to wait until the fierce lightning stopped flaring.

He checked his wristwatch in the flickering celestial light and was startled to see how late he had arrived. He had less than forty minutes to reach Laura before she was killed. If he screwed up and arrived too late, there would be no second chance.

Even while the last white flashes seared the overcast sky, while hard crashes of thunder still echoed back to him from distant peaks and ridges, he hurried away from the trees and down a sloping field where the snow was knee-deep from previous winter storms. There was a crust on the snow, through which he kept breaking with each step, and progress was as difficult as if he had been wading through deep water. He fell twice, and snow got down the tops of his boots, and the savage wind tore at him as if it possessed consciousness and the desire to destroy him. By the time he reached the end of the field and climbed over a snowbank onto the two-lane state highway that led to Arrowhead in one direction and Big Bear in the other, his pants and coat were crusted with frozen snow, his feet were freezing, and he had lost more than five minutes.

The recently plowed highway was clean except for the wispy snow snakes that slithered across the pavement on shifting currents of air. But already the tempo of the storm had increased. The flakes were much smaller than when he had arrived and were falling twice as fast as they had been minutes ago. Soon the road would be treacherous.

He noticed a sign by the side of the pavement—LAKE ARROWHEAD 1 MILE—and was shocked to discover how much farther he was from Laura than he had expected to be.

Squinting into the wind, looking north, he saw a warm glimmer of electric lighting in the dreary, iron-gray afternoon: a single-story building and parked cars about three hundred yards away, on the right. He headed immediately in that direction, keeping his head tucked down to protect his face from the icy teeth of the wind.

He had to find a car. Laura had less than half an hour to live, and she was ten miles away.

·3·

Five months after that first date, on Saturday, July 16, 1977, six weeks after graduating from UCI, Laura married Danny Packard in a civil ceremony before a judge in his chambers. The only guests in attendance, both of whom served as witnesses, were Danny's father, Sam Packard, and Thelma Ackerson.

Sam was a handsome, silver-haired man of about five ten, dwarfed by his son. Throughout the brief ceremony, he wept, and Danny kept turning around and saying, "You all right, Dad?" Sam nodded and blew his nose and told them to go on with it, but a moment later he was crying again, and Danny was asking him if he was all right, and Sam blew his nose as if imitating the mating calls of geese. The judge said, "Son, your father's tears are tears of joy, so if we could get on with this—I have three more ceremonies to perform."

Even if the groom's father had not been an emotional wreck, and even if the groom had not been a giant with the heart of a fawn, their wedding party would have been memorable because of Thelma. Her hair was cut in a strange, shaggy style, with a pompom-like spray in front that was tinted purple. In the middle of summer—and at a wedding, yet—she was wearing red high heels, tight black slacks, and tattered black blouse—carefully, purposefully tattered—gathered at the waist with a length of ordinary steel chain used as a belt. She was wearing exaggerated purple eye makeup, blood-red lipstick, and one earring that looked like a fishhook.

After the ceremony, as Danny was having a private word with his father, Thelma huddled with Laura in a corner of the courthouse lobby and explained her appearance. "It's called the punk look, the latest thing in Britain. No one's wearing it over here yet. In fact hardly anyone's wearing it in Britain, either, but in a few years everyone will dress like this. It's great for my act. I look freaky, so people want to laugh as soon as I step on the stage. It's also good for *me*. I mean, face it, Shane, I'm not exactly blossoming with age. Hell, if homely was a disease and had an organized charity, I'd be their poster child. But the two great things about punk style is you get to hide behind flamboyant makeup and hair, so no one can tell just how homely you are—and you're supposed to look weird, anyway. Jesus, Shane, Danny's a big guy. You've told me so much about him on the phone, but you never once said he was so huge. Put him in a Godzilla suit, turn him loose in New York, film the results, and you could make one of those movies without having to build expensive miniature sets. So you love him, huh?"

"I *adore* him," Laura said. "He's as gentle as he is big, maybe because of all the violence he saw and was a part of in Vietnam, or maybe because he's always been gentle at heart. He's sweet, Thelma, and he's thoughtful, and he thinks I'm one of the best writers he's ever read."

"And when he first started giving you toads, you thought he was a psychopath."

"A minor misjudgment."

Two uniformed police officers passed through the courthouse lobby, flanking a bearded young man in handcuffs, taking him to one of the courtrooms. The prisoner gave Thelma a looking over as he passed and said, "Hey, mama, let's get it on!"

"Ah, the Ackerson charm," Thelma said to Laura. "You get a guy who's a combination of a Greek god, a teddy bear, and Bennett Cerf, and I get crude propositions from the dregs of society. But come to think of it, I never even used to get that, so maybe my time is coming yet."

"You underrate yourself, Thelma. You always have. Some very special guy's going to see what a treasure you are—"

"Charles Manson when he's paroled."

"No. Someday you're going to be every bit as happy as I am. I know it. Destiny, Thelma."

"Good heavens, Shane, you've become a raging optimist! What about the lightning? All those deep conversations we had on the floor of our room at Caswell—you remember? We decided that life is just an absurdist comedy, and every once in a while it's suddenly interrupted with thunderbolts of tragedy to give the story balance, to make the slapstick seem funnier by comparison."

"Maybe it's struck for the last time in my life," Laura said.

Thelma stared hard at her. "Wow. I know you, Shane, and I know you realize what emotional risk you're putting yourself at by even just *wanting* to be this happy. I hope you're right, kid, and I bet you are. I bet there'll be no more lightning for you."

"Thank you, Thelma."

"And I think your Danny is a sweetheart, a jewel. But I'll tell you something that ought to mean a lot more than my opinion: Ruthie would have loved him too; Ruthie would have thought he was perfect."

They held each other tightly, and for a moment they were young girls again, defiant yet vulnerable, filled with both the cockeyed confidence and the terror of blind fate that had shaped their shared adolescence.

Sunday, July 24, when they returned from a week-long honeymoon in Santa Barbara, they went grocery shopping, then cooked dinner together—tossed salad, sourdough bread, microwave meatballs, and spaghetti—at the apartment in Tustin. She'd given up her own place and moved in with him a few days before the wedding. According to the plan that they had worked out, they would stay at the apartment for two years, maybe three. (They had talked about their future so often and in such detail that they now capitalized those two words in their minds—The Plan—as if they were referring to some cosmic owner's manual that had come with their marriage and that could be relied upon for an accurate picture of their destiny as husband and wife.) So after two years, maybe three, they would be able to afford the down payment on the right house without dipping into the tidy stock portfolio that Danny was building, and only then would they move.

They dined at the small table in the alcove off the kitchen, where they had a view of the king palms in the courtyard in the golden late-afternoon sun, and they discussed the key part of The Plan, which was for Danny to support them while Laura stayed home and wrote her first novel. "When you're wildly rich and famous," he said, twirling spaghetti on his fork, "then I'll leave the brokerage and spend my time managing our money."

"What if I'm never rich and famous?"

"You will be."

"What if I can't even get published?"

"Then I'll divorce you."

She threw a crust of bread at him. "Beast."

"Shrew."

"You want another meatball?"

"Not if you're going to throw it."

"My rage has passed. I make good meatballs, don't I?"

"Excellent," he agreed.

"That's worth celebrating, don't you think—that you have a wife who makes good meatballs?"

"Definitely worth celebrating."

"So let's make love."

Danny said, "In the middle of dinner?"

"No, in bed." She pushed back her chair and got up. "Come on. Dinner can always be reheated."

During that first year they made love frequently, and in their intimacies Laura found more than sexual release, something far more than she had expected. Being with Danny, holding him within her, she felt so close to him that at times it almost seemed as if they were one person—one body and one mind, one spirit, one dream. She loved him wholeheartedly, yes, but that feeling of oneness was more than love, or at least different from love. By their first Christmas together, she understood that what she felt was a sense of belonging not experienced in a long time, a sense of family; for this was her husband and she was his wife, and one day from their union would come children—after two or three years, according to The Plan—and within the shelter of the family was a peace not to be found elsewhere.

She would have thought that working and living in continuous happiness, harmony, and security day after day would lead to mental lethargy, that her writing would suffer from too much happiness, that she needed a balanced life with down days and miseries to keep the sharp edge on her work. But the idea that an artist needed to suffer to do her best work was a conceit of the young and inexperienced. The happier she grew, the better she wrote.

Six weeks before their first wedding anniversary, Laura finished a novel, *Jericho Nights,* and sent a copy to a New York literary agent, Spencer Keene, who had responded favorably to a query letter a month earlier. Two weeks later Keene called to say he would represent the book, expected a quick sale, and thought she had a splendid future as a novelist. With a swiftness that startled even the agent, he sold it to the first house to which it was submitted, Viking, for a modest but perfectly respectable advance of fifteen thousand dollars, and the deal was concluded on Friday, July 14, 1978, two days before Laura and Danny's anniversary.

·4·

The place he had seen from farther up the road was a restaurant and tavern in the shadows of enormous Ponderosa pines. The trees stood over two hundred feet tall, bedecked with clusters of six-inch cones, with beautifully fissured bark, some boughs bent low under the weight of snow from previous storms. The single-story building was made of logs; it was so sheltered by trees on three sides that its slate roof was covered with more pine needles than snow. The windows were either steamed over or frosted, and the light from within was pleasingly diffused by that translucent film on the glass.

In the parking lot in front of the building were two Jeep wagons, two pickup trucks, and a Thunderbird. Relieved that no one would be able to see him through the tavern windows, Stefan went directly to one of the Jeeps, tried the door, found it unlocked, and got in behind the steering wheel, closing the door after him.

He drew the Walther PPK/S .380 from the shoulder holster he was wearing inside his peacoat. He put it on the seat at his side.

His feet were painfully cold, and he wanted to pause and empty the snow out of his boots. But he had arrived late, and his original schedule was shot, so he dared not waste a minute. Besides, if his feet hurt, they weren't frozen; he wasn't in danger of frostbite yet.

The keys were not in the ignition. He slid the seat back, bent down, groped under the dashboard, located the ignition wires, and had the engine running in a minute.

Stefan sat up just as the owner of the Jeep, breath reeking of beer, pulled open the door. "Hey, what the hell you doing, pal?"

The rest of the snowswept parking lot was still deserted. They were alone.

Laura would be dead in twenty-five minutes.

The Jeep's owner reached for him, and he allowed himself to be dragged from behind the steering wheel, plucking his pistol off the seat as he went, and in fact he threw himself into the other man's grasp, using the momentum to send his adversary staggering backward on the slippery parking lot. They fell. As they hit the ground, he was on top, and he jammed the muzzle under the guy's chin.

"Jesus, mister! Don't kill me."

"We're getting up now. Easy, damn you, no sudden moves."

When they were on their feet Stefan moved behind the guy, quickly reversed his grip on the Walther, used it as a club, struck once, hard enough to knock the man unconscious without doing permanent damage. The owner of the Jeep went down again, stayed down, limp.

Stefan glanced at the tavern. No one else had come out.

He could hear no traffic approaching on the road, but then again the howling wind might mask the sound of an engine.

As the snow began to fall harder, he put the pistol in the deep pocket of his peacoat and dragged the unconscious man to the nearest other vehicle, the Thunderbird. It was unlocked, and he heaved the guy into the rear seat, closed the door, and hurried back to the Jeep.

The engine had died. He hot-wired it again.

As he put the Jeep in gear and swung it around toward the road, the wind shrieked at the window beside him. The falling snow grew denser, blizzard-thick, and clouds of yesterday's snow were whipped up from the ground and spun in sparkling columns. The giant, shadow-swaddled pines swayed and shuddered under winter's assault.

Laura had little more than twenty minutes to live.

·5·

They celebrated the publishing contract for *Jericho Nights* and the otherworldly harmony of their first year of marriage by spending their anniversary at a favorite place—Disneyland. The sky was blue, cloudless; the air was dry and hot. Virtually oblivious of the summer crowds, they rode the Pirates of the Caribbean, had their pictures taken with Mickey Mouse, got dizzy spinning in the Mad Hatter's teacups, had their portraits drawn by a caricaturist, ate hot dogs and ice cream and chocolate-covered frozen bananas on sticks, and danced that evening to a Dixieland band in New Orleans Square.

The park became even more magical after nightfall, and they rode the Mark Twain paddlewheel steamboat around Huck Finn Island for the third time, standing at the railing on the top level, near the bow, with their arms around each other. Danny said, "You know why we like this place so much? 'Cause it's of the world yet untainted *by* the world. And that's our marriage."

Later, over strawberry sundaes at the Carnation Pavilion, at a table beneath trees strung with white Christmas lights, Laura said, "Fifteen thousand bucks for a year's work . . . not exactly a fortune."

"It isn't slave wages either." He pushed his sundae aside, leaned forward, slid her sundae aside, too, and took her hands across the table. "The money will come eventually because you're brilliant, but money isn't what I care about. What I care about is that you've got something special to share. No. That's not exactly what I mean. You don't just *have* something special, you *are* something special. In some way I understand but can't explain, I know that what you *are,* when shared, will bring as much hope and joy to people in far places as it brings to me here at your side."

Blinking away sudden tears, she said, "I love you."

Jericho Nights was published ten months later, in May of 1979. Danny insisted she use her maiden name because he knew that through all the bad years in McIlroy Home and Caswell Hall, she had endured in part because she wanted to grow up and make something of herself as a testament to her father and perhaps, as well, to the mother she had never known. The book sold few copies, was not chosen by any book clubs, and was licensed by Viking to a paperback publisher for a small advance.

"Doesn't matter," Danny told her. "It'll come in time. It'll all come in time. Because of what you *are.*"

By then she was deep into her second novel, *Shadrach.* Working ten hours a day, six days a week, she finished it that July.

On a Friday she sent one copy to Spencer Keene in New York and gave the original script to Danny. He was the first to read it. He left work early and began reading at one o'clock Friday afternoon in his living-room armchair, then shifted to the bedroom, slept only four hours, and by ten o'clock Saturday morning he was back in the armchair and two-thirds of the way through the script. He would not talk about it, not a word. "Not until I'm done. It wouldn't be fair to you to start analyzing and reacting until I've finished, until I've grasped your entire pattern, and it wouldn't be fair to me, either, because in discussing it you're sure to give away some plot turn or other."

She kept peeking at him to see if he was frowning, smiling, or responding to the story in any way, and even when he was reacting she worried that it was the *wrong* reaction to whatever scene he might be reading. By ten-thirty Saturday, she couldn't bear to stay around the apartment any longer, so she drove to South Coast Plaza, browsed in bookstores, ate an early lunch though she was not hungry, drove to the Westminster Mall, window-shopped, ate a cone of frozen yogurt, drove to the Orange Mall, looked in a few shops, bought a square of fudge and ate half of it. "Shane," she told herself, "go home, or you'll be a double for Orson Welles by dinnertime."

As she parked in the carport at the apartment complex, she saw that Danny's car was gone. When she let herself into the apartment, she called his name but got no answer.

The script of *Shadrach* was piled on the dinette table.

She looked for a note. There was none.

"Oh, God," she said.

The book was bad. It stank. It reeked. It was mule puke. Poor Danny had gone out somewhere to have a beer and find the courage to tell her that she should study plumbing while she was still young enough to get launched on a new career.

She was going to throw up. She hurried to the bathroom, but the nausea passed. She washed her face with cold water.

The book was mule puke.

Okay, she would just have to live with that. She'd thought *Shadrach* was pretty good, better than *Jericho Nights* by a mile, but evidently she had been wrong. So she would write another book.

She went to the kitchen and opened a Coors. She had taken only two swallows when Danny came home with a gift-wrapped box about the right size to hold a basketball. He put it on the dinette table beside the manuscript, looked at her solemnly. "It's for you."

Ignoring the box, she said, "Tell me."

"Open your gift first."

"Oh, God, is it *that* bad? Is it so bad you have to soften the blow with a gift? Tell me. I can take it. Wait! Let me sit down." She pulled out a chair from the table and dropped into it. "Hit me with your best, big guy. I'm a survivor."

"You've got too strong a sense of drama, Laura."

"What're you saying? The book's melodramatic?"

"Not the book. You. Right now, anyway. Will you for God's sake stop being the shattered young artiste and open your gift?"

"All right, all right, if I've got to open the gift before you'll talk, then I'll open the bloody gift."

She put the box in her lap—it was heavy—and tore at the ribbon while Danny pulled up a chair and sat in front of her, watching.

The box was from an expensive shop, but she was not prepared for the contents: a large, gorgeous Lalique bowl; it was clear except for two handles that were partly clear green and partly frosted crystal; each handle was formed by two leaping toads, four toads altogether.

She looked up, wide-eyed. "Danny, I've never seen anything like this. It's the most beautiful piece ever."

"Like it, then?"

"Good God, how much was it?"

"Three thousand."

"Danny, we can't afford this!"

"Oh, yes, we can."

"No, we can't, really we can't. Just because I wrote a lousy book and you want to make me feel better—"

"You didn't write a lousy book. You wrote a toad-worthy book. A *four*-toad book on a scale of one to four, four being the best. We can afford that bowl precisely because you wrote *Shadrach*. This book is beautiful, Laura, infinitely better than the last one, and it's beautiful because it's you. This book is what you *are*, and it shines."

In her excitement and in her eagerness to hug him, she nearly dropped the three-thousand-dollar bowl.

·6·

A skin of new snow covered the highway now. The Jeep wagon had four-wheel drive and was equipped with tire chains, so Stefan was able to make reasonably good time in spite of the road conditions.

But not good enough.

He estimated that the tavern, where he had stolen the Jeep, was about eleven miles from the Packard house, which was just off state route 330 a few miles south of Big Bear. The mountain roads were narrow, twisty, full of dramatic rises and falls, and blowing snow ensured poor visibility, so his average speed was about forty miles an hour. He could not risk driving faster or more recklessly, for he would be of no use at all to Laura, Danny, and Chris if he lost control of the Jeep and plunged over an embankment to his death. At his current speed, however, he would arrive at their place at least ten minutes after they had left.

His intention had been to delay them at their house until the danger had passed. That plan was no longer viable.

The January sky seemed to have sunk so low under the weight of the storm that it was no higher than the tops of the serried ranks of massive evergreens that flanked both sides of the roadway. Wind shook the trees and hammered the Jeep. Snow stuck to the windshield wipers and became ice, so he turned up the defroster and hunched over the wheel, squinting through the inadequately cleaned glass.

When he next glanced at his watch, he saw that he had less than fifteen minutes. Laura, Danny, and Chris would be getting into their Chevy Blazer. They might even be pulling out of their driveway already.

He would have to intercept them on the highway, scant seconds ahead of Death.

He tried to squeeze slightly more speed out of the Jeep without shooting wide of a turn and into an abyss.

·7·

Five weeks after the day that Danny bought her the Lalique bowl, on August 15, 1979, a few minutes after noon, Laura was in the kitchen, heating a can of chicken soup for lunch, when she got a call from Spencer Keene, her literary agent in New York. Viking loved *Shadrach* and were offering a hundred thousand.

"*Dollars?*" she asked.

"Of course, dollars," Spencer said. "What do you think, Russian rubles? What would that buy you—a hat maybe?"

"Oh, God." She had to lean against the kitchen counter because suddenly her legs were weak.

Spencer said, "Laura, honey, only you can know what's best for you, but unless they're willing to let the hundred grand stand for a floor bid in an auction, I want you to consider turning this down."

"Turn down a hundred thousand dollars?" she asked in disbelief.

"I want to send this out to maybe six or eight houses, set an auction date, see what happens. I think I *know* what will happen, Laura, I think they'll all love this book as much as I do. On the other hand . . . maybe not. It's a hard decision, and you've got to go away and think about it before you answer me."

The moment Spencer said goodbye and hung up, Laura dialed Danny at work and told him about the offer.

He said, "If they won't make it a floor bid, turn it down."

"But, Danny, can we afford to? I mean, my car is eleven years old and falling apart. Yours is almost four years old—"

"Listen, what did I tell you about this book? Didn't I tell you that it was *you*, a reflection of what you are?"

"You're sweet, but—"

"Turn it down. Listen, Laura, You're thinking that scorning a hundred K is like spitting in the faces of all the gods of good fortune; it's like inviting that lightning you've spoken about. But you *earned* this payoff, and fate isn't going to cheat you out of it."

She called Spencer Keene and told him her decision.

Excited, nervous, already missing the hundred thousand dollars, she returned to the den and sat at her typewriter and stared at the unfinished short story for a while until she became aware of the odor of chicken soup and remembered she had left it on the stove. She hurried into the kitchen and found that all but half an inch of soup had boiled away; burnt noodles were stuck to the bottom of the pot.

At two-ten, which was five-ten New York time, Spencer called again to say that Viking had agreed to let the hundred thousand stand as a floor bid. "Now, that's the very least you make from *Shadrach*—a hundred grand. I think I'll set September twenty-sixth as the auction date. It's going to be a big one, Laura. I feel it."

She spent the remainder of the afternoon trying to be elated but unable to shake off her anxiety. *Shadrach* was already a big success, no matter what happened in the auction. She had no reason for her anxiety, but it held her in a tight grip.

Danny came home from work that day with a bottle of champagne, a bouquet of roses, and a box of Godiva chocolates. They sat on the sofa, nibbling chocolates, sipping champagne, and talking about the future, which seemed entirely bright; yet her anxiety lingered.

Finally she said, "I don't want chocolates or champagne or roses or a hundred thousand dollars. I want you. Take me to bed."

They made love for a long time. The late summer sun ebbed from the windows and the tide of night rolled in before they parted with a sweet, aching reluctance. Lying at her side in the darkness, Danny tenderly kissed her breasts, her throat, her eyes, and finally her lips. She realized that her anxiety had at last faded. It was not sexual release that expelled her fear. Intimacy, total surrender of self, and the sense of shared hopes and dreams and destinies had been the true medicines; the great, good feeling of *family* that she had with him was a talisman that effectively warded off cold fate.

On Wednesday, September 26, Danny took the day off from work to be at Laura's side as the news came in from New York.

At seven-thirty in the morning, ten-thirty New York time, Spencer Keene called to report that Random House had made the first offer above the auction floor. "One hundred and twenty-five thousand, and we're on our way."

Two hours later Spencer called again. "Everyone's off to lunch, so there'll be a lull. Right now, we're up to three hundred and fifty thousand and six houses are still in the bidding."

"Three hundred and fifty thousand?" Laura repeated.

At the kitchen sink where he was rinsing the breakfast dishes, Danny dropped a plate.

When she hung up and looked at Danny, he grinned and said, "Am I mistaken, or is this the book you were afraid might be mule puke?"

Four and a half hours later, as they were sitting at the dinette table pretending to be concentrating on a game of five-hundred rummy, their inattention betrayed by their mutual inability to keep score with any degree of mathematical accuracy whatsoever, Spencer Keene called again. Danny followed her into the kitchen to listen to her side of the conversation.

Spencer said, "You sitting down, honey?"

"I'm ready, Spencer. I don't need a chair. Tell me."

"It's over. Simon and Schuster. One million, two hundred and twenty-five thousand dollars."

Weak with shock, shaky, she spoke with Spencer for another ten minutes, and when she hung up, she wasn't sure of a thing that had been said after he had told her the price. Danny was staring at her expectantly, and she realized that he didn't know what had happened. She told him the name of the buyer and the figure.

For a moment they stared at each other in silence.

Then she said, "I think maybe now we can afford to have a baby."

·8·

Stefan topped a hill and peered ahead at the half-mile stretch of snowswept road on which it would happen. On his left, beyond the southbound lane, the tree-covered mountainside sloped steeply down to the highway. On his right the northbound lane was edged by a soft shoulder only about four feet wide, beyond which the mountainside fell away again into a deep gorge. No guardrails protected travelers from that deadly drop-off.

At the bottom of the slope, the road turned left, out of sight. Between that turn below and the crest of the hill, which he had just topped, the two-lane blacktop was deserted.

According to his watch, Laura would be dead in a minute. Two minutes at most.

He suddenly realized that he should never have tried to drive toward the Packards, not after he had arrived so late. Instead he should have given up the idea of stopping the Packards and should have tried instead to identify and stop the Robertsons' vehicle farther back on the road to Arrowhead. That would have worked just as well.

Too late now.

Stefan had no time to go back, nor could he risk driving farther north toward the Packards. He did not know the exact moment of their deaths, not to the second, but that catastrophe was now approaching swiftly. If he tried to go even another half mile and stop them before they arrived at this fateful incline, he might reach the bottom of the slope and, in taking the turn, pass them going the other way, at which point he would not be able to swing around and catch up with them and stop them before the Robertsons' truck hit them head-on.

He braked gently and angled across the ascending southbound lane, stopping the Jeep on a wide portion of that shoulder of the road about halfway down the slope, so close to the embankment that he could not get out of the driver's door. His heart was thudding almost painfully as he shifted the Jeep into park, put on the emergency brake, cut the engine, slid across the seat, and got out the passenger-side door.

The blowing snow and icy air stung his face, and all along the mountainside the wind shrieked and howled like many voices, perhaps the voices of the three sisters of Greek myth, the Fates, mocking him for his desperate attempt to prevent what they had ordained.

·9·

After receiving editorial suggestions, Laura undertook an easy revision of *Shadrach,* delivering the final version of the script in mid-December, 1979, and Simon and Schuster scheduled the book for publication in September, 1980.

It was such a busy year for Laura and Danny that she was only peripherally aware of the Iranian hostage crisis and presidential campaign, and even more vaguely cognizant of the countless fires, plane crashes, toxic spills, mass murders, floods, earthquakes, and other tragedies that constituted the news. That was the year the rabbit died. That was the year she and Danny bought their first house—a four-bedroom, two-and-a-half-bath, Spanish model in Orange Park Acres—and moved out of the apartment in Tustin. She started her third novel, *The Golden Edge,* and one day when Danny asked her how it was going, she said, "Mule puke," and he said, "That's great!" The first of September, upon receipt of a substantial check for the film rights to *Shadrach,* which had sold to MGM, Danny quit his job at the brokerage house and became her full-time financial manager. On Sunday, September 21, three weeks after it arrived in the stores, *Shadrach* appeared on the *New York Times* bestseller list at number twelve. On October 5, 1980, when Laura gave birth to Christopher Robert Packard, *Shadrach* was in a third printing, sitting comfortably at number eight on the *Times,* and received what Spencer Keene called a "thunderously good" review on page five of that same book section.

The boy entered the world at 2:23 P.M. in a greater rush of blood than that which usually carried babies out of their prenatal darkness. Pain-racked and hemorrhaging, Laura required three pints during the afternoon and evening. She spent a better night than expected, however, and by morning she was sore, weary, but well out of danger.

The following day during visiting hours, Thelma Ackerson came to see the baby and the new mother. Still dressed punkish and ahead of her time—hair long on the left side of her head, with a white streak like the bride of Frankenstein, and short on the right side, with no streak—she breezed into Laura's private room, went straight to Danny, threw her arms around him, hugged him hard, and said, "God, you're big. You're a mutant. Admit it, Packard, your mother might have been human, but your father was a grisly bear." She came to the bed where Laura was propped up against three pillows, kissed her on the forehead and then on the cheek. "I went to the nursery before I came here, had a peek at Christopher Robert through the glass, and he's adorable. But I think you're going to need all the millions you can make from your books, kiddo, because that boy is going to take after his father, and your food bill's going to run thirty thousand a month. Until you get him housebroken, he'll be eating your furniture."

Laura said, "I'm glad you came, Thelma."

"Would I miss it? Maybe if I was playing a Mafia-owned club in Bayonne, New Jersey, and had to cancel out part of a date to fly back, maybe *then* I'd miss it because if you break a contract with those guys they cut off your thumbs and make you use them as suppositories. But I was west of the Mississippi when I got the news last night, and only nuclear war or a date with Paul McCartney could keep me away."

Almost two years ago Thelma had finally gotten time on the stage at the Improv, and she'd been a hit. She landed an agent and began to get paid bookings in sleazy, third-rate—and eventually second-rate—clubs across the country. Laura and Danny had driven into Los Angeles twice to see her perform, and she had been hilarious; she wrote her own material and delivered it with the comic timing she had possessed since childhood but had honed in the intervening years. Her act had one unusual aspect that would either make her a national phenomenon or ensure her obscurity: Woven through the jokes was a strong thread of melancholy, a sense of the tragedy of life that existed simultaneously with the wonder and humor of it. In fact it was similar to the tone of Laura's novels, but what appealed to book readers was less likely to appeal to audiences who had paid for belly laughs.

Now Thelma leaned across the bed railing, peered closely at Laura and said, "Hey, you look pale. And those rings around your eyes . . ."

"Thelma, dear, I hate to shatter your illusions, but a baby isn't really brought by the stork. The mother has to expel it from her own womb, and it's a tight fit."

Thelma stared hard at her, then directed an equally hard stare at Danny, who had come around the other side of the bed to hold Laura's hand. "What's wrong here?"

Laura sighed and, wincing with discomfort, shifted her position slightly. To Danny, she said, "See? I told you she's a bloodhound."

"It wasn't an easy pregnancy, was it?" Thelma demanded.

"The pregnancy was easy enough," Laura said. "It was the delivery that was the problem."

"You didn't . . . almost die or anything, Shane?"

"No, no, no," Laura said, and Danny's hand tightened on hers. "Nothing that dramatic. We knew from the start there were going to be some difficulties along the way, but we found the best doctor, and he kept a close watch. It's just . . . I won't be able to have any more. Christopher will be our last."

Thelma looked at Danny, at Laura, and said quietly, "I'm sorry."

"It's all right," Laura said, forcing a smile. "We have little Chris, and he's beautiful."

They endured an awkward silence, and then Danny said, "I haven't had lunch yet, and I'm starved. I'm going to slip down to the coffee shop for a half hour or so."

When Danny left, Thelma said, "He's not really hungry, is he? He just knew we wanted a girl-to-girl talk."

Laura smiled. "He's a lovely man."

Thelma put down the railing on one side of the bed and said, "If I hop up here and sit beside you, I won't shake up your insides, will I? You won't suddenly bleed all over me, will you, Shane?"

"I'll try not to."

Thelma eased up onto the high hospital bed. She took one of Laura's hands in both of hers. "Listen, I read *Shadrach,* and it's damned good. It's what all writers try to do and seldom achieve."

"You're sweet."

"I'm a tough, cynical, hard-nosed broad. Listen, I'm serious about the book. It's brilliant. And I saw Bovine Bowmaine in there, and Tammy. And Boone, the child-welfare psychologist. Different names but I saw them. You've captured them perfectly, Shane. God, there were times you brought it all back, times when chills ran up and down my back so bad I had to put down the book and go for a walk in the sun. And there were times when I laughed like a loon."

Laura ached in every muscle, in every joint. She did not have the strength to lean away from the pillows and put her arms around her friend. She just said, "I love you, Thelma."

"The Eel wasn't there, of course."

"I'm saving him for another book."

"And me, damn it. I'm not in the book, though I'm the most colorful character you've ever known!"

"I'm saving you for a book all your own," Laura said.

"You mean it, don't you?"

"Yes. Not the one I'm working on now but the one after it."

"Listen, Shane, you better make me *gorgeous,* or I'll sue your ass off. You hear me?"

"I hear you."

Thelma chewed her lip, then said, "Will you—"

"Yes. I'm going to put Ruthie in it too."

They were silent a while, just holding hands.

Unshed tears clouded Laura's vision, but she saw that Thelma was blinking back tears too. "Don't. It'll streak all that elaborate punk eye makeup."

Thelma raised one of her feet. "Are these boots freaky or what? Black leather, pointy toes, stud-ringed heels. Makes me look like a damned dominatrix, doesn't it?"

"When you walked in, the first thing I wondered was how many men you've whipped lately."

Thelma sighed and sniffed hard to clear her nose. "Shane, listen and listen good. This talent of yours is maybe more precious than you think. You're able to capture people's lives on the page, and when the people are gone, the page is still there, the life is still *there*. You can put feelings on the page, and anyone, anywhere, can pick up that book and *feel* those same feelings, you can touch the heart, you can remind us what it means to be human in a world that's increasingly bent on forgetting. That's a talent and a reason to live that's more than most people ever have. So . . . well, I know how much you want to have a family . . . three or four kids, you've said . . . so I know how bad you must be hurting right now. But you've got Danny and Christopher and this amazing talent, and that's so very much to have."

Laura's voice was unsteady. "Sometimes . . . I'm just so afraid."

"Afraid of what, baby?"

"I wanted a big family because . . . then it's less likely they'll all be taken away from me."

"Nobody's going to be taken away from you."

"With just Danny and little Chris . . . just two of them . . . something might happen."

"Nothing will happen."

"Then I'd be alone."

"Nothing will happen," Thelma repeated.

"Something always seems to happen. That's life."

Thelma slid farther onto the bed, stretched out beside Laura, and put her head against Laura's shoulder. "When you said it was a hard birth . . . and the way you look, so pale . . . I was scared. I have friends in LA, sure, but all of them are show-biz types. You're the only *real* person I'm close to, even though we don't see each other that much, and the idea that you might have nearly . . ."

"But I didn't."

"Might've, though." Thelma laughed sourly. "Hell, Shane, once an orphan, always an orphan, huh?"

Laura held her and stroked her hair.

Shortly after Chris's first birthday, Laura delivered *The Golden Edge*. It was published ten months later, and by the boy's second birthday, the book was number one on the *Times* bestseller list, which was a first for her.

Danny managed Laura's book income with such diligence, caution, and brilliance that within a few years, in spite of the savage bite of income taxes, they would be not just rich—they were already rich by most standards—but seriously rich. She didn't know what she thought about that. She had never expected to be rich. When she considered her enviable circumstances, she thought perhaps she should be thrilled or, given the want of much of the world, appalled, but she felt nothing much one way or the other about the money. The security that money provided was welcome; it inspired confidence. But they had no plans to move out of their quite pleasant four-bedroom house, though they could have afforded an estate. The money was *there,* and that was the end of it; she gave it little thought. Life was not money; life was Danny and Chris and, to a lesser extent, her books.

With a toddler in the house, she no longer had the ability or desire to work sixty hours a week at her word processor. Chris was talking, walking, and he exhibited none of the moodiness or mindless rebellion that the child-rearing books described as normal behavior for the year between two and three. Mostly he was a pleasure to be with, a bright and inquisitive boy. She spent as much time with him as she could without risk of spoiling him.

The Amazing Appleby Twins, her fourth novel, was not published until October, 1984, two years after *The Golden Edge,* but there was none of the drop-off in audience that is sometimes the case when a writer does not publish a book each year. The advance sales were her biggest yet.

On October first, she was sitting with Danny and Chris on the sofa in the family room, watching old Road Runner cartoons on the VCR—"Vooom, vooom!" Christopher said each time Road Runner took off in a flash of speed—eating popcorn, when Thelma called from Chicago, in tears. Laura took the call on the kitchen phone, but on the TV in the adjoining room the beleaguered coyote was trying to blow up his nemesis and was blowing himself up instead, so Laura said, "Danny, I better take this in the den."

In the four years since Chris was born, Thelma's career had gone straight up. She had been booked in a couple of Vegas casino lounges. ("Hey, Shane, I must be pretty good because the cocktail waitresses are nearly naked, all boobs and butts, and sometimes the guys in the audience actually look at me instead of them. On the other hand maybe I only appeal to fags.") In the past year she had moved into the main showroom at the MGM Grand as an opening act for Dean Martin, and she had made four appearances on the *Tonight* show with Johnny Carson. There was talk of a movie or even a television series to be built around her, and she seemed poised for stardom as a comedienne. Now she was in Chicago, opening soon as the headliner at a major club.

Perhaps the long chain of positive developments in their lives was what panicked Laura when she heard Thelma crying. For some time she had been waiting for the sky to fall with a horrid suddenness that would have caught Chicken Little unaware. She dropped into the chair behind the desk in the den, snatched up the phone. "Thelma? What is it, what's wrong?"

"I just read . . . the new book."

Laura could not figure what in *The Amazing Appleby Twins* could have affected Thelma so profoundly, and then she suddenly wondered if something in the characterization of Carrie and Sandra Appleby had offended. Though none of the major events in the story mirrored those in the lives of Ruthie and Thelma, the Applebys were, of course, based on the Ackersons. But both characters had been drawn with great love and good humor; surely there was nothing about them that would offend Thelma, and in panic Laura tried to say as much.

"No, no, Shane, you hopeless fool," Thelma said between bouts of tears. "I'm not offended. The reason I can't stop crying is because you did the most wonderful thing. Carrie Appleby is Ruthie as sure as I ever knew her, but in your book you let Ruthie live a long time. You let Ruthie live, Shane, and that's a whole hell of a lot better job than God did in real life."

They talked for an hour, mostly about Ruthie, reminiscing, not with a lot of tears, now, but mostly with affection. Danny and Chris appeared in the open doorway of the den a couple of times, looking abandoned, and Laura blew them kisses, but she stayed on the telephone with Thelma because it was one of those rare times when remembering the dead was more important than tending to the needs of the living.

Two weeks before Christmas, 1985, when Chris was five and then some, the southern California rainy season started with a downpour that made palm fronds rattle like bones, battered the last remaining blossoms off the impatiens, and flooded streets. Chris could not play outside. His father was off inspecting a potential real estate investment, and the boy was in no mood to entertain himself. He kept finding excuses to bother Laura in her office, and by eleven o'clock she gave up trying to work on the current book. She sent him to the kitchen to get the baking sheets out of the cupboard, promising to let him help her make chocolate-chip cookies.

Before joining him, she got Sir Tommy Toad's webbed-foot boots, tiny umbrella, and miniature scarf from the dresser drawer in the bedroom, where she had been keeping them for just such a day as this. On her way to the kitchen she arranged those items near the front door.

Later, as she was slipping a tray of cookies into the oven, she sent him to the front door to see if the United Parcel deliveryman had left a package that she professed to be expecting, and Chris came back flushed with excitement. "Mommy, come look, come see."

In the foyer he showed her the three miniature items, and she said, "I suppose they belong to Sir Tommy. Oh, did I forget to tell you about the lodger we've taken in? A fine, upstanding toad from England here on the queen's business."

She had been eight when her father had invented Sir Tommy, and she had accepted the fabulous toad as a fun fantasy, but Chris was only five and took it more seriously. "Where's he going to sleep—the spare bedroom? Then what do we do when Grandpa comes to visit?"

"We've rented Sir Tommy a room in the attic," Laura said, "and we must not disturb him or tell anyone about him except Daddy because Sir Tommy is here on *secret* business for Her Majesty."

He looked at her wide-eyed, and she wanted to laugh but dared not. He had brown hair and eyes, like she and Danny, but his features were delicate, more his mother's than his father's. In spite of his smallness there was something about him that made her think he would eventually shoot up to be tall and solidly constructed like Danny. He leaned close and whispered: "Is Sir Tommy a *spy?*"

Throughout the afternoon, as they baked cookies, cleaned up, and played a few games of Old Maids, Chris was full of questions about Sir Tommy. Laura discovered that tale-telling for children was in some ways more demanding than writing novels for adults.

When Danny came home at four-thirty, he shouted a greeting on his way along the hall from the connecting door to the garage.

Chris jumped up from the breakfast-nook table, where he and Laura were playing cards, and urgently shushed his father. "Sssshhh, Daddy, Sir Tommy might be sleeping now, he had a long trip, he's the Queen of England, and he's spying in our attic!"

Danny frowned. "I go away from home for just a few hours, and while I'm gone we're invaded by scaly, transvestite, British spies?"

That night in bed, after Laura made love with a special passion that surprised even her, Danny said, "What's gotten into you today? All evening you were so . . . buoyant, so up."

Snuggling against him under the covers, enjoying the feel of his nude body against hers, she said, "Oh, I don't know, it's just that I'm *alive,* and Chris is alive, you're alive, we're all together. And it's this Tommy Toad thing."

"It tickles you?"

"Tickles me, yes. But it's more than that. It's . . . well, somehow it makes me feel that life goes on, that it always goes on, the cycle is renewed—does this sound crazy?—and that life is going to go on for us, too, for all of us, for a long time."

"Well, yeah, I think you're right," he said. "Unless you're that energetic *every* time you make love from now on, in which case you'll kill me in about three months."

In October, 1986, when Chris turned six, Laura's fifth novel, *Endless River,* was published to critical acclaim and bigger sales than any of her previous titles. Her editor had predicted the greater success: "It's got all the humor, all the tension, all the tragedy, that whole weird mix of a Laura Shane novel, but it's somehow not as *dark* as the others, and that makes it especially appealing."

For two years, Laura and Danny had been taking Chris up to the San Bernardino Mountains at least one weekend a month, to Lake Arrowhead and Big Bear, both during the summer and winter, to make sure he learned that the whole world was not like the pleasant but thoroughly urbanized and suburbanized realms of Orange County. With the continued flowering of her career and the success of Danny's investment strategies, and considering her recent willingness not only to entertain optimism but to *live* it, they decided it was time to indulge themselves, so they bought a second home in the mountains.

It was an eleven-room stone and redwood place on thirty acres just off state route 330, a few miles south of Big Bear. It was, in fact, a more expensive house than the one they lived in during the week in Orange Park Acres. The property was mostly covered with western juniper, Ponderosa pine, and sugar pine, and their nearest neighbor was far beyond sight. During their first weekend at the retreat, as they were making a snowman, three deer appeared at the edge of the looming forest, twenty yards away, and watched curiously.

Chris was thrilled at the sight of the deer, and by the time he had been tucked in bed that night, he was sure that they were Santa Claus's deer. *This* was where the jolly fat man went after Christmas, he insisted, and not, as legend had it, to the North Pole.

Wind and Stars appeared in October of '87, and it was a still bigger hit than any of her previous books. The movie of *Endless River* was released that Thanksgiving, enjoying the biggest opening-week box office of any film that year.

On Friday, January 8, 1988, buoyed by the knowledge that *Wind and Stars* would hold the number one spot on the *Times* list that Sunday for the fifth week in a row, they drove up to Big Bear in the afternoon, as soon as Chris came home from school. The following Tuesday was Laura's thirty-third birthday, and they intended to have an early celebration, just the three of them, high in the mountains, with the snow like icing on a cake and the wind to sing for her.

Accustomed to them, the deer ventured within twenty feet of their house on Saturday morning. But Chris was seven now, and in school he heard the rumor that Santa Claus was not real, and he was no longer so sure that these were more than ordinary deer.

The weekend was perfect, perhaps the best they had spent in the mountains, but they had to cut it short. They had intended to leave at six o'clock Monday morning, returning to Orange County in time to deliver Chris to school. However a major storm moved into the area ahead of schedule late Sunday afternoon, and though they were little more than ninety minutes from the balmy temperatures nearer the coast, the weather report called for two feet of new snow by morning. Not wanting to risk being snowbound and causing

Chris to miss a day of school—a possibility even with their four-wheel-drive Blazer—they closed up the big stone and redwood house and headed south on state route 330 at a few minutes past four o'clock.

Southern California was one of the few places in the world where you could drive from a winterscape to subtropical heat in less than two hours, and Laura always enjoyed—and marveled at—the journey. The three of them were dressed for snow—wool socks, boots, thermal underwear, heavy slacks, warm sweaters, ski jackets—but in an hour and a quarter they would be in milder climes where no one was bundled up, and in two hours they would be in shirtsleeve weather.

Laura drove while Danny, sitting in front, and Chris, sitting behind him, played a word-association game that they had devised on previous trips to amuse themselves. Rapidly falling snow found even those sections of the highway that were largely protected by trees on both sides, and in unsheltered areas the hard-driven flakes sheeted and whirled by the millions in the capricious currents of the high-mountain winds, sometimes half obscuring the way ahead. She drove with caution, not caring if the two-hour drive home required three hours or four; since they had left early, they had plenty of time to spare, all the time in the world.

When she came out of the big curve a few miles south of their house and entered the half-mile incline, she saw a red Jeep station wagon parked on the right shoulder and a man in a navy peacoat in the middle of the road. He was coming down the hill, waving both arms to halt them.

Leaning forward and squinting between the thumping windshield wipers, Danny said, "Looks like he broke down, needs help."

"Packard's Patrol to the rescue!" Chris said from the back seat.

As Laura slowed, the guy on the road began frantically gesturing for them to pull to the right shoulder.

Danny said uneasily, "Something odd about him. . . ."

Yes, odd indeed. He was her special guardian. The sight of him after all these years shocked and frightened Laura.

·10·

He had just gotten out of the stolen Jeep when the Blazer turned the bend at the bottom of the hill. As he rushed toward it, he saw Laura slow the Blazer to a crawl a third of the way up the slope, but she was still in the middle of the roadway, so he signaled her more frantically to get off onto the shoulder, as close to the embankment as possible. At first she continued to creep forward, as if unsure whether he was only a motorist in trouble or dangerous, but when they drew close enough to each other for her to see his face and perhaps recognize him, she immediately obeyed.

As she accelerated past him and whipped the Blazer onto the wider portion of the shoulder, only twenty feet downhill from Stefan's Jeep, he reversed direction and ran to her, yanked open her door. "I don't know if being off the road's good enough. Get out, up the embankment, quickly, *now!*"

Danny said, "Hey, wait just—"

"Do what he says!" Laura shouted. "Chris, come on, get out!"

Stefan gripped Laura's hand and helped her out of the driver's seat. As Danny and Chris also scrambled from the Blazer, Stefan heard a laboring engine above the skirling wind. He looked up the long hill and saw that a big pickup truck had topped the crest and was starting down toward them. Pulling Laura after him, he ran around the front of the Blazer.

Her guardian said, "Up the embankment, come on," and began to climb the hard-packed, ice-crusted snow that had been shoved there by plows and that sloped steeply toward the nearby trees.

Laura looked up the highway and saw the truck, a quarter-mile from them and only a hundred feet below the crest, beginning a long, sickening slide on the treacherous pavement until it was coming sideways down the road. If they had not stopped, if her guardian had not delayed them, they would have been just below the crest when the truck went out of control; already they would have been hit.

Beside her, with Chris riding him piggyback and holding on tight, Danny obviously had seen the danger. The truck might come all the way down the hill without the driver in control, might slam into the Jeep and Blazer. Lugging Chris, he scrambled up the snow-packed embankment, yelling for Laura to *move.*

She climbed, grabbing for handholds, kicking footholds as she went. The snow was not only ice-mantled but ice-marbled and rotten in places, breaking away in chunks, and a couple of times she nearly fell backward to the shoulder of the highway below. By the time she joined her guardian, Danny, and Chris fifteen feet above the highway, on a narrow but snow-free shelf of rock near the trees, it seemed as if she had been climbing for minutes. But in fact her sense of time must have been distorted by fear, for when she looked up the highway she saw that the truck was still sliding toward them, that it was two hundred feet away, had made one complete revolution, and was turning sideways again.

On it came through the streaming snow, as if in slow motion, fate in the form of a few tons of steel. A snowmobile stood in the big pickup's cargo bed, and it was apparently not secured by chains or in any way restrained; the driver foolishly had relied on inertia to keep it in place. But now the snowmobile was slamming from side to side against the walls of the cargo hold and forward into the back wall of the cab, and through the quarter-mile slide its violent shifts contributed to the destabilization of the vehicle under it, until it seemed as if the truck, leaning radically, would roll instead of spin through another complete turn.

Laura saw the driver fighting the wheel, and she saw a woman beside him, screaming, and she thought: Oh, my god, those poor people!

As if sensing her thoughts, her guardian shouted above the wind, "They're drunk, both of them, and no snow chains."

If you know that much about them, she thought, you must know who they are, so why didn't you stop them, why didn't you save them too?

With a terrible crash the front end of the truck rammed into the side of the Jeep, and unrestrained by a seat belt, the woman was thrown halfway through the windshield, where she hung partly in and partly out of the cab—

Laura yelled, "Chris!" But she saw that Danny had already taken the boy off his back and was holding him close, turning his head away from the ongoing accident.

—the collision didn't stop the truck; it had too much momentum, and the pavement was too slippery for chainless tread to grip. But the brutal impact did reverse the direction of the truck's slide: it abruptly whipped around to its driver's right, heading backward down the hill, and the snowmobile exploded through the tailgate, *flew* free, crashing onto the hood of the parked Blazer, smashing the windshield. An instant later the rear of the pickup slammed into the front of the Blazer with enough force to shove that vehicle ten feet backward in spite of its firmly engaged emergency brakes—

Though viewing the destruction from the safety of the embankment,

Laura gripped Danny's arm, horrified by the thought that they surely would have been injured and perhaps killed if they had taken refuge either in front of or behind the Blazer.

—now the pickup bounced off the Blazer; the bloodied woman fell back into the cab; and, sliding more slowly but still out of control, the battered truck turned three hundred and sixty degrees in an eerily graceful ballet of death, angling down the slope and across the snowy pavement and over the far shoulder, over the unguarded brink, out into emptiness, down, out of sight, gone.

Though no horror remained to be seen, Laura covered her face with her hands, perhaps trying to block out the mental image of the pickup carrying its occupants down the rocky, nearly treeless wall of that gorge, tumbling hundreds upon hundreds of feet. The driver and his companion would be dead before they hit bottom. Even above the raging wind, she heard the truck strike an outcropping of rock, then another. But in seconds the noise of its violent descent faded, and the only sound was the mad shrieking of the storm.

Stunned, they slid and groped their way down the embankment to the shoulder of the road between the Jeep and the Blazer, where bits of glass and metal littered the snowy surface. Steam rose from under the Blazer as hot radiator fluid drizzled onto the frozen ground, and the ruined vehicle creaked under the weight of the snowmobile embedded in its hood.

Chris was crying. Laura reached for him. He came into her arms, and she lifted him, held him, while he sobbed against her neck.

Dazed, Danny turned to their savior. "Who . . . who in the name of God are you?"

Laura stared at her guardian, finding it difficult to cope with the fact that he really was there. She had not seen him in over twenty years, since she was twelve, that day in the cemetery when she had spotted him watching her father's interment from the grove of Indian laurels. She had not seen him close up for almost twenty-*five* years, since the day he had killed the junkie in her father's grocery. When he failed to save her from the Eel, when he left her to handle *that* one on her own, a loss of faith set in, and doubt was encouraged when he did nothing to save Nina Dockweiler, either—or Ruthie. With the passage of so much time, he had become a dream figure, more myth than reality, and in the last couple of years she had not thought about him at all, had abandoned belief in him just as Chris was currently abandoning belief in Santa Claus. She still had the note that he'd left on her desk, after her father's funeral. But she had long ago convinced herself that it had not in fact been written by a magical guardian but perhaps by Cora or Tom Lance, her father's friends. Now he had saved her again, miraculously, and Danny wanted to know who in the name of God he was, and that was what Laura wanted to know as well.

The strangest part of it was that he looked the same as when he had shot the junkie. *Exactly the same.* She had recognized him at once, even after the passage of so much time, because he had not aged. He still appeared to be in his middle to late thirties. Impossibly, the years had left no mark on him, no hint of gray in his blond hair, no wrinkles in his face. Though he had been her father's age that bloody day in the grocery store, he now was of her own generation or nearly so.

Before the man could answer Danny's question or find a way to avoid an answer, a car topped the hill and started down toward them. It was a late-model Pontiac equipped with tire chains that sang on the pavement. The driver apparently saw the damage to the Jeep and the Blazer and noted the pickup's still fresh skid marks that had not yet been obliterated by wind and snow; he slowed—with reduced speed the song of the chains quickly changed to a clatter—and pulled across the pavement into the southbound lane. Instead of going all the way to the shoulder and out of traffic, however, the car continued north in the wrong lane, stopping only fifteen feet from them, near the back of the Jeep. When he threw open the door and got out of the Pontiac, the driver—a tall man in dark clothing—was holding an object that, too late, Laura identified as a submachine gun.

Her guardian said, "Kokoschka!"

Even as his name was spoken, Kokoschka opened fire.

Though he was more than fifteen years from Vietnam, Danny reacted with the instincts of a soldier. As bullets ricocheted off the red Jeep in front of them and off the Blazer behind them, Danny grabbed Laura, pushing her and Chris to the ground between the two vehicles.

As Laura dropped below the line of fire, she saw Danny struck in the back. He was hit at least once, maybe twice, and she jerked as if the slugs had hit her. He fell against the front of the Blazer, dropped to his knees.

Laura cried out and, holding Chris with one arm, reached for her husband.

He was still alive, and in fact he swung toward her on his knees.

His face was as white as the snow falling around them, and she had the bizarre and terrible feeling that she was looking into the countenance of a ghost rather than that of a living man. "Get under the Jeep," Danny said, pushing her hand away. His voice was thick and wet, as if something had broken in his throat. "Quick!"

One of the bullets had passed completely through him. Bright blood oozed down the front of his blue, quilted ski jacket.

When she hesitated, he moved to her on hands and knees, pushed her toward the Jeep just a few feet away.

Another loud burst of submachine-gun fire crackled through the wintry air.

The gunman would no doubt move cautiously forward toward the front of the Jeep and slaughter them as they cowered there. Yet they had nowhere to run: If they went up the embankment toward the trees, he would cut them down long before they reached the safety of the forest; if they crossed the road, he would blow them away before they reached the other side, and at the other side there was nothing but the steep-walled gorge, anyway; running uphill, they would be heading toward him; running downhill, they would be putting their backs to him, making even easier targets of themselves.

The submachine gun rattled. Windows burst. Bullets punctured sheet metal with a hard *pock-twang*.

Crawling to the front of the Jeep, dragging Chris with her, Laura saw her guardian slipping into the narrow space between that vehicle and the snow-packed embankment. He was crouched below the fender, out of sight of the man he had called Kokoschka. In his fear he no longer seemed magical, no guardian angel but merely a man; and in fact he was no longer a savior, either, but an agent of Death, for his presence here had attracted the killer.

At Danny's urging she frantically squirmed under the Jeep. Chris squirmed, too, not crying now, being brave for his father; but then he had not seen his father shot, for his face had been pressed to Laura's breast, buried in her ski jacket. It seemed useless to get under the Jeep because Kokoschka would find them anyway. He could not be so dim-witted as to fail to look under the Jeep when they could be found nowhere else, so at most they were just buying a little time, an extra minute of life at most.

When she was completely under the Jeep, pulling Chris against her to give him what little additional protection her body could provide, she heard Danny speak to her from the front of the vehicle.

"I love you." Anguish pierced her as she realized that those three short words also meant goodbye.

Stefan slipped between the Jeep and the dirty, mounded snow along the embankment. There was little space, not enough for him to have gotten out of the driver's door on that side when he had parked there, but barely enough to squeeze along toward the rear bumper where Kokoschka might not expect him to show up, where he might get off one good shot before Kokoschka swung around and sprayed him with the submachine gun.

Kokoschka. He had never been so surprised in his life as when Kokoschka had gotten out of that Pontiac. It meant they were aware of his traitorous activities at the institute. And they were also aware that he had interposed himself between Laura and her true destiny. Kokoschka had taken the Lightning Road with the intention of eliminating the traitor and evidently Laura as well.

Now, keeping his head down, Stefan urgently forced his way between the Jeep and the embankment. The submachine gun chattered and windows blew out above him. At his back the snowbank was ice-crusted in many places, jabbing painfully into him; when he endured the pain and pressed hard with his body, the ice cracked, and the snow beneath it compacted just enough to give him passage. Wind streamed through the narrow space he occupied, shrieking between sheet metal and snow, so it seemed that he was not alone there but was in the company of some invisible creature that hooted and gibbered in his face.

He had seen Laura and Chris wriggling under the Jeep, but he knew that cover would provide only an additional minute of safety, perhaps even less. When Kokoschka got to the front of the Jeep and didn't find them there, he would look under the vehicle, get down at road level, and open fire, chopping them to pieces in their confinement.

And what of Danny? He was such a big man, barrel-chested, surely too big to slide swiftly under the Jeep. And already he'd been shot; he must be stiff with pain. Besides, Danny wasn't the kind of man who hid from trouble, not even trouble like this.

At last Stefan reached the rear bumper. Cautiously he looked out and saw the Pontiac parked eight feet away in the southbound lane with its driver's door standing open, engine running. No

Kokoschka. So with his Walther PPK/S .380 in hand he eased away from the snowbank, moved behind the Jeep. He crouched against the tailgate and peered around the other rear bumper.

Kokoschka was in the middle of the roadway, moving toward the front of the Jeep where he believed everyone had taken cover. His weapon was an Uzi with an extended magazine, chosen for the mission because it would not be anachronistic. As Kokoschka reached the gap between the Jeep and the Blazer, he opened fire again, sweeping the submachine gun from left to right. Bullets screamed off metal, blew out tires, and thudded into the embankment.

Stefan fired at Kokoschka, missed.

Suddenly, with berserk courage, Danny Packard launched himself at Kokoschka, coming out from his hiding place tight up against the Jeep's grille, so low that he must have been lying flat, low enough to have been under the spray of bullets the submachine gun had just laid down. He was wounded from the initial burst of fire but still quick and powerful, and for a moment it seemed that he might even reach the gunman and disable him. Kokoschka was sweeping the Uzi from left to right, already moving away from his target when he saw Danny coming at him, so he had to reverse himself, bring the muzzle around. If he had been a few feet closer to the Jeep instead of in the middle of the highway, he would not have nailed Danny in time.

"Danny, no!" Stefan shouted, squeezing off three shots at Kokoschka even as Packard was going for him.

But Kokoschka had kept a cautious distance, and he brought the spitting muzzle around, straight at Danny, when they were still three or four feet apart. Danny was kicked backward by the impact of several slugs.

Stefan took no consolation from the fact that even as Danny was hit, Kokoschka was hit, too, taking two rounds from the Walther, one in his left thigh and one in his left shoulder. He was knocked down. He dropped the submachine gun as he fell; it spun along the pavement.

Under the Jeep, Laura was screaming.

Stefan rose from the cover of the rear bumper and ran toward Kokoschka, who was on the ground only thirty feet downslope, near the Blazer now. He slipped on the snowy pavement, struggled to keep his balance.

Badly wounded, no doubt in shock, Kokoschka nevertheless saw him coming. He rolled toward the Uzi carbine, which had come to rest by the rear tire of the Blazer.

Stefan fired three times as he ran, but he did not have the steadiness required for a good aim, and Kokoschka was rolling away from him, so he missed the son of a bitch. Then Stefan slipped again and fell to one knee in the middle of the road, landing so hard that pain shot up his thigh and into his hip.

Rolling, Kokoschka reached the submachine gun.

Realizing he'd never get to the man in time, Stefan dropped onto both knees and raised the Walther, holding it with both hands. He was twenty feet from Kokoschka, not far. But even a good marksman could miss at twenty feet if the circumstances were bad enough, and these were bad: a state of panic, a weird firing angle, gale-force wind to deflect the shot.

Downslope, lying on the ground, Kokoschka opened fire the instant he got his hands on the Uzi, even before he brought the weapon around, loosing the first twenty rounds under the Blazer, blowing out the front tires.

As Kokoschka swung the gun toward him, Stefan squeezed off his last three rounds with deliberation. In spite of the wind and the angle, he had to make them count, for if he missed he would have no time to reload.

The first round from the Walther missed.

Kokoschka continued to bring the submachine gun around, and the arc of fire reached the front of the Jeep. Laura was under the Jeep with Chris, and Kokoschka was shooting from ground level, so surely a couple of rounds had passed under the vehicle.

Stefan fired again. The slug hit Kokoschka in the upper body, and the submachine gun stopped firing. Stefan's next and last shot took Kokoschka in the head. It was over.

From beneath the Jeep, Laura saw Danny's incredibly brave charge, saw him go down again, flat on his back, unmoving, and she knew that he was dead, no possibility of a reprieve this time. A flash of grief like the terrible light from an explosion swept through her, and she glimpsed a future without Danny, a vision so starkly illuminated and of such dreadful power that she almost blacked out.

Then she thought of Chris, still alive and sheltering against her. She blocked out the grief, knowing she would return to it later—if she survived. The important thing right now was keeping Chris alive and, if possible, protecting him from the sight of his father's bullet-riddled corpse.

Danny's body blocked part of her view, but she saw Kokoschka hit by gunfire. She saw her guardian approaching the downed gunman, and for a moment it seemed the worst was over. Then her guardian slipped and fell to one knee, and Kokoschka rolled toward the submachine gun that he had dropped. More gunfire. A lot of it in a few seconds. She heard a couple of rounds passing under the Jeep, frighteningly close, lead cutting through the air with a deadly whisper that was louder than any other sound in the world.

The silence after the gunfire was at first perfect. Initially she could not hear the wind or her son's low sobbing. Gradually those sounds impinged upon her.

She saw her guardian was alive, and part of her was relieved, but part of her was irrationally angry that he had survived because he had drawn this Kokoschka with him, and Kokoschka had killed Danny. On the other hand Danny—and she and Chris—would surely have been killed in the collision with the truck, anyway, if her guardian had not come along. Who the hell was he? Where did he come from? Why was he so interested in her? She was frightened, angry, shocked, sick in her soul, and badly confused.

Clearly in pain, her guardian rose from his knees and hobbled to Kokoschka. Laura twisted farther around to look directly down the hill, just past Danny's unmoving head. She could not quite see what her guardian was doing, though he appeared to be tearing open Kokoschka's clothes.

After a while he hobbled back up the hill, carrying something he had taken off the corpse.

When he reached the Jeep, he crouched and looked under at her. "Come out. It's over." His face was pale, and in the past few minutes he seemed to have aged at least a couple of his twenty-five lost years. He cleared his throat. In a voice filled with what seemed like genuine, deeply felt remorse, he said, "I'm sorry, Laura. I'm so very sorry."

She squirmed on her belly toward the rear of the Jeep, bumping her head on the undercarriage. She pulled Chris and encouraged him to come with her, for if they wriggled out nearer the front, the boy might see his father. Her guardian pulled them into the open. Laura sat back against the rear bumper and clutched Chris to her.

Tremulously, the boy said, "I want Daddy."

I want him too, Laura thought. Oh, baby, I want him, too, I want him so bad, all I want in the world is your daddy.

The storm was a full-fledged blizzard now, pumping snow out of the sky under tremendous pressure. The afternoon was dying; light was fading, and all around the grim, gray day was succumbing to the queer, phosphorescent darkness of a snowy night.

In this weather few people would be traveling, but he was sure that someone would come along soon. No more than ten minutes had passed since he had stopped Laura in the Blazer, but even on this rural road in a storm, the gap in traffic would not last much longer. He needed to have a talk with her and leave before he got entangled in the aftermath of this bloody encounter.

Hunkering down in front of her and the weeping boy, behind the Jeep, Stefan said, "Laura, I've got to get out of here, but I'll be back soon, in just a couple of days—"

"Who are you?" she demanded angrily.

"There's no time for that now."

"I want to know, damn you. I have a right to know."

"Yes, you do, and I'll tell you in a few days. But right now we have to get your story straight, the way we did that day in the grocery store. Remember?"

"To hell with you."

Unfazed, he said, "It's for your own good, Laura. You can't tell the authorities the exact truth because it won't seem real, will it? They'll think you're making it all up. Especially when you see me leave . . . well, if you tell them how I went, they'll either be sure that you're somehow an accomplice to murder or a mad-woman."

She glared at him and said nothing. He did not blame her for being angry. Perhaps she even wanted him dead, but he understood that too. The only emotions she stirred in him, however, were love and pity and a profound respect.

He said, "You'll tell them that when you and Danny turned the curve at the bottom of the hill and started up, there were *three* cars in the roadway: the Jeep parked here along the embankment, the Pontiac in the wrong lane just where it is now, and another car was stopped in the northbound lane. There were . . . four men, two of them with guns, and they seemed to have forced the Jeep off the road. You just came along at the wrong time, that's all.

They pointed a submachine gun at you, made you pull off the road, made you and Danny and Chris get out of the car. At one point you heard talk about cocaine . . . somehow it involved drugs, you don't know how, but they were arguing over drugs, and they seemed to have chased down the man in the Jeep—"

"Drug dealers out here in the middle of nowhere?" she said scornfully.

"There could be processing labs out here—a cabin in the woods, processing PCP maybe. Listen, if the story makes at least *some* sense, they'll want to buy it. The *real* story makes no sense at all, so you can't rely on it. So you tell them the Robertsons came over the crest of the hill in their pickup—of course you don't know their name—and the road was blocked by all these cars, and when he braked the pickup it started to slide—"

"You've got an accent," she said angrily. "A slight one but I can hear it. Where are you from?"

"I'll tell you all of that in a few days," he said impatiently, looking up and down the snow-blasted road. "I really will, but now you've got to promise me you'll work with this false story, embellish it as best you can, and not tell them the truth."

"I don't have any choice, do I?"

"No," he said, relieved that she realized her position.

She clung to her son and said nothing.

Stefan had begun to feel the pain in his half-frozen feet again. The heat of action had dissipated, leaving him racked by shivers. He handed her the belt that he had taken off Kokoschka. "Put this inside your ski jacket. Don't let anyone see it. When you get home, put it away somewhere."

"What is it?"

"Later. I'll try to return in a few hours. Only a few hours. Right now just promise me you'll hide it. Don't get curious, don't put it on, and for God's sake don't push the yellow button on it."

"Why not?"

"Because you don't want to go where it'll take you."

She blinked at him in confusion. "Take me?"

"I'll explain but not now."

"Why can't you take it with you, whatever it is?"

"Two belts, one body—it's an anomaly, it'll cause a disruption of some kind in the energy field, and God only knows where I might wind up or in what condition."

"I don't understand. What're you talking about?"

"Later. But, Laura, if for some reason I'm unable to come back, you better take precautions.

"What kind of precautions."

"Arm yourself. Be prepared. There's no *reason* they should come after you if they get me, but they might. Just to teach me a lesson, to humble me. They thrive on vengeance. And if they come for you . . . there'll be a squad of them, well armed."

"Who the hell *are* they?"

Without answering, he got to his feet, wincing at the pain in his right knee. He backed away, taking one last, long look at her. Then he turned, leaving her on the ground, in the cold and snow, against the back of the battered and bullet-pocked Jeep, with her terrified child and her dead husband.

Slowly he walked out into the middle of the highway where more light seemed to come from the shifting snow on the pavement than from the sky overhead. She called to him, but he ignored her.

He holstered his empty gun beneath his coat. He reached inside his shirt, felt for and located the yellow button on his own travel belt, and hesitated.

They had sent Kokoschka to stop him. Now they would be waiting anxiously at the institute to learn the outcome. He would be arrested on arrival. He probably never again would have an opportunity to take the Lightning Road to return to her as he had promised.

The temptation to stay was great.

If he stayed, however, they would only send someone else to kill him, and he would spend the rest of his life running from one assassin after another—while watching the world around him change in ways that would be too horrible to endure. On the other hand, if he went back, there was a slim chance that he might still be able to destroy the institute. Dr. Penlovski and the others obviously knew everything about his meddling in the natural flow of events in this one woman's life, but perhaps they did not know that he had planted explosives in the attic and basement of the institute. In that case, if they gave him an opportunity to get into his office for just a moment, he could throw the hidden switch and blow the place—and all its files—to hell where it belonged. More likely than not, they had found the explosive charges and removed them. But as long as there was any possibility whatsoever that he could bring an end forever to the project and close the Lightning Road, he was morally obliged to return to the institute, even if it meant that he would never see Laura again.

As the day died, the storm seemed to come more fiercely alive. On the mountainside above the highway, the wind rumbled and keened through the enormous pines, and the boughs made an ominous rustling sound, as if some many-legged, giant creature were scuttling down the slope. The snowflakes had become fine and dry, almost like bits of ice, and they seemed to be abrading the world, smoothing it the way that sandpaper smoothed wood, until eventually there would be no peaks and valleys, nothing but a featureless, highly polished plain as far as anyone could see.

With his hand still inside his coat and shirt, Stefan pressed the yellow button three times in quick succession, triggering the beacon. With regret and fear he returned to his own time.

Holding Chris, whose sobbing had subsided, Laura sat on the ground at the back of the Jeep and watched her guardian walk into the slanting snow, past the rear of Kokoschka's Pontiac.

He stopped in the middle of the highway, stood for a long moment with his back to her, and then an incredible thing happened. First the air became heavy; she was aware of a strange pressure, something she had never felt before, as if the atmosphere of the earth were being condensed in some cosmic cataclysm, and abruptly she found it hard to draw breath. The air acquired a curious odor, too, exotic but familiar, and after a few seconds she realized it smelled like hot electrical wires and scorched insulation, much like what she had smelled in her own kitchen when a toaster plug had shorted out a few weeks ago; that stink was overlaid with the crisp but not unpleasant scent of ozone, which was the same odor that filled the air during any violent thunderstorm. The pressure grew greater, until she almost felt pinned to the ground, and the air shimmered and rippled as if it were water. With a sound like an enormous cork popping out of a bottle, her guardian vanished from the purple-gray, winter twilight, and simultaneously with that *pop* came a great *whoosh* of wind, as if massive quantities of air were rushing in to fill some void. Indeed for an instant she felt trapped in a vacuum, unable to breathe. Then the crushing pressure was gone, the air smelled only of snow and pine, and everything was normal again.

Except, of course, after what she had seen, nothing could ever be normal for her again.

The night grew very dark. Without Danny it was the blackest night of her life. Only one light remained to illuminate her struggle toward some distant hope of happiness: Chris. He was the last light in her darkness.

Later, at the top of the hill, a car appeared. Headlights bored through the gloom and the heavily falling snow.

She struggled to her feet and took Chris into the middle of the roadway. She waved for help.

As the descending car slowed, she suddenly wondered if when it stopped another man with another submachine gun would get out and open fire. She would never again feel safe.

Four

THE INNER FIRE

·1·

On Saturday, August 13, 1988, seven months after Danny was shot down, Thelma Ackerson came to the mountain house to stay for four days.

Laura was in the backyard, conducting target practice with her Smith & Wesson .38 Chief's Special. She had just reloaded, snapped the cylinder in place, and was about to put on her Hearing Guard headset when she heard a car approaching on the long gravel driveway from the state route. She picked up a pair of binoculars from the ground at her feet and took a closer look at the vehicle to be sure it was not an unwanted visitor. When she saw Thelma behind the wheel, she put the glasses down and continued firing at the target—an outline of a man's head and torso—that was lashed to a hay-bale backstop.

Sitting on the grass nearby, Chris plucked six more cartridges from the box and prepared to hand them to her when she had fired the last round currently in the cylinder.

The day was hot, clear, and dry. Wildflowers by the hundreds blazed along the edge of the yard where the mown area gave way to wild grass and weeds near the forest line. Squirrels had been at play on the grass a while ago, and birds had been singing, but the shooting had temporarily frightened them away.

Laura might have been expected to associate her husband's death with the high retreat and to sell it. Instead she had sold the house in Orange County four months ago and moved Chris to the San Bernardinos.

She believed that what had happened to them the previous January on route 330 could have happened anywhere. The place was not to blame; the fault lay in her destiny, in the mysterious forces at work in her strangely troubled life. Intuitively she knew that if her guardian had not stepped in to save her on that stretch of snowy highway, he would have entered her life elsewhere, at another moment of crisis. At *that* place Kokoschka would have shown up with a submachine gun, and the same set of violent, tragic events would have transpired.

Their other home had held more memories of Danny than did the stone and redwood place south of Big Bear. She was better able to deal with her grief in the mountains than in Orange Park Acres.

Besides, oddly enough, the mountains felt much safer to her. In the highly populated suburbs of Orange County, where the streets and freeways teemed with more than two million people, an enemy would not be perceived among the crowd until he chose to act. In the mountains, however, strangers were highly visible, especially since the house sat almost in the center of their thirty-acre property.

And she had not forgotten her guardian's warning: *Arm yourself. Be prepared. If they come for you . . . there'll be a squad of them.*

When Laura fired the last round in the .38 and pulled off the ear guards, Chris handed her six more cartridges. He removed his muffs, too, and ran to the target to check her accuracy.

The backstop consisted of hay bales piled seven feet high and four deep; it was fourteen feet wide. Behind it were acres of pine woods, her private land, so the need for an elaborate backstop was questionable, but she did not want to shoot anyone. At least not accidentally.

Chris lashed up a new target and returned to Laura with the old one. "Four hits out of six, Mom. Two deaders, two good wounds, but looks like you're pulling off to the left a little."

"Let's see if I can correct that."

"You're just getting tired, that's all," Chris said.

The grass around her was littered with over a hundred and fifty empty brass shell casings. Her wrists, arms, shoulders, and neck were beginning to ache from the cumulative recoil, but she wanted to get in another full cylinder before quitting for the day.

Back near the house, Thelma's car door slammed.

Chris put on his ear guards again and picked up the binoculars to watch the target while his mother fired.

Sorrow plucked at Laura as she paused to look at the boy, not merely because he was fatherless but because it seemed so unfair that a child two months short of his eighth birthday should already know how dangerous life was and should have to live in constant expectation of violence. She did her best to make sure there was as much fun in his life as possible: They still played with the Tommy Toad fantasy, though Chris no longer believed that Tommy was real; through a large personal library of children's classics, Laura also was showing him the pleasure and escape to be found in books; she even did her best to make target practice a game and thereby divert the focus from the deadly necessity of being able to protect themselves. Yet for the time being their lives were dominated by loss and danger, by a fear of the unknown. That reality could not be hidden from the boy, and it could not fail to have a profound and lasting effect on him.

Chris lowered the binoculars and looked at her to see why she was not shooting. She smiled at him. He smiled at her. He had such a sweet smile it almost broke her heart.

She turned to the target, raised the .38, gripped it with both hands, and squeezed off the first shot of the new series.

By the time Laura fired four rounds, Thelma stepped up beside her. She stood with her fingers in her ears, wincing.

Laura squeezed off the last two shots and removed her ear guards, and Chris retrieved the target. The roar of gunfire was still echoing through the mountains when she turned to Thelma and hugged her.

"What's all this gun stuff?" Thelma asked. "Are you going to write new movies for Clint Eastwood? No, hey, better yet, write the female equal of Clint's role—*Dirty Harriet*. And I'm just the broad to play it—tough, cold, with a sneer that would make Bogart cringe."

"I'll keep you in mind for the part," Laura said, "but what I'd really like to see is Clint play it in drag."

"Hey, you've still got a sense of humor, Shane."

"Did you think I wouldn't?"

Thelma frowned. "I didn't know what to think when I saw you blasting away, looking mean as a snake with fang decay."

"Self-defense," Laura said. "Every good girl should learn some."

"You were plinking away like a pro." Thelma noted the glitter of brass shell casings in the grass. "How often do you do this?"

"Three times a week, a couple of hours each time."

Chris returned with the target. "Hi, Aunt Thelma. Mom, you got four deaders out of six that time, one good wound, and a miss."

"Deaders?" Thelma said.

"Still pulling to the left, do you think?" Laura asked the boy.

He showed her the target. "Not so much as last time."

Thelma said, "Hey, Christopher Robin, is that all I get—just a lousy 'Hi, Aunt Thelma'?"

Chris put the target with the pile of others that he had taken down before it, went to Thelma, and gave her a big hug and a kiss. Noticing that she was no longer done up in punk style, he said, "Gee, what happened to you, Aunt Thelma? You look normal."

"I look normal? What is that—a compliment or an insult? Just you remember, kid, even if your old Aunt Thelma looks normal, she is no such a thing. She is a comic genius, a dazzling wit, a legend in her own scrapbook. Anyway, I decided punk was passé."

They enlisted Thelma to help them collect empty shell casings.

"Mom's a terrific shot," Chris said proudly.

"She better be terrific with all this practice. There's enough brass here to make balls for an entire army of Amazon warriors."

To his mother, Chris said, "What's that mean?"

"Ask me again in ten years," Laura said.

When they went into the house, Laura locked the kitchen door. Two deadbolts. She closed the Levelor blinds over the windows so no one could see them.

Thelma watched these rituals with interest but said nothing.

Chris put *Raiders of the Lost Ark* on the VCR in the family room and settled in front of the television with a bag of cheese popcorn and a Coke. In the adjacent kitchen Laura and Thelma sat at the table and drank coffee while Laura disassembled and cleaned the .38 Chief's Special.

The kitchen was big but cozy with lots of dark oak, used brick on two walls, a copper range hood, copper pots hung on hooks, and a dark blue, ceramic-tile floor. It was the kind of kitchen in which TV sitcom families worked out their nonsensical crises and attained transcendental enlightenment (with heart) in thirty minutes each week, minus commercials. Even to Laura it seemed like an odd place to be cleaning a weapon designed primarily to kill other human beings.

"Are you really afraid?" Thelma asked.

"Bet on it."

"But Danny was killed because you were unlucky enough to wander into the middle of a drug deal of some kind. Those people are long gone, right?"

"Maybe not."

"Well, if they were afraid that you might be able to identify them, they'd have come to get you long before this."

"I'm taking no chances."

"You got to ease up, kid. You can't live the rest of your life expecting someone to jump at you from the bushes. All right, you can keep a gun around the house. That's probably wise. But aren't you ever going to go out into the world again? You can't tote a gun with you everywhere you go."

"Yes, I can. I've got a permit."

"A permit to carry that cannon?"

"I take it in my purse wherever we go."

"Jesus, how'd you get a permit to carry?"

"My husband was killed under strange circumstances by persons unknown. Those killers tried to shoot my son and me—and they are still at large. On top of all that, I'm a rich and relatively famous woman. It'd be a little odd if I *couldn't* get a permit to carry."

Thelma was silent for a minute, sipping her coffee, watching Laura clean the revolver. Finally she said, "This is kind of spooky, Shane, seeing you so serious about this, so tense. I mean, it's seven months since . . . Danny died. But you're as skittish as if someone had shot at you yesterday. You can't maintain this level of tension or readiness or whatever you want to call it. That way lies madness. Paranoia. You've got to face the fact that you can't really be on guard the rest of your life, every minute."

"I can, though, if I have to."

"Oh, yeah? What about right now? Your gun's disassembled. What if some barbarian thug with tattoos on his tongue started kicking down the kitchen door?"

The kitchen chairs were on rubber casters, so when Laura suddenly shoved away from the table, she rolled swiftly to the counter beside the refrigerator. She pulled open a drawer and brought out another .38 Chief's Special.

Thelma said, "What—am I sitting in the middle of an arsenal?"

Laura put the second revolver back in the drawer. "Come on. I'll give you a tour."

Thelma followed her to the pantry. Hung on the back of the pantry door was an Uzi semiautomatic carbine.

"That's a machine gun. Is it legal to have one?"

"With federal approval, you can buy them at gunshops, though you can only get a semiautomatic; it's illegal to have them modified for full automatic fire."

Thelma studied her, then sighed. "Has this one been modified?"

"Yes. It's fully automatic. But I bought it that way from an illegal dealer, not a gunshop."

"This is too spooky, Shane. Really."

She led Thelma into the dining room and showed her the revolver that was clipped to the bottom of the sideboard. In the living room a fourth revolver was clipped under an end table next to one of the sofas. A second modified Uzi was hung on the back of the foyer door at the front of the house. Revolvers were also hidden in the desk drawer in the den, in her office upstairs, in the master bathroom, and in the nightstand in her bedroom. Finally, she kept a third Uzi in the master bedroom.

Staring at the Uzi that Laura pulled from under the bed, Thelma said, "Spookier and spookier. If I didn't know you better, Shane, I'd think you'd gone mad, a raving paranoid gun nut. But knowing you, if you're really *this* scared, you've got to have some reason. But what about Chris around all these guns?"

"He knows not to touch them, and I know he can be trusted. Most Swiss families have members in the militia—nearly every male citizen there is prepared to defend his country, did you know that?—with guns in almost every house, but they have the lowest rate of accidental shootings in the world. Because guns are a way of life. Children are taught to respect them from an early age. Chris'll be okay."

As Laura put the Uzi under the bed again, Thelma said, "How on earth do you find an illegal gun dealer?"

"I'm rich, remember?"

"And money can buy anything? Okay, maybe that's true. But, come on, how does a gal like you find an arms dealer? They don't advertise on Laundromat bulletin boards, I presume."

"I've researched the backgrounds to several complicated novels, Thelma. I've learned how to find anyone or anything I need."

Thelma was silent as they returned to the kitchen. From the family room came the heroic music that accompanied Indiana Jones on all of his exploits. While Laura sat at the table and continued cleaning the revolver, Thelma poured fresh coffee for both of them.

"Straight talk now, kiddo. If there's really some threat out there that justifies all this armament, then it's bigger than you can handle yourself. Why not bodyguards?"

"I don't trust anyone. Anyone but you and Chris, that is. And Danny's father, except he's in Florida."

"But you can't go on like this, alone, afraid. . . ."

Working a spiral brush into the barrel of the revolver, Laura said, "I'm afraid, yeah, but I feel good about being prepared. All my life I've stood by while people I love have been taken from me. I've done nothing about it but endure. Well, to hell with that. From now on, I fight. If anyone wants to take Chris from me, they're going to have to go *through* me to get him, they'll have to fight a war."

"Laura, I know what you're going through. But listen, let me play psychoanalyst here and tell you that you're reacting less to any real threat than you are *over*reacting to a sense of helplessness in the face of fate. You can't thwart Providence, kid. You can't play poker with God and expect to win because you've got a .38 in your purse. I mean, you lost Danny to violence, yeah, and maybe you could say that Nina Dockweiler would have lived if someone had put a bullet in the Eel when he first deserved it, but those are the only cases where lives of people you loved might've been saved with guns. Your mother died in childbirth. Your father died of a heart attack. We lost Ruthie to fire. Learning to defend yourself with guns is fine, but you've got to keep perspective, you've got to have a sense of humor about our vulnerability as a species, or you'll wind up in an institution with people who talk to tree stumps and eat their belly-button lint. God forbid, but what if Chris got cancer? You're all prepared to blow away anyone who touches him, but you can't kill cancer with a revolver, and I'm afraid you're so crazy determined to protect him that you'll fall to pieces if something like that happens, something you can't deal with, that no one can deal with. I worry about you, kid."

Laura nodded and felt a rush of warmth for her friend. "I know you do, Thelma. And you can put your mind at ease. For thirty-three years I just endured; now I'm fighting back as best I can. If cancer were to strike me or Chris, I'd hire all the best specialists, seek the finest possible treatment. But if all failed, if for example Chris died of cancer, then I'd accept defeat. Fighting doesn't preclude enduring. I can fight, and if fighting fails, I can still endure."

For a long time Thelma stared at her across the table. At last she nodded. "That's what I hoped to hear. Okay. End of discussion. On to other things. When do you plan to buy a tank, Shane?"

"They're delivering it Monday."

"Howitzers, grenades, bazookas?"

"Tuesday. What about the Eddie Murphy movie?"

"We closed the deal two days ago," Thelma said.

"Really. My Thelma is going to star in a movie with Eddie Murphy?"

"Your Thelma is going to *appear* in a movie with Eddie Murphy. I don't think I qualify as a star yet."

"You had fourth lead in that picture with Steve Martin, third lead in the picture with Chevy Chase. And this is second lead, right? And how many times have you hosted the *Tonight* show? Eight times, isn't it? Face it, you're a star."

"Low magnitude, maybe. Isn't it weird, Shane? Two of us come from nothing, McIlroy Home, and we make it to the top. Strange?"

"Not so strange," Laura said. "Adversity breeds toughness, and the tough succeed. And survive."

·2·

Stefan left the snow-filled night in the San Bernardino Mountains and an instant later was inside the gate at the other end of Lightning Road. The gate resembled a large barrel, not unlike one of those that were popular in carnival funhouses, except that its inner surface was of highly polished copper rather than wood, and it did not turn under his feet. The barrel was eight feet in diameter and twelve feet long, and in a few steps he walked out of it, into the main, ground-floor lab of the institute, where he was certain that he'd be met by armed men.

The lab was deserted.

Astonished, he stood for a moment in his snow-flecked peacoat and looked around in disbelief. Three walls of the thirty-by-forty-foot room were lined floor to ceiling with machinery that hummed and clicked unattended. Most of the overhead lamps were off, so the room was softly, eerily lit. The machinery supported the gate, and it featured scores of dials and gauges that glowed pale green or orange, for the gate—which was a breach in time, a tunnel to anywhen—was never shut down; once closed, it could be reopened only with great difficulty and a tremendous expenditure of energy, but once open it could be maintained with comparatively little effort. These days, because the primary research work was no longer focused on developing the gate itself, the main lab was attended by institute personnel only for routine maintenance of the machinery and, of course, when a jaunt was in progress. If different circumstance had pertained, Stefan would never have been able to make the scores of secret, unauthorized trips that he had taken to monitor—and sometimes correct—the events of Laura's life.

But though it was not unusual to find the lab deserted most times of the day, it was singularly strange now, for they had sent Kokoschka to stop him, and surely they would be waiting anxiously to learn how Kokoschka had fared in those wintry California mountains. They had to have entertained the possibility that Kokoschka would fail, that the wrong man would return from 1988, and that the gate would have to be guarded until the situation was resolved. Where were the secret police in their black trenchcoats with padded shoulders? Where were the guns with which he had expected to be greeted?

He looked at the large clock on the wall and saw that it was six minutes past eleven o'clock, local time. That was as it should have been. He'd begun the jaunt at five minutes till eleven that morning, and every jaunt ended exactly eleven minutes after it began. No one knew why, but no matter how long a time traveler spent at the other end of his journey, only eleven minutes passed at home base. He had been in the San Bernardinos for nearly an hour and a half, but only eleven minutes had transpired in his own life, in his own time. If he had stayed with Laura for months before pressing the yellow button on his belt, activating the beacon, he would still have returned to the institute only—and precisely—eleven minutes after he had left it.

But where were the authorities, the guns, his angry colleagues expressing their outrage? After discovering his meddling in the events of Laura's life, after sending Kokoschka to get him and Laura, why would they walk away from the gate when they had to wait only *eleven minutes* to learn the outcome of the confrontation?

Stefan took off his boots, peacoat, and shoulder holster, and tucked them out of sight in a corner behind some equipment. He had left his white lab coat in the same place when he had departed on the jaunt, and now he slipped into it again.

Baffled, still worried in spite of the lack of a hostile greeting committee, he stepped out of the lab into the ground-floor corridor and went looking for trouble.

•3•

At two-thirty Sunday morning Laura was at her word processor in the office adjacent to the master bedroom, dressed in pajamas and a robe, sipping apple juice, and working on a new book. The only light in the room came from the electronic-green letters on the computer screen and from a small desk lamp tightly focused on a printout of yesterday's pages. A revolver lay on the desk beside the script.

The door to the dark hallway was open. She never closed any but the bathroom door these days because sooner or later a closed door might prevent her from hearing the stealthy progress of an intruder in another part of the house. The house had a sophisticated alarm system, but she kept interior doors open just in case.

She heard Thelma coming down the hallway, and she turned just as her friend looked through the door. "Sorry if I've made any noise that's kept you awake."

"Nah. We nightclub types work late. But I sleep till noon. What about you? You usually up at this hour?"

"I don't sleep well any more. Four or five hours a night is good for me. Instead of lying in bed, fidgeting, I get up and write."

Thelma pulled up a chair, sat, and propped her feet on Laura's desk. Her taste in sleepwear was even more flamboyant than it had been in her youth: baggy silk pajamas in a red, green, blue, and yellow abstract pattern of squares and circles.

"I'm glad to see you're still wearing bunny slippers," Laura said. "It shows a certain constancy of personality."

"That's me. Rock-solid. Can't buy bunny slippers in my size any more, so I have to buy a pair of furry adult slippers *and* a pair of kids' slippers, snip the eyes and ears off the little ones and sew them on the big ones. What're you writing?"

"A bile-black book."

"Sounds like just the thing for a fun weekend at the beach."

Laura sighed and relaxed in her spring-backed armchair. "It's a novel about death, about the injustice of death. It's a fool's project because I'm trying to explain the unexplainable. I'm trying to explain death to my ideal reader because then maybe I can finally understand it myself. It's a book about why we have to struggle and go on in spite of that knowledge of our mortality, why we have to fight and endure. It's a black, bleak, grim, moody, depressing, bitter, deeply disturbing book."

"Is there a big market for that?"

Laura laughed. "Probably no market at all. But once an idea for a novel seizes a writer . . . well, it's like an inner fire that at first warms you and makes you feel good but then begins to eat you alive, burn you up from within. You can't just walk away from the fire; it keeps burning. The only way to put it out is to write the damned book. Anyway, when I get stuck on this one, I turn to a nice little children's book I'm writing all about Sir Tommy Toad."

"You're nuts, Shane."

"Who's wearing the bunny slippers?"

They talked about this and that, with the easy camaraderie they had shared for twenty years. Perhaps it was Laura's loneliness, more acute than in the days immediately following Danny's murder, or maybe it was fear of the unknown, but for whatever reason she began to speak of her special guardian. In all the world only Thelma might believe the tale. In fact Thelma was spellbound, soon lowering her feet from the desk and sitting forward on her chair, never expressing disbelief, as the story unrolled from the day the junkie was shot until the guardian vanished on the mountain highway.

When Laura had quenched *that* inner fire, Thelma said, "Why didn't you tell me about this . . . this guardian years ago? Back in McIlroy?"

"I don't know. It seemed like something . . . magical. Something I should keep to myself because if I shared it I'd break the spell and never see him again. Then after he left me to deal with the Eel on my own, after he had done nothing to save Ruthie, I guess I just stopped believing in him. I never told Danny about him because by the time I met Danny my guardian was no more real to me than Santa Claus. Then suddenly . . . there he was again on the highway."

"That night on the mountain, he said he'd be back to explain everything in a few days . . . ?"

"But I haven't seen him since. I've been waiting seven months, and I figure that when someone suddenly materializes it might be my guardian or, just as likely, another Kokoschka with a submachine gun."

The story had electrified Thelma, and she fidgeted on her chair as if a current were crackling through her. Finally she got up and paced. "What about Kokoschka? The cops find out anything about him?"

"Nothing. He was carrying no identification whatsoever. The Pontiac he was driving was stolen, just like the red Jeep. They ran his fingerprints through every file they've got, came up empty-handed. And they can't interrogate a corpse. They don't know who he was or where he came from or why he wanted to kill us."

"You've had a long time to think about all this. So any ideas? Who is this guardian? Where did he come from?"

"I don't know." She had one idea in particular that she focused on, but it sounded mad, and she had no evidence to support the theory. She withheld it from Thelma not because it was crazy, however, but because it would sound so egomaniacal. "I just don't know."

"Where's this belt he left with you?"

"In the safe," Laura said, nodding toward the corner where a floor-set box was hidden under the carpet.

Together they pulled the wall-to-wall carpet off its tack strip in that corner, revealing the face of the safe, which was a cylinder twelve inches in diameter and sixteen inches deep. Only one item reposed within, and Laura withdrew it.

They moved back to the desk to look at the mysterious article in better light. Laura adjusted the flexible neck of the lamp.

The belt was four inches wide and was made of a stretchy, black fabric, perhaps nylon, through which were woven copper wires that formed intricate and peculiar patterns. Because of its width, the belt required two small buckles rather than one; those were also made of copper. In addition, sewn on the belt just to the left of the buckles, was a thin box the size of an old-fashioned cigarette case—about four inches by three inches, only three-quarters of an inch thick—and this, too, was made of copper. Even on close examination no way to open the rectangular copper box could be discerned; its only feature was a yellow button toward the lower left corner, less than an inch in diameter.

Thelma fingered the odd material. "Tell me again what he said would happen if you pushed the yellow button."

"He just told me for God's sake not to push it, and when I asked why not, he said, 'You won't want to go where it'll take you.' "

They stood side by side in the glow of the desk lamp, staring at the belt that Thelma held. It was after four in the morning, and the house was as silent as any dead, airless crater on the moon.

Finally Thelma said, "You ever been tempted to push the button?"

"No, never," Laura said without hesitation. "When he mentioned the place to which it would take me . . . there was a terrible look in his eyes. And I know he returned there himself only with reluctance. I don't know where he comes from, Thelma, but if I didn't misunderstand what I saw in his eyes, the place is just one step this side of hell."

Sunday afternoon they dressed in shorts and T-shirts, spread a couple of blankets on the rear lawn, and made a long, lazy picnic of potato salad, cold cuts, cheese, fresh fruit, potato chips, and plump cinnamon rolls with lots of crunchy pecan topping. They played games with Chris, and he enjoyed the day enormously, partly because Thelma was able to shift her comic engine into a lower gear, producing one-liners designed for eight-year-olds.

When Chris saw squirrels frolicking farther back in the yard, near the woods, he wanted to feed them. Laura gave him a pecan roll and said, "Tear it into little pieces and toss the pieces to them. They won't let you get too near. And you stay close to me, you hear?"

"Sure, Mom."

"Don't you go all the way to the woods. Only about halfway."

He ran thirty feet from the blanket, only a little more than halfway to the trees, then dropped to his knees. He tore pieces from the cinnamon roll and threw them to the squirrels, making those quick and cautious creatures edge a bit closer for each successive scrap.

"He's a good kid," Thelma said.

"The best." Laura moved the Uzi to her side.

"He's only ten or twelve yards away," Thelma said.

"But he's closer to the woods than to me." Laura studied the shadows under the serried pines.

Plucking a few potato chips from the bag, Thelma said, "Never been on a picnic with someone who brought a submachine gun. I sort of like it. Don't have to worry about bears."

"It's hell on ants, too."

Thelma stretched out on her side on the blanket, her head propped up on one bent arm, but Laura continued to sit with her legs crossed Indian-fashion. Orange butterflies, as bright as condensed sunshine, darted through the warm August air.

"The kid seems to be coping," Thelma said.

"More or less," Laura agreed. "There was a very bad time. He cried a lot, wasn't emotionally stable. But that passed. They're flexible at his age, quick to adapt, to accept. But as good as he seems . . . I'm afraid there's a darkness in him now that wasn't there before and that isn't going to go away."

"No," Thelma said, "it won't go away. It's like a shadow on the heart. But he'll live, and he'll find happiness, and there'll be times when he's not aware of the shadow at all."

While Thelma watched Chris luring the squirrels, Laura studied her friend's profile. "You still miss Ruth, don't you?"

"Every day for twenty years. Don't you still miss your dad?"

"Sure," Laura said. "But when I think of him, I don't believe what I feel is like what you feel. Because we *expect* our parents to die before us, and even when they die prematurely, we can accept it because we've always known it was going to happen sooner or later. But it's different when the one who dies is a wife, husband, child . . . or sister. We don't expect them to die on us, not early in life. So it's harder to cope. Especially, I suppose, if she's a twin sister."

"When I get a piece of good news—career news, I mean—the first thing I always think of is how happy Ruthie would have been for me. What about you, Shane? You coping?"

"I cry at night."

"That's healthy now. Not so healthy a year from now."

"I lie awake at night and listen to my heartbeat, and it's a lonely sound. Thank God for Chris. He gives me purpose. And you. I've got you and Chris, and we're sort of family, don't you think?"

"Not just sort of. We *are* family. You and me—sisters."

Laura smiled, reached out, and rumpled Thelma's tousled hair.

"But," Thelma said, "being sisters doesn't mean you get to borrow my clothes."

·4·

In the corridors and through the open doors of the institute's offices and labs, Stefan saw his colleagues at work, and none of them had any special interest in him. He took the elevator to the third floor where just outside his office he encountered Dr. Wladyslaw Januskaya, who was Dr. Vladimir Penlovski's longtime protégé and second in charge of the time-travel research which originally had been called Project Scythe but which for several months now had been known by the apt code name Lightning Road.

Januskaya was forty, ten years younger than his mentor, but he looked older than the vital, energetic Penlovski. Short, overweight, balding, with a blotchy complexion, with two bright gold teeth in the front of his mouth, wearing thick glasses that made his eyes look like painted eggs, Januskaya should have been a comic figure. But his unholy faith in the state and his zeal in working for the totalitarian cause were sufficient to counteract his comic potential; indeed he was one of the more disturbing men involved with Lightning Road.

"Stefan, dear Stefan," Januskaya said, "I've been meaning to tell you how grateful we are for your timely suggestion, last October, that the power supply to the gate should be provided by a secure generator. Your foresight has saved the project. If we were still drawing from the municipal power lines . . . why, the gate would have collapsed half a dozen times by now, and we'd be woefully behind schedule."

Having returned to the institute in expectation of arrest, Stefan was confused to find his treachery undiscovered and startled to hear himself being praised by this evil worm. He had suggested switching the gate to a secure generator not because he wanted to see their vile project achieve success but because he had not wanted his own jaunts into Laura's life to be interrupted by the failure of the public power supply.

"I would not have thought last October that by this time we would have come to such a situation as this, with ordinary public services no longer to be trusted," Januskaya said, shaking his head sadly, "the social order so thoroughly disturbed. What must the people endure to see the socialist state of their dreams triumph, eh?"

"These are dark times," Stefan said, meaning very different things than Januskaya meant.

"But we will triumph," Januskaya said forcefully. His magnified eyes filled with the madness that Stefan knew too well. "Through the Lightning Road, we will triumph."

He patted Stefan on the shoulder and continued down the hall.

After Stefan watched the scientist walk nearly to the elevators, he said, "Oh, Dr. Januskaya?"

The fat white worm turned and looked at him. "Yes?"

"Have you seen Kokoschka today?"

"Today? No, not yet today."

"He's here, isn't he?"

"Oh, I'd imagine so. He's here pretty much as long as there's anyone working, you know. He's a diligent man. If we had more like Kokoschka we'd have no doubt of ultimate triumph. Do you need to talk to him? If I see him, should I send him to you?"

"No, no," Stefan said. "It's nothing urgent. I wouldn't want to interrupt him in other work. I'm sure I'll see him sooner or later."

Januskaya continued to the elevators, and Stefan went into his office, closing the door behind him.

He crouched beside the filing cabinet that he had repositioned slightly to cover one-third of the grille in the corner ventilation chase. In the narrow space behind it, a bundle of copper wires was barely visible, coming out of the bottom slot in the grille. The wires were connected to a simple dial-type timer that was in turn plugged into a wall outlet farther behind the cabinet. Nothing had been disconnected. He could reach behind the cabinet, set the timer, and in one to five minutes, depending on how big a twist he gave the dial, the institute would be destroyed.

What the hell is going on? he wondered.

He sat for a while at his desk, staring at the square of sky that he could see from one of his two windows: scattered, dirty gray clouds moving sluggishly across an azure backdrop.

Finally he left his office, went to the north stairs, and climbed quickly past the fourth floor to the attic. The door opened with only a brief squeak. He flipped the light switch and entered the long, half-finished room, stepping as softly as possible on the board floor. He checked three of the charges of plastique that he had hidden in the rafters two nights ago. The explosives had not been disturbed.

He had no need to examine the charges in the basement. He left the attic and returned to his office.

Obviously no one knew about either his intention of destroying the institute or his attempts to turn Laura's life away from a series of ordained tragedies. No one except Kokoschka. Damn it, Kokoschka *had* to know because he had shown up on the mountain road with an Uzi.

So why hadn't Kokoschka told anyone else?

Kokoschka was an officer of the state's secret police, a true fanatic, obedient and eager servant of the government, and personally responsible for the security of Lightning Road. On discovering a traitor at the institute, Kokoschka would not have hesitated to call in squads of agents to encircle the building, guard the gate, and interrogate everyone.

Surely he would not have allowed Stefan to go to Laura's aid on that mountain highway, then follow with the intent of killing them all. For one thing, he would want to detain Stefan and interrogate him to determine if Stefan had conspirators in the institute.

Kokoschka had learned of Stefan's meddling in the ordained flow of events in one woman's life. And he had either discovered or had not discovered the explosives in the institute—probably not, or he would have at least unwired them. Then for reasons of his own he had not reacted as a policeman but as an individual. This morning he had followed Stefan through the gate, to that wintry afternoon in January of '88, with intentions that Stefan did not now understand at all.

It made no sense. Yet that was what had to have happened.

What had Kokoschka been up to?

He would probably never know.

Now Kokoschka was dead on a highway in 1988, and soon someone at the institute would realize that he was missing.

This afternoon at two o'clock, Stefan was scheduled to take an approved jaunt under the direction of Penlovski and Januskaya. He had intended to blow the institute—in two senses—at one o'clock, an hour before the scheduled event. Now, at 11:43, he decided that he would have to move faster than he originally intended, before Kokoschka's disappearance caused alarm.

He went to one of the tall files, opened the bottom drawer, which was empty, and disconnected it from its slides, lifting it all the way out of the cabinet. Wired to the back of the drawer was a pistol, a Colt Commander 9mm Parabellum with a nine-round magazine, acquired on one of his illicit jaunts and brought back secretly to the institute. From behind another drawer he removed two high-tech silencers and four additional, fully loaded magazines. At his desk, working quickly lest someone enter without knocking, he screwed one of the silencers onto the pistol, flicked off the safety, and distributed the other silencer and magazines in the pockets of his lab coat.

When he left the institute by way of the gate for the last time, he could not trust to the explosives to kill Penlovski, Januskaya, and certain other scientists. The blast would bring down the building and no doubt destroy all machinery and paper files, but what if just one of the key researchers survived? The necessary knowledge to rebuild the gate was in Penlovski's and Januskaya's minds, so Stefan planned to kill them and one other man, Volkaw, before he set the timer on the explosives and entered the gate to return to Laura.

With the silencer attached, the Commander was too long to fit all the way in the pocket of his lab coat, so he turned the pocket inside out and tore the bottom of it. With his finger on the trigger, he shoved the gun into his now bottomless pocket and held it there as he opened his office door and went into the hallway.

His heart pounded furiously. This was the most dangerous part of his plan, the killing, because there were so many opportunities for something to go wrong before he finished with the gun and returned to his office to set the timer on the explosives.

Laura was a long way off, and he might never see her again.

·5·

On Monday afternoon Laura and Chris dressed in gray sweat suits. After Thelma helped them unroll the thick gym mats on the patio at the back of the house, Laura and Chris sat side by side and did deep-breathing exercises.

"When does Bruce Lee arrive?" Thelma asked.

"At two," Laura said.

"He's not Bruce Lee, Aunt Thelma," Chris said exasperatedly. "You keep calling him Bruce Lee, but Bruce Lee is dead."

Mr. Takahami arrived promptly at two o'clock. He was wearing a dark blue sweat suit, on the back of which was the logo for his martial arts school: QUIET STRENGTH. When introduced to Thelma, he said, "You're a very funny lady. I love your record album."

Glowing from the praise, Thelma said, "And I can honestly tell you that I sincerely wish Japan had won the war."

Henry laughed. "I think we did."

Sitting on a sun lounger, sipping iced tea, Thelma watched while Henry instructed Laura and Chris in self-defense.

He was forty years old, with a well-developed upper body and wiry legs. He was a master of judo and karate, as well as an expert kick boxer, and he taught a form of self-defense based on various martial arts, a system which he had devised himself. Twice a week he drove out from Riverside and spent three hours with Laura and Chris.

The kicking, punching, poking, grunting, twisting, throwing, off-the-hip rolling combat was conducted gently enough not to cause injury but with enough force to teach. Chris's lessons were less strenuous and less elaborate than Laura's, and Henry gave the boy plenty of breaks to pause and recoup. But by the end of the session, Laura was, as always, dripping sweat and exhausted.

When Henry left, Laura sent Chris upstairs to shower while she and Thelma rolled up the mats.

"He's cute," Thelma said.

"Henry? I guess he is."

"Maybe I'll take up judo or karate."

"Have your audiences been *that* dissatisfied lately?"

"That one was below the belt, Shane."

"Anything's fair when the enemy's formidable and merciless."

The following afternoon, as Thelma was putting her suitcase in the trunk of her Camaro for the return trip to Beverly Hills, she said, "Hey, Shane, you remember that first foster family you were sent to from McIlroy?"

"The Teagels," Laura said. "Flora, Hazel, and Mike."

Thelma leaned against the sun-warmed side of the car next to Laura. "You remember what you told us about Mike's fascination with newspapers like the *National Enquirer*?"

"I remember the Teagels as if I lived with them yesterday."

"Well," Thelma said, "I've been thinking a lot about what's happened to you—this guardian, the way he never ages, the way he disappeared into thin air—and I thought of the Teagels, and it all seems sort of ironic to me. All those nights at McIlroy, we laughed at nutty old Mike Teagel . . . and now what you find yourself in the middle of is a prime bit of exotic news."

Laura laughed softly. "Maybe I'd better reconsider all those tales of aliens living secretly in Cleveland, huh?"

"I guess what I'm trying to say is . . . life is full of wonders and surprises. Some of them are nasty surprises, yeah, and some days are as dark as the inside of the average politician's head. But just the same, there are moments that make me realize we're all here for some reason, enigmatic as it might be. It's not meaningless. If it was meaningless, there'd be no mystery. It'd be as dull and clear and lacking in mystery as the mechanism of a Mr. Coffee machine."

Laura nodded.

"God, listen to me! I'm torturing the English language to come up with a half-baked philosophical statement that ultimately means nothing more than 'keep your chin up, kid.' "

"You're not half-baked."

"Mystery," Thelma said. "Wonder. You're in the middle of it, Shane, and that's what life's all about. If it's dark right now . . . well, this too shall pass."

They stood by the car, hugging, not needing to say more, until Chris ran out from the house with a crayon drawing he had done for Thelma and that he wanted her to take back to LA with her. It was a crude but charming scene of Tommy Toad standing outside a movie theater, gazing up at a marquee on which Thelma's name was huge.

He had tears in his eyes. "But do you really have to go, Aunt Thelma? Can't you stay one more day?"

Thelma hugged him, then carefully rolled up the drawing as if in possession of a priceless masterwork. "I'd love to stay, Christopher Robin, but I can't. My adoring fans are crying for me to make this movie. Besides, I've got a big mortgage."

"What's a mortgage?"

"The greatest motivator in the world," Thelma said, giving him a last kiss. She got into the car, started the engine, put down the side window, and winked at Laura. "Exotic news, Shane."

"Mystery."

"Wonder."

Laura gave her the three-finger greeting from *Star Trek*.

Thelma laughed. "You'll make it, Shane. In spite of the guns and all I've learned since I came here on Friday, I'm less worried about you now than I was then."

Chris stood at Laura's side, and they watched Thelma's car until it went down the long driveway and disappeared onto the state route.

·6·

Dr. Vladimir Penlovski's large office suite was on the fourth floor of the institute. When Stefan entered the reception lounge, it was deserted, but he heard voices coming from the next room. He went to the inner door, which was ajar, pushed it all the way open, and saw Penlovski giving dictation to Anna Kaspar, his secretary.

Penlovski looked up, mildly surprised to see Stefan. He must have perceived the tension in Stefan's face, for he frowned and said, "Is something wrong?"

"Something's been wrong for a long time," Stefan said, "but it'll all be fine now, I think." Then, as Penlovski's frown deepened, Stefan pulled the silencer-equipped Colt Commander from the pocket of his lab coat and shot the scientist twice in the chest.

Anna Kaspar sprang up from her chair, dropping her pencil and dictation pad, a scream caught in her throat.

He did not like killing women—he did not like killing anyone—but there was no choice now, so he shot her three times, knocking her backward onto the desk, before the scream could tear free of her.

Dead, she slid off the desk and crumpled to the floor. The shots had been no louder than the hissing of an angry cat, and the sound of the body dropping had been insufficient to draw attention.

Penlovski was slumped in his chair, eyes and mouth open, staring sightlessly. One of the shots must have pierced his heart, for there was only a small spot of blood on his shirt; his circulation had been cut off in an instant.

Stefan backed out of the room, closed the door. He crossed the reception lounge and, stepping into the hall, shut the outer door too.

His heart was racing. With those two murders he had cut himself off forever from his own time, his own people. From here on, the only life for him was in Laura's time. Now there was no turning back.

With his hands—and the gun—jammed in his lab-coat pockets, he went down the hall toward Januskaya's office. As he neared the door, two of his other colleagues came out of it. They said hello as they passed him, and he stopped to see if they were heading for Penlovski's office. If they were, he'd have to kill them too.

He was relieved when they stopped at the elevators. The more corpses he left strewn around, the more likely someone would be to stumble across one of them and sound an alarm that would prevent him from setting the timer on the explosives and escaping by way of the Lightning Road.

He went into Januskaya's office, which also had a reception area. At the desk, the secretary—provided, as Anna Kaspar had been, by the secret police—looked up and smiled.

"Is Dr. Januskaya here?" Stefan asked.

"No. He's down in the documents room with Dr. Volkaw."

Volkaw was the third man whose overview of the project was great enough to require that he be eliminated. It seemed a good omen that he and Wladyslaw Januskaya were conveniently in the same place.

In the documents room, they stored and studied the many books, newspapers, magazines, and other materials that had been brought back by time travelers from scheduled jaunts. These days the men who had conceived of Lightning Road were engaged in an urgent analysis of the key points at which alterations in the natural flow of events could provide the changes in the course of history that they desired.

On the way down in the elevator, Stefan replaced the pistol's silencer with the unused spare. The first would muffle another dozen shots before its sound baffles were seriously damaged. But he did not want to overuse it. The second silencer was additional insurance. He also quickly exchanged the half-empty magazine for a full one.

The first-floor corridor was a busy place, with people coming and going from one lab and research room to another. He kept his hands in his pockets and went directly to the documents room.

When Stefan entered, Januskaya and Volkaw were standing at an oak table, bent over a copy of a magazine, arguing heatedly but in low voices. They glanced up, then immediately continued their discussion, assuming that he was there for research purposes of his own.

Stefan put two bullets in Volkaw's back.

Januskaya reacted with confusion and shock as Volkaw flew forward into the table, driven by the impact of the nearly silent gunfire.

Stefan shot Januskaya in the face, then turned and left the room, closing the door behind him. Not trusting himself to speak to one of his colleagues with any degree of self-control or coherence, he tried to appear to be lost in thought, hoping that would dissuade them from approaching him. He went to the elevators as quickly as possible without running, went to his third-floor office, reached behind the file cabinet, and twisted the dial on the timer as far as it would go, giving himself just five minutes to get to the gate and away before the institute was reduced to burning rubble.

·7·

By the time the school year began, Laura had won approval for Chris to receive his education at home, from a state-accredited tutor. Her name was Ida Palomar, and she reminded Laura of Marjorie Main, the late actress in the Ma and Pa Kettle movies. Ida was a big woman, a bit gruff, but with a generous heart, and she was a good teacher.

By the Thanksgiving school break, instead of feeling as if they were imprisoned, both she and Chris had accommodated to the relative isolation in which they lived. In fact they had actually come to enjoy the special closeness that developed between them as a result of having so few other people in their lives.

On Thanksgiving Day Thelma called from Beverly Hills to wish them a happy holiday. Laura took the call in the kitchen, which was full of the aroma of roasting turkey. Chris was in the family room, reading Shel Silverstein.

"Besides wishing you a happy holiday," Thelma said, "I'm calling to invite you down here to spend Christmas week with me and Jason."

"Jason?" Laura said.

"Jason Gaines, the director," Thelma said. "He's the guy who's directing this film I'm making. I've moved in with him."

"Does he know it yet?"

"Listen, Shane, *I* make the wisecracks."

"Sorry."

"He says he loves me. Is that crazy or what? I mean, Jeez, here's this decent-looking guy, only five years older than me, with no visible mutations, who's a *hugely* successful film director, worth many millions, who could just about have any stacked little starlet he wanted, and the only one he wants is me. Now obviously he's brain-damaged, but you wouldn't know it to talk to him, he could pass for normal. He says what he loves about me is I've got a *brain*—"

"Does he know how diseased it is?"

"There you go again, Shane. He says he loves my brain and sense of humor, and he's even excited by my body—or if he isn't excited then he's the first guy in history who could *fake* an erection."

"You've got a perfectly lovely body."

"Well, I'm beginning to consider the possibility that it's not as bad as I always thought. That is, if you consider *boniness* to be the sine qua non of feminine beauty. But even if I am able to look at my bod in a mirror now, it's still got *this* face perched atop it."

"You've got a perfectly lovely face—especially now that it's not surrounded by green and purple hair."

"It's not *your* face, Shane. Which means I'm mad for inviting you here for Christmas week. Jason will see you, and the next thing I'll be sitting in a Glad trash bag at the curb. But what about it? Will you come? We're shooting the film in and around LA, and we'll finish principal photography December tenth. Then Jason's got a lot of work to do, what with the editing, the whole schmear, but Christmas week we're just *stopping*. We'd like you to be here. Say you will."

"I'd sure like to meet the man smart enough to fall for you, Thelma, but I don't know. I feel . . . safe here."

"What do you think—we're dangerous?"

"You know what I mean."

"You can bring an Uzi."

"What will Jason think of that?"

"I'll tell him you're a radical leftist, save-the-sperm-whale, get-toxic-preservatives-out-of-Spam, parakeet liberationist and that you keep an Uzi with you at all times in case the revolution comes without warning. He'll buy it. This is Hollywood, kid. Most of the actors he works with are politically crazier than that."

Through the family-room archway, Laura could see Chris curled up in the armchair with his book.

She sighed. "Maybe it is time we got out in the world once in a while. And it's going to be a difficult Christmas if it's just Chris and me, this being the first without Danny. But I feel uneasy. . . ."

"It's been over ten months, Laura," Thelma said gently.

"But I'm not going to let down my guard."

"You don't have to. I'm serious about the Uzi. Bring your whole arsenal if that'll make you feel better. Just come."

"Well . . . all right."

"Fantastic! I can't wait for you to meet Jason."

"Do I detect that the love this brain-damaged Hollywood maven feels for you is reciprocated?"

"I'm crazy about him," Thelma admitted.

"I'm happy for you, Thelma. In fact I'm standing here now with a grin that won't stop, and nothing's made me feel so good in months."

Everything she said was true. But after she hung up, she missed Danny more than ever.

·8·

As soon as he set the timer behind the filing cabinet, Stefan left his third-floor office and went to the main lab on the ground floor. It was 12:14, and because the scheduled jaunt was not until two o'clock, the main lab was deserted. The windows were sealed, and most of the overhead lights were still off, as they had been little more than an hour ago, when he had returned from the San Bernardinos. The multitude of dials, gauges, and lighted graphs of the support machinery glowed green and orange. More in shadow than in the light, the gate awaited him.

Four minutes till detonation.

He went directly to the primary programming board and carefully adjusted the dials and switches and levers, setting the gate for the desired destination: southern California, near Big Bear, at eight o'clock on the night of January 10, 1988, just a few hours after

Danny Packard had been killed. He had done the necessary calculations days ago and had them on a sheet of paper to which he referred, so he was able to program the machinery in only a minute.

If he could have traveled to the afternoon of the tenth, prior to the accident and the shoot-out with Kokoschka, he would have done so in the hope of saving Danny. However, they had learned that a time traveler could not revisit a place if he scheduled his second arrival shortly *before* his previous jaunt; there was a natural mechanism that prevented a traveler from being in a place where he might encounter himself on a previous jaunt. He could return to Big Bear *after* he had left Laura that January night, for having already departed from the highway, he was no longer at risk of encountering himself there. But if he set the gate for an arrival time that would make it possible for him to meet himself, he would simply bounce back to the institute without going anywhere. That was one of many mysterious aspects of time travel which they had learned, around which they worked, but which they did not understand.

When he finished programming the gate, he glanced at the latitude and longitude indicator to confirm that he would arrive in the general area of Big Bear. Then he looked at the clock that noted his arrival time, and he was startled to see that it showed 8:00 P.M., January 10, 1989, instead of 1988. The gate was now set to deliver him to Big Bear not hours after Danny's death but a full year later.

He was sure that his calculations were correct; he'd had plenty of time to make them and recheck them over the past couple of weeks. Evidently, nervous as he was, he had made a mistake when entering the numbers. He would have to reprogram the gate.

Less than three minutes until detonation.

He blinked sweat out of his eyes and studied the numbers on the paper, the end product of his extensive calculations. As he reached for a control knob to cancel out the current program and re-enter the first of the figures again, a shout of alarm went up in the ground-floor corridor. The cries sounded as if they were coming from the north end of the building, in the general area of the document room.

Someone had found the bodies of Januskaya and Volkaw.

He heard more shouting. People running.

Glancing nervously at the closed door to the hall, he decided he had no time to reprogram. He would have to settle for returning to Laura one year after he had last left her.

With the silencer-fitted Colt Commander in his right hand, he rose from the programming console and headed toward the gate—

that eight-foot-high, twelve-foot-long, polished steel, open-ended barrel resting a foot off the floor on copper-plated blocks. He did not even want to risk taking time to recover his peacoat from the corner where he had left it an hour ago.

The commotion in the corridor was louder.

When he was only a couple of steps from the entrance to the gate, the lab door was thrown open behind him with such force that it hit the wall with a crash.

"Stop right there!"

Stefan recognized the voice, but he did not want to believe what he heard. He brought up the pistol as he swung around to confront his challenger: The man who had raced into the lab was Kokoschka.

Impossible. Kokoschka was dead. Kokoschka had followed him to Big Bear on the night of January 10, 1988, and he had killed Kokoschka on that snowswept highway.

Stunned, Stefan squeezed off two shots, both wide.

Kokoschka returned his fire. One slug took Stefan in the chest, high on the left side, knocking him backward against the edge of the gate. He stayed on his feet and got off three shots at Kokoschka, forcing the bastard to dive for cover and roll behind a lab bench.

They were less than two minutes from detonation.

Stefan felt no pain because he was in shock. But his left arm was useless; it hung limply at his side. And an insistent, oily blackness seeped in at the edges of his vision.

Only a few overhead lights had been left on, but suddenly even they flickered and went out, leaving the room vaguely illuminated by the wan glow of the many glass-covered dials and gauges. For an instant Stefan thought the dying light was a further surrender of his consciousness, a subjective development, but then he realized the public power supply had failed again, evidently due to the work of saboteurs, for there had been no sirens to warn of an air attack.

Kokoschka fired twice from darkness, the muzzle flash marking his position, and Stefan loosed the last three rounds in his pistol, though there was no hope of hitting Kokoschka through the marble lab bench.

Thankful that the gate was powered by a secure generator and still functional, Stefan threw away the pistol and with his good hand gripped the rim of the barrel-shaped portal. He pulled himself inside and crawled frantically toward the three-quarter point, where he would cross the energy field and depart this place for Big Bear, 1989.

As he hitched on two knees and one good arm through the gloomy interior of the barrel, he abruptly realized that the timer on the detonator in his office was connected to the public power supply. The countdown to destruction had been interrupted when the lights had gone out.

With dismay he understood why Kokoschka was not dead in Big Bear in 1988. *Kokoschka had not made that trip yet.* Kokoschka had only now learned of Stefan's perfidy, when he had discovered the bodies of Januskaya and Volkaw. Before the public power supply was restored, Kokoschka would search Stefan's office, find the detonator, and disarm the explosives. The institute would not be destroyed.

Stefan hesitated, wondering if he should go back.

Behind him he heard other voices in the lab, other security men arriving to reinforce Kokoschka.

He crawled forward.

And what of Kokoschka? The security chief evidently would travel to January 10, 1988, trying to kill Stefan on state route 330. But he would only manage to kill Danny before being killed himself. Stefan was pretty sure that Kokoschka's death was an immutable destiny, but he would need to think more about the paradoxes of time travel, to see if there was any way Kokoschka could escape being gunned down in 1988, a death that Stefan had already witnessed.

The complications of time travel were confusing even when one pondered them with a clear head. In his condition, wounded and struggling to remain conscious, he only grew dizzier thinking about such things. Later. He would worry about it later.

Behind him in the dark laboratory, someone began firing into the entrance of the gate, hoping to hit him before he reached the point of departure.

He crawled the last couple of feet. Toward Laura. Toward a new life in a distant time. But he had hoped to close forever the bridge between the era he was leaving and that to which he was now pledging himself. Instead the gate would remain open. And they could come across time to get him . . . and Laura.

•9•

Laura and Chris spent Christmas with Thelma at Jason Gaines's house in Beverly Hills. It was a twenty-two-room, Tudor-style mansion on six, walled acres, a phenomenally large property in an area where the cost per acre had long ago escalated far beyond reason. During construction in the '40s—it had been built by a producer of screwball comedies and war movies—no compromises had been made in quality, and the rooms were marked by beautiful detail work that could not have been duplicated these days at ten times the original cost: There were intricately coffered ceilings, some made of oak, some of copper; crown moldings were elaborately carved; the leaded windows were of stained or beveled glass, and they were set so deep in the castle-thick walls that one could comfortably sit on the wide sills; interior lintels were decorated with hand-carved panels—vines and roses, cherubs and banners, leaping deer, birds with ribbons trailing from their bills; exterior lintels were of carved granite, and in two were set mortared clusters of colorful della Robbia–style ceramic fruits. The six-acre property around the house was a meticulously maintained private park where winding stone pathways led through a tropical landscape of palms, benjaminas, ficus nidida, azaleas laden with brilliant red blossoms, impatiens, ferns, birds of paradise, and seasonal flowers of so many species that Laura could identify only half of them.

When Laura and Chris arrived early on Thursday afternoon, the day before Christmas, Thelma took them on a long tour of the house and grounds, after which they drank hot cocoa and ate miniature pastries prepared by the cook and served by the maid in the airy sun porch that looked out upon the swimming pool.

"Is this a crazy life, Shane? Can you believe that the same girl who spent almost ten years in holes like McIlroy and Caswell could end up living *here* without first having to be reincarnated as a princess?"

The house was so imposing that it encouraged anyone who owned it to feel Important with a capital I, and anyone in possession of it would be hard-pressed to avoid smugness and pomposity. But when Jason Gaines came home at four o'clock, he proved to be as unpretentious as anyone Laura knew, amazingly so for a man who had spent seventeen years in the movie business. He was thirty-eight, five years older than Thelma, and he looked like a younger Robert Vaughn, which was a lot better than "decent-looking," as Thelma had referred to him. He was home less than half an hour before he and Chris huddled in one of his three hobby rooms, playing with an electric train set that covered a fifteen-by-twenty-foot platform, complete with detailed villages, rolling countryside, windmills, waterfalls, tunnels, and bridges.

That night, with Chris asleep in the room adjoining Laura's, Thelma visited her. In their pajamas they sat cross-legged on her bed, as if they were girls again, though they ate roasted pistachios and drank Christmas champagne instead of cookies and milk.

"The weirdest thing of all, Shane, is that in spite of where I came from, I feel as if I belong here. I don't feel out of place."

She did not look out of place, either. Though she was still recognizably Thelma Ackerson, she had changed in the past few months. Her hair was better cut and styled; she had a tan for the first time in her life; and she carried herself more like a woman and less like a comic trying to win laughter—meaning approval—with each funny gesture and posture. She was wearing less flamboyant—and sexier—pajamas than usual: clingy, unpatterned, peach-colored silk. She was, however, still sporting bunny slippers.

"Bunny slippers," she said, "remind me of who I am. You can't get a swelled head if you wear bunny slippers. You can't lose your sense of perspective and start acting like a star or a rich lady if you keep on wearing bunny slippers. Besides, bunny slippers give me confidence because they're so jaunty; they make a statement; they say, 'Nothing the world does to me can ever get me so far down that I can't be silly and frivolous.' If I died and found myself in hell, I could endure the place if I had bunny slippers."

Christmas Day was like a wonderful dream. Jason proved to be a sentimentalist with the undiminished wonder of a child. He insisted they gather at the Christmas tree in pajamas and robes, that they open their gifts with as much popping of ribbons and noisy tearing of paper and as much general drama as possible, that they sing carols, that while opening gifts they abandon the idea of a healthy breakfast and instead eat cookies, candy, nuts, fruitcake, and caramel popcorn. He proved that he had not just been trying to be a good host when he had spent the previous evening with Chris at the trains, for all Christmas Day he engaged the boy in one form of play or another, both inside and outside the house, and it was clear that he had a love of and natural rapport with kids. By dinnertime Laura realized Chris had laughed more in one day than in the entire past eleven months.

When she tucked the boy into bed that night, he said, "What a great day, huh, Mom?"

"One of the all-time greats," she agreed.

"All I wish," he said as he dropped toward sleep, "is that Daddy could've been here to play with us."

"I wish the same thing, honey."

"But in a way he was here, 'cause I thought of him a lot. Will I always remember him, Mom, the way he was, even after dozens and dozens of years, will I remember him?"

"I'll help you remember, baby."

"Because sometimes already there are little things I don't quite remember about him. I have to think hard to remember them. But I don't want to forget 'cause he was my daddy."

When he was asleep, Laura went through the connecting door to her own bed. She was immensely relieved when a few minutes later Thelma came by for another girl-to-girl, because without Thelma, she would have had a few very bad hours there.

"If I had babies, Shane," Thelma said, climbing into Laura's bed, "do you think there's any chance at all that they'd be allowed to live in society, or would they be banished to some ugly-kid equivalent of a leper colony?"

"Don't be silly."

"Of course, I could afford *massive* plastic surgery for them. I mean, even if it turns out that their species is questionable, I could afford to have them made passably human."

"Sometimes your put-downs of yourself make me angry."

"Sorry. Chalk it up to not having a supportive mom and dad. I've got both the confidence and doubt of an orphan." She was quiet for a moment, then laughed and said, "Hey, you know what? Jason wants to marry me. I thought at first he was possessed by a demon and unable to control his tongue, but he assures me we've no need of an exorcist, though he's evidently suffered a minor stroke. So what do you think?"

"What do *I* think? What's that matter? But for what it's worth, he's a terrific guy. You are going to grab him, aren't you?"

"I worry that he's too good for me."

"No one's too good for you. Marry him."

"I worry that it won't work out, and then I'll be devastated."

"And if you don't give it a try," Laura said, "you'll be worse than devastated—you'll be alone."

·10·

Stefan felt the familiar, unpleasant tingle that accompanied time travel, a peculiar vibration that passed inward from his skin, through his flesh, into the marrow of his bones, then swiftly back out again from bones to flesh to skin. With a *pop-whoooosh* he left the gate, and in the same instant he was stumbling down a steep, snow-covered slope in the California mountains on the night of January 10, 1989.

He tripped, fell on his wounded side, rolled to the bottom of the slope, where he came to rest against a rotted log. Pain flashed through him for the first time since he had been shot. He cried out and flopped onto his back, biting his tongue to keep from passing out, blinking up at the tumultuous night.

Another thunderbolt ripped the sky, and light seemed to pulse from the jagged wound. By the spectral glow of the snow-covered earth and by the fierce but fitful flashes of lightning, Stefan saw that he was in a clearing in a forest. Leafless, black trees thrust bare limbs toward the fulminous sky, as if they were fanatical cultists praising a violent god. Evergreens, boughs drooping under surplices of snow, stood like the solemn priests of a more decorous religion.

Arriving in a time other than his own, a traveler disrupted the forces of nature in some way that required the dissipation of tremendous energy. Regardless of the weather at the point of arrival, the imbalance was corrected by a sky-shattering display of lightning, which was why the ethereal highway on which time travelers journeyed was called the Lightning Road. For reasons no one had been able to ascertain, a return to the institute, to the traveler's own era, was marked by no celestial pyrotechnics.

The lightning subsided, as it always did, from bolts worthy of the Apocalypse to distant flickerings. In a minute the night was dark and calm again.

As the thunderbolts had faded, his pain had increased. It almost seemed as if the lightning that had cracked the vaults of heaven was now captured within his chest, left shoulder, and left arm, too great a power for mortal flesh to contain or endure.

He got onto his knees and rose shakily to his feet, worried that he had little chance of getting out of the woods alive. But for the phosphorescent glow of the snow-mantled clearing, the cloudy night was cellar-black, forbidding. Though undisturbed by wind, the winter air was icy, and he was wearing only a thin lab coat over shirt and pants.

Worse, he might be miles from a highway or any landmark by which he could reckon his position. If the gate was considered as a gun, its accuracy was remarkable for the temporal distance covered to the target, but it was far from perfect in its aim. A traveler usually arrived within ten or fifteen minutes of the *time* he intended, but not always with the desired geographic precision. Sometimes he touched down within a hundred yards of his physical destination, but on other occasions he was as far as ten or fifteen miles off, as on the day that he had traveled to January 10, 1988, to save Laura, Danny, and Chris from the Robertsons' sliding pickup truck.

On all previous trips, he had carried both a map of the target area and a compass, lest he find himself in just such a place of isolation as he had arrived at now. But this time, having left his peacoat in the corner of the lab, he had neither compass nor map, and the occluded sky deprived him of the hope of finding his way out of the forest with the help of the stars.

He stood in snow almost to his knees, wearing street shoes, no boots, and he felt as if he must start moving immediately or freeze to the ground. He looked around the clearing, hoping for inspiration, for a twinge of intuition, but at last he chose a direction at random and headed to his left, searching for a deer trail or other natural course that would provide him a passage through the forest.

His entire left side from neck to waist throbbed with pain. He hoped that the bullet, in passing through him, had torn no arteries and that the rate of blood loss was slow enough to allow him at least to reach Laura and see her face, the face he loved, one last time before he died.

The one-year anniversary of Danny's death fell on a Sunday, which was the same day of the week that he had been murdered, and although Chris did not mention the significance of the date, he was aware of it. The boy was unusually quiet. He spent most of that somber day playing silently with his Masters of the Universe action figures in the family room, which was the kind of play ordinarily characterized by vocal imitations of laser weapons, clashing swords, and spaceship engines. Later he sprawled on his bed in his room, reading comic books. He resisted Laura's every effort to draw him out of his self-imposed isolation, which was probably for the best; any attempt she made to be cheerful would have been transparent, and he would have been further depressed by the perception that she was also struggling mightily to turn her thoughts away from their grievous loss.

Thelma, who had called only days before to report the good news that she had decided to marry Jason Gaines, called again at seven-fifteen that evening, just to chat, as if she were unaware of the importance of the date. Laura took the call in her office, where she was still struggling with the bile-black book that had occupied her for the past year.

"Hey, Shane, guess what? I met Paul McCartney! He was in LA to negotiate a recording contract, and we were at the same party Friday night. When I first saw him, he was stuffing an hors d'oeuvre in his mouth, he said hello, he had crumbs on his lip, and he was *gorgeous*. He said he'd seen my movies, thought I was very good, and we talked—you believe this?—we must've chatted twenty minutes, and gradually the strangest thing happened."

"You discovered that you'd undressed him while you were talking."

"Well, he still looks very good, you know, still that cherub face we swooned over twenty years ago but marked now by experience, *très* sophisticated and with an extremely appealing touch of sadness about his eyes, and he was enormously amusing and charming. At first maybe I did want to tear his clothes off, yeah, and live out the fantasy at last. But then the longer we talked, the less he seemed like a god, the more he seemed like a person, and in *minutes*, Shane, the myth evaporated, and he was just this very nice, attractive, middle-aged man. Now what do you make of that?"

"What am I supposed to make of it?"

"I don't know," Thelma said. "I'm a little disturbed. Shouldn't a living legend continue to awe you longer than twenty minutes after you meet him? I mean, I've met lots of stars by now, and none of them have remained godlike, but this was *McCartney*."

"Well, if you want my opinion, his swift loss of mythological stature says nothing negative about him, but it says plenty positive about you. You've achieved a new maturity, Ackerson."

"Does this mean I've got to give up watching old Three Stooges movies every Saturday morning?"

"The Stooges are permitted, but food fights are definitely a thing of the past for you."

By the time Thelma hung up at ten minutes till eight, Laura was feeling slightly better, so she switched from the bile-black book to the tale about Sir Tommy Toad. She had written only two sentences of the children's story when the night beyond the windows was lit by a bolt of lightning bright enough to spark dire thoughts of nuclear holocaust. The subsequent thunderclap shook the house from roof to foundation, as if a wrecker's ball had slammed into one of the walls. She came to her feet with a start, so surprised that she did not even hit the "save" key on the computer. A second bolt seared the night, making the windows as luminous as television screens, and the thunder that followed was louder than the first explosion.

"Mom!"

She turned and saw Chris standing in the doorway. "It's okay," she said. He ran to her. She sat in the spring-backed armchair and pulled him onto her lap. "It's all right. Don't be afraid, honey."

"But it's not raining," he said. "Why's it booming like that if it's not raining?"

Outside, an incredible series of lightning bolts and overlapping thunderclaps continued for nearly a minute, then subsided. The power of the event had been so great, Laura was able to imagine that in the morning they would find the broken sky lying about in huge chunks like fragments of a giant eggshell.

Before he walked five minutes from the clearing in which he had arrived, Stefan was forced to pause and lean against the thick trunk of a pine whose branches began just above his head. The pain of his wound wrung streams of sweat from him, yet he was shivering in the bitter January cold, too dizzy to stand up, yet terrified of sitting down and falling into an endless sleep. With the drooping boughs of that mammoth pine overhead and all around, he felt as if he had taken refuge under Death's black robe, from which he might not emerge.

Before putting Chris to bed for the night, she made sundaes for them with coconut-almond ice cream and Hershey's syrup. They ate at the kitchen table, and the boy's depression seemed to have lifted. Perhaps by marking the end of that sad anniversary with such drama, the bizarre weather phenomenon had startled him out of thoughts of death and into the contemplation of wonders. He was filled with talk of the lightning that had crackled down a kite string and into Dr. Frankenstein's laboratory in the old James Whale film, which he'd seen for the first time a week ago, and of the lightning that had frightened Donald Duck in a Disney cartoon, and of the stormy night in *101 Dalmations* during which Drusilla DeVille had posed such a dire threat to the title-role puppies.

By the time she tucked him in and kissed him goodnight, he was approaching sleep with a smile—a half smile, at least—rather than with the frown that had weighed upon his face all day. She sat in a chair by the side of his bed until he was fast asleep, though he was no longer afraid and did not require her presence. She stayed simply because she needed to look at him for a while.

She returned to her office at nine-fifteen, but before going to the word processor, she stopped at a window and stared out at the snow-swathed front lawn, at the black ribbon of the graveled driveway leading to the distant state route, and up at the starless, night sky. Something about the lightning deeply disturbed her: not that it had been so strange, not that it had been potentially destructive, but that the unprecedented and almost supernatural power of it had been somehow . . . familiar. She seemed to recall having witnessed a similar stormy display on another occasion, but she could not remember when. It was an uncanny feeling, akin to déjà vu, and it would not fade.

She went into the master bedroom and checked the security-control panel in her closet to be sure the perimeter alarm covering all the windows and doors was engaged. From beneath the bed, she withdrew the Uzi, which had an extended magazine holding four hundred rounds. She took the gun back to her office and put it on the floor by her chair.

She was about to sit down when lightning split the night again, frightening her, and it was followed at once by a crack of thunder she felt in her bones. Another bolt and another and another blazed in the windows like a series of leering, ghostly faces formed of ectoplasmic light.

As the heavens quaked with scintillant shudders, Laura hurried to Chris's room to calm him. To her surprise, though the lightning and thunder were shockingly more violent than they had been previously, the boy was not awakened, perhaps because the din seemed a part of some dream he was having about Dalmatian puppies on a stormy night of adventure.

Again, no rain fell.

The lightning and thunder quickly subsided, but her anxiety remained high.

He saw strange ebony shapes in the darkness, things that slipped between the trees and watched him with eyes blacker than their bodies, but though they startled and frightened him, he knew that they were not real, only phantoms spawned by his increasingly disoriented mind. He plodded onward in spite of outer cold, inner heat, prickling pine needles, sharp bramble thorns, icy ground that sometimes tilted out from beneath his feet and sometimes spun like a phonograph turntable. The pain in his chest and shoulder and arm was so intense that he was assailed by delirium images of rats gnawing at his flesh from within his body, though he could not figure how they had gotten *in* there.

After wandering for at least an hour—it seemed like many hours, even days, but it could not have been days because the sun had not risen—he came to the perimeter of the forest and, at the far end of a sloping half acre of snow-mantled lawn, he saw the house. Lights were vaguely visible at the edges of the blind-covered windows.

He stood, disbelieving, at first convinced that the house was no more real than the Stygian figures that had accompanied him through the woods. Then he began moving toward the mirage—in case it wasn't a fever dream, after all.

When he had taken only a few steps, a lash of lightning whipped the night, scarred the sky. The whip cracked repeatedly, and each time a stronger arm seemed to power it.

Stefan's shadow leaped and writhed on the snow around him, though he was temporarily paralyzed by fear. Sometimes he had two shadows because lightning silhouetted him simultaneously from two directions. Already well-trained hunters had followed him on the Lightning Road, determined to stop him before he had a chance to warn Laura.

He looked back at the trees out of which he had come. Under the stroboscopic sky, the evergreens seemed to jump toward him, then back, then toward him again. He saw no hunters there.

As the lightning faded, he staggered toward the house again. He fell twice, struggled up, kept moving, though he was afraid that if he fell again he would not be able to get to his feet or shout loud enough to be heard.

Staring at the computer screen, trying to think about Sir Tommy Toad and thinking instead of the lightning, Laura suddenly recalled when she previously had seen such a preternaturally stormy sky: the very day on which her father had first told her about Sir Tommy, the day that the junkie had come into the grocery, the day that she had seen her guardian for the first time, that summer of her eighth year.

She sat up straight in her chair.

Her heart began to hammer hard, fast.

Lightning of that unnatural power meant trouble of a specific nature, trouble for *her*. She could recall no lightning on the day that Danny died or when her guardian appeared in the cemetery during her father's burial service. But with an absolute certainty that she could not explain, she knew that the phenomenon she had witnessed tonight held a terrible meaning for her; it was an omen and not a good one.

She grabbed the Uzi and made a circuit of the upstairs, checking all the windows, looking in on Chris, making sure everything was as it should be. Then she hurried downstairs to inspect those rooms.

As she stepped into the kitchen, something thumped against the back door. With a gasp of surprise and fear, she whirled in that direction, swung the Uzi around, and nearly opened fire.

But it was not the determined sound of someone breaking in. It was an unthreatening thump, barely louder than a knock, repeated twice. She thought she heard a voice, too, weakly calling her name.

Silence.

She edged to the door and listened for perhaps half a minute.

Nothing.

The door was a high-security model with a steel core sandwiched between two inch-thick slabs of oak, so she was not worried about being shot by a gunman on the other side. Yet she hesitated to move directly to it and peer through the fisheye lens because she feared seeing an eye pressed to the other side, trying to peer in at *her*. When at last she had the courage for it, the peephole gave her a wide-angled view of the patio, and she saw a man sprawled on the concrete, his arms flung out at his sides, as if he had fallen backward after knocking on the door.

Trap, she thought. Trap, trick.

She switched on the outdoor spotlights and crept to the Levelor-covered window above the built-in writing desk. Cautiously she lifted one of the slats. The man on the concrete patio was her guardian. His shoes and trousers were caked with snow. He wore what appeared to be a white lab coat, the front darkly stained with blood.

As far as she could see, no one was crouched on the patio or on the lawn beyond, but she had to consider the possibility that someone had dumped his body there as a lure to bring her out of the house. Opening the door at night, under these circumstances, was foolhardy.

Nevertheless she could not leave him out there. Not her guardian. Not if he was hurt and dying.

She pressed the alarm bypass button next to the door, disengaged the dead-bolt locks, and reluctantly stepped into the wintry night with the Uzi at the ready. No one shot at her. On the dimly snow-illumined lawn, all the way back to the forest, nothing moved.

She went to her guardian, knelt at his side, and felt for his pulse. He was alive. She peeled back one of his eyelids. He was unconscious. The wound high in the left side of his chest looked bad, though it did not appear to be bleeding at the moment.

Her training with Henry Takahami and her regular exercise program had dramatically increased her strength, but she was not strong enough to lift the wounded man with one arm. She propped the Uzi by the back door and found she could not lift him even with both arms. It seemed dangerous to move a man who was so badly hurt, but more dangerous to leave him in the frigid night, especially when someone was apparently in pursuit of him. She managed to half lift and half drag him into the kitchen, where she stretched him out on the floor. With relief she retrieved the Uzi, relocked the door, and engaged the alarm again.

He was frighteningly pale and cold to the touch, so the immediate necessity was to strip off his shoes and socks, which were crusted with snow. By the time she dealt with his left foot and was unlacing his right shoe, he was mumbling in a strange language, the words too slurred for her to identify the tongue, and in English he muttered about explosives and gates and "phantoms in the trees."

Though she knew that he was delirious and very likely could not understand her any more than she could understand him, she spoke to him reassuringly: "Easy now, just relax, you'll be all right; as soon as I get your foot out of this block of ice, I'll call a doctor."

The mention of a doctor brought him briefly out of his confusion. He gripped her arm weakly, fixed her with an intense, fearful gaze. "No doctor. Get out . . . got to get out. . . ."

"You're in no condition to go anywhere," she told him. "Except by ambulance to a hospital."

"Got to get out. Quick. They'll be coming . . . soon coming. . . ."

She glanced at the Uzi. "Who will be coming?"

"Assassins," he said urgently. "Kill me for revenge. Kill you, kill Chris. Coming. Now."

At that moment there was no delirium in his eyes or voice. His pale, sweat-slick face was no longer slack but taut with terror.

All her training with guns and in the martial arts no longer seemed like hysterical precautions. "Okay," she said, "we'll get out as soon as I've had a look at that wound, see if it needs to be dressed."

"No! Now. Out now."

"But—"

"Now," he insisted. In his eyes was such a haunted look, she could almost believe that the assassins of whom he spoke were not ordinary men but creatures of some supernatural origin, demons with the ruthlessness and relentlessness of the soulless.

"Okay," she said. "We'll get out now."

His hand fell away from her arm. His eyes shifted out of focus, and he began to mumble thickly, senselessly.

As she hurried across the kitchen, intending to go upstairs and wake Chris, she heard her guardian speak dreamily yet anxiously of a "great, black, rolling machine of death," which meant nothing to her but frightened her nonetheless.

Part Two

PURSUIT

The long habit of living
indisposeth us for dying.

—SIR THOMAS BROWNE

Five

AN ARMY OF SHADOWS

·1·

Laura switched on a lamp and shook Chris awake. "Get dressed, honey. Quickly."

"What's happening?" he asked sleepily, rubbing his eyes with his small fists.

"Some bad men are coming, and we've got to get out of here before they arrive. Now hurry."

Chris had spent a year not only mourning his father but preparing for the moment when the deceptively placid events of daily life would be disrupted by another unexpected explosion of the chaos that lay at the heart of human existence, the chaos that from time to time erupted like an active volcano, as it had done the night his father had been murdered. Chris had watched his mother become a first-rate shot with a handgun, had seen her collect an arsenal, had taken self-defense classes with her, and through it all he had retained the point of view and attitudes of a child, had seemed pretty much like any other child, if understandably melancholy since the death of his father. But now in a moment of crisis he did not react like an eight-year-old; he did not whine or ask unnecessary questions; he was not quarrelsome or stubborn or slow to obey. He threw back the covers, got out of bed at once, and hurried to the closet.

"Meet me in the kitchen," Laura said.

"Okay, Mom."

She was proud of his responsible reaction and relieved that he would not delay them, but she was also saddened that at eight years of age he understood enough about the brevity and harshness of life to respond to a crisis with the swiftness and equanimity of an adult.

She was wearing jeans and a blue-plaid, flannel shirt. When she went to her bedroom, she only had to slip into a wool sweater, pull off her Rockport walking shoes, and put on a pair of rubberized hiking boots with lace-up tops.

She had gotten rid of Danny's clothes, so she had no coat for the wounded man in the kitchen. She had plenty of blankets, however, and she grabbed two of those from the linen closet in the hall.

As an afterthought, she went to her office, opened the safe, and removed the strange black belt with copper fittings that her guardian had given her a year ago. She jammed it in her satchel-like purse.

Downstairs she stopped at the front foyer closet for a blue ski jacket and the Uzi carbine that hung on the back of the door. As she moved she was alert for unusual noises—voices in the night beyond the house or the sound of a car engine—but all remained silent.

In the kitchen she put the submachine gun on the table with the other one, then knelt beside her guardian, who was unconscious again. She unbuttoned his snow-wet lab coat, then his shirt, and looked at the gunshot wound in his chest. It was high in his left shoulder, well above the heart, which was good, but he had lost a lot of blood; his clothes were soaked with it.

"Mom?" Chris was in the doorway, dressed for a winter night.

"Take one of those Uzis from the table, get the third one from the back of the pantry door, and put them in the Jeep."

"It's him," Chris said, wide-eyed with surprise.

"Yes, it is. He showed up like this, hurt bad. Besides the Uzis, get two of the revolvers—the one in the drawer over there and the one in the dining room. And be careful not to accidentally—"

"Don't worry, Mom," he said, setting off on the errands.

As gently as possible she rolled her guardian onto his right side—he groaned but did not awaken—to see if there was an exit wound in his back. Yes. The bullet had gone through him, exiting under the scapula. His back was soaked with blood, too, but neither the entry nor exit point was bleeding heavily any longer; if there was serious bleeding, it was internal, and she could not detect or treat it.

Under his clothing he wore one of the belts. She unbuckled it. The belt wouldn't fit in the center compartment of her purse, so she had to stuff it into a zippered side compartment after dumping out the items she usually kept in there.

She rebuttoned his shirt and debated whether she should take off his damp lab coat. She decided it would be too difficult to wrestle the sleeves down his arms. Rolling him gently from side to side, she worked a gray wool blanket under and around him.

While Laura bundled up the wounded man, Chris made a couple of trips to the Jeep with the guns, using the inner door that connected the laundry room to the garage. Then he came in with a two-foot-wide, four-foot-long, flat dolly—essentially a wooden platform on casters—that had accidentally been left behind by some furniture deliverymen almost a year and a half ago. Riding it like a skateboard toward the pantry, he said, "We gotta take the ammo box, but it's too heavy for me to carry. I'll put it on this."

Pleased by his initiative and cleverness, she said, "We have twelve rounds in the two revolvers and twelve *hundred* rounds in the three Uzis, so I don't think we'll need more than that, no matter what happens. Bring the board here. Quick now. I've been trying to figure how we can get him to the Jeep without shaking him up too bad. That looks like the ticket."

They were moving fast, as if they had drilled for just this particular emergency, yet Laura felt that they were taking too much time. Her hands were shaking, and her belly fluttered continuously. She expected someone to hammer on the door at any moment.

Chris held the dolly still while Laura heaved the wounded man onto it. When she got the board under his head, shoulders, back, and buttocks, she was able to lift his legs and push him as if he were a wheelbarrow. Chris scooted along at a crouch by the front wheels, one hand on the unconscious man's right shoulder to keep him from sliding off and to prevent the board from rolling out from beneath him. They had a little trouble easing across the door sill at the end of the laundry room, but they got him into the three-car garage.

The Mercedes was on the left, the Jeep wagon on the right, with the middle slot empty. They wheeled her guardian to the Jeep.

Chris had opened the tailgate. He had also unrolled a small gym mat in there for a mattress.

"You're a great kid," she told him.

Together they managed to transfer the wounded man from the dolly into the cargo bed by way of the open tailgate.

"Bring the other blanket and his shoes from the kitchen," she told Chris.

By the time the boy returned with those items, Laura had gotten her guardian stretched out flat on his back on the gym mat. They covered his bare feet with the second blanket and put his soggy shoes beside him.

As Laura shut the tailgate, she said, "Chris, get in the front seat and buckle up."

She hurried back into the house. Her purse, which contained all of her credit cards, was on the table; she slipped the straps over her shoulder. She picked up the third Uzi and headed back toward the laundry room, but before she had taken three steps, something hit the rear door with tremendous force.

She whirled, bringing up the gun.

Something slammed into the door again, but the steel core and Schlage deadbolts could not be defeated easily.

Then the nightmare began in earnest.

A submachine gun chattered, and Laura threw herself against the side of the refrigerator, sheltering there. They were trying to blow open the back door, but the heavy steel core held against that assault too. The door shook, however, and bullets pierced the wall on both sides of the reinforced frame, tearing holes in the drywall.

Family-room and kitchen windows exploded as a second submachine gun opened fire. The metal Levelors danced on their mountings. Metal slats twanged as slugs passed between them, and some slats bent, but most of the shattered window glass was contained behind the blinds, where it rained on sills and from there to the floor. Cabinet doors splintered and cracked as bullets pierced them, and chips of brick flew off one wall, and bullets ricocheted off the copper range hood, leaving it dented, creased. Hanging from ceiling hooks, the copper pots and pans took a lot of hits, producing a variety of *clinks* and *ponks*. One overhead light blew out. The Levelor at the window above the writing desk was torn off its mountings at last, and half a dozen slugs plowed into the refrigerator door just inches from her.

Her heart was racing, and a flood of adrenaline had made her senses almost painfully sharp. She wanted to run for the Jeep in the garage and try to get out before they realized she was in the process of leaving, but a primal warrior instinct told her to stay put. She pressed flat against the side of the refrigerator, out of the direct line of fire, hoping that she would not be hit by a ricochet.

Who the hell *are* you people? she wondered angrily.

The firing stopped, and her instinct proved true: The barrage was followed by the gunmen themselves. They stormed the house. The first one clambered through the imploded window above the kitchen desk. She stepped away from the refrigerator and opened fire, blowing him back out onto the patio. A second man, dressed in black like the first, entered by the shattered sliding door in the family room—she saw him through the archway a second before he saw her—and she swung the Uzi in that direction, spraying bullets, destroying the Mr. Coffee machine, tearing the hell out of the kitchen wall beside the archway, then cutting him down as he brought his weapon around toward her. She had practiced with the Uzi but not recently, and she was surprised at how controllable it was. She was also surprised at how sickened she was by the need to kill them, though they were trying to slaughter her and her child; like a wave of oily sludge, nausea washed through her, but she choked down the gorge that rose in her throat. A third man started into the family room, and she was ready to kill him, too, and a hundred like him, no matter how sick the killing made her, but he threw himself backward, out of the line of fire, when he saw his companion blown away.

Now the Jeep.

She didn't know how many killers were outside, maybe only the three, two dead and one still living, maybe four or ten or a hundred, but regardless of how many there were, they would not have expected to be met with such a bold response and certainly not with so much firepower, no way, not from a woman and a small boy, and they had known that her guardian was wounded and unarmed. So right now they were stunned, and they'd be taking cover, assessing the situation, planning their next move. This might be her first and last chance to get away in the Jeep wagon. She sprinted through the laundry room into the garage.

She saw that Chris had started the Jeep's engine when he'd heard the gunfire; bluish exhaust fumes billowed from the tailpipes. As she ran to the Jeep, the garage door started up; Chris had evidently used the Genie remote-control unit the moment he saw her.

By the time she got behind the wheel, the garage door was a third open. She shifted into gear. "Get down!"

As Chris instantly obeyed, sliding down in his seat below window level, Laura let up on the brakes. She rammed the accelerator against the floorboards, peeled rubber on the concrete, and roared out into the night, clearing the still rising garage door by only an inch or two, ripping off the radio antenna.

The Jeep's big tires, though not swaddled in chains, had heavy winter tread. They dug into the frozen slush and gravel that formed the surface of the driveway, finding traction with no trouble, spewing shrapnel of stone and ice.

From off to her left came a dark figure, a man in black, running across the front lawn, kicking up snow, forty or fifty feet away, and he was such a featureless shape that he might have been just a shadow, except that over the screaming of the engine she heard the rattle of automatic gunfire. Slugs slammed into the side of the Jeep, and the window behind her blew in, but the window beside her remained intact, and then she was speeding away, heading out of range, a few seconds from safety now, with wind shrieking at the broken window. She prayed none of the tires would be hit, and she heard more rounds striking sheet metal, or maybe it was gravel and ice churned up by the Jeep.

When she reached the state route at the end of the driveway, she was certain that she was out of range. As she braked hard for the left turn, she glanced into the rearview mirror and saw, far back, a pair of headlights at the open garage. The killers had arrived at her house without a vehicle—God only knew how they had traveled, perhaps with the use of those strange belts—and they were using her Mercedes to pursue her.

She had intended to turn left on the state route, head down past Running Springs, past the turnoff to lake Arrowhead, on to the superhighway and into the city of San Bernardino, where there were people and safety in numbers, where men dressed in black and toting automatic weapons would not stalk her so boldly, and where she could get medical treatment for her guardian. But when she saw the headlights behind her, she responded to an innate proclivity for survival, turning right instead, heading east-northeast toward Big Bear Lake.

If she had gone left they would have come to that fateful half mile of inclined highway on which Danny had been murdered a year ago; and Laura felt intuitively—almost superstitiously—that the most dangerous place in the world for them at the moment was that sloping length of two-lane blacktop. She and Chris had been meant to die twice on that hill: first, when the Robertsons' pickup slid out of control; second, when Kokoschka opened fire on them. Sometimes she perceived that there were both benign and ominous patterns in life and that, once thwarted, fate strove to reassert those predestined designs. Though she had no intellectually sound reason for believing that they would die if they headed down toward Running Springs, she knew in her heart that death in fact awaited them there.

As they pulled onto the state route and headed for Big Bear, tall evergreens rising darkly on both sides, Chris sat up and looked back.

"They're coming," Laura told him, "but we'll outrun them."

"Are they the ones that got Daddy?"

"Yes, I think so. But we didn't know about them then, and we weren't prepared."

The Mercedes was on the state route now, out of sight most of the time because the roadway rose and fell and twisted, putting hills and turns between the two vehicles. The car seemed to be about two hundred yards behind, but it was probably closing because it had a bigger engine and a lot more power than the Jeep.

"Who are they?" Chris asked.

"I'm not sure, honey. And I don't know why they want to hurt us, either. But I know *what* they are. They're thugs, they're scum, I learned all about their type a long time ago at Caswell Hall, and I know the only thing you can do with people like them is stand up to them, fight back, because they only respect toughness."

"You were terrific back there, Mom."

"You were darned good yourself, kiddo. That was very smart of you to start the Jeep when you heard the gunfire, and to have the garage door on the way up by the time I got behind the wheel. That probably saved us."

Behind them the Mercedes had closed the distance to about one hundred yards. It was a road-hugger, a 420 SEL, which handled as well as anything on the highway, much better than the Jeep.

"They're coming fast, Mom."

"I know."

"Real fast."

Approaching the eastern point of the lake, Laura pulled up behind a rattletrap Dodge pickup with one broken tailight and a rusted bumper that appeared to be held together by stickers with supposedly funny sayings—I BRAKE FOR BLONDES, MAFIA STAFF CAR. It chugged along at thirty miles an hour, below the speed limit. If Laura hesitated, the Mercedes would close the gap; when they were near enough the killers might use their guns again. They were in a no-passing zone, but she could see enough clear road ahead to risk the maneuver; she swung around the pickup, tramped the accelerator hard, got in front of the truck, and returned to the right lane. Immediately ahead was a Buick doing about forty, and she passed that, too, just before the road got too twisty to allow the Mercedes to get around the old truck.

"They're hung up back there!" Chris said.

Laura put the Jeep up to fifty-five, which was too fast for some of the turns, though she held it on the road and began to think they were going to escape. But the highway split at the lake, and neither the Buick nor the old Ford pickup followed her along the south shore toward Big Bear City; they both turned toward Fawnskin and the north shore, leaving the road empty between her and the Mercedes, which at once began to close the distance between them.

Houses were everywhere now, both on the high ground to the right and on the lower ground down toward the lake on her left. Some of them were dark, probably vacation homes used only on winter weekends and in the summers, but the lights of other places were visible among the trees.

She knew she could follow any of those lanes and driveways to a hundred different houses where she and Chris would have been taken in. People would open their doors without hesitation. This was not the city; in the small-town atmosphere of the mountains, people were not instantly suspicious of unannounced night visitors.

The Mercedes closed to within a hundred yards, and the driver flicked the headlights from low beam to high beam again and again, as if gleefully saying, *Hey, here we come, Laura, we're gonna get you, we're the boogeymen, the real thing, and nobody can run from us forever, here we come, here we come.*

If she tried to take refuge in one of the nearby houses, the killers probably would follow, murdering not only her and Chris but the people who sheltered them. The bastards might be reluctant to chase her to ground in the heart of San Bernardino or Riverside or even Redlands, where they were likely to encounter police response, but they would not be intimidated by a mere handful of bystanders because no matter how many people they slaughtered, they could no doubt elude capture by pushing the yellow buttons on their belts and vanishing as her guardian had vanished one year ago. She had no idea where they would be vanishing *to,* but she suspected that it was a place where the police could never touch them. She would not risk innocent lives, so she passed house after house without slowing.

The Mercedes was about fifty yards back, closing fast.

"Mom—"

"I see them, honey."

She was headed toward Big Bear City, but unfortunately the place was inaptly named. It was not only less than a city but not even much of a village, hardly a hamlet. There were not enough streets for her to hope to lose their pursuers, and the police presence was inadequate to deal with a couple of fanatics armed with submachine guns.

Light traffic passed them going the other way, and she got behind another car in their lane, a gray Volvo, around which she whipped on an almost blind stretch of road, but she had no choice because the Mercedes was within forty yards. The killers passed the Volvo with equal recklessness.

"How's our passenger?" she asked.

Without unfastening his safety harness, Chris turned to look into the back of the Jeep wagon. "He looks okay, I guess. He's getting bounced around a lot."

"I can't help that."

"Who is he, Mom?"

"I don't know much about him," she said. "But when we get out of this fix, I'm going to tell you what I do know. I haven't told you before because . . . I guess because I didn't know what was going on, and I was afraid it might be dangerous somehow for you to know anything about him at all. But it can't get more dangerous than this, huh? So I'll tell you later."

Assuming there was going to *be* a later.

When she was two-thirds of the way along the south shore of the lake, pushing the Jeep as fast as she dared, with the Mercedes just thirty-five yards behind, she saw the ridge-road turnoff ahead. It led up through the mountains past Clark's Summit, a ten-mile county road that cut off the thirty- or thirty-five-mile eastern loop of state route 38, rejoining that two-lane highway south near Barton Flats. As she recalled, the ridge road was paved for a couple of miles at each end but was only a graded dirt lane for six or seven miles in the middle. Unlike the Jeep, the Mercedes did not have four-wheel drive; it had winter tires, but they were not currently equipped with chains. The men driving the Mercedes were unlikely to know that the ridge road's pavement would give way to a rutted dirt surface patched with ice and in some places drifted over with snow.

"Hold on!" she told Chris.

She didn't use the brakes until the last moment, taking the right turn onto the ridge road so fast that the Jeep slid sideways with a tortured squeal of tires. It shuddered, too, as if it were an old horse that had been forced to make a frightening jump.

The Mercedes cornered better, though the driver had not known what she was going to do. As they headed into higher elevations and greater wilderness, the car closed the gap to about thirty yards.

Twenty-five. Twenty.

Thorny branches of lightning abruptly grew across the sky to the south. It was not as near to them as the lightning at the house but near enough to turn night to day around them. Even above the sound of the engine she could hear the roar of thunder.

Gaping at the stormy display, Chris said, "Mommy, what's going on? What's happening?"

"I don't know," she said, and she had to shout to be heard above the cacophony of the racing engine and clashing heavens.

She did not hear the gunfire itself but heard bullets smacking into the Jeep, and a slug punched a hole through the tailgate window and thudded into the back of the seat in which she and Chris were riding; she felt as well as heard its solid impact. She began to turn the wheel back and forth, weaving from one side of the road to the other, making as difficult a target as possible, which made her dizzy in the flickering light. Either the gunman stopped firing or missed them with every shot, because she did not hear any more incoming rounds. However, the weaving slowed her, and the Mercedes closed even faster.

She had to use the side mirrors instead of the rearview. Though most of the tailgate window was intact, the safety glass was webbed with thousands of tiny cracks that left it translucent and useless.

Fifteen yards, ten.

In the southern sky the lightning and thunder passed, as before.

She topped a rise, and the pavement ended halfway down the hill ahead of them. She stopped weaving, accelerated. When the Jeep left the blacktop, it shimmied for a moment, as if surprised by the change in road surface, but then streaked forward on the snow-spotted, ice-crusted, frozen dirt. They jolted across a series of ruts, through a short hollow where trees arched over them, and up the next hill.

In the side mirrors she saw the Mercedes cross the hollow on the dirt lane and start up the slope behind her. But as she reached the crest, the car began to founder in her wake. It slid sideways, its headlights swinging away from her. The driver overcorrected instead of turning the wheel into the slide, as he should have done. The car's tires began to spin uselessly. It slid not only off to the side but backward twenty yards, until the right rear wheel jolted into the drainage ditch that flanked the road; the headlight beams were canted up and angled across the dirt track.

"They're stuck!" Chris said.

"They'll need half an hour to get out of that mess." Laura continued over the crest, down the next slope of the dark ridge road.

Although she should have been exultant over their escape, or at least relieved, her fear was undiminished. She had a hunch that they were not yet safe, and she had learned to trust her hunches more than twenty years ago, when she had suspected the White Eel was going to come for her the night that she would have been alone in the end room by the stairs at McIlroy, the night when in fact he had left a Tootsie Roll under her pillow. After all, hunches were just messages from the subconscious, which was thinking furiously all the time and processing information she had not consciously noted.

Something was wrong. But what?

They made less than twenty miles an hour on that narrow, winding, potholed, rutted, frozen dirt track. For a while the road followed the rocky spine of a ridge where there were no trees, then traced the course of a declivity in the ridge wall, all the way to the floor of the parallel ravine, where trees were so thick on both sides that the headlights bouncing back from their trunks seemed to reveal phalanxes of pines as solid as board walls.

In the back of the wagon, her guardian murmured wordlessly in his fevered sleep. She was worried about him, and she wished that she could go faster, but she dared not.

For the first two miles after they lost their pursuers, Chris was silent. Finally he said, "At the house . . . did you kill any of them?"

She hesitated. "Yes. Two."

"Good."

Disturbed by the grim pleasure in the single word that he spoke, Laura said, "No, Chris, it isn't good to kill. It made me sick."

"But they deserved to be killed," he said.

"Yes, they did. But that doesn't mean it's pleasant to kill them. It's not. There's no satisfaction in it. Just . . . disgust at the necessity of it. And sadness."

"I wish I could've killed one of them," he said with tight, cold anger that was disturbing in a boy his age.

She glanced at him. With his face carved by shadows and the pale yellow light from the dashboard, he looked older than he was, and she had a glimpse of the man he would become.

When the ravine floor became too rocky to provide passage, the road rose again, following a shelf on the ridge wall.

She kept her eyes on the rude track. "Honey, we'll have to talk about this later at more length. Right now I just want you to listen carefully and try to understand something. There are a lot of bad philosophies in the world. You know what a philosophy is?"

"Sorta. No . . . not really."

"Then let's just say people believe in a lot of things that are bad for them to believe. But there are two things that different kinds of people believe that are the worst, most dangerous, *wrongest* of all. Some people believe the best way to solve a problem is with violence; they beat up or kill anyone who disagrees with them."

"Like these guys who're after us."

"Yes. Evidently that's the kind of people they are. That's a real bad way of thinking because violence leads to more violence. Besides, if you settle differences with a gun, there's no justice, no moment of peace, no hope. You follow me?"

"I guess so. But what's the other worst kind of bad thinking?"

"Pacifism," she said. "That's just the opposite of the first kind of bad thinking. Pacifists believe you should never lift a hand against another human being, no matter what he has done or what you know he's going to do. If a pacifist was standing beside his brother, and if he saw a man coming to kill his brother, he'd urge his brother to run, but he wouldn't pick up a gun and stop the killer."

"He'd let the guy go after his brother?" Chris asked, astonished.

"Yes. If worse came to worst, he'd let his brother be murdered rather than violate his own principles and become a killer himself."

"That's whacko."

They rounded the point of the ridge, and the road descended into another valley. The branches of overhanging pines were so low they scraped the roof; clumps of snow fell onto the hood and windshield.

Laura turned on the wipers and hunched over the steering wheel, using the change in terrain as an excuse not to talk until she had time to think how to make her point most clearly. They had endured a lot of violence in the past hour; much more violence no doubt lay ahead of them, and she was concerned that Chris develop a proper attitude toward it. She did not want him to get the idea that guns and muscle were acceptable substitutes for reason. On the other hand she did not want him to be traumatized by violence and learn to fear it at the cost of personal dignity and ultimate survival.

At last she said, "Some pacifists are cowards in disguise, but some really believe it's right to permit the murder of an innocent person rather than kill to stop it. They're wrong because by not fighting evil, they've become part of it. They're as bad as the guy who pulls the trigger. Maybe this is above your head right now, and maybe you'll have to do a lot of thinking before you understand, but it's important you realize there's a way to live that's in the middle, between killers and pacifists. You try to avoid violence. You never start it. But if someone else starts it, you defend yourself, friends, family, anyone who's in trouble. When I had to shoot those men at the house, it made me sick. I'm no hero. I'm not proud of having shot them, but I'm not ashamed of it, either. I don't want you to be proud of me for it, or think that killing them was satisfying, that revenge in any way makes me feel better about your dad's murder. It doesn't."

He was silent.

She said, "Did I dump too much on you?"

"No. I just gotta think about it a while," he said. "Right now, I'm thinking bad, I guess. 'Cause I want them all dead, all of them who had anything to do with . . . what happened to Dad. But I'll work on it, Mom. I'll try to be a better person."

She smiled. "I know you will, Chris."

During her conversation with Chris and for the few minutes of mutual silence that followed it, Laura continued to be plagued by the feeling that they were not yet out of imminent danger. They had gone about seven miles on the ridge road, with perhaps another mile of dirt track and two miles of pavement ahead before they connected with state route 38. The farther she drove, the more certain she became that she was overlooking something and that more trouble was drawing near.

She suddenly stopped on the spine of another ridge, just before the road dipped down again—and for the last time—toward lower land. She switched off the engine and the lights.

"What's wrong?" Chris asked.

"Nothing. I just need to think, have a look at our passenger."

She got out and went around to the back of the Jeep. She opened the tailgate, where a bullet had punched through the window. Chunks of safety glass broke out and fell on the ground at her feet. She climbed into the cargo bed and, lying next to her guardian, checked the wounded man's pulse. It was still weak, perhaps even slightly weaker than before, but it was regular. She put a hand to his head and found he was no longer cold; he seemed to be afire within. At her request Chris gave her the flashlight from the glove compartment. She pulled back the blankets to see if the man was bleeding worse than when they had loaded him into the Jeep. His wound looked bad, but there was not much fresh blood in spite of the bouncing that he had endured. She replaced the blankets, returned the flashlight to Chris, got out of the Jeep, and closed the tailgate.

She broke all of the remaining glass out of the tailgate window and out of the smaller rear window on the driver's side. With the glass missing completely, the damage was less conspicuous and less likely to draw the attention of a cop or anyone else.

For a while she stood in the cold air beside the wagon, staring out at the lightless wilderness, trying to force a connection between instinct and reason: Why was she so sure that she was heading for trouble and that the night's violence was not yet at an end?

The clouds were shredding in a high-altitude wind that harried them eastward, a wind that had not yet reached the ground, where the air was almost peculiarly still. Moonlight found its way through those ragged holes and eerily illuminated the snow-cloaked landscape of rising and falling hills, evergreens leeched of their color by the night, and clustered rock formations.

Laura looked south where in a few miles the ridge road led to state route 38, and everything in that direction seemed serene. She looked east, west, then back to the north from which they had come, and on all sides the San Bernardino Mountains were without a sign of human habitation, without a single light, and seemed to exist in primeval purity and peace.

She asked herself the same questions and gave the same answers that had been part of an interior dialogue for the past year. Where did the men with the belts come from? Another planet, another galaxy? No. They were as human as she was. So maybe they came from Russia. Maybe the belts acted like matter transmitters, devices akin to the teleportation chamber in that old movie, *The Fly*. That might explain her guardian's accent—if he'd teleported from Russia—but it didn't explain why he had not aged in a quarter of a century; besides, she did not seriously believe that the Soviet Union or anyone else had been perfecting matter transmitters since she was eight years old. Which left time travel.

She had been considering that possibility for some months, though she'd not even felt confident enough about her analysis to mention it to Thelma. But if her guardian had been entering her life at crucial points by time travel, he could have made all of his journeys in the space of a single month or week in his own era while many years had passed for her, so he would have appeared not to have aged. Until she could question him and learn the truth, the time-travel theory was the only one on which she could operate: Her guardian had traveled to her from some future world; and evidently it was an unpleasant future, because when speaking of the belt he had said, "You don't want to go where it'll take you," and there had been a bleak, haunted look in his eyes. She had no idea why a time traveler would come back from the future to protect her, of all people, from armed junkies and runaway pickup trucks, and she had no time to ponder the possibilities.

The night was quiet, dark, and cold.

They were heading straight into trouble.

She *knew* it, but she didn't know what it was or where it would come from.

When she got back into the Jeep, Chris said, "What's wrong now?"

"You're crazy about *Star Trek, Star Wars, Batteries Not Included,* all that stuff, so maybe what I've got here is the kind of background expert I seek out when I'm writing a novel. You're my resident expert in the weird."

The engine was switched off, and the interior of the Jeep was brightened only by the cloud-cloaked moonlight. But she was able to see Chris's face reasonably well because, during the few minutes she had been outside, her eyes had adapted to the night. He blinked at her and looked puzzled. "What're you talking about?"

"Chris, like I said earlier, I'm going to tell you all about the man lying back there, about the other strange appearances he's made in my life, but we don't have time for that now. So don't snow me under with lots of questions, okay? But just suppose my guardian—that's how I think of him, because he's protected me from terrible things when he could—suppose he was a time traveler from the future. Suppose he doesn't come in a big clumsy time machine. Suppose the whole machine is in a belt that he wears around his waist, under his clothes, and he just materializes out of thin air when he arrives here from the future. Are you with me so far?"

Chris was staring wide-eyed. "Is that what he is?"

"He might be, yes."

The boy freed himself from his safety harness, scrambled onto his knees on the seat, and looked back at the man lying in the compartment behind them. "Holy shit."

"Given the unusual circumstances," she said, "I'll overlook the foul language."

He glanced at her sheepishly. "Sorry. But a *time* traveler!"

If she had been angry with him, the anger would not have held, for she now saw in him a sudden rush of that boyish excitement and a capacity for wonder that he had not exhibited in a year, not even at Christmas when he had enjoyed himself immensely with Jason Gaines. The prospect of an encounter with a time traveler instantly filled him with a sense of adventure and joy. That was the splendid thing about life: Though it was cruel, it was also mysterious, filled with wonder and surprise; sometimes the surprises were so amazing that they qualified as miraculous, and by witnessing those miracles, a despondent person could discover a reason to live, a cynic could obtain unexpected relief from ennui, and a profoundly wounded boy could find the will to heal himself and medicine for melancholy.

She said, "Okay, suppose that when he wants to leave our time and return to his own, he presses a button on the special belt he wears."

"Can I see the belt?"

"Later. Remember, you promised not to ask a lot of questions just now."

"Okay." He looked again at the guardian, then turned and sat down, focusing his attention on his mother. "When he presses the button—what happens?"

"He just vanishes."

"Wow! And when he arrives from the future, does he just appear out of thin air?"

"I don't know. I've never seen him arrive. Though I think for some reason there's lightning and thunder—"

"The lightning tonight!"

"Yes, but there's not always lightning. All right. Suppose that he came back in time to help us, to protect us from certain dangers—"

"Like the runaway pickup."

"We don't know why he wants to protect us, can't know why until he tells us. Anyway, suppose other people from the future *don't* want us to be protected. We can't understand their motivations, either. But one of them was Kokoschka, the man who shot your father—"

"And the guys who showed up tonight at the house," Chris said, "they're from the future, too."

"I think so. They were planning to kill my guardian, you, and me. But we killed some of them instead and left two of them stranded in the Mercedes. So . . . what are they going to do next, kiddo? You're the resident expert on the weird. Do you have any ideas?"

"Let me think."

Moonlight gleamed dully on the dirty hood of the Jeep.

The interior of the station wagon was growing cold; their breath issued in frosty plumes, and the windows were beginning to fog over. Laura switched on the engine, heater, defroster, but not the lights.

Chris said, "Well, see, their mission failed, so they won't hang around. They'll go back to the future where they came from."

"Those two guys in our car?"

"Yeah. They probably already pushed the buttons on the belts of the guys you killed, sent the bodies back to the future, so there're no dead men at the house, no proof time travelers were ever there. Except maybe some blood. So when the last two or three guys got stuck in the ditch, they probably gave up and went home."

"So they aren't back there any more? They wouldn't walk back to Big Bear maybe, steal a car, and try to find us?"

"Nope. That would be too hard. I mean, they have an easier way to find us than to just drive around looking for us like regular bad guys would have to do."

"What way?"

The boy screwed up his face and squinted through the windshield at the snow and moonglow and darkness ahead. "See, Mom, as soon as they lost us, they'd push the buttons on their belts, go home to the future, and then make a *new* trip back to our time to set another trap for us. They knew we took this road. So what they probably did was make another trip back to our time, but earlier tonight, and they set a trap at the other end of this road, and now they're waiting there for us. Yeah, that's where they are! I'll just bet that's where they are."

"But why couldn't they come back even earlier tonight, earlier than they came the first time, back to the house, and attack us before my guardian ever showed up to warn us?"

"Paradox," the boy said. "You know what that means?"

The word seemed too complex for a boy his age, but she said, "Yes, I know what a paradox is. Anything that's self-contradictory but possibly true."

"See, Mom, the neat thing is that time travel is full of all kinds of possible paradoxes. Things that couldn't be true, shouldn't be true—but then might be." Now he was talking in that excited voice with which he described scenes in his favorite fantastic films and comic books, but with more intensity than she had ever heard before, probably because this was not a story but reality even more amazing than fiction. "Like suppose you went back in time and married your own grandfather. See, then you'd be your own grandmother. If time travel was possible, maybe you could do that—but then how could you have ever been born if your *real* grandmother had never married your grandfather in the first place? Paradox! Or what if you went back in time and met up with your mom when she was a kid and accidentally killed her? Would you just cease to exist—*pop!*—like you'd never been born? But if you ceased to exist—then how could you have gone back in time in the first place? Paradox! Paradox!"

Staring at him in the moon-painted darkness of the Jeep, Laura felt as though she was looking at a different boy from the one she had always known. Of course, she had been aware of his great fascination with space-age tales, which seemed to preoccupy most kids these days, regardless of age. But until now she hadn't gotten a deep look inside the mind shaped by those influences. Evidently the American children of the late twentieth century not only lived interior fantasy lives richer than those of children at any other time in history, but they seemed to have gotten from their fantasies something not provided by the elves and fairies and ghosts with which earlier generations of kids had entertained themselves: the ability to think about abstract concepts like space and time in a manner far beyond their intellectual and emotional age. She had the peculiar feeling that she was speaking to a little boy and a rocket scientist coexisting in one body.

Disconcerted, she said, "So . . . when these men failed to kill us on their first trip tonight, why wouldn't they make a second trip *earlier* than the first, to kill us before my guardian warned us that they were coming?"

"See, your guardian already showed up in the time stream to warn us. So if they came back *before* he warned us—then how could he have warned us in the first place, and how could we be here where we are now, alive? Paradox!"

He laughed and clapped his hands like a gnome chortling over some particularly amusing side-effect of a magical spell.

In contrast to his good humor, Laura was getting a headache from trying to sort out the complexities of this thing.

Chris said, "Some people believe time travel isn't even possible 'cause of all the paradoxes. But some believe it's possible so long as the trip you make into the past doesn't create a paradox. Now if *that's* true, see, then the killers couldn't come back on a second, earlier trip 'cause two of them had already been killed on the *first* trip. They couldn't do it because they were already dead, and it was a paradox. But the guys you didn't kill and maybe some *new* time travelers could make another trip to cut us off at the end of this road." He leaned forward to peer through the streaked windshield again. "That's what all that lightning was off to the south when we were weaving to keep them from shooting us—more guys from the future were arriving. Yeah, I'll bet they're waiting for us down there somewhere, down there in the dark."

Rubbing her temples with her fingertips, Laura said, "But if we turn around and go back, if we don't drive into the trap ahead, then they'll realize we've outthought them. And so they'll make a *third* trip back in time and return to the Mercedes and shoot us when we try to drive back that way. They'll get us no matter which way we go."

He shook his head vigorously. "No. Because by the time they realize we're on to them, maybe half an hour from now, we'll already have turned around and driven back past the Mercedes." The boy was bouncing up and down in his seat with excitement now. "So if they try to make a *third* trip in time to go back to the beginning of this road and trap us there, they can't do it, because we'll already have driven back that way and out, we'll already be safe. Paradox! See, they got to play by the rules, Mom. They're not magical. They got to play by the rules, and they can be beat!"

In thirty-three years she had never had a headache that had gone from a mild throb to a pounding skull-splitter as quickly as this one. The more she tried to puzzle out the difficulties of avoiding a pack of time-traveling hitmen, the deeper rooted the pain became.

Finally she said, "I give up. I guess I should've been watching *Star Trek* and reading Robert Heinlein all these years instead of being a serious adult, because I'm just not able to cope with this.

So I'll tell you what: I'm going to rely on *you* to outsmart them. You'll have to try to keep one step ahead of them. They want us dead. So how can they try to kill us without creating one of these paradoxes? Where will they show up next . . . and next? Right now, we're going to go back the way we came, past the Mercedes, and if you're right, no one will be waiting there for us. So where will they show up after that? Will we see them again tonight? Think about those things, and when you have any ideas, let me know what they are."

"I will, Mom." He slumped down in his seat, grinning broadly for a moment, then chewing on his lip as he settled deeper into the game.

Except it was not a game, of course. Their lives were really at stake. They had to elude killers with nearly superhuman abilities, and they were pinning their hopes of survival on nothing more than the richness of an eight-year-old boy's imagination.

Laura started the Jeep, put it in reverse, and backed up a couple of hundred yards until she found a place in the road wide enough to turn around. Then they headed back the way they had come, toward the Mercedes in the ditch, toward Big Bear.

She was beyond terror. Their situation contained such a large element of the unknown—and unknowable—that terror could not be sustained. Terror was not like happiness or depression; it was an *acute* condition that by its very nature had to be of a short term. Terror wilted fast. Or it escalated until you passed out or until you died of it, frightened to death; you screamed until a blood vessel burst in your brain. She wasn't screaming, and in spite of her headache she didn't think any vessels were going to burst. She settled into a low-key, chronic fear, hardly more than anxiety.

What a day this had been. What a year. What a life.

Exotic news.

·2·

They passed the stranded Mercedes and drove all the way to the north end of the ridge road without encountering men with submachine guns. At the intersection with the lakeside highway, Laura stopped and looked at Chris. "Well?"

"As long as we're driving around," he said, "and as long as we go to a place where we've never been and don't usually go, we're pretty safe. They can't find us if they don't have any idea where we might be. Just like your regular-type scumbags."

Scumbags? she thought. What is this—H. G. Wells meets *Hill Street Blues*?

He said, "See, now that we've given them the slip, these guys are going to go back to the future and look over the records they've got about you, Mom, your history, and they're going to see where you show up next—like when you want to go live in the house again. Or if you hid out for a year and wrote another book and then went on a tour for it, they'd show up at a store where you're signing books because, see, there'd be a *record* of that in the future; they'd know you could be found in that store at a certain time on a certain day."

She frowned. "You mean the only way to avoid them for the rest of my life is to change my name, go on the run forever, and leave no trace of myself on any public records, just vanish from recorded history from here on out?"

"Yeah, I think maybe that's what you'll have to do," he said excitedly.

He was smart enough to have figured out how to defeat a pack of time-traveling hitmen but not adult enough to perceive how hard it would be for them to forsake everything they owned and start with only the cash in their pockets. In a way he was like an idiot savant, tremendously insightful and gifted in one narrow area, but naive and severely limited in all other ways. In matters of time-travel theory, he was a thousand years old, but otherwise he was going on nine.

She said, "I can never write another book because I'd have to have contact with editors, agents, even if by phone. So there'd be phone records that could be traced. And I can't collect royalties because no matter how many blinds I use, no matter how many different bank accounts I shift the money through, sooner or later I have to collect the funds personally, which would leave a public record. So then they'd have that record in the future, and they'd travel back to the bank to wipe me out when I showed up. How am I supposed to get my hands on the money we *already* have? How can I cash a check anywhere without leaving a record that they would have in the future?" She blinked at him. "Good God, Chris, we're in a box!"

Now it was the boy's turn to be baffled. He looked at her with little understanding of where money came from, how it was put aside for future use, or how difficult it was to obtain. "Well, for a couple of days, we can just drive around, sleep in motels—"

"We can only sleep in motels if I pay cash. A credit card record might be all they need to find us. Then they'd come back in time to the night I used the credit card, and they'd kill us at the motel."

"Yeah, so we use cash. Hey, we can eat at McDonald's all the time! That doesn't take much money, and it's *good.*"

They drove down from the mountains, out of the snow, into San Bernardino, a city of about 300,000, without encountering assassins. She needed to get their guardian to a doctor, not only because she owed him a debt of life, but also because without him she might never learn the truth of what was happening and might never find a way out of the box they were in.

She could not take him to a hospital because hospitals kept records, which might give her enemies from the future a way of finding her. She would have to obtain medical care secretly, from someone who would not have to be told her name or anything about the patient.

Shortly before midnight she stopped at a telephone booth near a Shell service station. The phone was at the corner of the property, away from the station itself, which was ideal because she could not risk an attendant noticing the Jeep's broken windows or the unconscious man.

In spite of the hour-long nap the boy had gotten earlier and in spite of the excitement, Chris had dozed off. In the compartment behind the front seat, their guardian was sleeping, too, but his sleep was neither restful nor natural. He was not mumbling much any more, but for minutes at a stretch he drew breath with a dismaying wheeze and rattle.

She left the Jeep in park, the engine running, and went into the telephone booth to look through the directory. She tore out the Yellow Pages' listings for physicians.

After obtaining a street map of San Bernardino from the attendant in the service station, she began searching for a doctor who did not operate out of a clinic or medical office building but from an office attached to his home, which was how most doctors in small towns and cities had worked in years gone by, though these days few continued to keep home and office together. She was acutely aware that the longer she took to find help, the smaller the chance that their guardian would survive.

At a quarter past one, in a quiet residential neighborhood of older homes, she pulled in front of a two-story, white, Victorian house built in another era, in a lost California, before everything had been constructed of stucco. It stood on a corner lot, with a two-car garage, shaded by alders that were leafless in the middle of winter, a touch that made it seem like a place transported entirely, landscaping and all, from the East. According to the pages she had torn from the telephone directory, this was the address for Dr. Carter Brenkshaw, and beside the driveway a small sign suspended between two wrought-iron posts confirmed the directory's accuracy.

She drove to the end of the block and parked at the curb. She got out of the Jeep, scooped a handful of damp earth from a flowerbed in front of a nearby house, and smeared the dirt over the front and back license plates as best she could.

By the time she wiped her hand in the grass and got back in the Jeep, Chris had awakened but was groggy and confused after being asleep for more than two hours. She patted his face and pushed his hair back from his forehead and rapidly talked him awake. The cold night air, flowing through the broken windows, helped too.

"Okay," she said when she was sure he was awake, "listen closely, partner. I've found a doctor. Can you act sick?"

"Sure." He made a face as if he was going to puke, then gagged and moaned.

"Don't overplay it." She explained what they were going to do.

"Good plan, Mom."

"No, it's nuts. But it's the only plan I've got."

She swung the car around and drove back to Brenkshaw's, where she parked in the driveway in front of the closed garage, which was set back from the house. Chris slid out by the driver's door, and she picked him up and held him against her left side, his head against her shoulder. He held on to her, so she only needed her left arm to keep him in place, though he was quite heavy; her baby was not a baby any more. In her free hand she gripped the revolver.

As she carried Chris along the walk, past the stark alders, with no light except a purplish glow from one of the widely spaced mercury-vapor streetlamps out at the curb, she hoped no one was at a window in any of the nearby houses. On the other hand it probably wasn't unusual for someone to visit a doctor's house in the middle of the night, needing treatment.

She went up the front steps, across the porch, and rang the bell three times, quick, as a frantic mother might do. She waited only a few seconds before ringing it three more times.

In a couple of minutes, after she had rung the bell again and was beginning to think that no one was home, the porch lights came on. She saw a man studying her through the three-pane, fan-shaped window in the top third of the door.

"Please," she said urgently, holding the revolver at her side where it could not be seen, "my boy, poison, he's swallowed poison!"

The man opened the door inward, and there was an outward-opening glass storm door, as well, so Laura stepped out of its way.

He was about sixty-five, white-haired, with a face that was Irish except for a strong Roman nose and dark brown eyes. He was dressed in a brown robe, white pajamas, and slippers. Peering at her over the rims of tortoiseshell glasses, he said, "What's wrong?"

"I live two blocks down, you're so close, and my boy—poison." At the height of her hysteria, she let go of Chris, and he got out of her way as she shoved the muzzle of the .38 against the man's belly. "I'll blow your guts out if you call for help."

She had no intention of shooting him, but she apparently sounded convincing, for he nodded and said nothing.

"Are you Dr. Brenkshaw?" He nodded again, and she said, "Who else is in the house, Doctor?"

"No one. I'm alone here."

"Your wife?"

"I'm a widower."

"Children?"

"All grown and gone."

"Don't lie to me."

"I've made a lifetime habit of not lying," he said. "It's gotten me in trouble a few times, but telling the truth generally makes life simpler. Look, it's chilly, and this robe's thin. You can intimidate me as well if you come inside."

She stepped across the threshold, keeping the gun in his belly and pushing him backward with it. Chris followed her. "Honey," she whispered, "go check out the house. Quietly. Start upstairs, and don't miss a room. If there's anyone here, tell them the doctor has an emergency patient and needs their help."

Chris headed for the stairs, and Laura kept Carter Brenkshaw in the foyer at gunpoint. Nearby a grandfather clock was ticking softly.

"You know," he said, "I've been a lifelong reader of thrillers."

She frowned. "What do you mean?"

"Well, I've often read a scene in which a gorgeous villainness held the hero against his will. As often as not, when he finally turned the tables on her, she surrendered to the inevitability of masculine triumph, and they made wild, passionate love. So when it happens to me, why do I have to be too old to enjoy the prospect of the second half of this little showdown?"

Laura held back a smile because she could not continue to pretend to be dangerous once she allowed herself to smile. "Shut up."

"Surely you can do better than that."

"Just shut up, all right? Shut up."

He did not go pale or begin to tremble. He smiled.

Chris returned from upstairs. "Nobody, Mom."

Brenkshaw said, "I wonder how many dangerous thugs have pint-size accomplices who call them Mom?"

"Don't misjudge me, Doctor. I'm desperate."

Chris disappeared into the downstairs rooms, turning on lights as he went.

To Brenkshaw, Laura said, "I've got a wounded man in the car—"

"Of course, a gunshot."

"—I want you to treat him and keep your mouth shut about it, 'cause if you don't, we'll come back some night and blow you away."

"This," he said almost merrily, "is perfectly delicious."

As Chris returned, he switched off the lights he had switched on moments ago. "Nobody, Mom."

"You have a stretcher?" Laura asked the physician.

Brenkshaw stared at her. "You really do have a wounded man?"

"What the hell else would I be doing here?"

"How peculiar. Well, all right, how badly is he bleeding?"

"A lot earlier, not so much now. But he's unconscious."

"If he's not bleeding badly now, we can roll him in. I've got a collapsible wheelchair in my office. Can I get an overcoat," he said, pointing to the foyer closet, "or do tough molls like you get a thrill out of making old men shiver in their peejays?"

"Get your coat, Doctor, but damn it, don't underestimate me."

"Yeah," Chris said. "She shot two guys already tonight." He imitated the sound of an Uzi. "She just cut 'em down, and they never had a chance to lay a hand on her."

The boy sounded so sincere that Brenkshaw looked at Laura with new concern. "There's nothing but coats in the closet. Umbrellas. A pair of galoshes. I don't keep a gun in there."

"Just be careful, Doctor. No fast moves."

"No fast moves—yes, I knew you'd say that." Though he still

seemed to find the situation to some degree amusing, he was not quite as lighthearted about it as he had been.

When he had pulled on his overcoat, they went with him through a door to the left of the foyer. Without snapping on a light, relying on the glow from the foyer and on his familiarity with the place, Dr. Brenkshaw led them through a patients' waiting room that contained straight-backed chairs and a couple of end tables. Another door led into his office—a desk, three chairs, medical books—where he did turn on a light, and a door from the office led farther back in the house to his examination room.

Laura had expected to see an examination table and equipment that had been in use and well maintained for thirty-odd years, a homely den of medicine straight out of a Norman Rockwell painting, but everything looked new. There was even an EKG machine, and at the far end of the room was a door with a sign that warned X-RAY: KEEP CLOSED IN USE.

"You have X-ray equipment here?" she asked.

"Sure. It's not as expensive as it once was. Every clinic has X-ray equipment these days."

"Every clinic, yes, but this is just a one-man—"

"I may look like Barry Fitzgerald playing at being a doctor in an old movie, and I may prefer the old-fashioned convenience of an office in my home, but I don't give patients outdated care just to be quaint. I dare say, I'm a more serious physician than you are a desperado."

"Don't bet on that," she said harshly, though she was getting tired of pretending to be cold-blooded.

"Don't worry," he said. "I'll play along. Seems like it'll be more fun if I do." To Chris, he said, "When we came through my office, did you notice a big, red-ceramic jar on the desk? It's full of orange-slice candies and Tootsie Pops if you want some."

"Wow, thanks!" Chris said. "Uh . . . can I have a piece, Mom?"

"A piece or two," she said, "but don't make yourself sick."

Brenkshaw said, "When it comes to giving sweet treats to young patients, I'm old-fashioned, I guess. No sugar-free gum here. What the hell fun is that stuff? Tastes like plastic. If their teeth rot out after they visit me, that's their dentist's problem."

While he talked, he got a folding wheelchair from the corner, unfolded it, and rolled it to the middle of the room.

Laura said, "Honey, you stay here while we go out to the Jeep."

"Okay," Chris said from the next room, where he was peering into the red-ceramic jar, selecting his treat.

"Your Jeep in the driveway?" Brenkshaw asked. "Then let's go out the back. Less conspicuous, I think."

Pointing the revolver at the physician but feeling foolish, Laura followed him out of a side door in the examination room, which opened onto a ramp, so there was no need to descend stairs.

"Handicapped entrance," Brenkshaw said quietly over his shoulder as he pushed the wheelchair along a walk toward the back of the house. His bedroom slippers made a crisp sound on the concrete.

The physician had a large property, so the neighboring house did not loom over them. Instead of being planted with alders as was the front lawn, the side yard was graced with ficus and pines, which were green all year. In spite of the screening branches and the darkness, however, Laura could see the blank windows of the neighboring place, so she supposed that she could be seen, as well, if anyone looked.

The world had the hushed quality that it possessed only between midnight and dawn. Even if she had not known it was going on two in the morning, she would have been able to guess the time within half an hour. Though faint city noises echoed in the distance, there was a cemeterial stillness that would have made her feel like a woman on a secret mission even if she had only been taking out the garbage.

The walk led around the house, crossing another walk that extended to the back of the property. They went past the rear porch, through an areaway between house and garage, into the driveway.

Brenkshaw halted at the back of the Jeep and chuckled. "Mud on the license plates," he whispered. "Convincing touch."

After she put the tailgate down, he got into the back of the Jeep to have a look at the wounded man.

She looked out toward the street. All was silent. Still.

But if a San Bernardino Police cruiser happened to drive by now on a routine patrol, the officer would surely stop to see what was up at kindly old Doc Brenkshaw's place. . . .

Brenkshaw was already crawling out of the Jeep. "By God, you *do* have a wounded man in there."

"Why the hell do you keep being surprised? Would I pull this kind of stunt for laughs?"

"Let's get him inside. Quickly," Brenkshaw said.

He could not handle her guardian by himself. In order to help him, Laura had to stick the .38 in the waistband of her jeans.

Brenkshaw made no attempt to run or to knock her down and get the weapon away from her. Instead, as soon as he had the wounded man in the wheelchair, he rolled him out of the drive, through the areaway, and around the house to the handicapped entrance at the far side.

She grabbed one of the Uzis from the front seat and followed Brenkshaw. She didn't think she'd have any use for the automatic carbine, but she felt better with it in her hands.

Fifteen minutes later, Brenkshaw turned from the developed X-rays that hung on a lightboard in a corner of his examination room. "The bullet didn't fragment, made a clean exit. Didn't nick any bones, so we don't have chips to worry about."

"Terrific," Chris said from a corner chair, happily sucking on a Tootsie Pop. In spite of the warm air in the house, Chris was still wearing his jacket, as was Laura, because she wanted them to be ready to get out on short notice.

"Is he in a coma or what?" Laura asked the doctor.

"Yes, he's comatose. Not from any fever associated with a bad infection of the wound. Too early for that. And now that he's gotten treatment, there probably won't be an infection. It's traumatic coma from being shot, the loss of blood, the shock and all. He shouldn't have been moved, you know."

"I had no choice. Will he come out of it?"

"Probably. In this case a coma is the body's way of shutting down to conserve energy, facilitate healing. He's not lost as much blood as it appears; he's got a good pulse, so this probably won't last long. When you see his shirt and lab coat soaked like that, you think he's bled quarts, but he hasn't. Not that it was a spoonful, either. He's had a bad time of it. But no major blood vessels were torn, or he'd be in worse shape. Still, he should be in a hospital."

"We've already been through that," Laura said impatiently. "We can't go to a hospital."

"What bank did you rob?" the physician asked teasingly, but with noticeably less twinkle in his eyes than there had been when he had made his other little jokes.

While he waited for the pictures to develop, he had cleaned the wound, flooded it with iodine, dusted it with antibiotic powder, and prepared a bandage. Now he got a needle, another implement she could not identify, and heavy thread from a cabinet and put them on a stainless-steel tray that he had hung on the side of the examination table. The wounded man lay there, unconscious, propped on his right side with the help of several foam pillows.

"What're you doing?" Laura asked.

"Those holes are fairly large, especially the exit wound. If you insist on endangering his life by keeping him out of a hospital, then the least I can do is throw a few stitches in him."

"Well, all right, but be quick about it."

"You expect G-men to break down the door any minute?"

"Worse than that," she said. "Far worse than that."

Since they had arrived at Brenkshaw's, she had been expecting a sudden, night-shattering display of lightning, thunder like the giant hooves of apocalyptic horsemen, and the arrival of more well-armed time travelers. Fifteen minutes ago, as the doctor had been X-raying her guardian's chest, she'd thought she heard thunder so distant that it was barely audible. She hurried to the nearest window to search the sky for far-off lightning, but she saw none through the breaks in the trees, perhaps because the sky over San Bernardino already had a ruddy glow from city lights or perhaps because she had not heard thunder in the first place. She had finally decided that she might have heard a jet passing overhead and, in her panic, had misinterpreted it as a more distant sound.

Brenkshaw stitched up his patient, snipped the thread—"sutures will dissolve"—and bound the bandages in place with wide adhesive tape that he repeatedly wound around the guardian's chest and back.

The air had a pungent, medicinal smell that made Laura slightly ill, but it did not bother Chris. He sat in the corner, happily working on another Tootsie Pop.

While waiting for the X-rays, Brenkshaw also had administered an injection of penicillin. Now he went to the tall, white, metal cabinets along the far wall and poured capsules from a large jar into a pill bottle, then from another large jar into a second small bottle. "I keep some basic drugs here, sell them to poorer patients at cost so they don't have to go broke at the pharmacy."

"What're these?" Laura asked when he returned to the examination table, where she stood, and gave her the two small plastic bottles.

"More penicillin in this one. Three a day, with meals—if he can take meals. I *think* he'll come around soon. If he doesn't he'll begin to dehydrate, and he'll need intravenous fluid. Can't give him liquid by mouth when he's in a coma—he'd choke. This other is a painkiller. Only when needed, and no more than two a day."

"Give me more of these. In fact give me your whole supply." She pointed to two quart jars that contained hundreds of both capsules.

"He won't need that much of either one. He—"

"No, I'm sure he won't," she said, "but I don't know what the hell other problems we're going to have. We may need both penicillin and painkillers for me—or my boy."

Brenkshaw stared at her for a long moment. "What in the name of God have you gotten into? It's like something in one of your books."

"Just give me—" Laura stopped, stunned by what he had said. "Like something in one of my books? *In one of my books!* Oh, my God, you know who I am."

"Of course. I've known almost from the moment I saw you on the porch. I read thrillers, as I said, and although your books aren't strictly in that genre, they're very suspenseful, so I read them, too, and your photograph's on the back of the jacket. Believe me, Ms. Shane, no man would forget your face once he'd seen it, even if he'd seen it only in pictures and even if he was an old crock like me."

"But why didn't you say—"

"At first I thought it was a joke. After all, the melodramatic way you appeared on my doorstep in the dead of night, the gun, the corny, hard-boiled dialogue . . . it all seemed like a gag. Believe me, I have certain friends who might think of such an elaborate hoax and, if they knew you, might be able to persuade you to join in the fun."

Pointing to her guardian, she said, "But when you saw him—"

"Then I knew it was no joke," the physician said.

Hurrying to his mother's side, Chris pulled the Tootsie Pop from his mouth. "Mom, if he tells on us . . ."

Laura had drawn the .38 from her waistband. She began to raise it, then lowered her hand as she realized the gun no longer had any power to intimidate Brenkshaw; in fact it had never frightened him. For one thing she now realized he was not the kind of man who could be intimidated, and for another thing she could not convincingly portray a lawless, dangerous woman when he knew who she really was.

On the examination table her guardian groaned and tried to shift in his unnatural sleep, but Brenkshaw put a hand upon his chest and stilled him.

"Listen, Doctor, if you tell anyone what happened here tonight, if you can't keep my visit a secret for the rest of your life, it'll be the death of me and my boy."

"Of course the law requires a physician to report any gunshot wounds he treats."

"But this is a special case," Laura said urgently. "I'm not on the run from the law, Doctor."

"Who are you running from?"

"In a sense . . . from the same men who killed my husband, Chris's father."

He looked surprised and pained. "Your husband was killed?"

"You must've read about it in the papers," she said bitterly. "It made a sensational story there for a while, the kind of thing the press loves."

"I'm afraid I don't read newspapers or watch television news," Brenkshaw said. "It's all fires, accidents, and crazed terrorists. They don't report real news, just blood and tragedy and politics. I'm sorry about your husband. And if these people who killed him, whoever they are, want to kill you now, you should go straight to the police."

Laura liked this man and thought they shared more views and sympathies than not. He seemed reasonable, kind. Yet she had little hope of persuading Brenkshaw to keep his mouth shut. "The police can't protect me, Doctor. No one can protect me except *me*—and maybe that man whose wounds you just sewed up. These people who're after us . . . they're relentless, implacable, and they're beyond the law."

He shook his head. "No one is beyond the law."

"*They* are, Doctor. It'd take me an hour to explain to you why they are, and then you probably wouldn't believe me. But I beg of you, unless you want our deaths on your conscience, keep your mouth shut about our being here. Not just for a few days but forever."

"Well . . ."

Studying him, she knew it was no use. She remembered what he had told her in the foyer earlier, when she had warned him not to lie about the presence of other people in the house: He did not lie, he said, because always telling the truth made life simpler; telling the truth was a lifelong habit. Hardly forty-five minutes later, she knew him well enough to believe that he was indeed an unusually truthful man. Even now, as she begged him to keep their visit secret, he was not able to tell the lie that would placate her and get her out of his office. He stared at her guiltily and could not tease the falsehood from his tongue. He would do his duty when she left; he would file a police report. The cops would look for her at her house near Big Bear, where they would discover the blood if not the bodies of the time travelers, and where they would find hundreds of expended bullets, shattered windows, slug-pocked walls. By tomorrow or the next day the story would be splashed across the newspapers. . . .

The airliner that had flown overhead more than half an hour ago might not have been a passing jet, after all. It might well have been what she had first thought it was—very distant thunder, fifteen or twenty miles away.

More thunder on a night without rain.

"Doctor, help me get him dressed," she said, indicating her guardian on the table beside them. "Do at least that much for me, since you're going to betray me later."

He winced visibly at the word *betray*.

Earlier she'd sent Chris upstairs to get one each of Brenkshaw's shirts, sweaters, jackets, slacks, a pair of his socks, and shoes. The physician was not as muscular and trim as her guardian, but they were approximately the same size.

At the moment the wounded man was wearing only his blood-stained pants, but Laura knew there would not be time to put all the clothes on him. "Just help me get him into the jacket, Doctor. I'll take the rest and dress him later. The jacket will be enough to protect him from the cold."

Reluctantly lifting the unconscious man into a sitting position on the examination table, the doctor said, "He shouldn't be moved."

Ignoring Brenkshaw, struggling to pull the wounded man's right arm through the sleeve of the warmly lined corduroy jacket, Laura said, "Chris, go to the waiting room at the front of the house. It's dark in there. Don't turn on the lights. Go to the windows and give the street a good looking over, and for God's sake don't let yourself be seen."

"You think they're here?" the boy asked fearfully.

"If not now, they will be soon," she said, working her guardian's left arm through the other jacket sleeve.

"What're you talking about?" Brenkshaw asked, as Chris dashed into the adjoining office and on into the dark waiting room.

Laura didn't answer. "Come on, let's get him in the wheelchair."

Together, they lifted the wounded man off the examination table, into the chair, and buckled a restraining strap around his waist.

As Laura was gathering up the other clothes and the two quart-sized jars of drugs, making a bundle, padding the clothes around the jars and tying it all together in the shirt, Chris raced back from the waiting room. "Mom, they're just pulling up outside, it must be them, two cars full of men across the street, six or eight of 'em, anyway. What're we going to do?"

"Damn," she said, "we can't get to the Jeep now. And we can't go out the side door because they might see us from the front."

Brenkshaw headed toward his office. "I'll call the police—"

"No!" She put the bundle of clothes and drugs on the wheelchair between her guardian's legs, put her purse there, too, and snatched up the Uzi and .38 Chief's Special. "There's no time, damn you. They'll be in here in a couple of minutes, and they'll kill us. You've got to help me get the wheelchair out the back, down the rear porch steps."

Apparently her terror was at last conveyed to the physician, for he did not hesitate or continue to work at cross purposes to her. He grabbed the chair and wheeled it swiftly through a door that connected the examination room to the downstairs hall. Laura and Chris followed him along the gloomy corridor, then across a kitchen lit only by the illuminated digital clocks on the oven and microwave oven. The chair thumped over the sill between the kitchen and the back porch, badly jarring the wounded man, but he had been through worse.

Slinging the Uzi over her shoulder and jamming the revolver into her waistband, Laura hurried around Brenkshaw to the bottom of the porch steps. She took hold of the wheelchair from the front, helping him trundle it to the concrete walk below.

She glanced at the areaway between the house and garage, half expecting to see an armed man coming through there already, and she whispered to Brenkshaw, "You'll have to go with us. They'll kill you if you stay here, I'm sure they will."

Again he offered no argument but followed Chris, as the boy led the way down the walk that struck across the rear lawn to the gate in the redwood fence at the back of the long property. Having unslung the Uzi from her shoulder, Laura came last, ready to turn and open fire if she heard a noise from the house behind them.

As Chris reached the gate, it opened in front of him, and a man dressed in black stepped through from the alley, darker than the night around them except for his moon-pale face and white hands, every bit as surprised by them as they were by him. He'd come along the street beside the house and into the alley to cover the place from the back. In his left hand, gleaming darkly, was a submachine gun, not at the ready, but he started to bring it up—Laura could not blow him away, not without cutting her son down as well—but Chris reacted as Henry Takahami had spent months teaching him to react. The boy spun and kicked the assassin's right arm, knocking the gun out of his grasp—it hit the lawn with a thump and soft clatter—then kicked again at his adversary's crotch, and with a grunt of pain, the man in black fell backward against the gatepost.

By then Laura had stepped around the wheelchair and interposed herself between Chris and the killer. She reversed the Uzi, raised it overhead, and brought the stock of it down on the assassin's skull, struck him again with all her might, and he dropped to the lawn, away from the walk, without having had a chance to cry out.

Events were moving fast now, too fast, they were on a downhill ride, and already Chris was going through the gate, so Laura followed, and they surprised a second man in black, eyes like holes in his white face, a vampiric figure, but this one was beyond the reach of a karate kick, so she had to open fire before he could use his own weapon. She shot over Chris's head, a tightly placed burst that pounded into the assassin's chest, throat, and neck, virtually decapitating him as it catapulted him backward onto the alley pavement.

Brenkshaw had come through the gate behind them, pushing the wheelchair into the alley, and Laura felt bad about having gotten him into this, but there was no going back now. The back street was narrow, flanked by the fenced yards of houses on both sides, with a few garages and clusters of garbage cans behind each property, poorly revealed by the lamps on the intersecting streets at each end of the block, with no lights of its own.

To Brenkshaw, Laura said, "Wheel him across the alley and down a couple of doors. Find a gate that's open and get him into somebody else's yard, out of sight. Chris, you go with them."

"What about you?"

"I'll follow you in a second."

"Mom—"

"Go, Chris!" she said, for the physician had already rolled the wheelchair fifty feet, angling across the alleyway.

As the boy reluctantly followed the doctor, Laura returned to the open redwood gate at the rear of Brenkshaw's property. She was just in time to see two dark figures scuttle out of the areaway between the house and garage, thirty yards from her, barely visible, noticeable only because they were moving. They ran crouched, one of them heading toward the porch and the other toward the lawn because they didn't yet know exactly where the trouble was, where the gunfire had come from.

She stepped through the gate, onto the walk, and opened up on them before they saw her, spraying the back of the house with bullets. Though she was not on top of her targets, she was in range—ninety feet was not far—and they dove for cover. She could not tell if she hit them, and she didn't continue to fire because even with a magazine of four hundred rounds expended in short bursts, the Uzi could empty quickly; and now it was the only automatic weapon she still possessed. She backed out of the gate and ran after Brenkshaw and Chris.

They were just going through a wrought-iron gate at the back of a property on the other side of the alley, two doors down. When she got there and stepped into the yard, she found that old eugenias were planted along the iron fence to the left and right of the gate; they had grown into a dense hedge, so no one would spot her easily from the alley unless they were directly in front of the gate itself.

The physician had pushed the wheelchair all the way to the back of the house. It was Tudor, not Victorian like Brenkshaw's, but also built at least forty or fifty years ago. The doctor was starting around the side of the place, into the driveway, heading toward the next major street.

Lights winked on in houses all over the neighborhood. She was sure that faces were pressed to windows, including those where lights had not appeared, but she didn't think anyone would see much.

She caught up with Brenkshaw and Chris at the front of the house and halted them in shadows near some overgrown shrubbery. "Doc, I'd like you to wait here with your patient," she whispered.

He was shaking, and she hoped to God he didn't have a heart attack, but he was still game. "I'll be here."

She took Chris out to the next street, where at least a score of cars were parked at the near and far curbs along that block. In the rain of bluish light from the streetlamps, the boy looked bad but not as awful as she had feared, not as frightened as the physician; he was growing accustomed to terror. She said, "Okay, let's start trying car doors. You take this side, I'll take the far side. If the door is open, check the ignition, under the driver's seat, and behind the sun visor for keys."

"Gotcha."

Having once done research for a book in which a character had been a car thief, she had learned among other things that on average one out of seventeen drivers left his keys in his car overnight. She hoped the figure might be even more in their favor in a place like San Bernardino; after all, in New York and Chicago and LA and other big cities, nobody but masochists left their keys in their cars, so for the average to work out to one in seventeen, there had to be more trusting people among other Americans.

She attempted to keep an eye on Chris as she tried the doors of the cars along the far side of the street, but she soon lost track of him. Out of the first eight vehicles, four were unlocked, but no keys were in any of them.

In the distance rose the wail of sirens.

That would probably drive off the men in black. Anyway, they were most likely still searching along the alleyway behind Brenkshaw's house, moving cautiously, expecting to be fired upon again.

Laura moved boldly, with no caution whatsoever, not concerned about being seen by residents in the flanking houses. The street was lined with mature but squat, stunted date palms that provided a lot of cover. Anyway, if anyone had been aroused at this dead hour of the night, they were probably at second-floor windows, not trying to look down at their own street through the palms but over toward the next street, toward Brenkshaw's place, where all the shooting had been.

The ninth vehicle was an Oldsmobile Cutlass, and there were keys under the seat. Just as she started the engine and pulled her door shut, Chris opened the door on the passenger's side and showed her a set of keys that he had found.

"Brand new Toyota," he said.

"This'll do," she said.

The sirens were closer.

Chris pitched the Toyota's keys away, hopped into the car, and rode with her to the driveway of the house on the other side of the street, farther up toward the corner, where the doctor was waiting in the shadows along the driveway of a house in which no lights had yet come on. Maybe they were in luck; maybe no one was home at that place. They lifted her guardian out of the wheelchair and laid him on the rear seat of the Cutlass.

The sirens were very close now, and in fact a police cruiser shot past at the far end of that block, on the side street, red beacons flashing, heading toward Brenkshaw's block.

"You'll be okay, Doctor?" she asked, turning to him as she closed the back door of the Cutlass.

He had dropped into the wheelchair. "No apoplexy, if that's what you're afraid of. What the *hell* is going on with you, girl?"

"No time, Doc. I have to split."

"Listen," he said, "maybe I won't tell them anything."

"Yes, you will," she said. "You may think you won't, but you'll tell them everything. If you weren't going to tell them, then there wouldn't have been a police report or a newspaper story, and without that record in the future, those gunmen couldn't have found me."

"What're you jibbering about?"

She leaned down and kissed his cheek. "No time to explain, Doc. Thanks for your help. And, sorry, but I'd better take that wheelchair too."

He folded it and put it in the trunk for her.

The night was full of sirens now.

She got behind the wheel, slammed her door. "Buckle up, Chris."

"Buckled," he said.

She turned left at the end of the driveway and drove to the far corner of the block, away from Brenkshaw's end of the neighborhood, to the intersecting street on which a cruiser had flashed by only a moment ago. She figured that if police were converging in answer to reports of automatic-weapons fire, they would be coming from different areas of the city, from different patrols, so maybe no other car would approach by that same route. The avenue was nearly deserted, and the only other vehicles she saw were not fitted with rooftop emergency beacons. She turned right, heading steadily farther away from the Brenkshaw place, across San Bernardino, wondering where she would find sanctuary.

·3·

Laura reached Riverside at 3:15 in the morning, stole a Buick from a quiet residential street, shifted her guardian to it with the wheelchair, and abandoned the Cutlass. Chris slept through the entire operation and had to be carried from one car to the other.

Half an hour later, in another neighborhood, exhausted and in need of sleep, she used a screwdriver from a tool pouch in the Buick's trunk to steal a set of license plates from a Nissan. She put the Nissan's plates on the Buick and put the Buick's plates in the trunk because they would eventually turn up on a police hot sheet.

A couple of days might pass before the Nissan's owner noticed his plates were missing, and even when he reported them stolen, the police would not treat that news with the same attention they gave to stolen cars. Plates were usually taken by kids playing a stupid prank or vandals, and their recovery was not a high priority for overworked police laboring under heavy caseloads of major crimes. That was one more useful fact she had learned while researching the book in which a car thief had played a secondary role.

She also paused long enough to dress her guardian in wool socks, shoes, and a pullover sweater to keep him from catching a chill. At one point he opened his eyes, blinked at her, and said her name, and she thought he was coming around, but then he slipped away again, muttering in a language that she could not identify because she could not hear any of the words clearly.

She drove from Riverside to Yorba Linda in Orange County, where she parked in a corner of a Ralph's Supermarket lot, behind a Goodwill collection station, at 4:50 in the morning. She killed the engine and lights, unbuckled her safety harness. Chris was still buckled up, leaning against the door, sound asleep. Lying on the back seat, her guardian was still unconscious, though his breathing was not quite as wheezy as it had been before they had visited Carter Brenkshaw. Laura did not think she would be able to doze off; she hoped just to collect her wits and rest her eyes, but in a minute or two she was asleep.

After killing at least three men, after being shot at repeatedly, after stealing two cars, after surviving a chase that had harried her through three counties, she might have expected to dream of death, of blasted bodies and blood, with the cold chatter of automatic-weapons fire as background music to the nightmare. She might have expected to dream of losing Chris, for he was one of the two remaining lights in her personal darkness, he and Thelma, and she dreaded the thought of going on without him. But instead she dreamed of Danny, and they were lovely dreams, not nightmares. Danny was alive again, and they were reliving the sale of *Shadrach* for more than one million dollars, but Chris was there, too, and he was eight years old, though in fact Chris had not been born at that time, and they were celebrating their good fortune by spending the day at Disneyland, where the three of them had their picture taken with Mickey Mouse, and in the Carnation Pavilion Danny told her he'd love her forever, while Chris pretended that he could speak in an all-snort pig language that he had learned from Carl Dockweiler, who was sitting at the next table with Nina and with Laura's father, and at another table the amazing Ackerson twins were eating strawberry sundaes. . . .

She woke more than three hours later at 8:26, feeling rested as much because of that familial communion, provided by her subconscious, as because of the sleep itself. Sunlight from a cloudless sky sparkled on the car's chrome and fell in a bright, brassy shaft through the rear window. Chris was still dozing. In the back seat the wounded man had not regained consciousness.

She risked a quick walk to a telephone booth beside the market, which was within sight of the car. With change she had in her purse, she called Ida Palomar, Chris's tutor in Lake Arrowhead, to tell her they would be away from home all week. She did not want poor Ida to walk unsuspecting into the bullet-riddled, blood-spattered house near Big Bear, where police forensic teams were no doubt hard at work. She did not tell Ida where she was calling from; nevertheless, she did not intend to remain in Yorba Linda much longer.

After she returned to the car, she sat yawning, stretching, and massaging the back of her neck, as she watched early shoppers entering and leaving the supermarket a couple of hundred feet away. She was hungry. With sleep-matted eyes and sour breath, Chris woke less than ten minutes later, and she gave him money to go into the market and buy a package of sweet rolls and two pints of orange juice, not the most nutritional breakfast but energy-giving.

"What about him?" Chris asked, indicating her guardian.

She remembered Dr. Brenkshaw's warning about the patient's risk of dehydration. But she also knew that she could not force-feed him liquids when he was comatose; he would choke to death. "Well . . . bring a third orange juice. Maybe I can coax him awake." As Chris got out of the car, she said, "Might as well get us something for lunch, something that won't spoil—say a loaf of bread and a jar of peanut butter. And get a can of spray deodorant and a bottle of shampoo."

He grinned. "Why won't you let me eat this way at home?"

"Because if you don't get good nutrition, you're going to wind up with a brain even more twisted than the one you've got now, kiddo."

"Even on the lam from hired killers, I'm surprised you didn't pack a microwave, fresh vegetables, and a bottle of vitamins."

"Are you saying I'm a good mother but a fussbudget? Compliment noted and point taken. Now go."

He started to close his door.

She said, "And, Chris . . ."

"I know," the boy said. "Be careful."

While Chris was gone, she started the engine and switched on the radio to listen to the nine o'clock news. She heard a story about herself: the scene at her house near Big Bear, the shoot-out in San Bernardino. Like most news stories it was inaccurate, disjointed, and made little sense. But it confirmed that the police were looking for her throughout southern California. According to the reporter, the authorities expected to locate her soon, largely because her face was already widely known.

She had been shocked last night when Carter Brenkshaw recognized her as Laura Shane, famous writer. She did not think of herself as a celebrity; she was only a storyteller, a weaver of tales, who worked with a loom of language, making a special fabric from words. She had done only one book tour for an early novel, had loathed that dreary trek, and had not repeated the experience. She was not a regular guest on television talkshows. She had never endorsed a product in a TV commercial, had never gone public in support of a politician, and had in general attempted to avoid being part of the media circus. She observed the tradition of having a dust jacket photograph on her books because it seemed harmless, and by the age of thirty-three she could admit without severe embarrassment that she was an unusually striking woman, but she never imagined, as the police put it, that her face was widely known.

Now she was dismayed not only because her loss of anonymity made her easier quarry for the police but because she knew that becoming a celebrity in modern America was tantamount to a loss of one's self-critical faculties and a severe decline of artistic power. A few managed to be both public figures and worthwhile writers, but most seemed to be corrupted by the media attention. Laura dreaded that trap almost as much as she dreaded being picked up by the police.

Suddenly, with some surprise, she realized that if she could worry about becoming a celebrity and losing her artistic center, she must still believe in a safe future in which she would write more books. At times during the night, she had vowed to fight to the death, to struggle to a bloody end to protect her son, but throughout she had felt that their situation was virtually hopeless, their enemy too powerful and unreachable to be destroyed. Now something had changed her, had brought her around to a dim, guarded optimism.

Maybe it had been the dream.

Chris returned with a large package of pecan-cinnamon rolls, three one-pint containers of orange juice, and the other items. They ate the rolls and drank the juice, and nothing had ever tasted better.

When she finished her own breakfast, Laura got in the back seat and tried to wake her guardian. He could not be roused.

She gave the third carton of orange juice to Chris and said, "Keep it for him. He'll probably wake up soon."

"If he can't drink, he can't take his penicillin," Chris said.

"He doesn't need to take any for a few hours yet. Dr. Brenkshaw gave him a pretty potent shot last night; it's still working."

But Laura was worried. If he did not regain consciousness, they might never learn the true nature of the dangerous maze in which they were now lost—and might never find a way out of it.

"What next?" Chris asked.

"We'll find a service station, use the rest rooms, then stop at a gunshop and buy ammunition for the Uzi and the revolver. After that . . . we start looking for a motel, just the right kind of motel, a place where we can hide out."

When they settled in somewhere, they would be at least fifty miles from Dr. Brenkshaw's place, where their enemies had last found them. But did distance matter to men who measured their journeys strictly in days and years rather than miles?

Parts of Santa Ana, neighborhoods on the south side of Anaheim, and adjoining areas offered the greatest number of motels of the type she was seeking. She did not want a modern, gleaming Red Lion Inn or Howard Johnson's Motor Lodge with color television sets, deep-pile carpet, and a heated swimming pool, because reputable establishments required valid ID and a major credit card, and she dared not risk leaving a paper trail that would bring either the police or the assassins down on her. Instead she was seeking a motel that was no longer clean enough or in good enough repair to attract tourists, a seedy place where they were happy to get the business, eager to take cash, and reluctant to ask questions that would drive away guests.

She knew she would have a hard time finding a room, and she was not surprised to discover that the first twelve places she tried were unable or unwilling to accommodate her. The only people who could be seen going from or coming to those dead-end motels were young Mexican women with babies in their arms or young children in tow, and young or middle-aged Mexican men in sneakers, chinos, flannel shirts, and lightweight denim or corduroy jackets, some wearing straw cowboy hats and some baseball caps, and all of them with an air of watchfulness and suspicion. Most decrepit motels had become boarding houses for illegal immigrants, hundreds of thousands of whom had taken up not-so-secret residence in Orange County alone. Whole families lived in a single room, five or six or seven of them crowded into that cramped space, sharing one ancient bed and two chairs and a bathroom with minimally functional plumbing, for which they paid a hundred and fifty dollars or more every week, with no linen or maid service or amenities of any kind, but with cockroaches by the thousands. Yet they were willing to endure those conditions and let themselves be outrageously exploited as underpaid workers rather than return to their homeland and live under the rule of the "revolutionary people's government" that for decades had given them no brotherhood but that of despair.

At the thirteenth motel, The Bluebird of Happiness, the owner-manager still hoped to serve the lower end of the tourist trade, and he had not yet succumbed to the temptation to squeeze a rich living from the blood of poor immigrants. A few of the twenty-four units were obviously rented to illegals, but the management still provided fresh linen daily, maid service, television sets, and two spare pillows in every closet. However the fact that the desk clerk took cash, did not press her for ID, and avoided meeting her eyes was sad proof that in another year The Bluebird of Happiness would be one more monument to political stupidity and human avarice in a world as crowded with such monuments as any old, city cemetery was crowded with tombstones.

The motel had three wings in a U-shape, with parking in the middle, and their unit was in the right rear corner of the back wing. A big fan palm flourished near the door to their room, not visibly touched by smog or limited by its small patch of ground midst so much concrete and blacktop, bristling with new growth even in winter, as if nature had chosen it as a subtle omen of her intention to seize every corner of the earth again when humankind passed on.

Laura and Chris unfolded the wheelchair and got the wounded man into it, making no effort to conceal what they were doing, as if they were simply caring for a disabled person. Fully dressed, with his wounds concealed, her guardian could pass for a paraplegic—except for the way his head lolled against his shoulder.

Their room was small though passably clean. The carpet was worn but recently shampooed, and a pair of dustballs in one corner were far from the size of tumbleweeds. The maroon-plaid spread on the queen-size bed was tattered at the edges, and its pattern was not quite busy enough to conceal two patches, but the sheets were crisp and smelled faintly of detergent. They moved her guardian from the wheelchair to the bed and put two pillows under his head.

The seventeen-inch television set was firmly bolted to a table with a scarred, laminated top, and the back legs of the table were in turn bolted to the floor. Chris sat in one of the two mismatched chairs, switched on the set, and turned the cracked dial in search of either a cartoon show or reruns of an old sitcom. He settled for *Get Smart* but complained that it was "too stupid to be funny," and Laura wondered how many boys his age would have thought so.

She sat in the other chair. "Why don't you get a shower?"

"Then just get back in these same clothes?" he asked doubtfully.

"I know it sounds like purest folly, but try it. I guarantee you'll feel cleaner even without fresh clothes."

"But all that trouble to shower, then get into *wrinkled* clothes?"

"When did you become such a fashion plate that you're offended by a few wrinkles?"

He grinned, got up from his chair, and pranced to the bathroom as he thought a hopeless fop might prance. "The king and queen would be shocked to see me such a mess."

"We'll make them put on blindfolds when they visit," she said.

He returned from the bathroom in a minute. "There's a dead bug in the toilet bowl. I think it's a cockroach, but I'm not really sure."

"Does the species matter? Will we be notifying next of kin?"

Chris laughed. God, she loved to hear him laugh. He said, "What should I do—flush him?"

"Unless you want to fish him out, put him in a matchbox, and bury him in the flowerbed outside."

He laughed again. "Nope. Burial at sea." In the bathroom, he hummed "Taps," then flushed the john.

While the boy was showering, *Get Smart* ended and a movie came on, *The Harlem Globetrotters on Gilligan's Island*. Laura was not actually watching the set; she left it on for background, but there were limits to what even a woman on the lam could endure, so she quickly switched to channel eleven and *Hour Magazine*.

She stared at her guardian for a while, but his unnatural slumber depressed her. From her chair she reached to the drapes a few times, parting them far enough to scan the motel's parking lot, but no one on earth could know where she was; she was in no imminent danger. So she stared at the TV screen, uninterested in what it offered, until she was half hypnotized by it. The *Hour Magazine* host was interviewing a young actor who droned on about himself, not always making much sense, and after a while she was vaguely aware that he kept saying something about water, but now she was beginning to doze off, and his insistent talk of water was both mesmeric and annoying.

"Mom?"

She blinked, sat up, and saw Chris in the bathroom doorway. He'd just gotten out of the shower. His hair was damp, and he was dressed only in his briefs. The sight of his thin, boyish body—all ribs and elbows and knees—pulled at her heart, for he looked so innocent and vulnerable. He was so small and fragile that she wondered how she could ever protect him, and renewed fear rose in her.

"Mom, he's talking," Chris said, pointing to the man on the bed. "Didn't you hear him? He's talking."

"Water," her guardian said thickly. "Water."

She went quickly to the bed and bent over him. He was no longer comatose. He was trying to sit up, but he had no strength. His blue eyes were open, and although they were bloodshot, they focused on her, alert and observant.

"Thirsty," he said.

She said, "Chris—"

He was already there with a glass of water from the bathroom.

She sat on the bed beside her guardian, lifted his head, took the water from Chris, and helped the wounded man drink. She allowed him only small sips; she didn't want him to choke. His lips were fever-chapped, and his tongue was coated with a white film, as if he had eaten ashes. He drank more than a third of a glass of water, then indicated that he'd had enough.

After she lowered his head to the pillow, she put a hand to his forehead. "Not so hot as he was."

He rolled his head from side to side, trying to look at the room. In spite of the water, his voice was dry, burnt out. "Where are we?"

"Safe," she said.

"Nowhere . . . is safe."

"We may have figured out more of this crazy situation than you realize," she told him.

"Yeah," Chris said, sitting on the bed beside his mother. "We know you're a time traveler!"

The man looked at the boy, managed a weak smile, winced in pain.

"I've got drugs," Laura said. "A painkiller."

"No," he said. "Not now. Later maybe. More water?"

Laura lifted him once more, and this time he drank most of what remained in the glass. She remembered the penicillin and put a capsule between his teeth. He washed it down with the last two swallows.

"When do you come from?" Chris asked, intensely interested, oblivious of the droplets of bathwater that tracked out of his damp hair and down his face. "When?"

"Honey," Laura said, "he's very weak, and I don't think we should bother him with too many questions just yet."

"He can tell us that much, anyway, Mom." To the wounded man, Chris said, "When do you come from?"

He stared at Chris, then at Laura, and the haunted look was in his eyes again.

"When do you come from? Huh? The year 2100? 3000?"

In his paper-dry voice, her guardian said, "Nineteen forty-four."

The little bit of activity had clearly tired him already, for his eyelids looked heavy, and his voice was fainter than it had been, so Laura was certain that he had lapsed into delirium again.

"When?" Chris repeated, baffled by the answer he had been given.

"Nineteen forty-four."

"That's impossible," Chris said.

"Berlin," her guardian said.

"He's delirious," Laura told Chris.

His voice was slurred now as weariness dragged him down, but what he said was unmistakable: "Berlin."

"Berlin?" Chris said. "You mean—Berlin, Germany?"

Sleep claimed the wounded man, not the unnatural sleep of a coma but restful sleep that was immediately marked by soft snoring, though in the moment before he slipped away, he said, "*Nazi* Germany."

·4·

One Life to Live was on the television, but neither she nor Chris was paying any attention to the soap opera. They had drawn the two chairs closer to the bed, where they could watch the sleeping man. Chris was dressed, and his hair was mostly dry, though it remained damp at the nape of his neck. Laura felt grimy and longed for a shower, but she was not going to leave her guardian in case he woke again and was able to talk. She and the boy spoke in whispers:

"Chris, it just occurred to me, if these people were from the future, why wouldn't they have been carrying laser guns or something futuristic when they came for us?"

"They wouldn't want everyone to *know* they were from the future," Chris said. "They'd bring weapons and wear clothes that wouldn't be out of place here. But, Mom, he said he was from—"

"I know what he said. But it doesn't make sense, does it? If they had time travel in 1944, we'd know about it by now, wouldn't we?"

At one-thirty her guardian woke and seemed briefly confused as to his whereabouts. He asked for more water, and Laura helped him drink. He said he was feeling a little better, though very weak and still surprisingly sleepy. He asked to be propped up higher. Chris got the two spare pillows from the closet and helped his mother raise the wounded man.

"What is your name?" Laura asked.

"Stefan. Stefan Krieger."

She repeated the name softly, and it was all right, not melodic but solid, a masculine-sounding name. It was just not the name of a guardian angel, and she was mildly amused to realize that after so many years, including two decades during which she had professed to have no belief in him, she still expected his name to be musical and unearthly.

"And you really come from—"

"Nineteen forty-four," he repeated. Just the effort required to move to a sitting position had wrung fine beads of perspiration from his brow—or perhaps the sweat resulted in part from thoughts of the time and place where his long journey had begun. "Berlin, Germany. There was a brilliant Polish scientist, Vladimir Penlovski, considered a madman by some, and very likely mad in fact—very mad, I think—but also a genius. He was in Warsaw, working on certain theories about the nature of time for more than twenty-five years before Germany and Russia collaborated to invade Poland in 1939. . . ."

Penlovski, according to Stefan Krieger, was a Nazi sympathizer and welcomed Hitler's forces. Perhaps he knew that from Hitler he would receive the kind of financial backing for his researches that he could not get from sources more rational. Under the personal patronage of Hitler himself, Penlovski and his closest assistant, Wladyslaw Januskaya, went to Berlin to establish an institute for temporal research, which was so secret that it was given no name. It was simply called the institute. There, in association with German scientists no less committed and no less farsighted than he, financed by a seemingly inexhaustible river of funds from the Third Reich, Penlovski had found a way to pierce the artery of time and move at will through that bloodstream of days and months and years.

"*Blitzstrasse,*" Stefan said.

"*Blitz*—that part of it means lightning," Chris said. "Like *Blitzkrieg*—lightning war—in all those old movies."

"Lightning Road in this case," Stefan said. "The road through time. The road to the future."

It literally could have been called *Zukunftstrasse,* or Future Road, Stefan explained, for Vladimir Penlovski had been unable to discover a way to send men backward in time from the gate he had invented. They could travel only forward, into their future, and return automatically to their own era.

"There seems to be some cosmic mechanism that prohibits time travelers from meddling with their own pasts in order to change their present-day circumstances. You see, if they *could* travel back in time to their own past, there would develop certain—"

"Paradoxes!" Chris said excitedly.

Stefan looked surprised to hear the boy speak that word.

Smiling, Laura said, "As I told you, we've had rather a long discussion about your possible origins, and time travel turned out to be the most logical. And in Chris here, you're looking at my resident expert on the weird."

"Paradox," Stefan agreed. "It's the same word in English and German. If a time traveler could go back in time to his own past and affect some event in history, that change would have tremendous ramifications. It would alter the future from which he had come. Therefore he wouldn't be able to return to the same world he'd left—"

"Paradox!" Chris said gleefully.

"Paradox," Stefan agreed. "Apparently nature abhors a paradox and generally will not permit a time traveler to create one. And thank God for that. Because . . . suppose, for example, Hitler sent an assassin back in time to kill Franklin Roosevelt and Winston Churchill long before they rose to high office, which would have resulted in the election of different men in the U.S. and England, men who might have been less brilliant and more easily dealt with, leading to Hitler's triumph by '44 or sooner."

He was speaking now with a passion that his physical condition would not allow him to sustain, and Laura could see it taking a toll of him word by word. The perspiration had almost dried on his brow; but now, although he was not even gesturing, a new thin film of sweat silvered his pale forehead again. The circles of fatigue around his eyes appeared to grow darker. But she could not stop him and order him to rest, because she wanted and needed to hear everything he had to say—and because he would not have allowed her to stop him.

"Suppose *der Führer* could send back assassins to kill Dwight Eisenhower, George Patton, Field Marshal Montgomery, kill them in their *cradles,* when they were babies, eliminating them and others, all the best military minds the Allies possessed. Then most of the world would have been his by '44, in which case time travelers would have been going back in time to kill those men *who had already long been dead and posed no threat.* Paradox, you see. And thank God that nature permits no such paradox, no such tampering with the time traveler's own past, for otherwise Adolf Hitler would have turned the entire world into a concentration camp, a crematorium."

They were silent a while, as the possibility of such hell on earth struck each of them. Even Chris responded to the picture of an altered world that Stefan painted, for he was a child of the eighties, in which the villains of film and television melodramas were usually either voracious aliens from a distant star or Nazis. The Swastika, the silver death's-head symbol and black uniforms of the SS, and that strange fanatic with the small mustache were to Chris especially terrifying because they were part of the media-created mythology on which he had been raised. Laura knew that real people and events, once subsumed by mythology, were somehow *more* real to a child than the very bread he ate.

Stefan said, "So from the institute we could go only forward in time, but that had its uses too. We could leap forward a few decades to discover if Germany had held on in the dark days of the war and had somehow turned the tide. But of course we found that Germany had not done any such thing, that the Third Reich had been defeated. Yet with all the knowledge of the future to draw from, could not that tide be turned, after all? Surely there were things Hitler could do to save the Reich even as late as '44. And there were things that might be brought back from the future with which the war might be won—"

"Such as," Chris said, "atomic bombs!"

"Or the knowledge of how they were built," Stefan said. "The Reich already had a nuclear research program, you know, and if they'd had a breakthrough early enough, had split the atom . . ."

"They'd have won the war," Chris said.

Stefan asked for water and drank half a glass this time. He wanted to hold the glass in his good hand, but he was shaking too much; water slopped on the bedclothes, and Laura had to help him.

When he spoke again, Stefan's voice wavered at times. "Because the time traveler exists *outside* of time during his journey, he is not only able to move in time but geographically, as well. Picture him hanging above the earth, unmoving, as the globe turns below him. That's not what he does, of course, but it's easier to see that image than to imagine him hovering in another dimension. Now, as he hangs above the world, it turns below him, and if his journey to the future is gauged properly, he can travel to a precise time at which he will find himself in Berlin, the same city he left years before. But if he chooses to travel a few hours more or less, the world will have turned that much more beneath him, and he will arrive at a different place on its surface. The calculations to achieve a precise arrival are monumentally difficult in my era, 1944—"

"But they'd be easy these days," Chris said, "with computers."

Shifting in discomfort against the pillows that propped him up, putting his trembling right hand against his wounded left shoulder as if to quell the pain by his own touch, he said, "Teams of German physicists, accompanied by Gestapo, were sent secretly to various cities in Europe and the United States in the year 1985, to accumulate vital information on the making of nuclear weapons. The material they were after was not classified or difficult to find. With what they already knew from their own researches, they could obtain the rest from textbooks and scientific publications readily available at any major university library in '85. Four days before I departed the institute for the last time, those teams returned from '85 to March, 1944, with material that would give the Third Reich a nuclear arsenal before the autumn of that year. They were to spend a few weeks studying the material at the institute before deciding how and where to introduce that knowledge into the German nuclear program without revealing how it had been obtained. I knew then that I had to destroy the institute and everything it contained, key personnel as well as files, to prevent a future shaped by Adolf Hitler."

As Laura and Chris listened, rapt, Stefan Krieger told them how he had planted explosives in the institute, how on the last of his days in '44 he had shot Penlovski, Januskaya, and Volkaw, and had programmed the time gate to bring him to Laura in present-day America.

But something had gone wrong at the last minute, as Stefan was leaving. The public power supply failed. The RAF had bombed Berlin for the first time in January that year, and U.S. bombers had made the first daylight runs on March 6, so the power supply had been interrupted often, not merely due to bomb damage but also because of the work of saboteurs. It was to guard against such interruptions that the gate itself was powered by a secure generator. Stefan heard no bombers that day when, wounded by Kokoschka, he had crawled into the gate, so apparently the power failed because of saboteurs.

"And the timer on the explosives stopped. The gate was not destroyed. It's still open back there, and they can come after us. And . . . they can still win the war."

Laura was getting another headache. She put her fingertips to her temples. "But wait. Hitler can't have succeeded in building atomic weapons and winning World War Two, because we don't live in a world where that happened. You don't have to worry. Somehow, in spite of all the knowledge they took back through the gate, they obviously failed to develop a nuclear arsenal."

"No," he said. "They've failed so far, but we can't assume they will continue to fail. To those men at the institute in Berlin in 1944, their past is immutable, as I have said. They cannot travel backward in time and change their own past. But they can change their future and ours, because a time traveler's future is mutable; he can take steps to alter it."

"But *his* future is *my* past," Laura said. "And if the past can't be changed, how can he change mine?"

"Yeah," Chris said. "Paradox."

Laura said, "Listen, I haven't spent the last thirty-four years in a world ruled by Adolf Hitler and his heirs; therefore, in spite of the gate, Hitler failed."

Stefan's expression was dismal. "If time travel were invented now, in 1989, that past of which you speak—World War Two and every event since—would be unalterable. You could not change it, for nature's rule against backward time-travel and time-travel paradoxes would apply to you. But time travel has not been discovered here—or rediscovered. The time travelers at the institute in Berlin in '44 are free to change *their* future, apparently, and though they will simultaneously be changing your past, nothing in the laws of nature will stop them. And there you have the greatest paradox of all—the only one that for some reason nature seems to allow."

"You're saying they could still build nuclear weapons back then with the information they got in '85," Laura said, "and win the war?"

"Yes. Unless the institute is destroyed first."

"And what then? Suddenly, all around us, we find things changed, find ourselves living under Nazism?"

"Yes. And you won't even know what's happened, because you will be a different person than you are now. Your entire past will never have occurred. You will have lived a *different* past altogether, and you will remember nothing else, none of what has happened to you in *this* life because this life will never have existed. You will think the world has always been as it is, that there was never a world in which Hitler lost."

What he was proposing terrified and appalled her because it made life seem even more fragile than she had always thought it was. The world under her feet suddenly seemed no more real than the world of a dream; it was apt to dissolve without warning and send her tumbling into a great, dark void.

With growing horror she said, "If they change the world in which I grew up, I might never have met Danny, never married."

"I might never have been born," Chris said.

She reached to Chris and put a hand on his arm, not only to reassure him but to reassure herself of his current solidity. "I might not have been born myself. Everything I've seen, the good and bad of the world that's been since 1944 . . . it'll all wash away like an elaborate sandcastle, and a new reality will exist in its place."

"A new and worse reality," Stefan said, clearly exhausted by the effort he had made to explain what was at stake.

"In that new world, I might never have written my novels."

"Or if you wrote novels," Stefan said, "they would be different from those you've done in this life, grotesque works produced by an artist laboring under the rule of an oppressive government, in the iron fist of Nazi censorship."

"If those guys build the atom bomb in 1944," Chris said, "then we'll all just crumble into dust and blow away."

"Not literally. But like dust, yes," Stefan Krieger agreed. "Gone, with no trace that we've ever been."

"We've gotta stop them," Chris said.

"If we can," Stefan agreed. "But first we've got to stay alive in *this* reality, and that might not be easy."

Stefan needed to relieve himself, and Laura helped him into the motel bathroom, handling him as if she were a nurse accustomed to matter-of-fact dealings with the plumbing of sick men. By the time she returned him to the bed, she was worried about him again; though he was muscular, he felt limp, clammy, and he was frighteningly weak.

She told him briefly about the shoot-out at Brenkshaw's, through which he had remained comatose. "If these assassins are coming from the past instead of the future, how do they know where to find us? How did they know in 1944 that we'd be at Dr. Brenkshaw's when we were, forty-five years later?"

"To find you," Stefan said, "they made two trips. First, they went farther into the future, a couple of days farther, to this coming weekend perhaps, to see if you had shown up anywhere by then. If you hadn't—and apparently you had not—then they started checking the public record. Back issues of newspapers, for one thing. They looked for the stories about the shooting at your house last night, and in those stories they read that you'd taken a wounded man to Brenkshaw's place in San Bernardino. So they simply returned to '44 and made a second trip—this time to Dr. Brenkshaw's in the early hours of this morning, January 11."

"They can hopscotch around us," Chris told Laura. "They can pop ahead in time to see where we show up, then they pick and choose the easiest place along the time stream to ambush us. It's sorta like . . . if we were cowboys and the Indians were all psychic."

"Who was Kokoschka?" Chris wanted to know. "Who was the man who killed my dad?"

"Head of institute security," Stefan said. "He claimed to be a distant relation of Oskar Kokoschka, the noted Austrian expressionist painter, but I doubt if it was true because in *our* Kokoschka there was no hint of an artist's sensitivity. *Standartenführer*—which means Colonel—Heinrich Kokoschka was an efficient killer for the Gestapo."

"Gestapo," Chris said, awestruck. "Secret police?"

"State police," Stefan said. "Widely known to exist but allowed to operate in secrecy. When he showed up on that mountain road in 1988, I was as surprised as you. There'd been no lightning. He must have arrived far away from us, fifteen or twenty miles, in some other valley of the San Bernardinos, and the lightning had been beyond our notice." The lightning associated with time travel was in fact a very localized phenomenon, Stefan explained. "After Kokoschka showed up there, on my trail, I thought I would return to the institute and find all of my colleagues outraged at my treason, but when I got there, no one took special notice of me. I was confused. Then after I killed Penlovski and the others, when I was in the main lab preparing for my final jaunt into the future, Heinrich Kokoschka burst in and shot me. He wasn't dead! Not dead on that highway in 1988. Then I realized that Kokoschka had obviously only just learned of my treason when he'd found the men I'd shot. He would travel to 1988 and try to kill me—and all of you—at a later time. Which meant that the gate would have to remain open to allow him to do so, and that I was destined to fail to destroy it. At least at that time."

"God, this headache," Laura said.

Chris seemed to have no trouble whatsoever following the tangled threads of time travel. He said, "So after you traveled to our house last night, Kokoschka traveled to 1988 and killed my dad. Jeez! In a way, Mr. Krieger, you killed Kokoschka forty-three years *after* he shot you in that lab . . . yet you had shot him *before* he shot you. This is wild stuff. Mom, isn't this wild? Isn't this great?"

"It's something," she agreed. "And how did Kokoschka know to find you on that mountain road?"

"After he discovered I'd shot Penlovski, and after I escaped through the gate, Kokoschka must have found the explosives in the attic and basement. Then he must have dug into the automatic records the machinery keeps of all the times the gate is used. That was a bit of data tracking that was *my* responsibility, so no one previously had noticed all my jaunts into your life, Laura. Anyway, Kokoschka must have done some time traveling of his own, must have taken a lot of trips to see where I'd been going, secretly watching me watch you, watching me alter your destiny for the better. He must have been watching the day I came to the cemetery when your father was buried, and he must have been watching when I beat Sheener, but I never saw him. So from all the trips I made into your life, from all the times I just observed you and the times I acted to save you, he picked a place at which to kill us. He wanted to kill me because I was a traitor, and he wanted to kill you and your family because . . . well because he realized you were so important to me."

Why? she thought. *Why am I so important to you, Stefan Krieger? Why have you intruded in my destiny, trying to give me a better life?*

She would have asked those questions then, but he had more to say about Kokoschka. His strength seemed to be fading fast, and he was having some difficulty holding on to the thread of his reasoning. She did not want to interrupt and confuse him.

He said, "From the clocks and graphs on the gate's programming board, Kokoschka could have discovered my final destination: last night, your house. But, you see, I actually had intended to return to the night that Danny died, as I promised you I would, and instead I returned one year later only because I made some mistake when entering my calculations in the machine. After I left through the gate, wounded, Heinrich Kokoschka would have found those calculations. He would have realized my mistake, and would have known where to find me not only last night but on the night that Danny died. In a way, by coming to save you from that runaway truck last year, I brought Danny's killer with me. I feel responsible for that, even though Danny would have died in the accident, anyway. At least you and Chris are alive. For now."

"Why wouldn't Kokoschka have followed you to 1989, to our house last night? He knew you were already wounded, easy prey."

"But he also knew that I would expect him to follow me, and he was afraid I was armed and would be prepared for him. So he went to 1988, where I was not expecting him, where he had the advantage of surprise. Also, Kokoschka probably figured if he followed me to 1988 and killed me there, I would not therefore have ever returned to the institute from that mountain highway and would not have had a chance to kill Penlovski. He no doubt thought he could pull a trick with time and *undo* those murders, thereby saving the head of the project. But of course he could not do so, because then he would be altering his *own* past, an impossibility. Penlovski and the others were already dead by then and would stay dead. If Kokoschka had better understood the laws of time travel, he would have known that I would kill him in 1988 when he followed me there, because by the time he made that jaunt to avenge Penlovski, I had already returned to the institute from that night, safe!"

Chris said, "Are you all right, Mom?"

"Do they make Excedrin in one-pound tablets?" she asked.

"I know it's a lot to absorb," Stefan said. "But that's who Heinrich Kokoschka is. Or who he was. He removed the explosives I'd planted. Because of him—and that inconvenient power failure that stopped the timer on the detonator—the institute still stands, the gate is still open, and Gestapo agents are trying to track us here in our own time—and kill us."

"Why?" Laura asked.

"For revenge," Chris said.

"They're crossing forty-five years of time to kill us just for revenge?" Laura said. "Surely there's more than that."

"There is," Stefan said. "They want to kill us because they believe we are the only people in existence who can find a way to close the gate before they win the war and alter their future. And in that assumption, they're correct."

"How?" she asked, astounded. "How can we destroy the institute forty-five years ago?"

"I'm not sure yet," he said. "But I'll think about it."

She began to ask more questions, but Stefan shook his head. He pleaded exhaustion and soon drifted off to sleep again.

Chris made a late lunch of peanut butter sandwiches with the fixings he had bought at the supermarket. Laura had no appetite.

She could see that Stefan was going to sleep for a few hours, so she showered. She felt better afterward, even in wrinkled clothes.

Throughout the afternoon the television fare was relentlessly idiotic: soap operas, game shows, more soap operas, reruns of *Fantasy Island, The Bold and the Beautiful,* and Phil Donahue dashing back and forth through the studio audience, exhorting them to raise their consciousness about—and find compassion for—the singular plight of transvestite dentists.

She replenished the Uzi's magazine with the ammunition she had bought at a gunshop that morning.

Outside, as the day waned, clots of dark clouds formed and grew until no blue sky could be seen. The fan palm beside the stolen Buick seemed to pull its fronds closer together in expectation of a storm.

She sat in one of the chairs, propped her feet up on the edge of the bed, closed her eyes, and dozed for a while. She woke from a bad dream in which she had discovered she was made of sand and was swiftly dissolving in a rainstorm. Chris was sleeping in the other chair, and Stefan was still snoring softly on the bed.

Rain was falling, drumming hollowly on the motel roof, pattering in the puddles on the parking lot outside, a sound like bubbling-hot grease, though the day was cool. It was a typical southern California storm, tropically heavy and steady but lacking thunder and lightning. Occasionally such pyrotechnics accompanied rain in this part of the world, but less often than elsewhere. Now Laura had special reason to be thankful for that climatological fact, because if there had been thunder and lightning, she would not have known whether it was natural or signaled the arrival of Gestapo agents from another era.

Chris woke at five-fifteen, and Stefan Krieger came around five minutes later. Both said they were hungry, and in addition to his appetite, Stefan showed other signs of recovery. His eyes had been bloodshot and watery; now they were clear. He was able to raise himself up in bed with his good arm. His left hand, which had been numb and virtually useless, was full of feeling now, and he was able to flex it, wriggle his fingers, and make a weak fist.

Instead of dinner she wanted answers to her questions, but she'd led a life that had taught her patience—among other things. When they had checked into the motel shortly after eleven that morning, Laura had noticed a Chinese restaurant across the street. Now, though reluctant to leave Stefan and Chris, she went out into the rain to get some take-out food.

She carried the .38 under her jacket and left the Uzi on the bed with Stefan. Though the carbine was too big and powerful for Chris to handle, Stefan might be able to brace himself against the headboard and trigger a burst even with just his right hand, though the shock of recoil would shatter through his wound.

When she returned, dripping rain, they put the waxed-cardboard containers of food on the bed—except for the two orders of egg-flower soup, which were for Stefan, and which she put on the night-stand near him. Upon walking into the aromatic restaurant, she had found her own appetite, and naturally she had ordered far too much food: lemon chicken, beef with orange flavor, brown-pepper shrimp, moo goo gai pan, moo shu pork, and two containers of rice.

As she and Chris sampled all of the dishes with plastic forks and washed the food down with Cokes that she had gotten from the motel's soda machine, Stefan drank his soup. He had thought he could not hold down more solid food, but with the soup disposed of, he cautiously began to try the moo goo gai pan and the lemon chicken.

At Laura's request he told them about himself while they ate. He had been born in 1909 in the German town of Gittelde in the Harz Mountains, which made him thirty-five years old. ("Well," Chris said, "on the other hand, if you count the forty-five years you skipped when you traveled in time from '44 to '89, you're actually eighty years old!" He laughed, pleased with himself. "Boy, you sure look *good* for an eighty-year-old geezer!") After moving the family to Munich following the First World War, Stefan's father, Franz Krieger, had been an early supporter of Hitler in 1919, a member of the German Workers' Party from the very week that Hitler began his political career in that organization. He even worked with Hitler and Anton Drexler to write the platform with which that group, essentially a debating society, was eventually transformed into a true political party, later to become the National Socialists.

"I was one of the first members of the Hitler Youth in 1926, when I was seventeen," he said. "Less than a year later I joined the *Sturmabteilung* or the SA, the brown shirts, the enforcement arm of the party, virtually a private army. By 1928, however, I was a member of the *Schutzstaffel*—"

"The SS!" Chris said, speaking in the same tone of horror mixed with strange attraction that he would have used if he had been talking of vampires or werewolves. "You were a member of the SS? You wore the black uniform and the silver death's-head, carried the dagger?"

"I'm not proud of it," Stefan Krieger said. "Oh, at the time I was proud, of course. I was a fool. My father's fool. In the early days the SS was a small group, the essence of elitism, and our purpose was to protect *der Führer* with our own lives if that was necessary. We were all eighteen to twenty-two, young and ignorant and hot-headed. In my own defense I'll say that I was not particularly hot-headed, not as committed as those around me. I was doing what my father wanted, but of ignorance I'll admit to having more than my fair share."

Windblown rain rattled against the window and gurgled noisily in a downspout beyond the outside wall against which the bed stood.

Since awakening from his nap, Stefan had looked healthier, and he had perked up even more with the hot soup. But now, as he recalled a youth spent in a cauldron of hatred and death, he paled again, and his eyes seemed to sink deeper into the darkness under his brow. "I never left the SS because it was such a desired position and there was no way to leave without arousing suspicion that I'd lost my faith in our revered leader. But year by year, month by month, then day by day I became sickened by what I saw, by the madness and murder and terror."

Neither the brown-pepper shrimp nor the lemon chicken tasted too good any longer, and Laura's mouth was so dry that the rice stuck to the roof of it. She pushed the food aside, sipped her Coke. "But if you never left the SS . . . when did you go to college, when did you get involved in scientific research?"

"Oh," he said, "I wasn't at the institute as a researcher. I've no university education. Except . . . for two years I received intensive instruction in English, trying to learn to speak with an acceptable American accent. I was part of a project that dropped hundreds of deep-cover agents into Britain and the United States. But I never could quite cast off the accent, so I was never sent overseas; besides, because my father was an early supporter of Hitler, they felt I was trustworthy, so they found other uses for me. I was on special assignment to *der Führer's* staff, where I was given sensitive jobs, usually as a liaison between squabbling factions of the government. It was an excellent position from which to obtain information useful to the British, which I did from 1938 on."

"You were a spy?" Chris asked excitedly.

"Of a sort. I had to do what little I could to bring down the Reich, to make up for ever having been a willing part of it. I had to atone—though atoning seemed impossible. And then, in the autumn of 1943, when Penlovski began to have some success with his time gate, sending animals off to God-knew-where and bringing them back, I was assigned to the institute as an observer, as *der Führer's* personal representative. Also as a guinea pig, as the first human to be sent forward in time. You see, when they were ready to send a man into the future, they did not want to risk Penlovski or Januskaya or Helmut Volkaw or Mitter or Shenck or one of the other scientists whose loss would damage the project. No one knew if a man would come back as reliably as the animals did—or if he would come back sane and whole."

Chris nodded solemnly. "It's possible time travel might've been painful or mentally unbalancing or something, yeah. Who could know?"

Who could know indeed? Laura thought.

Stefan said, "They also wanted whomever they sent to be reliable and capable of keeping his mission a secret. I was the ideal choice."

"An SS officer, a spy, and the first chrononaut," Chris said. "Wow, what a fascinating life."

"May God give you a life far less eventful," Stefan Krieger said. Then he looked at Laura more directly than previously. His eyes were a beautiful, pure blue, yet they revealed a tortured soul. "Laura . . . what do you think of your guardian now? Not an angel but an aide to Hitler, an SS thug."

"No thug," she said. "Your father, your time, and your society may have tried to make a thug of you, but there was an inner core they couldn't bend. Not a thug, Stefan Krieger. Never. Not you."

"No angel, though," he said. "Far from an angel, Laura. Upon my death, when the stains on my soul are read by He who sits in judgment, I'll be given my own small space in hell."

The rain drumming on the roof seemed like time flowing away, many millions of precious minutes, hours and days and years pouring through gutters and downspouts, draining away, wasted.

After she had gathered up the unfinished food and thrown it in a dumpster behind the motel office, after she'd gotten three more Cokes from the machine, one for each of them, she at last asked her guardian the question she had wanted to ask him from the moment he had come out of his coma: "Why? Why did you focus on me, on my life, and why did you want to help me along, to save my butt now and then? For God's sake, how does my fate tie up with Nazis, time travelers, the fate of the world?"

On his third trip into the future, he explained, he had traveled to California in 1984. California because his previous two trips—two weeks in 1954, two weeks in 1964—had shown him that California was perhaps the coming cultural and current scientific center of the most advanced nation on earth. Nineteen eighty-four because it was a neat forty years from his own time. He was not the only man going through the gate by then; four others began making jaunts as soon as it was proved safe. On that third trip Stefan had still been scouting the future, learning in detail what had happened to the world during and after the war. He was also learning what scientific developments of the intervening forty years would most likely be taken back to Berlin in '44 to win the war for Hitler, not because he intended to help in that design but because he hoped to sabotage it. His researches involved reading newspapers, watching television, and just circulating in American society, getting a feel for the late twentieth century.

Leaning back on his pillows now, recalling that third journey in a voice utterly different from the gloom with which he had described his grim life up to 1944, he said, "You can't imagine what it was like for me to walk the streets of Los Angeles for the first time. If I had traveled one thousand years into the future instead of forty, it couldn't have seemed more wondrous. The cars! Cars everywhere—and so many of them German, which seemed to indicate a certain forgiveness for the war, acceptance of the new Germany, and I was moved by that."

"We have a Mercedes," Chris said. "It's neat, but I like the Jeep better."

"The cars," Stefan said, "the styles, the amazing advancements everywhere: digital watches, home computers, videotape recorders for watching movies in your own living room! Even after five days of my visit had passed, I was in a state of pleasant shock, and looked forward each morning to new wonders. On the sixth day, as I passed a bookstore in Westwood, I saw a line of people waiting to have copies of a novel signed by the author. I went inside to browse and to see what kind of book was so popular, to help me a bit in understanding American society. And there you were, Laura, at a table piled with copies of your third novel and your first major success, *Ledges.*"

Laura leaned forward, as if puzzlement were a force drawing her to the edge of her chair. "*Ledges?* But I've never written a book with that title."

Again, Chris understood. "That was a book you wrote in the life you would've lived if Mr. Krieger hadn't meddled in it."

"You were twenty-nine years old when I saw you for the first time at that book-signing party in Westwood," Stefan said. "You were in a wheelchair because your legs were twisted, useless. Your left arm was partly paralyzed, as well."

"Crippled?" Chris said. "Mom was crippled?"

Laura was literally on the edge of her chair now, for though what her guardian said seemed too fantastic to be believed, she sensed that it was true. On a deep level even more primitive than instinct, she perceived a *rightness* to the image of herself in a wheelchair, her legs useless and wasted; perhaps what she apprehended was the faint echo of destiny thwarted.

"You'd been that way since birth," Stefan said.

"Why?"

"I only learned that much later, after conducting much research into your life. The doctor who had delivered you in Denver, Colorado, in 1955—Markwell was his name—had been an alcoholic. Yours was a difficult birth anyway—"

"My mother died delivering me."

"Yes, in *that* reality she died too. But in that reality Markwell botched the delivery, and you received a spinal injury that crippled you for life."

A shudder passed through her. As if to prove to herself that she had indeed escaped the life that fate had originally planned for her, she got up and walked to the window, using her legs, her undamaged and blessedly useful legs.

To Chris, Stefan said, "That day I saw her in the wheelchair, your mother was so beautiful. Oh, so very beautiful. Her face, of course, was the same as it is now. But it wasn't the face alone that made her beautiful. There was such an aura of *courage* about her, and she was in such good humor in spite of her handicaps. Each person who came to her with *Ledges* was sent away not only with a signature but with a laugh. In spite of being condemned to a life in a wheelchair, your mother was so amusing, lighthearted. I watched from a distance and was charmed and profoundly moved, as I'd never been before."

"She's great," Chris said. "Nothing scares my mom."

"Everything scares your mom," Laura said. "This whole crazy conversation is scaring your mom half to death."

"You never run from anything or hide," Chris said, turning to look at her. He blushed; a boy his age was supposed to be cool, at a stage where he was beginning to wonder if he was not infinitely wiser than his mother. In an ordinary relationship, such expressions of admiration for one's mother seldom were expressed so directly short of the child's fortieth birthday or the mother's death, whichever came first. "Maybe you're afraid, but you never *act* afraid."

She had learned young that those who showed fear were seen as easy targets.

"I bought a copy of *Ledges* that day," Stefan said, "and took it back to the hotel where I was staying. I read it overnight, and it was so beautiful that in places I wept . . . and so amusing that in other places I laughed out loud. The next day I got your other two books, *Silverlock* and *Fields of Night,* which were as fine, as moving, as the book that made you famous, *Ledges*."

It was strange to listen to favorable reviews of books that in this life she had never written. But she was less concerned about learning the storylines of those novels than hearing the answer to a chilling question that had just occurred to her: "In this life I was meant to live, in this other 1984 . . . was I married?"

"No."

"But I'd met Danny and—"

"No. You had never met Danny. You had never married."

"I'd never been born!" Chris said.

Stefan said, "All of those things happened because I went back to Denver, Colorado, in 1955, and prevented Dr. Markwell from delivering you. The doctor who took Markwell's place couldn't save your mother, but he brought you into the world whole and sound. And everything in your life changed from that point on. It was your past that I was changing, yes, but it was *my* future, therefore flexible. And thank God for that peculiarity of time travel, for otherwise I wouldn't have been able to save you from a life as a paraplegic."

The wind gusted, and another barrage of rain rattled against the window at which Laura stood.

She was plagued again by the feeling that the room in which she stood, the earth on which it was built, and the universe in which it turned were as insubstantial as smoke, subject to sudden change.

"I monitored your life thereafter," Stefan said. "Between mid-January of '44 and mid-March, I made over thirty secret jaunts to see how you were getting along. On the fourth of those trips, when I went to 1964, I discovered you had been dead for one year, you and your father, killed by that junkie who had held up the grocery store. So I journeyed to 1963 and killed him before he could kill you."

"Junkie?" Chris said, baffled.

"I'll tell you about it later, honey."

Stefan said, "And until the night that Kokoschka showed up on that mountain road, I was pretty successful, I think, at making your life easier and better. Yet my interference did not deprive you of your art or result in books that were any less beautiful than the ones that you'd written in that other life. Different books but not lesser ones, books in the same voice, in fact, that you write in now."

Feeling weak-kneed, Laura returned to her chair. "But *why?* Why did you go to such great lengths to improve my life?"

Stefan Krieger looked at Chris, then at her, then closed his eyes when he finally spoke. "After seeing you in that wheelchair, signing copies of *Ledges,* and after reading your books, I fell in love with you . . . deeply in love with you."

Chris squirmed in his chair, obviously embarrassed to hear such feelings expressed when the object of affection was his own mother.

"Your mind was even more beautiful than your face," Stefan said softly. His eyes were still closed. "I fell in love with your great courage, perhaps because real courage was something I'd seen none of in my own world of strutting, uniformed fanatics. They committed atrocities in the name of the people and called that courage. They were willing to die for a twisted totalitarian ideal, and they called *that* courage when it was really stupidity, insanity. And I fell in love with your dignity, for I had none of my own, no self-respect like that I saw shining in you. I fell in love with your compassion, which was so rich a part of your books, for in my world I had seen little compassion. I fell in love, Laura, and realized that I could do for you what all men would do for those they loved if they had the power of gods: I did my best to spare you the worst that fate had planned for you."

He opened his eyes at last.

They were a beautiful blue. And tortured.

She was immeasurably grateful to him. She did not love him in return, for she hardly knew him. But in stating the depth of his love, a passion that had caused him to transform her destiny and that had driven him to sail across vast tides of time to be with her, he had to some degree restored the magical aura in which she had once viewed him. Again he seemed larger than life, a demigod if not a god, elevated from mere mortal status by the degree of his selfless commitment to her.

That night Chris shared the creaky-springed bed with Stefan Krieger. Laura tried to sleep in one chair with her feet propped on the other.

Rain fell in ceaseless, lulling rhythms that soon put Chris to sleep. Laura could hear him snoring softly.

After she sat for perhaps an hour in darkness, she said quietly, "Are you asleep?"

"No," Stefan said at once.

"Danny," she said. "My Danny . . ."

"Yes?"

"Why didn't you . . ."

"Make a second trip to that night in 1988 and kill Kokoschka before he could kill Danny?"

"Yes. Why didn't you?"

"Because . . . you see, Kokoschka was from the world of 1944, so his killing of Danny and his own death were a part of *my* past, which I could not undo. If I'd attempted to travel again to that night in '88, to an earlier point in the evening, to stop Kokoschka *before* he killed Danny—I would have bounced immediately back through the gate, back to the institute, without going anywhere; nature's law against paradox would have prevented me from going in the first place."

Laura was silent.

Stefan said, "Do you understand?"

"Yes."

"Do you accept it?"

"I'll never accept his death."

"But . . . do you believe me."

"I think I do, yes."

"Laura, I know how much you loved Danny Packard. If I could have saved him, even at the cost of my own life, I would have done so. I would not have hesitated."

"I believe you," she said. "Because without you . . . I'd never have had Danny at all."

"The Eel," she said.

"Destiny struggles to reassert the pattern that was meant to be," Stefan said in the darkness. "When you were eight years old, I shot that junkie, prevented him from raping and killing you, but inevitably fate brought you to another pedophile who had the potential to be a murderer. Willy Sheener. The Eel. But fate also determined that you would be a writer and a successful one, that you would bring the same message to the world in your books regardless of what I did to change your life. That's a *good* pattern. There's something frightening yet reassuring in the way some power tries to reestablish destiny's broken designs . . . almost as if there's meaning in the universe, something that in spite of its insistence on our suffering, we might even call God."

For a while they listened to the rain and wind sweep clean the world outside.

She said, "But why didn't you take care of the Eel for me?"

"I waited for him one night in his apartment—"

"You gave him a bad beating. Yes, I knew that was you."

"Beat him and warned him to stay away from you. I told him I'd kill him the next time."

"But the beating only made him more determined to have me. Why didn't you kill him right off?"

"I should have. But . . . I don't know. Perhaps I'd seen so much killing and participated in enough of it that . . . I just hoped for once that killing wouldn't be necessary."

She thought of his world of war, concentration camps, genocide, and she could understand why he might have hoped to avoid murder even though Sheener had hardly deserved to live.

"But when Sheener came after me at the Dockweilers' house, why weren't you there to stop him?"

"The next time I monitored your life was when you were thirteen, after you'd already killed Sheener yourself and survived, so I decided not to go back and deal with him for you."

"I survived," she said. "But Nina Dockweiler didn't. Maybe if she hadn't come home and seen the blood, the body . . ."

"Maybe," he said. "And maybe not. Destiny struggles to restore the ordained pattern as best it can. Maybe she'd have died anyway. Besides, I couldn't protect you from every trauma, Laura. I would have needed ten thousand trips through time to have done that. And perhaps that degree of tampering wouldn't have been good for you. Without any adversity in your life, perhaps you wouldn't have become the woman with whom I fell in love."

Silence settled between them.

She listened to the wind, the rain.

She listened to her heartbeat.

At last she said, "I don't love you."

"I understand."

"Seems like I should—a little."

"You don't even really know me yet."

"Maybe I can never love you."

"I know."

"In spite of all you've done for me."

"I know. But if we live through this . . . well, there's always time."

"Yes," she said, "I suppose there's always time."

Six

NIGHT'S COMPANION

·1·

On Saturday, March 18, 1944, in the main, ground-floor lab of the institute, SS *Obersturmführer* Erich Klietmann and his squad of three highly trained men were prepared to jump into the future and eliminate Krieger, the woman, and the boy. They were dressed to pass as young California executives in 1989: pinstripe suits by Yves St. Laurent, white shirts, dark ties, black Bally loafers, black socks, and Ray-Ban sunglasses if the weather required them; they had been told that in the future this was called the "power look," and though Klietmann didn't know what that meant exactly, he liked the sound of it. Their clothes had been purchased in the future by institute researchers on previous jaunts; nothing about them, down to their underwear, was anachronistic.

Each of the four was carrying a Mark Cross attaché case, as well, a smart-looking model made of calfskin with gold-plated fixtures. The cases had also been brought back from the future, as had the modified Uzi carbine and spare magazines that were packed in each attaché.

A team of institute researchers had been on a mission to the U.S. in the year and month when John Hinckley had attempted to assassinate Ronald Reagan. While watching the film of the attack on television, they had been immensely impressed by the compact automatic weapons that the Secret Service agents had been carrying in attaché cases. The agents had been able to withdraw those submachine guns and bring them into firing position in but a second or two. Now the Uzi was not only the automatic carbine of choice in many of the police agencies and armies of 1989, but was the preferred weapon of the time-traveling *Schutzstaffel* commandos.

Klietmann had practiced with the Uzi. He regarded the weapon with as much affection as he had ever lavished upon a human being. The only thing about it that bothered him was the fact that it was an Israeli-designed and manufactured gun, the product of a bunch of Jews. On the other hand, within a few days the new directors of the institute were likely to approve the integration of the Uzi into the world of 1944, and German soldiers equipped with it would be better able to drive back the subhuman hordes who would depose *der Führer*.

He looked at the clock on the gate's programming board and saw that seven minutes had passed since the research team had left for California on February 15, 1989. They were there to search public records—mostly back issues of newspapers—to discover if Krieger, the woman, and the boy had been found by police and detained for questioning in the month following the shoot-outs at Big Bear and San Bernardino. Then they would return to '44 and tell Klietmann the day, time, and place where Krieger and the woman could be found. Because every time traveler returned from a jaunt exactly eleven minutes after departing, regardless of how long he spent in the future, Klietmann and his squad had only four more minutes to wait.

·2·

Tuesday, January 12, 1989, was Laura's thirty-fourth birthday, and they spent it in the same room at The Bluebird of Happiness Motel. Stefan needed another day of rest to regain his strength and let the penicillin do its work. He also needed the time to think; he had to devise a plan for destroying the institute, and that problem was sufficiently knotty to require hours of intense concentration.

The rain had stopped, but the sky still looked bruised, swollen. The forecast was for another storm to follow the first by midnight.

They watched the local five o'clock television news and saw a story about her and Chris and the wounded mystery man they had taken to Dr. Brenkshaw. Police were still looking for her, and the best guess anyone could make about the situation was that the drug dealers who had killed her husband were after her and her son, either because they were afraid she would eventually identify them in a police lineup or because she was somehow involved in drug traffic herself.

"My mom a drug dealer?" Chris said, offended by that insinuation. "What a bunch of bozos!"

Although no bodies had been found at Big Bear or San Bernardino, there had been a sensational development that guaranteed the media's continued interest. Reporters had learned that considerable blood had been found at both scenes—and that a man's severed head had been discovered in the alleyway behind the Brenkshaw house, between two garbage cans.

Laura remembered stepping through the redwood gate behind Carter Brenkshaw's property, seeing the second surprised gunman, and opening fire on him with the Uzi. The burst had taken him in the throat and head, and at the time she had thought that the concentrated automatic fire might well have decapitated him.

"The surviving SS men pushed the call-home button on the dead man's belt," Stefan said, "and sent his body back."

"But why not his head?" Laura said, sickened by the subject but too curious not to ask the question.

"It must've rolled away from the body, between the garbage cans," Stefan said, "and they couldn't find it in the few seconds they had to look. If they'd located it, they could have laid it on the corpse and folded his arms around it. Anything a time traveler wears or carries is taken with him on a jaunt. But with the sirens approaching and the darkness in the alley . . . they didn't have time to find the head."

Chris, who might have been expected to revel in these bizarre complications, slumped in his chair, legs curled up under him, and was silent. Perhaps the hideous image of a severed head had made Death's presence more real for him than had all the gunfire directed at him.

Laura made a special point of hugging him and subtly reassuring him that they were going to come out of this together and unscathed. The hugs, however, were as much for her as for him, and the pep talks she gave him must have seemed at least somewhat false, for she had not yet convinced herself that in fact they would triumph.

For lunch and dinner she got take-out from the Chinese restaurant just across the street. The previous night none of the restaurant's employees recognized her as either the famous author or the fugitive, so she felt reasonably safe there. It seemed foolish to go elsewhere and risk being spotted.

At the end of dinner, while Laura was cleaning up the cardboard containers, Chris produced two chocolate cupcakes with a yellow candle on each. He had bought the packet of Hostess pastries and a box of birthday candles at the Ralph's supermarket yesterday morning and had hidden them until now. With great ceremony he carried the cupcakes from the bathroom, where he had secretly inserted and lit the candles, and golden reflections of the two flames shimmered brightly in his eyes. He grinned when he saw that he had surprised and delighted her. In fact she had to strive to hold back tears. She was moved that even in the thrall of fear, in the midst of danger, he'd still had the presence of mind to think of her birthday, and the desire to please her; it seemed, to her, to be the essence of what mothers and children were all about.

The three of them ate wedges of the cupcakes. In addition five fortune cookies had come with the take-out food.

From his pillowed perch upon the bed, Stefan opened his cookie. "If only this were true: 'You'll live in times of peace and plenty.' "

"It might turn out to be true," Laura said. She cracked her cookie and withdrew the slip of paper. "Oh, well, I think I've had enough of this, thank you: 'Adventure will be your companion.' "

When Chris opened his cookie, there was no slip of paper inside, no fortune.

A flicker of fear passed through Laura, as if the empty cookie actually meant that he had no future. Superstitious nonsense. But she could not suppress her sudden anxiety.

"Here," she said, quickly handing him both of the remaining cookies. "Getting none in that one just means you get *two* fortunes."

Chris opened the first, read it to himself, laughed, then read it to them: " 'You will achieve fame and fortune.' "

"When you're stinking rich, will you support me in my old age?" Laura asked.

"Sure, Mom. Well . . . as long as you'll still cook for me, and especially your vegetable soup."

"Going to make your old mom *earn* her way, huh?"

Smiling at the interplay between Laura and Chris, Stefan Krieger said, "He's a tough customer, isn't he?"

"He'll probably have me scrubbing his floors when I'm eighty," Laura said.

Chris opened the second cookie. " 'You'll have a good life of little pleasures—books, music, art.' "

Neither Chris nor Stefan seemed to notice that the two fortunes made opposed predictions, effectively canceling each other, which in a way confirmed the ominous meaning of the empty cookie.

Hey, you're losing your mind, Shane, you really are, she thought. They're just fortune cookies. They don't *really* predict anything.

Hours later, after the lights were out and Chris was asleep, Stefan spoke to Laura from the darkness. "I've devised a plan."

"A way to destroy the institute?"

"Yes. But it's very complicated, and there are many things we'll need. I don't know for sure . . . but I suspect some of these items can't be purchased by private citizens."

"I can get anything you need," she said confidently. "I have the contacts. Anything."

"We'll have to have quite a lot of money."

"That's thorny. I've only got forty bucks left, and I can't go to the bank and withdraw funds because that would leave a record—"

"Yes. That would draw them straight to us. Is there someone you can trust and who trusts you, someone who would give you a lot of their own money and tell no one they'd seen you?"

"You know all about me," Laura said, "so you know about Thelma Ackerson. But, God, I don't want to drag her into this. If anything happened to Thelma—"

"It can be arranged without risk to her," he insisted.

Outside, the promised rain arrived in a sudden downpour.

Laura said, "No."

"But she's our only hope."

"No."

"Where else can you raise the money?"

"We'll find another way that doesn't require a lot of financing."

"Whether we come up with another plan or not, we'll need money. Your forty dollars won't last another day. And I have nothing."

"I won't risk Thelma," she said adamantly.

"As I said, we can do it without risk, without—"

"No."

"Then we're defeated," he said dismally.

She listened to the rain, which in her mind became the heavy roar of World War II bombers—and then the sound of a chanting, maddened crowd.

At last she said, "But even if we could arrange it without any risk to Thelma, what if the SS has a tail on her? They must know she's my best friend—my only real friend. So why wouldn't they have sent one of their teams forward in time to just keep a watch on Thelma with the hope she'd lead them to me?"

"Because that's an unnecessarily tedious way to find us," he said. "They can just send research teams into the future, to February of this year and then March and April, month after month, to check the newspapers until they find out where we first showed up. Each of those jaunts only takes eleven minutes in *their* time, remember, so it's quick; and that method is almost certain to work sooner or later because it's doubtful we could stay in hiding the rest of our lives."

"Well . . ."

He waited a long time. Then he said, "You're like sisters, you two. And if you can't turn for help to a sister at a time like this, who can you turn to, Laura?"

"If we can get Thelma's help without putting her at risk . . . I guess we have to try."

"First thing in the morning," he said.

That was a night of rain, and rain also filled her dreams, and in those dreams were explosive thunderclaps and lightning, as well. She woke in terror, but the rainy night in Santa Ana was unmarred by those bright, noisy omens of death. It was a comparatively peaceful storm, without thunder, lightning, and wind, though she knew that it would not always be so.

·3·

The machinery clicked and hummed.

Erich Klietmann looked at the clock. In just three minutes the research team would return to the institute.

Two scientists, heirs of Penlovski and Januskaya and Volkaw, stood at the programming board, studying the myriad dials and gauges.

All the light in the room was unnatural, for the windows were not merely blacked out to avoid providing beacons for night-flying enemy bombers, but were bricked in for security reasons. The air was stuffy.

Standing in one corner of the main lab, near the gate, Lieutenant Klietmann anticipated his trip to 1989 with excitement, not because that future was filled with wonders but because the mission gave him an opportunity to serve *der Führer* in a way that few men ever could. If he succeeded in killing Krieger, the woman, and the boy, he would have earned a personal meeting with Hitler, a chance to see the great man face to face, to know the touch of his hand and through that touch to feel the power, the tremendous power of the German state and people and history and destiny. The lieutenant would have risked death ten times, a thousand times, for the chance to be brought to the personal attention of *der Führer,* to make Hitler aware of him, not aware of him as just another SS officer, but aware of him as an individual, as Erich Klietmann, the man who saved the Reich from the dire fate that it had almost been forced to endure.

Klietmann was not the Aryan ideal, and he was acutely aware of his physical shortcomings. His maternal grandfather had been Polish, a disgusting slavic mongrel, which made Klietmann only three-quarters German. Furthermore, though his other three grandparents and both of his parents had been blond, blue-eyed, with Nordic features, Erich had hazel eyes, dark hair, and the heavier, more sensuous features of his barbarian grandfather. He loathed the way he looked, and he tried to compensate for his physical shortcomings by being the most vigilant Nazi, most courageous soldier, and most ardent supporter of Hitler in the entire *Schutzstaffel,* which was tough because he had so much competition for that honor. Sometimes he had despaired of ever being singled out for glory. But he never gave up, and now here he was, on the brink of heroism that would earn him Valhalla.

He wanted to kill Stefan Krieger personally, not only because that would win *der Führer's* favor but because Krieger *was* the Aryan ideal, blond and blue-eyed, every feature truly Nordic, and from fine breeding stock. With every advantage, the hateful Krieger had chosen to betray his *Führer,* and that enraged Klietmann, who had to labor toward greatness under the burden of mongrel genes.

Now, with little more than two minutes left before the research team would return through the gate from 1989, Klietmann looked at his three subordinates, all dressed as young executives of another age, and he felt both a fierce and a sentimental pride in them so strong it almost brought tears to his eyes.

They had all come from humble beginnings. *Unterscharführer* Felix Hubatsch, Klietmann's sergeant and second in command of the unit, was the son of an alcoholic lathe operator and a slattern mother, both of whom he despised. *Rottenführer* Rudolph von Manstein was the son of a poor farmer whose lifetime of failure shamed him, and *Rottenführer* Martin Bracher was an orphan. In spite of coming from four different corners of Germany, the two corporals, the sergeant, and lieutenant Klietmann shared one thing that made them as close as brothers: They understood that a man's truest, deepest, and dearest relationship was not to his family but to the state, to the fatherland, and to their leader in whom the fatherland was embodied; the state was the only family that mattered; this single bit of wisdom elevated them and made them worthy fathers of the superrace to come.

Klietmann discreetly dabbed at the corners of his eyes with his thumb, blotting the nascent tears that he was not able to suppress.

In one minute the research team would return.

The machinery clicked and hummed.

·4·

At three o'clock, Wednesday afternoon, January 13, a white pickup entered the rainswept motel lot, came straight to the rear wing, and parked next to the Buick that bore a Nissan's license plates. The truck was about five or six years old. The passenger-side door was dented, and that rocker panel was spotted with rust. The owner was evidently refinishing the pickup in a patchwork fashion, because some spots had been sanded and primed but not yet repainted.

Laura watched the truck from behind the barely parted drapes at the motel-room window. She held the Uzi in one hand at her side.

The truck's headlights blinked off, and its windshield wipers stopped, and a moment later a woman with frizzy blond hair got out and walked to the door of Laura's unit. She rapped three times.

Chris was standing behind the door, looking at his mother.

Laura nodded.

Chris opened the door and said, "Hi, Aunt Thelma. Jeez, that's an ugly wig."

Stepping inside, hugging Chris fiercely, Thelma said, "Well, thanks a lot. And what would you say if I told you that was a monumentally ugly nose you were born with, but you're stuck with it, while I'm not stuck with the wig? Huh? What would you say then?"

Chris giggled. "Nothing. 'Cause I know I've got a cute nose."

"Cute nose? God, kid, you've got an actor's ego." She let go of him, glanced at Stefan Krieger, who was sitting in one of the chairs near the TV set, then turned to Laura. "Shane, did you see the heap I pulled up in? Am I clever? As I was getting in my Mercedes, I said to myself, Thelma—I call myself Thelma—I said, Thelma, isn't it going to draw a hell of a lot of attention at that sleazy motel when you pull up in a sixty-five-thousand-dollar car? So I tried to borrow the butler's car, but you know what *he* drives? A Jaguar. Is Beverly Hills the Twilight Zone, or what? So I had to borrow the gardener's truck. But here I am, and what do you think of this disguise?"

She was wearing a kinky blond wig glittering with droplets of rain, horn-rimmed glasses, and a pair of false dentures that gave her an overbite.

"You look better this way," Laura said, grinning.

Thelma popped out the fake teeth. "Listen, once I turned up a set of wheels that wouldn't draw attention, I realized that I'd draw some attention myself, being a major star and everything. And since the media's already dug up the fact that you and I are friends and have tried to ask me some pointed questions about you, the famous machine-gun-packing authoress, I decided to come incognito." She dropped her purse and the stage teeth on the bed. "This getup was for a new character I created in my nightclub act, tried it about eight times at Bally's in Vegas. It was a primo flop, that character. The audience *spat* at me, Shane, they brought in the casino's security guard and tried to have me arrested, they questioned my right to share the same planet with them—oh, they were rude, Shane, they were—"

Suddenly she halted in the middle of her patter and burst into tears. She rushed to Laura, threw her arms around her. "Oh, Jesus, Laura, I was scared, I was so scared. When I heard the news about San Bernardino, machine guns, and then the way they found your house at Big Bear, I thought you . . . or maybe Chris . . . I was so worried . . ."

Holding Thelma as tightly as Thelma was holding her, Laura said, "I'll tell you all about it, but the main thing is we're all right, and we think maybe we have a way to get out of the hole we're in."

"Why didn't you call me, you silly bitch?"

"I did call you."

"Only this morning! Two *days* after you're splashed all over the newspapers. I nearly went crazy."

"I'm sorry. I should've called sooner. I just didn't want to get you involved if I could avoid it."

Reluctantly Thelma let go of her. "I'm inevitably, deeply, and hopelessly involved, you idiot, because *you're* involved." She pulled a Kleenex from a pocket of her suede jacket and blotted her eyes.

"You have another one of those?" Laura asked.

Thelma gave her a Kleenex, and they both blew their noses.

"We were on the lam, Aunt Thelma," Chris said. "It's hard to stay in touch with people when you're on the lam."

Taking a deep, shuddery breath, Thelma said, "So, Shane, where are you keeping your collection of severed heads? In the bathroom? I heard you left one behind in San Bernardino. Sloppy. Is this a new hobby of yours, or have you always had an appreciation for the beauty of the human head unencumbered by all the messy extremities?"

"I want you to meet someone," Laura said. "Thelma Ackerson, this is Stefan Krieger."

"Pleased to meet you," Thelma said.

"You'll excuse me if I don't get up," Stefan said. "I'm still recuperating."

"If you can excuse this wig, I can excuse anything." To Laura, Thelma said, "Is he who I think he is?"

"Yes."

"Your guardian?"

"Yes."

Thelma went to Stefan and kissed him wetly on both cheeks. "I've no idea where you come from or who the hell you are, Stefan Krieger, but I love you for all the times you've helped my Laura." She stepped back and sat on the foot of the bed beside Chris. "Shane, this man you have here is gorgeous. Look at him, he's a hunk. I'll bet *you* shot him just so he couldn't get away. He looks just like a guardian angel ought to look." Stefan was embarrassed, but Thelma would not be stopped. "You're a real dish, Krieger. I want to hear all about you. But first, here's the money you asked for, Shane." She opened her voluminous purse and withdrew a thick wad of hundred-dollar bills.

Examining the money, Laura said, "Thelma, I asked you for four thousand. There's at least twice that here."

"Ten or twelve thousand, I think." Thelma winked at Chris and said, "When my friends are on the lam, I *insist* they go first class."

Thelma listened to the story, never expressing disbelief. Stefan was surprised by her open-mindedness, but she said, "Hey, once you've lived at McIlroy Home and Caswell Hall, the universe holds no more surprises. Time travelers from 1944? Pah! At McIlroy I could've shown you a woman as big as a sofa, who wore clothes made of bad upholstery fabric, and who was paid a handsome civil-service wage to treat orphaned children like vermin. Now *there* is an amazement." She was clearly affected by Stefan's origins, chilled and amazed by the trap they were in, but even under these circumstances she was Thelma Ackerson, always looking for the laugh in everything.

At six o'clock she put in the stage teeth again and went up the street to get take-out from a Mexican restaurant. "When you're on the run from the law, you need beans in your belly, tough-guy food." She came back with rain-dampened bags of tacos, containers of enchiladas, two orders of nachos, burritos, and chimichangas. They spread the food out on the bottom half of the bed, and Thelma and Chris sat on the top half. Laura and Stefan sat in chairs at the foot of the bed.

"Thelma," Laura said, "there's enough food here for ten."

"Well, I figured that would feed us and the cockroaches. If we didn't have food for the cockroaches, they might get mean, might go outside and overturn my gardener's pickup. You *do* have cockroaches here, don't you? I mean, after all, a swell place like this without cockroaches would be like the Beverly Hills Hotel without tree rats."

As they ate, Stefan outlined the plan he had devised for closing the gate and destroying the institute. Thelma interrupted with wisecracks, but when he was finished, she was solemn. "This is damned dangerous, Stefan. Brave enough to be foolish, maybe."

"There's no other way."

"I can see that," she said. "So what can I do to help?"

Pausing with a wad of corn chips halfway to his mouth, Chris said, "We need you to buy the computer, Aunt Thelma."

Laura said, "An IBM PC, their best model, the same one I have at home, so I'll know how to use all the software. We don't have time to learn the operating procedures of a new machine. I've written it all down for you. I could go buy it myself, I guess, with money you gave me, but I'm afraid of showing my face too many places."

"And we'll need a place to stay," Stefan said.

"We can't stay here," Chris said, enjoying being a part of the discussion, "not if we're going to be doing stuff with a computer. The maid would see it no matter how hard we tried to hide it, and she'd talk about it because that would be weird, people holing up in a place like this with a computer."

Stefan said, "Laura tells me that you and your husband have a second house in Palm Springs."

"We have a house in Palm Springs, a condo in Monterey, another condo in Vegas, and it wouldn't surprise me if we owned—or at least had time shares in—our very own Hawaiian volcano. My husband is too rich. So take your pick. My houses are your houses. Just don't use the towels to polish the hubcaps on your car, and if you must chew tobacco and spit on the floors, try to keep it in the corners."

"I thought the house in Palm Springs would be ideal," Laura said. "You've told me it's fairly secluded."

"It's on a large property with lots of trees, and there're other show-biz people on that block, all of 'em busy, so they don't tend to drop over for a cup of coffee. No one'll disturb you there."

"All right," Laura said, "there's just a few other things. We need changes of clothes, comfortable shoes, some basic necessities. I've made a list, sizes and everything. And, of course, when this is all over, I'll pay you back the cash you gave me and whatever you spend on the computer and these other things."

"Damn right you will, Shane. And forty percent interest. Per week. Compounded hourly. Plus your child. Your child will be mine."

Chris laughed. "My Aunt Rumpelstiltskin."

"You won't make smart remarks when you're *my* child, Christopher Robbin. Or at least you'll call me Mother Rumpelstiltskin, Sir."

"Mother Rumpelstiltskin, Sir!" Chris said, and saluted her.

At eight-thirty Thelma prepared to leave with the shopping list that Laura had composed and the information about the computer. "I'll be back tomorrow afternoon, as soon as I can," she said, giving Laura and then Chris one last hug. "You'll really be safe here, Shane?"

"I think we will. If they'd discovered we were staying here, they would've shown up sooner."

Stefan said, "Remember, Thelma, they're time travelers; once they discover where we've been hiding, they could just jaunt forward to the moment when we first arrived here. In fact they could've been waiting for us when we pulled into the motel on Monday. The fact that we've stayed here so long unmolested is almost proof there'll never be public knowledge that this was our hideout."

"My head spins," Thelma said. "And I thought reading a major studio's contract was complicated!"

She went out into the night and rain, still wearing the wig and the horn-rimmed glasses but carrying her stage teeth in her pocket, and she drove away in her gardener's truck.

Laura, Chris, and Stefan watched her from the big window, and Stefan said, "She's a special person."

"Very," Laura said. "I hope to God I haven't endangered her."

"Don't worry, Mom," Chris said. "Aunt Thelma's a tough broad. She always says so."

That night at nine o'clock, shortly after Thelma left, Laura drove to Fat Jack's place in Anaheim. The rain was not as heavy as it had been but fell in a steady drizzle. The macadamized pavement glistered silver-black, and gutters still overflowed with water that looked like oil in the queer light of the sodium-vapor streetlamps. Fog had crept in, too, not on little cat feet but slithering like a snake on its belly.

She had been loath to leave Stefan at the motel. But it was not wise for him to spend much time in the chilly, rainy January night in his debilitated condition. Besides, he could do nothing to help her.

Though Stefan remained behind, Chris accompanied Laura, for she would not be separated from him for the time it would take to cut a deal for the weapons. The boy had gone with her when she had first visited Fat Jack a year ago, when she'd bought the illegally modified Uzis, so the fat man would not be surprised to see him. Displeased, yes, since Fat Jack was no lover of children, but not surprised.

As she drove, Laura looked frequently in the rearview mirror, in the side mirrors, and took the measure of the other drivers around her with a diligence that gave new meaning to the term defensive driving. She could not afford to be broadsided by a dunderhead who was driving too fast for the road conditions. Police would put in an appearance at the scene of the crash, would routinely check out her license plates, and before they even arrested her, men carrying submachine guns would materialize and kill her and Chris.

She had left her own Uzi with Stefan, although he had protested. However, she was unable to abandon him with no means of self-defense. She still carried the .38 Chief's Special. And fifty spare rounds were distributed in the zippered pockets of her ski jacket.

Near Disneyland, when the neon-drenched phantasmagoria of Fat Jack's Pizza Party Palace appeared in the fog like the starship in *Close Encounters of the Third Kind* descending from clouds of its own making, Laura was relieved. She pulled into the crowded parking lot and switched off the engine. The windshield wipers stopped thumping, and rain washed down the glass in rippling sheets. Orange, red, blue, yellow, green, white, purple, and pink reflections of neon glimmered in that flowing film of water, so Laura felt curiously as if she were inside one of those old-fashioned, gaudy jukeboxes from the 1950s.

Chris said, "Fat Jack's put up more neon since we were here."

"I think you're right," Laura said.

They got out of the car and looked up at the blinking, flashing, rippling, winking, grotesquely flamboyant façade of Fat Jack's Pizza Party Palace. Neon was not reserved solely for the name of the place. It was also used to outline the building, the roofline, every window, and the front doors. In addition there were a pair of giant neon sunglasses on one end of the roof, and a huge neon rocketship poised for takeoff on the other end, with neon vapors perpetually curling and sparkling beneath its exhaust jets. The ten-foot-diameter neon pizza was an old feature, but the grinning neon clown's face was new.

The quantity of neon was so great that every falling raindrop was brightly tinted, as if it was part of a rainbow that had broken apart at nightfall. Every puddle shimmered with rainbow fragments.

The effect was disorienting, but it prepared the visitor for the inside of Fat Jack's, which seemed to be a glimpse of the chaos out of which the universe had formed trillions of years ago. The waiters and waitresses were dressed as clowns, ghosts, pirates, spacemen, witches, gypsies, and vampires, and a singing trio in bear costumes moved from table to table, delighting young children with pizza-smeared faces. In alcoves off the main room, older kids were at banks of videogames, so the *beep-zing-zap-bong* of that electronic play served as background music to singing bears and shouting children.

"Asylum," Chris said.

They were met inside the front door by the host, Dominick, who was Fat Jack's minority partner. Dominick was tall, cadaverous, with mournful eyes, and he seemed out of place midst the forced hilarity.

Raising her voice to be heard over the din, Laura asked for Fat Jack and said, "I called earlier. I'm an old friend of his mother's," which was what you were to say to indicate you wanted guns not pizza.

Dominick had learned to project his voice clearly through the cacophony without shouting. "You've been here before, I believe."

"Good memory," she said. "A year ago."

"Please follow me," Dominick said in a funereal voice.

They did not have to go through the cyclonic commotion of the dining room, which was good because that meant Laura was less likely to be seen and recognized by one of the customers. A door off the other side of the host's foyer opened onto a corridor that led past the kitchen and the storeroom to Fat Jack's private office. Dominick knocked on the door, ushered them inside, and said to Fat Jack, "Old friends of your mother," then left Laura and Chris with the big man.

Fat Jack took his nickname seriously and tried to live up to it. He was five feet ten and weighed about three hundred and fifty pounds. Wearing immense gray sweatpants and sweatshirt that fit him almost as tightly as Spandex, he looked like the fat man in that magnetized photograph that dieters could buy to put on refrigerators to scare them off food; in fact he looked like the refrigerator.

He sat in a baronial swivel chair behind a desk sized for him, and he did not get up. "Listen to the little beasts." He spoke to Laura, ignored Chris. "I put my office at the back of the building, had it specially soundproofed, and I can still hear them out there, shrieking, squealing; it's as if I'm just down the hall from hell."

"They're only children having fun," Laura said, standing with Chris in front of the desk.

"And Mrs. O'Leary was just an old lady with a clumsy cow, but she burned down Chicago," Fat Jack said sourly. He was eating a Mars bar. In the distance children's voices, insulated by soundproofing, rose in a dull roar, and as if talking to that unseen multitude, the fat man said, "Ah, choke on it, you little trolls."

"It's a nuthouse out there," Chris said.

"Who asked you?"

"Nobody, sir."

Jack had a grainy complexion with gray eyes nearly buried in a puff-adder face. He focused on Laura and said, "You see my new neon?"

"The clown is new, isn't it?"

"Yeah. Isn't it a beauty? I designed it, had it made, and then had it erected in the dead of night, so the next morning it was too late for anybody to get a restraining order to stop me. The damn city council just about croaked, all of them at once."

Fat Jack had been embroiled in a decade-long legal battle with the Anaheim Zoning Commission and the city council. The authorities disapproved of his garish neon displays, especially now that the area around Disneyland was slated for urban renewal. Fat Jack had spent tens if not hundreds of thousands of dollars fighting them in the courts, paying fines, being sued, countersuing, and he had even spent time in jail for contempt of court. He was a former libertarian who now claimed to be an anarchist, and he would not tolerate infringement on his rights—real and imagined—as a free-thinking individual.

He dealt in illegal weapons for the same reason he erected neon signs that violated city codes: as a statement against authority, to champion individual rights. He could talk for hours about the evils of government, any kind of government, in any degree whatsoever, and on Laura's last visit with Chris, in order to get the modified Uzis she wanted, she had listened to a lengthy explanation of why the government did not even have the right to pass laws forbidding murder.

Laura had no great love of big government, whether of the left or right, but she had little sympathy with Fat Jack, either. He did not acknowledge the legitimacy of any authority whatsoever, not that of proven institutions, not even that of family.

Now, after she gave Fat Jack her new shopping list, after he quoted a price and counted her money, he led her and Chris through the hidden door in the back of his office closet, down a narrow stairwell—he seemed in danger of becoming wedged tight—to the basement where he kept his illegal stock. Though his restaurant was a madhouse, his arsenal was stored with fetishistic neatness: cartons upon cartons of handguns and automatic weapons were stacked on metal shelves, arranged according to caliber and also according to price; he kept at least a thousand guns in the basement of the Pizza Party Palace.

He was able to provide her with two modified Uzis—"An immensely popular gun since the attempt to kill Reagan," he said—and another .38 Chief's Special. Stefan had hoped to obtain a Colt Commander 9mm Parabellum with a nine-round magazine and the barrel machined for a silencer. "Don't have it," Fat Jack said, "but I can let you have a Colt Commander Mark IV in .38 Super, which has a nine-round magazine, and I've got two of those machined for silencers. Got the silencers, too, plenty of 'em." She already knew that he wasn't able to provide her with ammunition, but as he finished his Mars bar, he explained anyway: "Don't stock ammunition or explosives. Look, I don't believe in authority, but I'm not totally irresponsible. I got a restaurant full of shrieking, snot-faced kids upstairs, and I can't risk blowing them to bits, even if that'd bring more peace to the world. Besides, I'd destroy all my pretty neon too."

"All right," Laura said, putting one arm around Chris to keep him at her side, "what about the gas on my list?"

"You sure you don't mean tear gas?"

"No. Vexxon. That's the stuff I want." Stefan had given her the name of the gas. He said it was one of the chemical weapons that was on the list of items the institute hoped to bring back to 1944 and introduce into the German military arsenal. Now perhaps it could be used *against* the Nazis. "We need something that will kill fast."

Fat Jack leaned his backside against the metal worktable in the middle of the room, where he had laid out the Uzis, revolvers, pistol, and silencers. The table creaked ominously. "Well, what we're talking about here is army ordnance, tightly controlled stuff."

"You can't get it?"

"Oh, sure, I can get you some Vexxon," Fat Jack said. He moved away from the table, which creaked in relief as his weight was lifted from it, and went to a set of metal shelves where he withdrew a couple of Hershey bars from between boxes of guns, a secret stash. He did not offer one to Chris, but put the second bar in the side pocket of his sweatpants and began to eat the other. "I don't have that sort of crap here; just as dangerous as explosives. But I can have it for you late tomorrow, if that's not inconvenient."

"That'll be fine."

"It'll cost you."

"I know."

Fat Jack grinned. Bits of chocolate were stuck between his teeth. "Don't get much call for this kind of thing, not from someone like yourself, a small buyer. Tickles me to try to figure what you'd be up to with it. Not that I expect you to tell me. But usually it's big buyers from South America or the Middle East who want these neuroactive and respiractive gases. Iraq and Iran used plenty the last few years."

"Neuroactive, respiractive? What's the difference?"

"Respiractive—they have to breathe it in; it kills them seconds after it hits the lungs and spreads through the bloodstream. When you release it, you've got to be wearing a gas mask. Your neuroactive, on the other hand, kills even quicker, just on touching the skin, and with certain types of it—like Vexxon—you won't need a gas mask or protective clothing, 'cause you can take a couple of pills before you use it, and they're like an advance antidote."

"Yes, I was supposed to ask for the pills, too," Laura said.

"Vexxon. Easiest-to-use gas on the market. You're a real smart shopper," Fat Jack said.

Already he had finished the candy bar, and he appeared to have grown noticeably since Laura and Chris had entered his office half an hour ago. She realized that Fat Jack's commitment to political anarchy was reflected not only in the atmosphere of his pizza parlor but in the condition of his body, for his flesh swelled unrestrained by social or medical considerations. He seemed to revel in his size, as well, frequently patting his gut or grabbing the rolls of fat on his sides and kneading them almost affectionately, and he walked with belligerent arrogance, pushing the world away from him with his belly. She had a vision of Fat Jack growing ever more huge, soaring past four hundred pounds, past five hundred, even as the wildly pyramiding neon structures on the roof grew ever more elaborate, until one day the roof collapsed and Fat Jack exploded simultaneously.

"I'll have the gas by five o'clock tomorrow," he said as he put the Uzis, .38 Chief's Special, Colt Commander, and silencers in a box labeled BIRTHDAY PARTY FAVORS, which had probably contained paper hats or noisemakers for the restaurant. He slipped the lid on the box and indicated that Laura was to carry it upstairs; among other things, Fat Jack did not believe in chivalry.

Back in Fat Jack's office, when Chris opened the door to the hall for his mother, Laura was pleased by the squealing of the children in the pizza parlor. That sound was the first normal, sane thing she had heard in more than half an hour.

"Listen to the little cretins," Fat Jack said. "They're not children;

they're shaved baboons trying to pass for children." He slammed his soundproofed office door behind Chris and Laura.

In the car on the way back to the motel, Chris said, "When this is all over . . . what're you going to do about Fat Jack?"

"Turn his butt in to the cops," Laura said. "Anonymously."

"Good. He's a nut."

"He's worse than a nut, honey. He's a fanatic."

"What's a fanatic exactly?"

She thought for a moment, then said, "A fanatic is a nut who has something to believe in."

·5·

Lieutenant Erich Klietmann, SS, watched the second hand on the programming-board clock, and when it neared the twelve, he turned and looked at the gate. Inside that twelve-foot-long, gloom-filled tube, something shimmered, a fuzzy gray-black patch that resolved into the silhouette of a man—then three more men, one behind the other. The research team came out of the gate, into the room, and were met by the three scientists who had been monitoring the programming board.

They had returned from February, 1989, and were smiling, which made Klietmann's heart pound because they would not be smiling if they had not located Stefan Krieger, the woman, and the boy. The first two assassination squads that had been sent into the future—the one that had attacked the house near Big Bear and the one in San Bernardino—had been composed of Gestapo officers. Their failures had led *der Führer* to insist the third team be *Schutzstaffel*, and now Erich judged the researchers' smiles to mean that his squad was going to have a chance to prove the SS was filled with better men than the Gestapo.

The failures of the two previous squads were not the only black marks on the Gestapo's record in this affair. Heinrich Kokoschka, the head of the institute's security, had been a Gestapo officer, as well, and he had apparently turned traitor. Available evidence seemed to support the theory that two days ago, on March 16, he had defected to the future with five other members of the institute's staff.

On the evening of March 16, Kokoschka had jaunted alone to the San Bernardino Mountains with the claimed intention of killing

Stefan Krieger there in the future before Krieger returned to 1944 and killed Penlovski, thereby undoing the deaths of the project's best men. But Kokoschka never came back. Some argued that Kokoschka had been killed up there in 1988, that Krieger had won the confrontation—but that did not explain what had happened to the five other men in the institute that evening: the two Gestapo agents waiting for Kokoschka's return and the three scientists monitoring the gate's programming board. All vanished, and five homing belts were missing; so the evidence pointed to a group of traitors within the institute who had become convinced that Hitler would lose the war even with the advantage of exotic weapons brought back from the future, and who had defected to another age rather than stay in a doomed Berlin.

But Berlin was not doomed. Klietmann would not entertain that possibility. Berlin was the new Rome; the Third Reich would last a thousand years. Now that the SS was being given the chance to find and kill Krieger, *der Führer's* dream would be protected and fulfilled. Once they had eliminated Krieger, who was the main threat to the gate and whose execution was the most urgent task before them, they would then focus on finding Kokoschka and the other traitors. Wherever those swine had gone, in whatever distant year and place they had taken refuge, Klietmann and his SS brethren would exterminate them with extreme prejudice and great pleasure.

Now Dr. Theodore Juttner—director of the institute since the murders of Penlovski, Januskaya, and Volkaw, and the disappearances on March 16—turned to Erich and said, "We've perhaps found Krieger, *Obersturmführer* Klietmann. Get your men ready to go."

"We're ready, Doctor," Erich said. Ready for the future, he thought, ready for Krieger, ready for glory.

·6·

At three-forty on Thursday afternoon, January 14, little more than one day after her first visit, Thelma returned to The Bluebird of Happiness Motel in her gardener's battered white pickup. She had two changes of clothes for each of them, suitcases in which to pack all the stuff, and a couple of thousand rounds of ammunition for the revolvers and the Uzis. She also had the IBM PC in the truck, plus a printer, a variety of software, a box of diskettes, and everything else they would need to make the system work for them.

With the wound in his shoulder only four days old, Stefan was recuperating surprisingly fast, although he was not ready to do any lifting, heavy or otherwise. He stayed in the motel room with Chris and packed the suitcases while Laura and Thelma moved the computer boxes to the trunk and back seat of the Buick.

The storm had passed during the night. Shredded gray clouds hung beardlike from the sky. The day had warmed to sixty-five degrees, and the air smelled clean.

Closing the Buick's trunk on the last of the boxes, Laura said, "You went shopping in that wig and those glasses, those *teeth?*"

"Nah," Thelma said, removing the stage teeth and putting them in a jacket pocket because they made her lisp when she talked. "Up close a salesclerk might've recognized me, and being disguised would arouse more attention than if I shopped as myself. But after I'd bought everything, I drove the truck to the deserted end of another shopping center's parking lot and made myself look like a cross between Harpo Marx and Bucky Beaver before heading here, just in case someone in another car looked over at me in traffic. You know, Shane, I sorta like this kind of intrigue. Maybe I'm the reincarnation of Mata Hari, 'cause when I think about seducing men to learn their secrets and then selling the secrets to a foreign government, I get delicious chills."

"It's the part about seducing men that gives you chills," Laura said, "not the secret-selling part. You're no spy, just a lech."

Thelma gave her the keys to the house in Palm Springs. "There's no full-time staff there. We just call a housekeeping service to spruce the place up a couple of days before we go. I didn't call them this time, of course, so you're liable to find some dust, but no real filth, and none of the severed heads *you* tend to leave behind."

"You're a love."

"There's a gardener. Not full-time like the one at our house in Beverly Hills. This guy just comes around once a week, Mondays, to mow the lawn, trim the hedges, and trample some flowers so he can charge us to replace them. I'd advise staying away from windows and keeping a low profile on Monday, until he comes and goes."

"We'll hide under the beds."

"You'll notice a lot of whips and chains under the bed, but don't get the idea Jason and I are kinky. The whips and chains belonged to his mother, and we keep them strictly for sentimental reasons."

They brought the packed suitcases out of the motel room and put those in the back seat with the other packages that would not fit in the Buick's trunk. After a round of hugs, Thelma said, "Shane, I'm between nightclub appearances for the next three weeks, so if you need me for anything more, you can get hold of me at the house in Beverly Hills, night or day. I'll stay by the phone." Reluctantly she left.

Laura was relieved when the truck disappeared in traffic; Thelma was safe, out of it. She dropped the room keys at the motel office, then drove away in the Buick with Chris in the other front seat and Stefan in the back seat with the luggage. She regretted leaving The Bluebird of Happiness because they had been safe there for four days, and there was no guarantee they'd be safe anywhere else in the world.

They stopped at a gunshop first. Because it was best to keep Laura out of sight as much as possible, Stefan went in to buy a box of ammunition for the pistol. They had not put that item on the shopping list they had given Thelma, for at that time they had not known whether they would get the 9mm Parabellum that Stefan wanted. And in fact they had gotten the .38 Colt Commander Mark IV instead.

After the gunshop they drove to Fat Jack's Pizza Party Palace to pick up two canisters of deadly nerve gas. Stefan and Chris waited in the car, under neon signs that were already burning at twilight, though they would not be in their full glory until nightfall.

The canisters were on Jack's desk. They were the size of small household fire extinguishers with a stainless-steel finish instead of fire-red, with a skull-and-crossbones label that said VEXXON/AEROSOL/WARNING—DEADLY NERVE TOXIN/UNAUTHORIZED POSSESSION IS A FELONY UNDER U.S. LAW, followed by a lot of fine print.

With a finger as plump as an overstuffed sausage, Jack pointed to a half-dollar-size dial on the top of each cylinder. "These here are timers, calibrated in minutes, one to sixty. If you set the timer and push the button in the center of it, you can release the gas remote, sort of like setting off a time bomb. But if you want to release it manually, then you hold the bottom of the canister in one hand, take this pistol-grip handle in your other hand, and just squeeze this loop the way you would a trigger. This crap, released under pressure, will disperse through a five-thousand-square-foot building in a minute and a half, faster if the heating or air conditioning is running. Exposed to light and air, it breaks down fast into nontoxic components, but it remains deadly for forty to sixty minutes. Just three milligrams on the skin kills in thirty seconds."

"The antidote?" Laura asked.

Fat Jack smiled and tapped the sealed, four-inch-square, blue-plastic bags that were fixed to the handles of the cylinders. "Ten capsules in each bag. Two will protect one person. Instructions are in the bag, but I was told you have to take the pills at least one hour before dispersing the gas. Then they'll protect you for three to five hours."

He took her money and put the Vexxon cylinders in a cardboard box labeled MOZZARELLA CHEESE—KEEP REFRIGERATED. As he put the lid on the box, he laughed and shook his head.

"What's wrong?" Laura asked.

"It just tickles me," Fat Jack said. "A looker like you, clearly well educated, with a little boy . . . if someone like *you* is involved in shit like this, society must be really coming apart at the seams a lot faster than I ever hoped. Maybe I will live to see the day when the establishment falls, when anarchy rules, when the only laws are those that individuals make between themselves and seal with a handshake."

As an afterthought, he lifted the lid on the box, plucked a few green slips of paper from a desk drawer, and dropped them on top of the cylinders of Vexxon.

"What're those?" Laura asked.

"You're a good customer," Fat Jack said, "so I'm throwing in a few coupons for free pizza."

Thelma and Jason's house in Palm Springs was indeed secluded. It was a curious but attractive cross between Spanish and Southwest adobe-style architecture on a one-acre property surrounded by a nine-foot-tall, peach-colored stucco wall that was interrupted only by the entrance and exit from the circular driveway. The grounds were heavily planted with olive trees, palms, and ficus, so neighbors were screened out on three sides, with only the front of the house revealed.

Though they arrived at eight o'clock that Thursday night, after driving into the desert from Fat Jack's place in Anaheim, the house and grounds were visible in detail because they were illuminated by cunningly designed, photocell-controlled landscape lighting that provided both security and aesthetic value. Palm and fern shadows made dramatic patterns on stucco walls.

Thelma had given them the remote garage door opener, so they drove the Buick into the three-car garage and entered the house through the connecting door to the laundry room—after deactivating the alarm system with the code Thelma had also given them.

It was far smaller than the Gaines's mansion in Beverly Hills, but still sizable, with ten rooms and four baths. The unique stamp of Steve Chase, the interior designer of choice in Palm Springs, was on every room: dramatic spaces dramatically lit; simple colors—warm apricot, dusty salmon—accented with turquoise here and there; suede walls, cedar ceilings; here, copper tables with a rich patina; there, granite tables contrasting interestingly with comfortably upholstered furniture in a variety of textured fabrics; elegant yet livable.

In the kitchen Laura found most of the pantry bare except for one shelf of canned goods. As they were all too tired to go grocery shopping, they made a dinner of what was at hand. Even if Laura had broken into the house without a key and had not known who owned the place, she would have realized it belonged to Thelma and Jason as soon as she looked in the pantry, for she could not imagine that any other pair of millionaires would still be so childlike at heart as to stock their larder with Chef Boyardee canned ravioli and spaghetti. Chris was delighted. For dessert they finished off two boxes of chocolate-covered Klondike ice-cream nuggets that they found in the otherwise empty freezer.

Laura and Chris shared the king-size bed in the master bedroom, and Stefan bunked across the hall in a guest room. Though she had reengaged the perimeter alarm system that monitored every door and window, though a loaded Uzi was on the floor beside her, though a loaded .38 was on the nightstand, and though no one in the world but Thelma could know where they were, Laura slept only fitfully. Each time she woke, she sat straight up in bed, listening for noises in the night—stealthy footsteps, whispering voices.

Toward morning, when she could not get back to sleep, she stared at the shadowy ceiling for a long time, thinking about something that Stefan had said a couple of days ago when explaining some of the fine points of time travel and the changes that travelers could effect in their futures: *Destiny struggles to reassert the pattern that was meant to be.* When Stefan had saved her from the junkie in the grocery store in 1963, fate eventually had brought her to another pedophile, Willy Sheener, in 1967. She had been destined to be an orphan, so when she found a new home with the Dockweilers, fate had conspired to shock Nina Dockweiler with a fatal heart attack, sending Laura back to the orphanage again.

Destiny struggles to reassert the pattern that was meant to be.

What next?

In the pattern that was meant to be, Chris had never been born.

Therefore would fate arrange his death soon, to bring events back as close as possible to those which had been ordained and with which Stefan Krieger had meddled? She had been destined to spend her life in a wheelchair before Stefan held Dr. Paul Markwell at gunpoint and prevented him from delivering her. So perhaps now fate would put her in the way of Gestapo gunfire that would sever her spine and render her paraplegic in accordance with the original plan.

How long did the forces of destiny strive to reassert the pattern after a change had been made in it? Chris had been alive for more than eight years. Was that long enough for destiny to decide that his existence was acceptable? She had lived thirty-four years out of a wheelchair. Was destiny still troubling itself with that unnatural squiggle in the ordained design?

Destiny struggles to reassert the pattern that was meant to be.

As dawn's light glowed softly at the edges of the drapes, Laura tossed and turned, growing angry but not sure at whom or what her anger could be directed. What *was* destiny? What was the power that shaped the patterns and attempted to enforce them? God? Should she be raging at God—or begging Him to let her son live and to spare her from the life of a cripple? Or was the power behind destiny merely a natural mechanism, a force no different in origin from gravity or magnetism?

Because there was no logical target at which her emotions could be vented, Laura felt her anger slowly metamorphosing to fear. They seemed to be safe at the Gaines's Palm Springs house. After passing one uneventful night in the place, they almost could be assured that their presence would never be public knowledge, for otherwise killers from the past no doubt already would have appeared. Yet Laura was afraid.

Something bad was going to happen. Something very bad.

Trouble was coming, but she did not know from what direction.

Lightning. Soon.

Too bad the old saw wasn't true: In fact lightning did strike twice in the same place, three times, a hundred, and she was the reliable rod that drew it.

·7·

Dr. Juttner entered the last of the numbers in the programming board that controlled the gate. To Erich Klietmann, he said, "You and your men will be traveling to the vicinity of Palm Springs, California, in January, 1989."

"Palm Springs?" Klietmann was surprised.

"Yes. Of course, we had expected you'd have to go somewhere in the Los Angeles or Orange County area, where you would have found your young-executive dress more appropriate than in a resort town, but you'll still pass without notice. For one thing, it's winter there, and even in the desert dark suits will be appropriate for the season." Juttner handed Klietmann a sheet of paper on which he had written directions. "Here's where you'll find the woman and the boy."

Folding the paper and putting it in an inside coat pocket, the lieutenant said, "What about Krieger?"

"The researchers didn't find mention of him," Juttner said, "but he must be with the woman and the boy. If you don't see him, then do your best to take the woman and boy captive. If you have to torture them to learn Krieger's whereabouts, so be it. And if worse comes to worst and they won't give you Krieger—kill them. That might draw him into the open somewhere down the time line."

"We'll find him, Doctor."

Klietmann, Hubatsch, von Manstein, and Bracher were all wearing their homing belts beneath their Yves St. Laurent suits. Carrying their Mark Cross attaché cases, they walked to the gate, stepped up into that giant barrel, and moved toward the two-thirds point where they would pass in a wink from 1944 to 1989.

The lieutenant was afraid but also exhilarated. He was the iron fist of Hitler, from which Krieger could not hide even forty-five years in the future.

·8·

On their first full day in the Palm Springs house, Friday the fifteenth of January, they set up the computer, and Laura instructed Stefan in its use. IBM's operating program and the software for the tasks they needed to perform were extremely user-friendly, and though by nightfall Stefan was far from expert at operating the computer, he was able to understand how it functioned, how it thought. He would not be doing most of the work with the machine, anyway; that would be left to Laura, who was already experienced with the system. His job would be to explain to her the calculations that would have to be done, so she would be able to apply the computer to the solution of the many problems ahead of them.

Stefan's intention was to go back to 1944, using the gate-homing belt he had taken off Kokoschka. The belts were not time machines. The gate itself was the machine, the vehicle of transport, and it remained always in 1944. The belts were in tune with the temporal vibrations of the gate, and they simply brought the traveler home when he pushed the button to activate that link.

"How?" Laura asked when he explained the use of the belt. "How does it take you back?"

"I don't know. Would you know *how* a microchip functions inside a computer? No. But that doesn't prevent you from using the computer any more than my ignorance prevents me from using the gate."

Having returned to the institute in 1944, having seized control of the main lab, Stefan would make two crucial jaunts, each only days into the future from March of '44, to arrange the destruction of the institute. Those two trips had to be meticulously planned, so he would arrive at each destination in *exactly* the geographical location and *precisely* at the time that he desired. Such refined calculations were impossible to make in 1944, not only because computer assistance was unavailable but because in those days marginally—but vitally—less was known then about the angle and rate of rotation of the earth and about other planetary factors that affected a jaunt, which was why time travelers from the institute frequently arrived off schedule by minutes and out of place by miles. With the ultimate numbers provided by the IBM, he could program the gate to deliver him within one yard and within a split second of his desired point of arrival.

They used all of the books that Thelma had bought. These were not merely science and mathematics texts, but histories of the Second World War, in which they could pinpoint the whereabouts of certain major figures on certain dates.

In addition to performing complex calculations for the jaunts, they had to allow time for Stefan to heal. When he returned to 1944, he would be reentering the wolf's lair, and even equipped with nerve gas and a first-rate firearm, he would have to be quick and agile to avoid being killed. "Two weeks," he said. "I think I'll have enough flexibility in the shoulder and arm to go back in two more weeks."

It did not matter if he took two weeks or ten, for when he used Kokoschka's homing belt, he would return to the institute only eleven minutes after Kokoschka had left it. His date of departure from current time would not affect his date of return in 1944.

The only worry was that the Gestapo would find them first and send a hit squad to 1989 to eliminate them before Stefan could return to his era to implement his plan. Though it was their only worry—it was worry enough.

With considerable caution, more than half expecting a sudden flash of lightning and a roll of thunder, they took a break and went grocery shopping Friday afternoon. Laura, still the object of media attention, remained in the car while Chris and Stefan went into the market. No lightning struck, and they returned to the house with a trunkful of groceries.

Unpacking the market bags in the kitchen, Laura discovered that a third of the sacks contained nothing but snack food: three different kinds of ice-cream bars, plus one quart each of chocolate, rocky road, butter almond, and almond fudge; family-size bags of M&Ms, Kit Kats, Reese's Cups, and Almond Joys; potato chips, pretzels, tortilla chips, cheese popcorn, peanuts; four kinds of cookies; one chocolate cake, one cherry pie, one box of doughnuts, four packages of Ding Dongs.

Stefan was helping her put things away, and she said, "You must have the world's biggest sweet tooth."

"See, this is another thing I find so amazing and wonderful about this future of yours," he said. "Just imagine—there's no longer any nutritional difference between a chocolate cake and a steak. Just as many vitamins and minerals in these potato chips as in a green salad. You can eat nothing but desserts and remain as healthy as a man who eats balanced meals. Incredible! How was this advance achieved?"

Laura turned in time to see Chris slinking out of the kitchen. "Whoa, you little con artist."

Looking sheepish, he said, "Doesn't Mr. Krieger get some funny ideas about our culture?"

"I know where he got this one," she said. "What a sneaky thing to have done."

Chris sighed and tried to sound mournful. "Yeah. But I figure . . . if we're being hunted down by Gestapo agents, we ought to be able to eat as many Ding Dongs as we want, at least, 'cause every meal could be our last." He looked at her sideways to see if she was buying his condemned-man routine.

In fact what the boy said contained enough truth to make his trickery understandable if not excusable, and she could not find the will to punish him.

That night after dinner, Laura changed the dressing on Stefan's wound. The impact of the slug had left an enormous bruise on his chest with the bullet hole at its approximate center, a smaller bruise around the exit point. The suture threads and the inside of the old bandage were crusted with fluid that had seeped from him and dried. After she carefully bathed the wounds, cleaning that material away as much as possible without disturbing the scab, she gently palpated the flesh, producing a trace of clear seepage, but there was no sign of pus formation that would indicate a serious infection. Of course, he might have an abscess within the wound, draining internally, but that was not likely because he had no fever.

"Keep taking the penicillin," she said, "and I think you'll be fine. Doc Brenkshaw did a good job."

While Laura and Stefan spent long hours at the computer Saturday and Sunday, Chris watched television, looked through the bookshelves for something to read, puzzled over a hardcover collection of old Barbarella cartoons—

"Mom, what does orgasm mean?"

"What're you reading? Give me that."

—and generally entertained himself without a fuss. He came to the den once in a while and stood for a minute or two at a time, watching them use the computer. After about a dozen visits he said, "In *Back to the Future* they just had this time-traveling car, and they pushed a few buttons on the dashboard, and they were *off—Pow!*—like that. How come nothing in real life's ever as easy as it is in the movies?"

On Monday, January 18, they kept a low profile while the gardener mowed the lawn and trimmed some shrubbery. In four days he was the only person they had seen; no door-to-door salesmen had called, not even a Jehovah's Witness pushing *Watchtower* magazine.

"We're safe here," Stefan said. "Obviously, our presence in the house never becomes public knowledge. If it did, the Gestapo would have visited us already."

Nevertheless Laura kept the perimeter alarm system switched on nearly twenty-four hours a day. And at night she dreamed of destiny reasserting itself, of Chris erased from existence, of waking up to find herself in a wheelchair.

·9·

They were supposed to arrive at eight o'clock to give them plenty of time to reach the location at which the researchers had pinpointed the woman and the boy, if not Krieger. But when Lieutenant Klietmann blinked and found himself forty-five years beyond his own era, he knew at once that they were a couple of hours late. The sun was too high above the horizon. The temperature was about seventy-five, too warm for an early, winter morning in the desert.

Like a white crack in a blue-glazed bowl, lightning splintered down the sky. Other cracks opened, and sparks flashed above as if struck from the hooves of a bull loose in some celestial china shop.

As the thunder faded, Klietmann turned to see if von Manstein, Hubatsch, and Bracher had made the journey safely. They were with him, all carrying attaché cases, with sunglasses stuck in the breast pockets of their expensive suits.

The problem was that thirty feet beyond the sergeant and the two corporals, a pair of elderly, white-haired women in pastel stretch pants and pastel blouses were standing at a white car near the rear door to a church, staring in astonishment at Klietmann and his squad. They were holding what appeared to be casseroles.

Klietmann glanced around and saw that he and his men had arrived in the parking lot behind the church. There were two other cars in addition to the one that seemed to belong to the women, but there were no other onlookers. The lot was encircled by a wall, so the only way out was past the women and along the side of the church.

Deciding that boldness was the best course, Klietmann walked straight toward the women, as if there was nothing whatsoever unusual about his having materialized out of thin air, and his men followed him. Mesmerized, the women watched them approach.

"Good morning, ladies." Like Krieger, Klietmann had learned to speak English with an American accent in hopes of serving as a deep-cover agent, but he'd been unable to lose his accent entirely, no matter how hard he studied and practiced. Though his own watch was set to local time, he knew he could no longer trust it, so he said, "Could you please be so kind as to tell me what time it is?"

They stared at him.

"The time?" he repeated.

The woman in yellow pastel twisted her wrist without letting go of the casserole, looked at her watch, and said, "Uh, it's ten-forty."

They were two hours and forty minutes late. They couldn't waste time searching for a car to hot-wire, especially not when a perfectly good one was available, with keys, right in front of them. Klietmann was prepared to kill both women for the car. He could not leave their bodies in the parking lot; an alarm would go up when they were found, and shortly thereafter the police would be looking for their car—a nasty complication. He'd have to stuff the bodies in the trunk and take them with him.

The woman in blue pastels said, "Why've you come to us, are you angels?"

Klietmann wondered if she was senile. Angels in pinstripe suits? Then he realized that they were in the vicinity of a church and had appeared miraculously, so it might be logical for a religious woman to assume they were angels, regardless of their clothing. Maybe it would not be necessary to waste time killing them, after all. He said, "Yes, ma'am, we are angels, and God needs your car."

The woman in yellow said, "My Toyota here?"

"Yes, ma'am." The driver's door was standing open, and Klietmann put his attaché on the front seat. "We're on an urgent mission for God, you saw us step through the pearly gate from Heaven right before your eyes, and we must have transportation."

Von Manstein and Bracher had gone around to the other side of the Toyota, opened those doors, and gotten inside.

The woman in blue said, "Shirley, you've been *chosen* to give your car."

"God will return it to you," Klietmann said, "when our work here is done." Remembering the gasoline shortages of his own war-torn era and not sure how plentiful fuel was in 1989, he added: "Of course, no matter how much gas is in the tank now, it'll be full when we return it and perpetually full thereafter. The loaves and fishes thing."

"But there's potato salad in there for the church brunch," the woman in yellow said.

Felix Hubatsch had already opened the rear door on the driver's side and had found the potato salad. Now he took it out of the car and put it on the macadam at the woman's feet.

Klietmann got in, closed the door, heard Hubatsch slam the door behind him, found the keys in the ignition, started the car, and drove out of the church lot. When he looked in the rearview mirror just before turning into the street, the old women were still back there, holding their casseroles, staring after him.

·10·

Day by day they refined their calculations, and Stefan exercised his left arm and shoulder as much as he dared, trying to prevent it from growing stiff as it healed, hoping to maintain as much muscle tone as possible. On Thursday afternoon, January 21, as their first week in Palm Springs drew to a close, they completed the calculations and arrived at the precise time and space coordinates that Stefan would require for the jaunts he would make once he returned to 1944.

"Now I just need a bit more time to heal," he said, as he stood up from the computer and testingly moved his left arm in circles.

She said, "It's been eleven days since you were shot. Do you still have pain?"

"Some. A deeper, duller pain. And not all the time. But the strength isn't back. I think I'd better wait a few days yet. If it feels all right by next Wednesday, the twenty-seventh, I'll return to the institute then. Sooner, if I improve faster, but certainly no later than next Wednesday."

That night, Laura woke from a nightmare in which she was confined yet again to a wheelchair and in which destiny, in the form of a faceless man in a black robe, was busily erasing Chris from reality, as if the boy was only a crayon drawing on a pane of glass. She was soaked in sweat, and for a while she sat up in bed, listening for noises in the house but hearing nothing other than her son's steady, low breathing on the bed beside her.

Later, unable to get back to sleep, she lay thinking about Stefan Krieger. He was an interesting man, extremely self-contained and at times hard to figure.

Since Monday of the previous week, when he explained that he had become her guardian because he had fallen in love with her and wanted to improve the life she had been meant to live, he'd said nothing more of love. He had not restated his feelings for her, had not subjected her to meaningful looks, had not played the part of a pining suitor. He made his case and was willing to give her time to think about him and get to know him before she decided what she thought of him. She suspected he would wait years, if necessary, and without complaint. He had the patience born of extreme adversity, which was something she understood.

He was quiet, pensive a lot of the time, occasionally downright melancholy, which she supposed was a result of the horrors he had seen in his long-ago Germany. Perhaps that core of sadness had its roots in things he had done himself and had come to regret, things for which he felt he could never atone. After all, he had said that a place in hell was reserved for him. He had revealed no more about his past than what he had told her and Chris in the motel room more than ten days ago. She sensed, however, that he was willing to tell her all the details, those that were a discredit to him as well as those that reflected well on him; he would not conceal anything from her; he was merely waiting for her to decide what she thought of him and whether, in any case, she wanted to know more.

In spite of the sorrow in him, deep as marrow and dark as blood, he had a quiet sense of humor. He was good with Chris and could make the boy laugh, which Laura counted in his favor. His smile was warm and gentle.

She still did not love him, and she did not think that she ever would. She wondered how she could be so sure of that. In fact she lay in the dark bedroom for a couple of hours, wondering, until at last she began to suspect that the reason she could not love him was because he was not Danny. Her Danny had been a unique man, and with him she had known a love as close to perfection as the world allowed. Now, in seeking her affections, Stefan Krieger would be forever in competition with a ghost.

She recognized the pathos in their situation, and she was glumly aware of the loneliness that her attitude assured. In her heart she wanted to be loved and to love in return, but in her relationship with Stefan, she saw only his passion unrequited, her hope unfulfilled.

Beside her, Chris murmured in his sleep, then sighed.

I love you, honey, she thought. I love you so much.

Her son, the only child she could ever have, was the center of her existence now and for the foreseeable future, her primary reason for going on. If anything happened to Chris, Laura knew she would no longer be able to find relief in the dark humor of life; this world in which tragedy and comedy were married in all things would become, for her, exclusively a place of tragedy, too black and bleak to be endured.

·11·

Three blocks from the church Erich Klietmann pulled the white Toyota to the curb and parked on a side street off Palm Canyon Drive in Palm Springs's main shopping district. Scores of people strolled along the sidewalks, window-shopping. Some of the younger women were wearing shorts and brief tops that Klietmann found not only scandalous but embarrassing, casually displaying their bodies in a way unknown in his own age. Under the iron rule of *der Führer's* National Socialist Workers' Party, such shameless behavior wouldn't be permitted; Hitler's triumph would result in a different world, where morality would be strictly enforced, where these bare-limbed, brassiereless women would parade themselves only at the risk of imprisonment and reeducation, where decadent creatures wouldn't be tolerated. As he watched their buttocks clench and flex beneath their tight shorts, as he watched unrestrained breasts swaying under the thin fabric of T-shirts, what most disturbed Klietmann was that he desperately wanted to lay with every one of these women even if they were representatives of the deviant strains of humanity that Hitler would abolish.

Beside Klietmann, Corporal Rudy von Manstein had unfolded the map of Palm Springs provided by the team of researchers that had located the woman and the boy. He said, "Where do we make the hit?"

From an inside pocket of his suit jacket, Klietmann withdrew the folded paper that Dr. Juttner had given him in the lab. He opened it and read aloud: "On state route 111, approximately six miles north of the Palm Springs city limits, the woman will be arrested by an officer of the California Highway Patrol at eleven-twenty, Wednesday morning, January 27. She will be driving a black Buick Riviera. The boy will be with her and will be taken into protective custody. Apparently Krieger is there, but we're not sure; apparently he escapes from the police officer, but we don't know how."

Von Manstein had already traced a route on the map that would take them out of Palm Springs and onto highway 111.

"We've got thirty-one minutes," Klietmann said, glancing at the dashboard clock.

"We'll make it easily," von Manstein said. "Fifteen minutes at the most."

"If we get there early," Klietmann said, "we can kill Krieger before he slips away from the highway-patrol officer. In any event we have to get there before the woman and boy are taken into custody because it'll be far more difficult to get at them once they're in jail." He turned around to look at Bracher and Hubatsch in the back seat. "Understood?"

They both nodded, but then Sergeant Hubatsch patted the breast pocket of his suit and said, "Sir, what about these sunglasses?"

"What about them?" Klietmann asked impatiently.

"Should we put them on now? Will that help us blend with the local citizenry? I've been studying the people on the street, and though a lot of them are wearing dark glasses, many of them aren't."

Klietmann looked at the pedestrians, trying not to be distracted by scantily clad women, and he saw that Hubatsch was correct. More to the point, he realized that not even one of the men in sight was dressed in the power look preferred by young executives. Maybe all young executives were in their offices at this hour. Whatever the reason for the lack of dark suits and black Bally loafers, Klietmann felt conspicuous even though he and his men were in a car. Because many pedestrians were wearing sunglasses, he decided that wearing his own would give him one thing in common with some of the locals.

When the lieutenant put on his Ray-Bans, so did von Manstein, Bracher, and Hubatsch.

"All right, let's go," Klietmann said.

But before he could pop the emergency brake and put the car in gear, someone knocked on the driver's window beside him. It was a Palm Springs police officer.

·12·

Laura sensed that, one way or the other, their ordeal was soon coming to an end. They would succeed in destroying the institute or die trying, and she had almost reached the point at which an end to fear was desirable regardless of how it was achieved.

Wednesday morning, January 27, Stefan still suffered deep-muscle soreness in his shoulder but no sharp pain. No numbness remained in his hand or arm, which meant the bullet had not damaged any nerves. Because he cautiously had exercised every day, he had more than half of his usual strength in his left arm and shoulder, just enough to make him confident that he would be able to implement his plan. But Laura could see that he was afraid of the trip ahead of him.

He put on Kokoschka's gate-homing belt, which Laura had taken from her safe the night that Stefan had arrived wounded on her doorstep. His fear remained apparent, but the moment that he put on the belt, his anxiety was overlaid with a steely determination.

In the kitchen at ten o'clock, each of them, including Chris, took two of the capsules that would render them impervious to the effects of the nerve gas, Vexxon. They washed down the preventive with glasses of Hi-C orange drink.

The three Uzis, one of the .38 revolvers, the silencer-equipped Colt Commander Mark IV, and a small nylon backpack full of books had been loaded into the car.

The two pressurized, stainless-steel bottles of Vexxon were still in the Buick's trunk. After studying the informational pamphlets in the blue plastic bags attached to the containers, Stefan had decided he would need only one cylinder for the job. Vexxon was a designer gas tailored primarily for use indoors—to kill the enemy in barracks, shelters, and bunkers deep underground—rather than against troops in the field. In the open air the stuff dispersed too fast—and broke down too quickly in sunlight—to be effective beyond a radius of two hundred yards from point of release. However, when opened full-cock, a single cylinder could contaminate a fifty-thousand-square-foot structure in a few minutes, which was good enough for his purposes.

At 10:35 they got in the car and left the Gaines's house, heading for the desert off route 111, north of Palm Springs. Laura made sure Chris's safety harness was buckled, and the boy said, "See, if you had a car that was a time machine, we'd drive back to 1944 in comfort."

Days ago they had taken a night drive to the open desert to find a spot suitable for Stefan's departure. They needed to know the exact geographical location in advance in order to do the calculations that would make it possible for him to return conveniently to them after his work in 1944 was done.

Stefan intended to open the valve on the Vexxon cylinder *before* he pushed the button on the gate-homing belt, so the nerve gas would be dispersing even as he returned through the gate to the institute, killing everyone who was in the lab at the 1944 end of the Lightning Road. Therefore he would be releasing a quantity of the toxin at his point of departure, too, and it seemed prudent to do so only in an isolated place. The street in front of the Gaines's house was less than two hundred yards away, within Vexxon's effective range, and they did not want to kill innocent bystanders.

Besides, though the gas was supposed to remain poisonous only for forty to sixty minutes, Laura was concerned that the deactivated residue, although not lethal, might have unknown, long-range toxic effects. She did not intend to leave any such substance in Thelma and Jason's house.

The day was clear, blue, serene.

When they had driven only a couple of blocks and were descending into a hollow where the road was flanked by huge date palms, Laura thought she saw a strange pulse of light in the fragment of sky that was captured by her rearview mirror. What would lightning be like in a bright, cloudless sky? Not as dramatic as on a storm-clouded day, for it would be competing with the brightness of the sun. What it might look like in fact was the very thing she thought she had seen—a strange, brief *pulse* of brightness.

Though she braked, the Buick was into the bottom of the hollow, and she could no longer see the sky in the rearview mirror, just the hill behind them. She thought she heard a rumble, too, like distant thunder, but she could not be sure because of the roar of the car's air conditioner. She pulled quickly to the side of the road, fumbling with the ventilation controls.

"What's wrong?" Chris asked as she put the car in park, threw open her door, and got out.

Stefan opened the rear door and got out too. "Laura?"

She was looking at the limited expanse of sky that she could see from the bottom of the hollow, using her flattened hand as a visor over her eyes. "You hear that, Stefan?"

In the warm, desert-dry day, a faraway rumble slowly died.

He said, "Could be jet noise."

"No. The last time I thought it might be a jet, it was *them*."

The sky pulsed again, one last time. She did not actually see the lightning itself, not the jagged bolt scored on the heavens, but just the reflection of it in the upper atmosphere, a faint wave of light flushing across the blue vault above.

"They're here," she said.

"Yes," he agreed.

"Somewhere on our way out to route 111, someone's going to stop us, maybe a traffic cop, or maybe we'll be in an accident, so there'll be a public record, and then *they'll* show up. Stefan, we've got to turn around, go back to the house."

"It's no use," he said.

Chris had gotten out of the other side of the car. "He's right, Mom. It doesn't matter what we do. Those time travelers came here 'cause they've already peeked into the future and know where they're gonna find us maybe half an hour from now, maybe ten minutes from now. It doesn't matter if we go back to the house or go on ahead; they've already seen us someplace—maybe even back at the house. See, no matter how much we change our plans, we'll cross their path."

Destiny.

"Shit!" she said and kicked the side of the car, which didn't do any good, didn't even make her feel better. "I *hate* this. How can you hope to win against goddamn time travelers? It's like playing blackjack when the dealer is God."

No more lightning flared.

She said, "Come to think of it, all of life is a blackjack game with God as the dealer, isn't it? So this is no worse. Get in the car, Chris. Let's get on with it."

As she drove through the western neighborhoods of the resort city, Laura's nerves were as taut as garroting wire. She was alert for trouble on all sides, though she knew it would come when and where she least expected it.

Without incident they connected with the northern end of Palm Canyon Drive, then state route 111. Ahead lay twelve miles of mostly barren desert before 111 intersected Interstate 10.

·13·

Hoping to avoid catastrophe, Lieutenant Klietmann lowered the driver's window and smiled up at the Palm Springs policeman who had rapped on the glass to get his attention and who was now bending down, squinting in at him. "What is it, officer?"

"Didn't you see the red curb when you parked here?"

"Red curb?" Klietmann said, smiling, wondering what the hell the cop was talking about.

"Now, sir," the officer said in a curiously playful tone, "are you telling me you didn't see the red curb?"

"Yes, sir, of course I saw it."

"I didn't think *you'd* fib," the cop said as if he knew Klietmann and trusted his reputation for honesty, which baffled the lieutenant. "So if you saw the red curb, sir, why'd you park here?"

"Oh, I see," Klietmann said, "parking is restricted to curbs that aren't red. Yes, of course."

The patrolman blinked at the lieutenant. He shifted his attention to von Manstein in the passenger's seat, then to Bracher and Hubatsch in the rear, smiled and nodded at them.

Klietmann did not have to look at his men to know they were on edge. The air in the car was heavy with tension.

When he shifted his gaze to Klietmann, the police officer smiled tentatively and said, "Am I right—you fellas are four preachers?"

"Preachers?" Klietmann said, disconcerted by the question.

"I've got a bit of a deductive mind," the cop said, his tentative smile still holding. "I'm no Sherlock Holmes. But the bumper stickers on your car say 'I Love Jesus' and 'Christ Has Risen.' And there's a Baptist convention in town, and you're all dressed in dark suits."

That was why he had thought he could trust Klietmann not to fib: He believed they were Baptist ministers.

"That's right," Klietmann said at once. "We're with the Baptist convention, officer. Sorry about the illegal parking. We don't have red curbs where I come from. Now if—"

"Where *do* you hail from?" the cop asked, not with suspicion but in an attempt to be friendly.

Klietmann knew a lot about the United States but not enough to carry on a conversation of this sort when he did not control its direction to any degree whatsoever. He believed that Baptists were from the southern part of the country; he wasn't sure if there were any of them in the north or west or east, so he tried to think of a southern state. He said, "I'm from Georgia," before he realized how unlikely that claim seemed when spoken in his German accent.

The smile on the cop's face faltered. Looking past Klietmann to von Manstein, he said, "And where you from, sir?"

Following his lieutenant's lead, but speaking with an even stronger accent, von Manstein said, "Georgia."

From the back seat, before they could be asked, Hubatsch and Bracher said, "Georgia, we're from Georgia," as if that word was magic and would cast a spell over the patrolman.

The cop's smile had vanished altogether. He frowned at Erich Klietmann and said, "Sir, would you mind stepping out of the car for a moment?"

"Certainly, officer," Klietmann said, as he opened his door, noticing how the cop backed up a couple of steps and rested his right hand on the butt of his holstered revolver. "But we're late for a prayer meeting—"

In the back seat Hubatsch snapped open his attaché case and

snatched the Uzi from it as quickly as a presidential bodyguard might have done. He did not roll down the window but put the muzzle against the glass and opened fire on the cop, giving him no time to draw his revolver. The car window blew out as bullets pounded through it. Struck by at least twenty rounds at close range, the cop pitched backward into traffic. Brakes squealed as a car made a hard stop to avoid the body, and across the street display windows shattered as bullets hit a men's clothing shop.

With the cool detachment and quick thinking that made Klietmann proud to be in the *Schutzstaffel,* Martin Bracher got out of the Toyota on his side and loosed a wide arc of fire from the Uzi to add to the chaos and give them a better chance of escaping. Windows imploded in the exclusive shops not only on the side street at the end of which they were parked but all the way across the intersection on the east flank of Palm Canyon Drive as well. People screamed, dropped to the pavement, scuttled for the cover of doorways. Klietmann saw passing cars hit by bullets out on Palm Canyon, and maybe a few drivers were hit or maybe they only panicked, but the vehicles swung wildly from lane to lane; a tan Mercedes sideswiped a delivery truck, and a sleek, red sportscar jumped the curb, crossed the sidewalk, grazed the bole of a palm tree, and plowed into the front of a gift shop.

Klietmann got behind the wheel again and released the emergency brake. He heard Bracher and Hubatsch leap into the car, so he threw the white Toyota in gear and shot forward onto Palm Canyon, hanging a hard left, heading north. He discovered at once that he was on a one-way street, going in the wrong direction. Cursing, he dodged oncoming cars. The Toyota rocked wildly on bad springs, and the glove compartment popped open, emptying its contents in von Manstein's lap. Klietmann turned right at the next intersection. A block later he ran a red light, narrowly avoiding pedestrians in the crosswalk, and turned left onto another avenue that allowed northbound traffic.

"We only have twenty-one minutes," von Manstein said, pointing at the dashboard clock.

"Tell me where to go," Klietmann said. "I'm lost."

"No, you're not," von Manstein said, brushing the contents of the glove compartment—spare keys, paper napkins, a pair of white gloves, individual packets of catsup and mustard, documents of various kinds—off the map that he was still holding open in his lap. "You're not lost. This will connect with Palm Canyon where it becomes a two-way street. From there we head straight north onto route 111."

·14·

Approximately six miles north of Palm Springs, where the barren land looked particularly empty, Laura pulled to the shoulder of the highway. She slowly proceeded a few hundred yards until she found the place where the embankment declined almost to the level of the surrounding desert and sloped sufficiently to allow her to drive out onto the flat plain. Aside from a little bunchgrass that bristled in dry clumps and a few gnarly mesquite bushes, the only vegetation was tumbleweed—some green and rooted, some dry and rolling free. The fixed weeds scraped softly against the Buick, and the loose ones flew away on the wind that the car created.

The hard ground had a shale base over which an alkaline sand was drifted and whorled in places. As she had done when they found the place a few nights ago, Laura stayed away from the sand, kept to the bare gray-pink shale. She did not stop until she was three hundred yards from the highway, putting that well-traveled road beyond the radius of Vexxon's open-air effectiveness. She parked not far from an arroyo, a twenty-foot-wide and thirty-foot-deep natural drainage channel formed by flash floods during hundreds of the desert's brief rainy seasons; previously, at night, proceeding with caution but guided only by headlights, they'd been fortunate not to drive into that enormous ditch.

Though the lightning had not been followed by any sign of armed men, urgency informed the moment; Laura, Chris, and Stefan moved as if they could hear a clock ticking toward an impending detonation. While Laura removed one of the thirty-pound Vexxon cylinders from the trunk of the Buick, Stefan put his arms through the straps on the small, green nylon backpack that was full of books, pulled the chest strap in place, and pressed the Velcro fasteners together. Chris carried one of the Uzis twenty feet from the car to the center of a circle of utterly barren shale where not even a tuft of bunchgrass grew, which looked like a good staging area for Stefan's debarkation from 1989. Laura joined the boy there, and Stefan followed, holding the silencer-fitted Colt Commander in his right hand.

North of Palm Springs on state route 111, Klietmann was pushing the Toyota as hard as it would go, which was not hard enough.

The car had forty thousand miles on the odometer, and no doubt the old woman who owned it never drove faster than fifty, so it wasn't responding well to the demands Klietmann made on it. When he tried to go faster than sixty, the Toyota began to shimmy and sputter, forcing him to ease up.

Nevertheless, just two miles north of the Palm Springs city limits, they fell in behind a California Highway Patrol cruiser, and Klietmann knew they must have caught up with the officer who was going to encounter and arrest Laura Shane and her son. The cop was doing just under fifty-five in a fifty-five-mile-per-hour zone.

"Kill him," Klietmann said over his shoulder to Corporal Martin Bracher, who was in the right rear seat.

Klietmann glanced in the rearview mirror, saw no traffic behind; there was oncoming traffic, but it was in the southbound lanes. He swung into the northbound passing lane and began to move around the patrol car at sixty.

In the back Bracher rolled down his window. The other rear window was already open because Hubatsch had shot it out when he had killed the Palm Springs cop, so wind roared noisily through the back of the Toyota and reached into the front seat to flutter the map that was still in von Manstein's lap.

The CHP officer glanced over in surprise, for motorists probably seldom dared pass a policeman who was already driving within a couple of miles of the speed limit. When Klietmann pressed the Toyota past sixty, it shimmied and coughed, still accelerating but grudgingly. The policeman took note of this indication of Klietmann's determined breaking of the law, and he tapped his siren lightly, making it whoop and die, which apparently meant that Klietmann was to fall back and pull to the shoulder of the road.

Instead the lieutenant nursed the protesting Toyota up to sixty-four miles an hour, where it seemed in danger of shaking itself apart, and that was just fast enough to pull slightly ahead of the startled CHP officer, bringing Bracher's rear window in line with the patrol car's front window. The corporal opened fire with his Uzi.

The police cruiser's windows imploded, and the officer was dead in an instant. He had to be dead, for he had not seen the attack coming and surely had taken several rounds in the head and upper body. The patrol car swung toward the Toyota and brushed it before Klietmann could get out of the way, then veered toward the shoulder of the road.

Klietmann braked, falling back from the out-of-control cruiser.

The four-lane highway was elevated about ten feet above the desert floor, and the patrol car shot past the unguarded brink of the shoulder. It was airborne for a few seconds, then came down so hard that some of its tires no doubt blew out on impact. Two doors popped open, including that on the driver's side.

As Klietmann moved into the right lane and drove slowly by the wreckage, von Manstein said, "I can see him in there, slumped over the wheel. He's no more trouble to us."

Oncoming drivers had witnessed the patrol car's spectacular flight. They pulled to the verge on their side of route 111. When Klietmann glanced in his rearview mirror, he saw people getting out of those vehicles, good Samaritans hurrying across the highway to the CHP officer's rescue. If some of them realized why the cruiser had crashed, they had decided not to pursue Klietmann and bring him to justice. Which was wise.

He accelerated again, glanced at the odometer, and said, "Three miles from here, that cop would've arrested the woman and boy. So be on the lookout for a black Buick. Three miles."

Standing in the bright desert sun on the patch of barren shale near the Buick, Laura watched Stefan slip the strap of the Uzi over his right shoulder. The carbine hung freely and did not interfere with the backpack full of books.

"But now I wonder if I should take it," he said. "If the nerve gas works as well as it ought to, I probably won't even need the pistol, let alone a submachine gun."

"Take it," Laura said grimly.

He nodded. "You're right. Who knows."

"Too bad you don't have a couple of grenades too," Chris said. "Grenades would be good."

"Let's hope it doesn't get *that* nasty back there," Stefan said.

He switched off the pistol's safeties and held it ready in his right hand. Gripping the canister of Vexxon by its heavy-duty, fire-extinguisher-type handle, he picked it up with his left hand and tested its weight to see how his injured shoulder would react.

"Hurts a little," he said. "Pulls at the wound. But it's not bad, and I'll be able to control it."

They had cut the wire on the canister's trigger, which allowed the manual venting of the Vexxon. He curled his finger through that release loop.

When he finished his work in 1944, he would make a final jaunt to their time again, 1989, and the plan was for him to arrive only five minutes after he departed. Now he said, "I'll see you very soon. You'll hardly know I'm gone."

Suddenly Laura was afraid that he would never return. She put a hand to his face and kissed him on the cheek. "Good luck, Stefan."

It was not a kiss that a lover might have given, nor was there even a promise of passion; it was just the affectionate kiss of a friend, the kiss of a woman who owed eternal gratitude but who did not owe her heart. She saw an awareness of that in his eyes. At the core, in spite of flashes of humor, he was a melancholy man, and she wished that she could make him happy. She regretted that she could not at least pretend to feel more for him; yet she knew he would see through any such pretense.

"I want you to come back," she said. "I really do. Very much."

"That's enough." He looked at Chris and said, "Take care of your mother while I'm gone."

"I'll try," Chris said. "But she's pretty good at taking care of herself."

Laura pulled her son to her side.

Stefan lifted the thirty-pound Vexxon cylinder higher, squeezed the release loop.

As the gas vented under high pressure with a sound like a dozen snakes hissing at once, Laura was seized by a brief panic, certain that the capsules they had taken would not protect them from the nerve toxin, that they would drop to the ground, twitching in the grip of muscle spasms and convulsions, where they would die in thirty seconds. Vexxon was colorless but not odorless or tasteless; even in the open air, where it dispersed quickly, she detected a sweet odor of apricots and a tart, nauseating taste that seemed half lemon juice and half spoiled milk. But in spite of what she could smell and taste, she felt no adverse effects.

Holding the pistol across his body, Stefan reached beneath his shirt with a free finger of his gun hand and pressed the button on the homing belt three times.

Von Manstein was the first to spot the black car standing in that expanse of white sand and pale rock, a few hundred yards east of the highway. He called it to their attention.

Of course, Lieutenant Klietmann could not see the make of the car from so far away, but he was sure it was the one for which they were searching. Three people stood together near the car; they were hardly more than stick figures at that distance, and they appeared to shimmer like mirages in the desert sun, but Klietmann could see that two of them were adults, the other a child.

Abruptly one of the adults vanished. It was not a trick of the desert air and light. The figure did not shimmer into view again a moment later. It was gone, and Klietmann knew that it had been Stefan Krieger.

"He went back!" Bracher said, astonished.

"Why would he go back," von Manstein said, "when everyone at the institute wants his ass?"

"Worse," Hubatsch said from behind the lieutenant. "He came to 1989 days before we did. So that belt of his will have taken him back to the same point, to the day that Kokoschka shot him—to just eleven minutes after Kokoschka shot him. Yet we know for a fact he never returned that day. What the hell's going on here?"

Klietmann was worried, too, but he didn't have time to figure out what was going on. His job was to kill the woman and her son if not Krieger. He said, "Get ready," and he slowed the Toyota to look for a way down the embankment.

Hubatsch and Bracher had already withdrawn the Uzis from their attaché cases in Palm Springs. Now von Manstein armed himself with his weapon.

The land rose to meet the highway. Klietmann swung the Toyota off the pavement, down the sloped embankment, and onto the desert floor, heading toward the woman and the boy.

When Stefan activated the homing belt, the air became heavy, and Laura felt a great, invisible weight pressing on her. She grimaced at the stench of hot electrical wiring and burnt insulation, overlaid by the scent of ozone, underlaid by the apricot smell of the Vexxon. The air pressure grew, the blend of odors intensified, and Stefan left her world with a sudden, loud *pop*. For an instant there seemed to be no air to breathe, but the brief vacuum was followed by a blustery inrush of hot wind tainted by the faintly alkaline smell of the desert.

Standing close at her side and holding fast to her, Chris said, "Wow! Wasn't that something, Mom, wasn't that great?"

She did not answer because she noticed a white car driving off state route 111, onto the desert floor. It turned toward them and leaped forward as its driver accelerated.

"Chris, get in front of the Buick. Stay down!"

He saw the oncoming vehicle and obeyed her without question.

She ran to the open door of the Buick and snatched one of the submachine guns off the seat. She stepped to the rear, standing by the open trunk, and faced the oncoming car.

It was less than two hundred yards away, closing fast. Sunlight starred and flashed off the chrome, coruscated across the windshield.

She considered the possibility that the occupants were not German agents from 1944 but innocent people. However that was so unlikely, she could not allow the possibility to inhibit her.

Destiny struggles to reassert the pattern that was meant to be.

No. Damn it, no.

When the white car was within one hundred yards, she squeezed off two solid bursts from the Uzi and saw bullets punch at least two holes in the windshield. The rest of the tempered glass instantly crazed.

The car—she could see now that it was a Toyota—spun out, turning a full three hundred and sixty degrees, then ninety degrees more, throwing up clouds of dust, tearing through a couple of still green tumbleweeds. It came to rest about sixty yards away, the front end pointed north, the passenger's side toward her.

Doors flew open on the far side, and Laura knew the occupants were scrambling out of the car where she could not see them, staying low. She opened fire again, not with the hope of hitting them through the Toyota but with the intention of puncturing the fuel tank; then perhaps a lucky spark, struck by a bullet passing through sheet metal, might ignite the gasoline and catch some or all of those men in the sudden flames as they huddled against the far flank of the vehicle. But she emptied the Uzi's extended magazine without igniting a fire, even though she had almost certainly riddled the fuel tank.

She threw down the gun, pulled open the back door of the Buick, and snatched up the other, fully loaded Uzi. She got the .38 Chief's Special from the front seat, too, never taking her eyes off the white Toyota for more than a second or two. She wished that Stefan had left the third submachine gun, after all.

From the other car, sixty yards away, one of the gunmen opened fire with an automatic weapon, and now there was no doubt who they were. As Laura crouched against the side of the Buick, bullets thudded into the open trunk lid, blew out the rear window, tore into the rear fenders, ricocheted off the bumper, bounced off surrounding shale with sharp *cracks*, and kicked up puffs of powdery, white sand.

She heard a couple of rounds cutting the air close to her head—deadly, high-pitched, whispery whines—and she began to edge backward toward the front of the Buick, staying close to it, trying to make as small a target of herself as possible. In a moment she joined Chris where he huddled against the Buick's grille.

The gunman at the Toyota ceased firing.

"Mom?" Chris said fearfully.

"It's all right," she said, trying hard to believe what she told him. "Stefan will be back in less than five minutes, honey. He's got another Uzi, and that'll even the odds a lot. We'll be okay. We only have to hold them off for a few minutes. Just a few minutes."

·15·

Kokoschka's belt returned Stefan to the institute in a blink, and he entered the gate with the nozzle on the Vexxon cylinder wide open. He was squeezing the handle and trigger so hard that his hand ached, and the pain already was beginning to travel up his arm into his wounded shoulder.

From within the gloom of the barrel, he could see only a small portion of the lab. He glimpsed two men in dark suits, who were peering in the far end of the gate. They very much resembled Gestapo agents—all of the bastards looked as if they'd been cloned from the same small group of degenerates and fanatics—and he was relieved to know that they could not see him as clearly as he could see them; for a moment at least they would think he was Kokoschka.

He moved forward, the noisily hissing canister of Vexxon held before him in his left hand, the pistol in his right hand, and before the men in the lab realized something was wrong, the nerve gas hit them. They dropped to the floor, below the elevated gate, and by the time Stefan stepped down into the laboratory, they were writhing in agony. They had vomited explosively. Blood was running from their nostrils. One of them was on his side, kicking his legs and clawing at his throat; the other was curled fetally on his side and, with fingers hooked like claws, was ripping horribly at his eyes. Near the gate-programming board three men in lab coats—Stefan knew them: Hoepner, Eicke, Schmauser—had collapsed. They tore at themselves as if mad or rabid. All five dying men were trying to scream, but their throats had swollen shut in an instant; they were able to make only faint, pathetic, chilling sounds like the mewling of small, tortured animals. Stefan stood among them, physically unaffected but appalled, horrified, and in thirty to forty seconds they were dead.

A cruel justice was served in the use of Vexxon against these men, for it had been Nazi-sponsored researchers who had synthesized the first nerve gas in 1936, an organophosphorous ester called tabun. Virtually all subsequent nerve gases—which killed by interfering with the transmission of electrical nerve impulses—had been related to that original chemical compound. Including Vexxon. These men in 1944 had been killed by a futuristic weapon, yet it was a substance that had its origins in their own twisted, death-centered society.

Nevertheless Stefan took no satisfaction from these five deaths. He had seen so much killing in his life that even the extermination of the guilty to protect the innocent, even murder in the service of justice, repulsed him. But he could do what he had to do.

He put the pistol on a lab bench. He shrugged the Uzi off his shoulder and put that aside as well.

From a pocket of his jeans, he withdrew a few inches of wire, which he used to lock open the trigger on the Vexxon. He stepped into the ground-floor corridor and put the canister in the center of that hallway. In a few minutes the gas would spread through the building by way of stairwells, elevator shafts, and ventilation ducts.

He was surprised to see that only the night lights illuminated the hallway and that the other labs on the ground floor appeared to be deserted. Leaving the gas to disperse, he returned to the gate-programming board in the main lab to learn the date and time to which Heinrich Kokoschka's homing device had brought him. It was eleven minutes past nine o'clock on the night of March 16.

This was a piece of singularly good luck. Stefan had expected to return to the institute at an hour when most of its staff—some of whom began work as early as six in the morning and some of whom stayed as late as eight o'clock—would be in residence. That would have meant as many as a hundred bodies scattered throughout the four-floor building; and when they were discovered, it would be known that only Stefan Krieger, using Kokoschka's belt and penetrating the institute from the future by way of the gate, could have been responsible. They would realize that he had not come back merely to kill as many of the staff as were on the premises, that he had been up to something else, and they would launch a major investigation to discover the nature of his scheme and undo what damage he had done. But now . . . if the building was mostly empty, he might be able to dispose of the few bodies in a fashion that would cover his presence and direct all suspicion to these dead men.

After five minutes the Vexxon cylinder was empty. The gas had spread throughout the structure, with the exception of the two guard foyers at the front and back entrances, which did not share even ventilation ducts with the rest of the building. Stefan went from floor to floor, room to room, looking for more victims. The only bodies he found were those of the animals in the basement, the first time-travelers, and the sight of their pathetic corpses disturbed him as much or more than the five gassed men.

Stefan returned to the main lab, took five of the special belts from a white cabinet, and buckled the devices on the dead men, over their clothes. He quickly reprogrammed the gate to send the bodies roughly six billion years into the future. He had read somewhere that the sun would have gone nova or would have died in six billion years, and he wanted to dispose of the five men in a place where no one would exist to notice them or to use their belts to home in on the gate.

Dealing with the dead in that silent, deserted building was an eerie business. Repeatedly he froze, certain that he'd heard stealthy movement. A couple of times he even paused in his labors to go in search of the imagined sound but found nothing. Once he looked at one of the dead men behind him, half convinced that the lifeless thing had started to rise, that the soft scrape he'd heard had been its cool hand clawing for a grip on the machinery, as it tried to drag itself erect. That was when he realized how deeply disturbed he had been by bearing witness to so many deaths over so many years.

One by one he dragged the reeking corpses into the gate, shoved them along to the point of transmission, and heaved them across that energy field. Tumbling through the invisible doorway in time, they vanished. At an unimaginably distant point they would reappear—either on an earth long cold and dead, where not even one plant or insect lived, or in the airless and empty space where the planet had existed before being consumed by the exploding sun.

He was exceedingly careful not to venture across the transmission point. If he was suddenly transported to the vacuum of deep space, six billion years hence, he would be dead before he had a chance to press the button on his homing belt and return to the lab.

By the time he disposed of the five cadavers and cleaned up all traces of their messy deaths, he was weary. Fortunately the nerve gas left no apparent residue; there was no need to wipe down every surface in the institute. His wounded shoulder throbbed as badly as in the days immediately after he had been shot.

But at least he had cleverly covered his trail. In the morning it might appear as if Kokoschka, Hoepner, Eicke, Schmauser, and the two Gestapo agents had decided that the Third Reich was doomed and had defected to a future in which peace and plenty could be found.

He remembered the animals in the basement. If he left them in their cages, tests would be run to discover what had killed them, and perhaps the results would cast doubt on the theory that Kokoschka and the others had defected through the gate. Then once again the primary suspect would be Stefan Krieger. Better the animals should disappear. That would be a mystery, but it would not point directly toward the truth, as would the condition of their carcasses.

The hot, pounding pain in his shoulder became hotter, as he used clean lab coats for burial shrouds, bundling groups of animals together, tying them up with cord. Without belts he sent them six billion years into the future. He retrieved the empty nerve-gas canister from the hall and sent that to the far end of time as well.

At last he was ready to make the two crucial jaunts that he hoped would lead to the utter destruction of the institute and the certain defeat of Nazi Germany. Moving to the gate-programming board again, he took a folded sheet of paper from the hip pocket of his jeans; it contained the results of days of calculations that he and Laura had done on the IBM PC in the house in Palm Springs.

If he had been able to return from 1989 with enough explosives to reduce the institute to smoldering rubble, he would have done the job himself, right here, right now. However, in addition to the heavy canister of Vexxon, the rucksack filled with six books, the pistol, and the Uzi, he would have been unable to carry more than forty or fifty pounds of plastique, which was insufficient to the task. The explosives he had planted in the attic and basement had been removed by Kokoschka a couple of days ago, of course, in local time. He might have come back from 1989 with a couple of cans of gasoline, might have attempted to burn the place to the ground; but many research documents were locked in fireproof file cabinets to which even he did not have access, and only a devastating explosion would split them open and expose their contents to flames.

He could no longer destroy the institute alone.

But he knew who could help him.

Referring to the numbers arrived at with the aid of the IBM PC, he reprogrammed the gate to take him three and a half days into the future from that night of March 16. Geographically, he would be arriving on British soil in the heart of the extensive underground shelters beneath the government offices overlooking St. James's Park by Storey's Gate, where bombproof offices and quarters for the prime minister and other officials had been constructed during the Blitz, and where the War Room was still located. Specifically, Stefan hoped to arrive in a particular conference room at 7:30 A.M., a jaunt of such precision that only the knowledge and computers available in 1989 could allow the complex calculations to determine the necessary time and space coordinates.

Carrying no weapons, taking with him only the rucksack full of books, he entered the gate, crossed the point of transmission, and materialized in the corner of a low-ceilinged conference room in the center of which stood a large table encircled by twelve chairs. Ten of the chairs were empty. Only two men were present. The first was a male secretary in a British army uniform, a pen in one hand and a pad of paper in the other. The second man, engaged in the dictation of an urgent message, was Winston Churchill.

·16·

As he crouched against the Toyota, Klietmann decided they could not have been more inappropriately dressed for their mission if they had been made up as circus clowns. The surrounding desert was mostly white and beige, pale pink and peach, with little vegetation and only a few rock formations significant enough to provide cover. In their black suits, as they tried to circle and get behind the woman, they would be as visible as bugs on a wedding cake.

Hubatsch, who had been standing near the front of the Toyota, directing short barrages of automatic fire at the Buick, dropped down. "She's gone to the front of the car with the boy, out of sight."

"Local authorities will show up soon," Bracher said, looking west toward state route 111, then southwest in the general direction of the patrol car they had blown off the road four miles back.

"Remove your coats," Klietmann said, stripping out of his own. "White shirts will blend with the landscape better. Bracher, you stay here, prevent the bitch from doubling back this way. Von Manstein and Hubatsch, try to circle around on the right side. Stay well apart and don't move from one point of cover until you've picked out the next. I'll go north and east, around on the left."

"Do we kill her without trying to find out what Krieger is up to?" Bracher asked.

"Yes," Klietmann said at once. "She's too heavily armed to be taken alive. Anyway, I'd bet my honor that Krieger will be coming back to them, returning here through the gate in a few minutes, and we'll be better able to deal with him when he arrives if we've already taken out the woman. Now go. *Go.*"

Hubatsch, followed a few seconds later by von Manstein, left the cover of the Toyota, staying low, moving fast, and heading south-southeast.

Lieutenant Klietmann went north from the Toyota, holding his submachine gun in one hand, running in a crouch, making for the meager cover of a sprawling mesquite bush upon which a few tumbleweeds had gotten hung up.

Laura rose slightly and peered around the front fender of the Buick just in time to see two men in white shirts and black trousers sprint away from the Toyota, heading east toward her but also angling to the south, obviously intending to circle behind her. She stood and squeezed off a short burst at the first man, who made for the cover of a toothlike formation of rock, behind which he safely vanished.

At the sound of gunfire, the second man sprawled flat in a shallow depression that did not entirely conceal him, but the angle of fire and the distance made him a hard target. She did not intend to waste any more rounds.

Besides, even as she saw where the second man had gone to ground, a third gunman opened fire on her from behind the Toyota. Bullets cracked off the Buick, missing her by inches, and she was forced to drop down again.

Stefan would be back in just three or four minutes. Not long. Not long at all. But an eternity.

Chris was sitting with his back against the front bumper of the Buick, his knees drawn up against his chest, hugging himself, and shaking visibly.

"Hang on, kiddo," she said.

He looked at her but said nothing. Through all the terrors they had endured in the past couple of weeks, she had not seen him look so dispirited. His face was pale and slack. He realized that this game of hide and seek had never been a game at all for anyone but him, that nothing *was* in fact as easy as in the movies, and this frightening perception brought to his gaze a bleak detachment that scared Laura.

"Hang on," she repeated, then scrambled past him to the other front fender, on the driver's side, where she crouched to study the desert to the north of them.

She was worried that other men were circling her on that flank. She could not let them do that because then the Buick would be of no use as a barricade, and there would be no place to run except into the open desert, where they would kill her and Chris within fifty yards. The Buick was the only good cover around. She had to keep the Buick between her and them.

She could see no one out there on her north flank. The land was more uneven in that direction, with a few low spines of rock, a few drifts of white sand, and no doubt many man-size depressions in the desert floor that were not visible from her position, places where a stalker might even now be taking cover. But the only things that moved were three dry tumbleweeds; they rolled slowly, erratically, in the mild, inconstant breeze.

She slipped past Chris and returned to the other fender in time to see that the two men to the south were already on the move again. They were thirty yards south of her but only twenty yards in front of the Buick, closing with frightening speed. Though the leader was staying low and weaving as he ran, the follower was bolder; perhaps he thought Laura's attention would be focused on the front man.

She fooled him, stood up, leaned out from the Buick as far as she had to, using it for cover as best she could, and squeezed off a two-second burst. The gunman at the Toyota opened fire on her, giving his buddies cover, but she hit the second running man hard enough to lift him off his feet and pitch him through a bristling manzanita.

Though not dead, he was clearly out of action, for his screams were so shrill and agonized, there could be no doubt he was mortally wounded.

As she dropped down below the line of fire again, she found that she was grinning fiercely. She was intensely pleased by the pain and horror that the wounded man's screams conveyed. Her savage reaction, the primitive power of her thirst for blood and revenge, startled her, but she held fast to it because she sensed that she would be a better and more clever fighter while in the spell of that primal rage.

One down. Perhaps only two more to go.

And soon Stefan would be here. No matter how long his work required in 1944, Stefan would program the gate to bring him back here shortly after he had left. He would rejoin her—and enter the fight—in only two or three minutes.

·17·

The prime minister happened to be looking directly at Stefan when he materialized, but the man in uniform—a sergeant—became aware of him because of the discharge of electrical energy that accompanied his arrival. Thousands of bright snakes of blue-white light wriggled away from Stefan, as if his very flesh had generated them. Perhaps deep crashes of thunder and bolts of lightning shattered the sky in the world above these underground rooms, but some of the displaced energy of time travel was expended here, as well, in a sizzling display that brought the uniformed man straight to his feet in surprise and fear. The hissing serpents of electricity streaked across the floor, up the walls, coalesced briefly on the ceiling, then dissipated, leaving everyone unharmed; the only damage was to a large wall map of Europe, which had been seared in several places but not set aflame.

"Guards!" the sergeant shouted. He was unarmed but evidently quite sure that his cry would be heard and answered swiftly, for he repeated it only once and made no move toward the door. "Guards!"

"Mr. Churchill, please," Stefan said, ignoring the sergeant, "I'm not here to do you any harm."

The door flew open and two British soldiers entered the room, one holding a revolver, the other an automatic carbine.

Speaking hastily, afraid he was about to be shot, Stefan said, "The future of the world depends on your hearing me out, sir, please."

Throughout the excitement, the prime minister had remained seated in the armchair at the end of the table. Stefan believed that he had seen a brief flash of surprise and perhaps even a glimmer of fear on the great man's face, but he would not have bet on it. Now the prime minister looked as bemused and implacable as in every photograph that Stefan had ever seen of him. He raised one hand to the guards: "Hold a moment." When the sergeant began to protest, the prime minister said, "If he had meant to kill me, certainly he would have done so already, on arrival." To Stefan he said, "And that was *some* entrance, sir. As dramatic as any that young Olivier has ever made."

Stefan could not help but smile. He stepped out of the corner, but when he moved toward the table, he saw the guards stiffen, so he stopped and spoke from a distance. "Sir, by the very manner that I've arrived here, you know I'm no ordinary messenger and that what I have to tell you must be . . . unusual. It's also highly sensitive, and you may not wish to have my information conveyed to any ears but yours."

"If you expect us to leave you alone with the PM," the sergeant said, "you're . . . you're mad!"

"He may be mad," the prime minister said, "but he's got flair. You must admit that much, Sergeant. If the guards search him and find no weapons, I'll give the gentleman a bit of my time, as he asks."

"But, sir, you don't know who he is. You don't know *what* he is. The way he exploded into—"

Churchill cut him off. "I know how he arrived, Sergeant. And please remember that only you and I *do* know. I will expect you to remain as tight-lipped about what you've seen here as you would about any other bit of war information that might be considered classified."

Chastened, the sergeant stood to one side and glowered at Stefan while the guards conducted a body search.

They found no weapons, only the books in the rucksack and a few papers in Stefan's pockets. They returned the papers and stacked the books in the middle of the long table, and Stefan was amused to see that they had not noticed the nature of the volumes they'd handled.

Reluctantly, carrying his pencil and dictation pad, the sergeant accompanied the guards out of the room, as the prime minister had instructed. When the door closed, Churchill motioned Stefan to the chair that the sergeant had vacated. They sat in silence a moment, regarding each other with interest. Then the prime minister pointed to a steaming pot that stood on a serving tray. "Tea?"

Twenty minutes later, when Stefan had told only half of the condensed version of his story, the prime minister called for the sergeant in the corridor. "We'll be here a while yet, Sergeant. I will have to delay the War Cabinet meeting by an hour, I'm afraid. Please see that everyone is informed—and with my apologies."

Twenty-five minutes after *that,* Stefan finished.

The prime minister asked a few more questions—surprisingly few but well-thought and to the heart of the matter. Finally he sighed and said, "It's terribly early for a cigar, I suppose, but I'm in the mood to have one. Will you join me?"

"No, thank you, sir."

As he prepared the cigar for smoking, Churchill said, "Aside from your spectacular entrance—which really proves nothing but the existence of a revolutionary means of travel, which might or might not be *time* travel—what evidence do you have to convince a reasonable man that the particulars of your story are true?"

Stefan had expected such a test and was prepared for it. "Sir, because I have been to the future and read portions of your account of the war, I knew you would be in this room at this hour on this day. Furthermore I knew what you would be doing here in the hour before your meeting with the War Cabinet."

Drawing on his cigar, the prime minister raised his eyebrows.

"You were dictating a message to General Alexander in Italy, expressing your concerns about the conduct of the battle for the town of Cassino, which has been dragging on at a terrible cost of life."

Churchill remained inscrutable. He must have been surprised by Stefan's knowledge, but he would not provide encouragement even with a nod or a narrowing of his eyes.

Stefan needed no encouragement because he knew that what he said was correct. "From the account of the war that you will eventually write, I memorized the opening of that message to General Alexander—which you had not even finished dictating to the sergeant when I arrived a short while ago: 'I wish you would explain to me why this passage by Cassino Monastery Hill, etcetera, all on a front of two or three miles, is the only place which you must keep butting at.' "

The prime minister drew on his cigar again, blew out smoke, and studied Stefan intensely. Their chairs were only a few feet apart, and being the object of Churchill's thoughtful scrutiny was more unnerving than Stefan would have expected.

At last the prime minister said, "And you got that information from something I will write in the future?"

Stefan rose from his chair, retrieved the six thick books that the guards had taken from his rucksack—Houghton Mifflin Company's trade-paperback reprints published at $9.95 each—and spread them out on the end of the table in front of Winston Churchill. "This, sir, is your six-volume history of the Second World War, which will stand as the definitive account of that conflict and be hailed as both a great work of history and literature." He was going to add that those books were largely responsible for Churchill's being awarded the Nobel Prize for literature in 1953, but decided not to make that revelation. Life would be less interesting if robbed of such grand surprises.

The prime minister examined the covers of all six books, front and back, and permitted himself a smile when he read the three-line excerpt from the review that had appeared in the *Times Literary Supplement*. He opened one volume and swiftly riffled the pages, not pausing to read anything.

"They aren't elaborate forgeries," Stefan assured him. "If you will read any page at random, you'll recognize your own unique and unmistakable voice. You will—"

"I've no need to read them. I believe you, Stefan Krieger." He pushed the books away and leaned back in his chair. "And I believe I understand why you've come to me. You want me to arrange an aerial bombardment of Berlin, targeted tightly to the district in which this institute of yours is located."

"Yes, Prime Minister, that's exactly right. It must be done before the scientists working at the institute have finished studying the material on nuclear weapons that's been brought back from the future, before they agree upon a means of introducing that information into the German scientific community at large—which they may do any day now. You must act before they come back from the future with something else that might turn the tide against the Allies. I'll give you the precise location of the institute. American and RAF bombers have been making both daylight and night runs on Berlin since the first of the year, after all—"

"There has been considerable uproar in Parliament about bombing cities, even enemy cities," Churchill noted.

"Yes, but it's not as if Berlin can't be hit. Because of the narrowly defined target, of course, this mission will have to take place in daylight. But if you strike that district, if you utterly pulverize that block—"

"Several blocks on all sides of it would have to be reduced to rubble," the prime minister said. "We can't strike with sufficient accuracy to surgically remove the buildings on one block alone."

"Yes, I understand. But you *must* order it, sir. More tons of explosives must be dropped on that district—and within the next few days—than will be dropped on any other scrap of land in the entire European theater at any time in the entire war. Nothing must be left of the institute but *dust*."

The prime minister was silent for a minute or so, watching the thin, bluish plume of his cigar smoke, thinking. Finally: "I'll need to consult with my advisers, of course, but I believe the earliest we could prepare and launch the bombardment would be two days hence, on the twenty-second, but perhaps as late as the twenty-third."

"I think that'll be soon enough," Stefan said with great relief. "But no later. For God's sake, sir, no later."

·18·

As the woman crouched by the driver's-side fender of the Buick and surveyed the desert to the north of her position, Klietmann was watching her from behind a tangle of mesquite and tumbleweed. She did not see him. When she moved to the other fender and turned her back to Klietmann, he got up at once and ran in a crouch toward the next bit of cover, a wind-scalloped knob of rock narrower than he was.

The lieutenant silently cursed the Bally loafers he was wearing, because the soles were too slippery for this kind of action. It now seemed foolish to have come on a mission of assassination dressed like young executives—or Baptist ministers. At least the Ray-Bans were useful. The bright sun glared off every stone and slope of drifted sand; without the sunglasses, he would not have been able to see the ground ahead of him as clearly as he could now, and he certainly would have put a foot wrong and fallen more than once.

He was about to dive for cover again when he heard the woman open fire in the other direction. With this proof that she was distracted, he kept going. Then he heard screaming so shrill and ululant that it hardly sounded like the screaming of a man; it was more like the cry of a wild animal gutted by another creature's claws but still alive.

Shaken, he took cover in a long, narrow basin of rock that was below the woman's line of sight. He crawled on his belly to the end of that trough and lay there, breathing hard. When he raised his head to bring his eyes up to the level of the surrounding ground, he saw that he was fifteen yards directly north of the Buick's rear door. If he could move just a few more yards east, he would be behind the woman, in the perfect position to cut her down.

The screaming faded.

Figuring that the other man to the south of her would lie low for a while because he would be spooked by the death of his partner, Laura shifted again to the other front fender. As she passed Chris, she said, "Two minutes, baby. Two minutes at most."

Crouching against the corner of the car, she surveyed their north flank. The desert out there still seemed untenanted. The breeze had died, and not even the tumbleweed moved.

If there were only three of them, they surely would not leave one man at the Toyota while the other two tried to circle her from the *same* direction. If there were only three, then the two on her south side would have split, one of them going north. Which meant there had to be a fourth man, perhaps even a fifth, out there in the shale and sand and desert scrub to the northwest of the Buick.

But where?

·19·

As Stefan expressed his gratitude to the prime minister and got up to leave, Churchill pointed to the books on the table and said, "I wouldn't want you to forget those. If you left them behind—what a temptation to plagiarize myself!"

"It's a mark of your character," Stefan said, "that you haven't importuned me to leave them with you for that very purpose."

"Nonsense." Churchill put his cigar in an ashtray and rose from his chair. "If I possessed those books now, all written, I'd not be content to have them published just as they are. Undoubtedly I would find things needing improvement, and I'd spend the years immediately after the war tinkering endlessly with them—only to find, upon completion and publication, that I had destroyed the very elements of them that in your future have made them classics."

Stefan laughed.

"I'm quite serious," Churchill said. "You've told me that my history will be the definitive one. That's enough foreknowledge to suit me. I'll write them as I wrote them, so to speak, and not risk second-guessing myself."

"Perhaps that's wise," Stefan agreed.

As Stefan packed the six books in the rucksack, Churchill stood with his hands behind his back, rocking slightly on his feet. "There are so many things I'd like to ask you about the future that I'm helping to shape. Things that are of more interest to me than whether I will write successful books or not."

"I really must be going, sir, but—"

"I know, yes," the prime minister said. "I won't detain you. But tell me at least one thing. Curiosity's killing me. Let's see . . . well, for instance, what of the Soviets after the war?"

Stefan hesitated, closed the rucksack, and said, "Prime Minister, I'm sorry to tell you that the Soviets will become far more powerful than Britain, rivaled only by the United States."

Churchill looked surprised for the first time. "That abominable system of theirs will actually produce economic success, abundance?"

"No, no. Their system will produce economic ruin—but tremendous military power. The Soviets will relentlessly militarize their entire society and eliminate all dissidents. Some say their concentration camps rival those of the Reich."

The expression on the prime minister's face remained inscrutable, but he could not conceal the troubled look in his eyes. "Yet they are allies of ours now."

"Yes, sir. And without them perhaps the war against the Reich wouldn't have been won."

"Oh, it would be won," Churchill said confidently, "just not as quickly." He sighed. "They say politics makes strange bedfellows, but the alliances necessitated by war make stranger ones yet."

Stefan was ready to depart.

They shook hands.

"Your institute shall be reduced to pebbles, splinters, dust, and ashes," the prime minister said. "You've my word on that."

"That's all the assurance I need," Stefan said.

He reached beneath his shirt and pushed three times on the button that activated the homing belt's link with the gate.

In what seemed like the same instant, he was in the institute in Berlin. He stepped out of the barrel-like gate and returned to the programming board. Exactly eleven minutes had elapsed on the clock since he had departed for those bombproof rooms below London.

His shoulder still ached, but the pain had not increased. The relentless throbbing, however, was gradually taking a toll on him, and he sat in the programmer's chair for a while, resting.

Then, using more numbers provided by the IBM computer in

1989, he programmed the gate for his next-to-last jaunt. This time he would go five days into the future, arriving at eleven o'clock at night, March 21, in other bombproof, underground quarters—not in London but in his own city of Berlin.

When the gate was ready, he entered it, taking no weapons. This time he did not take the six volumes of Churchill's history, either.

When he crossed the point of transmission inside the gate, the familiar unpleasant tingle passed inward from his skin, through his flesh, into his marrow, then instantly back out again from marrow to flesh to skin.

The windowless, subterranean room in which Stefan arrived was lit by a single lamp on the corner desk and briefly by the crackling light he brought with him. In that weird glow Hitler was clearly revealed.

·20·

One minute.

Laura huddled with Chris against the Buick. Without shifting her position she looked first toward the south where she knew one man was hiding, then to the north where she suspected that other enemies lay concealed.

A preternatural calm had befallen the desert. Windless, the day had no more breath than a corpse. The sun had shed so much of itself upon the arid plain that the land seemed as full of light as the sky; at the far edges of the world, the bright heavens blended into the bright earth with so little demarcation that the horizon effectively disappeared. Though the temperature was only in the high seventies, everything—every bush and rock and weed and sweep of sand—appeared to have been welded by the heat to the object beside it.

One minute.

Surely only a minute or less remained until Stefan would return from 1944, and somehow he would be of great help to them, not only because he had an Uzi but because he was her guardian. Her *guardian*. Although she understood his origins now and was aware that he was not supernatural, in some ways he remained for her a figure larger than life, capable of working wonders.

No movement to the south.

No movement to the north.

"They're coming," Chris said.

"We'll be okay, honey," she said softly. However, her heart not only raced with fear but ached with a sense of loss, as if she knew on some primitive level that her son—the only child she could ever have, the child who had never been meant to live—was already dead, not because of her failure to protect him so much as because destiny would not be thwarted. No. Damn it, no. She would beat fate this time. She would hold on to her boy. She would not lose him as she had lost so many people she had loved over the years. He was hers. He did not belong to destiny. He did not belong to fate. He was hers. He was *hers*. "We'll be okay, honey."

Only half a minute now.

Suddenly she saw movement to the south.

·21·

In the private study of Hitler's Berlin bunker, the displaced energy of time travel hissed and squirmed away from Stefan in snakes of blazing light, tracing hundreds of serpentine paths across the floor and up the concrete walls, as it had done in the subterranean conference room in London. That bright and noisy phenomenon did not draw guards from other chambers, however, for at that moment Berlin was enduring another bombing by Allied planes; the bunker shook with the impact of blockbusters in the city far above, and even at that depth the thunder of the attack masked the particular sounds of Stefan's arrival.

Hitler turned in his swivel chair to face Stefan. He showed no more surprise than Churchill, though of course he knew about the work of the institute, as Churchill had not, and he understood at once how Stefan had materialized within these private quarters. Furthermore he knew Stefan both as the son of a loyal and early supporter and as an SS officer who had worked long for the cause.

Though Stefan had not expected to see surprise on Hitler's face, he had hoped to see those vulturine features twist with fear. After all, if *der Führer* had read Gestapo reports on recent events at the institute—which he had certainly done—he knew that Stefan stood accused of having killed Penlovski, Januskaya, and Volkaw six days ago, on March 15, fleeing thereafter into the future. He probably thought that Stefan had made this trip illicitly just six days ago, shortly before killing those scientists, and was going to kill him as well. Yet if he was frightened, he controlled his fear; remaining seated, he calmly opened a desk drawer and withdrew a Luger.

Even as the last of the electricity discharged, Stefan threw his arm forth in the Nazi salute, and said with all the false passion he could muster, "Heil Hitler!" To prove quickly that his intentions were not hostile, he dropped to one knee, as if genuflecting before the altar of a church, and bowed his head, making of himself an easy and unresisting target. "*Mein Führer,* I come to you to clear my name and to alert you to the existence of traitors in the institute and in the Gestapo contingent responsible for the institute's security."

For a long moment the dictator did not speak.

From far above, the shockwaves of the night bombardment passed through the earth, through twenty-foot-thick steel and concrete walls, and filled the bunker with a continuous, low, ominous sound. Each time that a blockbuster hit nearby, the three paintings—removed from the Louvre following the conquest of France—rattled against the walls, and on *der Führer's* desk a hollow, vibrant sound rose from a tall copper pot filled with pencils.

"Get up, Stefan," Hitler said. "Sit there." He indicated a maroon leather armchair, one of only five pieces of furniture in the cramped, windowless study. He put the Luger on his desk—but within easy reach. "Not just for your honor but for your father's honor and that of the SS, as well, I hope you're as innocent as you claim."

Stefan spoke forcefully because he knew Hitler greatly admired forcefulness. But at all times he also spoke with feigned reverence, as if he truly believed he was in the presence of the man in whom the very spirit of the German people, past and present and future, was embodied. Even more than forcefulness, Hitler was pleased by the awe in which certain of his subordinates held him. It was a thin line to tread, but this was not Stefan's first encounter with the man; he'd had some practice ingratiating himself with this megalomaniac, this viper cloaked in a human disguise.

"*Mein Führer,* it was not I who killed Vladimir Penlovski, Januskaya, and Volkaw. It was Kokoschka. He was a traitor to the Reich, and I caught him in the documents room at the institute just after he had shot Januskaya and Volkaw. He shot me there, as well." Stefan put his right hand against the upper left side of his chest. "I can show you the wound if you wish. Shot, I fled from him to the main lab. I was stunned, not sure how many in the institute were involved in his subversion. I didn't know to whom I could safely turn, so there was only one way to save myself—I fled through the gate to the future before Kokoschka could catch me and finish me off."

"Colonel Kokoschka's report tells a quite different story. He said that he shot you *as* you fled through the gate, after *you* had killed Penlovski and the others."

"If that were so, *Mein Führer,* would I have returned here to attempt to clear my name? If I were a traitor with more faith in the future than I have in you, would I not have stayed in that future, where I was safe, rather than return to you?"

"But were you safe there, Stefan?" Hitler said, and smiled slyly. "As I understand, two Gestapo squads and later an SS squad were sent after you in that distant time."

Stefan was jolted by the mention of an SS squad because he knew it must have been the group that arrived in Palm Springs less than an hour before he left, the group that had occasioned the lightning in the clear desert sky. He was suddenly more worried for Laura and Chris than he had been, because his respect for the dedication and murderous abilities of the SS was far greater than that with which he regarded the Gestapo.

He also realized Hitler had not been told that the Gestapo squads had been outgunned by a woman; he thought Stefan had gone up against them himself, not realizing that Stefan had been comatose throughout those encounters. That played into the lies that Stefan intended to tell, so he said, "My *Führer,* I dealt with those men when they came after me, yes, and did so in good conscience because I knew they were all traitors to you, intent on killing me so that I would not be able to return to you and warn you of the nest of subversives who were—and still are—at work within the institute. Kokoschka has since vanished—am I correct? And so have five other men at the institute, as I understand. They had no faith in the future of the Reich, and fearing that their roles in the murders of March fifteenth would soon be revealed, they fled to the future, to hide in another era."

Stefan paused to let what he had said sink in.

As the explosions far overhead subsided and a lull developed in the bombardment, Hitler studied him intently. This man's scrutiny was every bit as direct as that of Winston Churchill, but there was none of the clean, straightforward, man-to-man assessment in it that had marked the prime minister's attitude. Instead Hitler appraised Stefan from the perspective of a self-appointed god viewing one of his own creations for indications of a dangerous mutation.

And this was a malign god who had no love for his creatures; he loved only the fact of their obedience.

At last *der Führer* said, "If there are traitors at the institute, what is their goal?"

"To mislead you," Stefan said. "They are presenting you with false information about the future in hopes of encouraging you to make serious military blunders. They've told you that in the last year and a half of the war, virtually all of your military decisions will prove to be mistakes, but that's not true. As the future stands now, you will lose the war by only the thinnest of margins. With but a few changes in your strategies, you can *win*."

Hitler's face hardened, and his eyes narrowed, not because he was suspicious of Stefan but because suddenly he was suspicious of all those at the institute who had told him he would make fatal military misjudgments in the days ahead. Stefan was encouraging him to believe again in his infallibility, and the madman was only too eager to trust once more in his genius.

"With a few *small* changes in my strategies?" Hitler asked. "And what might those changes be?"

Stefan quickly summarized six alterations in military strategy that he claimed would be decisive in certain key battles to come; in fact those changes would make no difference to the outcome, and the battles of which he spoke were not to be the major engagements of the remainder of the war.

But *der Führer* wanted to believe that he had been very nearly a winner rather than a certain loser, and now he seized upon Stefan's advice as the truth, for it suggested bold strategies only slightly different from those the dictator would have endorsed himself. He rose from his chair and paced the small room in excitement. "From the first reports presented to me by the institute, I've felt there was a *wrongness* in the future they portrayed. I sensed that I could not have managed this war as brilliantly as I have—then suddenly be plagued by such a long string of misjudgments. Oh, yes, we are in a dark period now, but this will not last. When the Allies launch their long-awaited invasion of Europe, they will fail; we will drive them back into the sea." He spoke almost in a whisper, though with the mesmerizing passion so familiar from his many public speeches. "In that failed assault they will have expended most of their reserves; they will have to retreat on a broad front, and they will not be able to regain their strength and mount a new offensive for many months. During that time we will strengthen our hold on

Europe, defeat the Russian barbarians, and be stronger than we have ever been!" He stopped pacing, blinked as if rising from a self-induced trance, and said, "Yes, what of the invasion of Europe? D-Day as I'm told it came to be called. Reports from the institute tell me that the Allies will land at Normandy."

"Lies," Stefan said. Now they had come to the issue that was the entire purpose behind Stefan's trip to this bunker on this night in March. Hitler had learned from the institute that the beaches of Normandy would be the site of the invasion. In the future that fate had ordained for him, *der Führer* would misjudge the Allies and would prepare for a landing elsewhere, leaving Normandy inadequately defended. He must be encouraged to stick with the strategy that he would have followed had the institute never existed. He must lose the war as fate intended, and it was up to Stefan to undermine the influence of the institute and thereby assure the success of the Normandy invasion.

·22·

Klietmann had managed to ease a few more yards east, past the Buick, outflanking the woman. He lay prone behind a low spine of white rock veined with pale blue quartz, waiting for Hubatsch to make a move on the south of her. When the woman was thus distracted, Klietmann would spring from concealment and close on her, firing the Uzi as he ran. He would cut her to pieces before she even had a chance to turn and see the face of her executioner.

Come on, Sergeant, don't huddle out there like a cowardly Jew, Klietmann thought savagely. Show yourself. Draw her fire.

An instant later Hubatsch broke from cover, and the woman saw him running. As she focused on Hubatsch, Klietmann leaped up from behind the quartz-veined rock.

·23·

Leaning forward in the leather armchair in the bunker, Stefan said, "Lies, all lies, my *Führer*. This attempt to misdirect you toward Normandy is the key part of the plot by the subversives at the institute. They want to force you to make the sort of major mistake that you're not really destined to make. They want you to focus on Normandy, when the real invasion will come at—"

"Calais!" Hitler said.

"Yes."

"I have believed it will be in the area of Calais, farther north than Normandy. They will cross the Channel where it's narrowest."

"You're correct, my *Führer,*" Stefan said. "Troops *will* be put ashore at Normandy on June seventh—"

Actually it would be June 6, but the weather would be so bad on the sixth that the German High Command would not believe the Allies capable of conducting the operation in such rough seas.

"—but that will be a minor force, a diversion, to pull your elite Panzer divisions to the Normandy coast while the real front subsequently opens near Calais."

This information played to all of the dictator's prejudices and to his belief in his own infallibility. He returned to his chair and thumped his desk with one fist. "*This* has the feel of reality, Stefan. But . . . I have seen documents, selected pages from histories of the war that were brought back from the future—"

"Forgeries," Stefan said, counting on the man's paranoia to make the lie seem plausible. "Rather than show you the real documents from the future, they created forgeries to mislead you."

With luck, Churchill's promised bombardment of the institute would take place tomorrow, eradicating the gate, everyone who knew how to re-create the gate, and every scrap of material that had been brought back from the future. Then *der Führer* would never have the opportunity to conduct a thorough investigation to test Stefan's truthfulness.

Hitler sat in silence for perhaps a minute, staring at the Luger on his desk, thinking intently.

Overhead the bombing began to escalate once more, rattling the paintings on the walls and the pencils in the copper pot.

Stefan waited anxiously to discover if he would be believed.

"How have you come to me?" Hitler asked. "How could you use the gate now? I mean, it has been so closely guarded since the defection of Kokoschka and the other five."

"I didn't come to you by way of the gate," Stefan said. "I came to you straight from the future, using only the time-travel belt."

This was the boldest lie of all, for the belt was not a time machine, only a homing device that could do nothing but bring the wearer back to the institute. He was counting on the ignorance of politicians to save him: They knew a little bit about everything that was done under their rule, but there were no matters that they understood in depth. Hitler knew of the gate and of the nature of time travel, of course, but perhaps only in a general sense; he might lack knowledge of most of the details, such as how the belts actually functioned.

If Hitler realized that Stefan had come from the institute after returning there with Kokoschka's device, he would know that Kokoschka and the other five had been dispatched by Stefan and had not been defectors, after all, at which point the entire elaborate tale of conspiracy would collapse. And Stefan would be a dead man.

Frowning, the dictator said, "You used the belt without the gate? Is that possible?"

Dry-mouthed with fear but speaking with conviction, Stefan said, "Oh, yes, my *Führer,* it is quite simple to . . . adjust the belt and use it not merely to home in on the beacon of the gate but to skip through time as one wishes. And we are fortunate that such is the case, for otherwise, if I'd had to return to the gate to get here, I would have been stopped by the Jews who control it."

"Jews?" Hitler said, startled.

"Yes, sir. The conspiracy within the institute is organized, I believe, by staff members who have Jewish blood but have concealed their heritage."

The madman's face hardened further in a look of sudden anger. "Jews. Always the same problem. Everywhere, the same problem. Now in the institute as well."

Upon hearing that statement, Stefan knew that he had pushed the course of history back toward the proper path.

Destiny struggles to reassert the pattern that was meant to be.

·24·

Laura said, "Chris, I think you better hide under the car."

Even as she spoke, the gunman to the southwest of her rose from concealment and sprinted along the edge of the arroyo, angling toward her and toward the meager cover offered by another low dune.

She leaped to her feet, confident that the Buick would shelter her from the man at the Toyota, and opened fire. The first dozen rounds kicked up sand and chips of shale at the running man's heels, but then the bullets caught up with him, tearing into his legs. He went down, screaming, and was hit on the ground as well. He rolled twice and fell over the edge of the arroyo to the floor thirty feet below.

Even as the gunman slipped over that brink, Laura heard automatic fire, not from the Toyota but behind her. Before she could turn to meet the threat, she took several bullets in the back and was thrown forward, facedown on the hard shale.

·25·

"Jews," Hitler said again, angrily. Then: "What of this nuclear weapon that they say may win the war for us?"

"Another lie, my *Führer*. Though many attempts to develop such a weapon were made in the future, there were never any successes. This is a fantasy the conspirators have created to further misdirect the resources and energies of the Reich."

A rumbling came through the walls, as if they were not underground but suspended high in the heavens, in a thunderstorm.

The heavy frames of the paintings thumped against the concrete.

The pencils jiggled in the copper pot.

Hitler met Stefan's eyes and studied him for a long time. Then: "I suppose that if you were not loyal to me, you'd simply have come armed and would have killed me the instant you arrived."

He had considered doing just that, for only in killing Adolf Hitler might he expunge some of the stain on his own soul. But that would have been a selfish act, for by killing Hitler he would have radically changed the course of history and would have put the future as he knew it at extreme risk. He could not forget that his future was also Laura's past; if he meddled sufficiently to change the series of events that fate ordained, perhaps he would change the world for the worse in general and for Laura in particular. What if he killed Hitler here and, upon returning to 1989, found a world so drastically altered that for some reason Laura had never even been born?

He wanted to kill this snake in human skin, but he could not take the responsibility for the world that might follow. Common sense said that only a better world could result, but he knew that common sense and fate were mutually exclusive concepts.

"Yes," he said, "had I been a traitor, my *Führer,* I could've done just that. And I worry that the *real* traitors at the institute may sooner or later think of just such a method of assassination."

Hitler paled. "Tomorrow, I shut the institute down. The gate will be closed until I know the staff is purged of traitors."

Churchill's bombers may beat you to the punch, Stefan thought.

"We will win, Stefan, and we'll do so by retaining faith in our great destiny, not by playing fortune teller. We will win because it is our fate to win."

"It's our destiny," Stefan agreed. "We're on the side of truth."

Finally the madman smiled. Overcome by a sentimentality that was strange because of the extremely sudden change of mood, Hitler spoke of Stefan's father, Franz, and the early days in Munich: the secret meetings in Anton Drexler's apartment, the public meetings at the beer halls—the *Hofbräuhaus* and *Eberlbräu.*

Stefan listened for a while, pretending to be enthralled, but when Hitler expressed his continued and unshakable faith in the son of Franz Krieger, Stefan seized the opportunity to leave. "And I, my *Führer,* have undying faith in you and will be, forever, your loyal disciple." He stood, saluted the dictator, put one hand under his shirt to the button on the belt, and said, "Now I must return to the future, for I've more work to do in your behalf."

"Go?" Hitler said, rising from the desk chair. "But I thought you'd stay now in your own time? Why go there now that you've cleared your name with me?"

"I think I may know where the traitor Kokoschka has gone, in what corner of the future he's taken refuge. I've got to find him, bring him back, for perhaps only Kokoschka knows the names of the traitors at the institute and can be made to reveal them."

He saluted quickly, pushed the button on the belt, and left the bunker before Hitler could respond.

He returned to the institute on the night of March 16, the night that Kokoschka had set out for the San Bernardinos in pursuit of him, never to return. To the best of his ability, he had arranged for the destruction of the institute and had almost ensured Hitler's distrust of any information that came from it. He would have been exhilarated if he had not been so worried about the SS squad that apparently was stalking Laura in 1989.

At the programming board, he entered the computer-derived numbers for the last jaunt that he would ever make: to the desert outside of Palm Springs, where Laura and Chris waited for him on the morning of January 27, 1989.

·26·

Even as she fell to the ground, Laura knew that her spinal column had been severed or shattered by one of the bullets, for she felt no pain whatsoever—nor any sensation of any kind in any part of her body below the neck.

Destiny struggles to reassert the pattern that was meant to be.

The gunfire ceased.

She could move only her head, and only enough to turn and see Chris on his feet in front of the Buick, as paralyzed by terror as she was by the bullet that had cracked her spine. Beyond the boy, hurrying toward them from the north, only fifteen yards away, was a man in sunglasses, a white shirt, and black slacks, carrying a submachine gun.

"Chris," she said thickly, "run! *Run!*"

His face twisted with an expression of purest grief, as if he knew he was leaving her to die. Then he ran as fast as his small legs would carry him, east into the desert, and he was smart enough to weave back and forth as he ran, making as difficult a target of himself as possible.

Laura saw the killer raise the submachine gun.

In the main lab, Stefan opened the hinged panel that covered the automatic jaunt-recorder.

A spool of two-inch-wide paper indicated that tonight's uses of the gate had included a jaunt to January 10, 1988, which was the trip Heinrich Kokoschka had made to the San Bernardinos, when he had killed Danny Packard. The tape additionally recorded eight trips to the year A.D. 6,000,000,000—the five men and three bundles of lab animals. Also noted were Stefan's own jaunts: to March 20, 1944, with the latitudes and longitudes of the bombproof underground facility near St. James's Park in London; to March 21, 1944, with the precise latitudes and longitudes of Hitler's bunker; and the destination of the jaunt that he had just programmed but not yet made—Palm Springs, January 27, 1989. He tore the tape, pocketed the evidence, and respooled the blank paper. He'd already set the programming-board clocks to clear themselves and reset to zero when he passed through the gate. They would know someone had tampered with the records, but they would think it had been Kokoschka and the other defectors covering their trail.

He closed the panel and strapped on the backpack that was filled with Churchill's books. He slipped the strap of the Uzi over his shoulder and picked up the silencer-fitted pistol from the lab bench.

He quickly scanned the room to see if he had left anything behind that might betray his presence here tonight. The IBM printouts were folded away in the pockets of his jeans again. The Vexxon cylinder had long ago been sent into a future where the sun was dead or dying. As far as he could see, he had overlooked nothing.

He stepped into the gate and approached the point of transmission with more hope than he had dared entertain in many years. He had been able to assure the destruction of the institute and the defeat of Nazi Germany through a series of Machiavellian manipulations of time and people, so surely he and Laura would be able to deal with that single squad of SS gunmen who were somewhere in Palm Springs in 1989.

Lying paralyzed upon the desert shale, Laura screamed, "No!" The word came out as a whisper, for she didn't have the strength or lung power to make more of it.

The submachine gun opened fire on Chris, and for a moment she was sure that the boy was going to weave his way out of range, which was a last desperate fantasy, of course, because he was only a small boy, such a very small boy, with short legs, and he was well within range when the bullets found him, stitching a pattern across the center of his frail back, pitching him into the sand where he lay motionless in spreading blood.

All the unfelt pain of her ruined body would have been as a pinprick compared to the anguish that wrenched her at the sight of her little boy's lifeless body. Through all the tragedies of her life, she had known no pain to equal this. It was as if all the losses she had experienced—the mother she had never known, her sweet father, Nina Dockweiler, gentle Ruthie, and Danny, for whom she would gladly have sacrificed herself—were manifested again in this new brutality that fate insisted she endure, so she felt not only the shattering grief at Chris's death but felt anew the terrible agony of all the deaths that had come before it. She lay paralyzed and unfeeling but in torment, spiritually lacerated, at last emotionally broken on the hateful wheel of fate, no longer able to be brave, no longer able to hope or care. Her boy was dead. She had failed to save him, and with him all prospects of joy had died. She felt horribly alone in a cold and hostile universe, and all she hoped for now was death, emptiness, infinite nothingness, and at last an end to all loss and grief.

She saw the gunman approaching her.

She said, "Kill me, please kill me, finish me," but her voice was so faint that he probably did not hear her.

What had been the point of living? What had been the point of enduring all the tragedies that she had endured? Why had she suffered and gone on with life if it was all to end like this? What cruel consciousness lay behind the workings of the universe that it could even conceive of forcing her to struggle through a troubled life that turned out, in the end, to have no apparent meaning or purpose?

Christopher Robin was dead.

She felt hot tears spilling down her face, but that was all she could feel physically—that and the hardness of the shale against the right side of her face.

In a few steps the gunman reached her, stood over her, and kicked her in the side. She knew he kicked her, for she was looking back along her own immobile body and saw his foot land in her ribs, but she felt nothing whatsoever.

"Kill me," she murmured.

She was suddenly terrified that destiny would try too faithfully to reassert the pattern that was meant to be, in which case she might be permitted to live but only in the wheelchair that Stefan had saved her from when he had meddled with the ordained circumstances of her birth. Chris was the child who had never been a part of destiny's plans, and now he had been scrubbed from existence. But she might not be erased, for it had been *her* destiny to live as a cripple. Now she had a vision of her future: alive, paraplegic or quadriplegic, confined to a wheelchair, but trapped in something else far worse—trapped in a life of tragedy, of bitter memories, of endless sorrow, of unendurable longing for her son, her husband, her father, and all the others she had lost.

"Oh, God, please, please kill me."

Standing over her, the gunman smiled and said, "Well, I must be God's messenger." He laughed unpleasantly. "Anyway, I'm answering your prayer."

Lightning flashed and thunder crashed across the desert.

Thanks to the calculations performed on the computer, Stefan returned to the precise spot in the desert from which he had departed for 1944, exactly five minutes after he had left. The first thing he saw in the too-bright desert light was Laura's bloody body and the SS gunman standing over it. Then beyond them, he saw Chris.

The gunman reacted to the thunder and lightning. He began to turn in search of Stefan.

Stefan pushed the button on his homing belt three times. The air pressure instantly increased; the odor of hot electric wires and ozone filled the day.

The SS thug saw him, brought up the submachine gun, and opened fire, wide of him at first, then bringing the muzzle around to bear straight on him.

Before the bullets hit, Stefan popped out of 1989 and back to the institute on the night of March 16, 1944.

"Shit!" Klietmann said when Krieger slipped into the time stream and away, unhurt.

Bracher was running over from the Toyota, shouting, "That was him! That was him!"

"I know it was him," Klietmann said when Bracher arrived. "Who else would it be—Christ on His second coming?"

"What's he up to?" Bracher said. "What's he doing back there, where's he been, what's this all about?"

"I don't know," Klietmann said irritably. He looked down at the badly wounded woman and said to her, "All I know is that he saw you and your boy's dead body, and he didn't even make an attempt to kill me for what I'd done to you. He cut and ran to save his own skin. What do you think of your hero now?"

She only continued to beg for death.

Stepping back from the woman, Klietmann said, "Bracher, get out of the way."

Bracher moved, and Klietmann squeezed off a burst of perhaps ten or twenty rounds, all of which pierced the woman, killing her instantly.

"We could have questioned her," Corporal Bracher said. "About Krieger, about what he was doing here—"

"She was paralyzed," Klietmann said impatiently. "She could feel nothing. I kicked her in the side, must've broken half her ribs, and she didn't even cry out. You can't torture information from a woman who can feel no pain."

March 16, 1944. The institute.

His heart hammering like a blacksmith's sledge, Stefan jumped down from the gate and ran to the programming board. He pulled the list of computer-derived numbers from his pocket and spread it out on the small programmer's desk that filled a niche in the machinery.

He sat in the chair, picked up a pencil, pulled a tablet from the drawer. His hands shook so badly that he dropped the pencil twice.

He already had the numbers that would put him in that desert five minutes after he had first left it. He could work backward from those figures and find a new set that would put him in the same place four minutes and fifty-five seconds earlier, only five seconds after he had originally left Laura and Chris.

If he was gone only five seconds, the SS assassins would not yet have killed her and the boy by the time Stefan returned. He would be able to add his firepower to the fight, and perhaps that would be enough to change the outcome.

He had learned the necessary mathematics when first assigned to the institute in the autumn of 1943. He could do the calculations. The work was not impossible because he didn't have to begin from scratch; he had only to refine the computer's numbers, work backward a few minutes.

But he stared at the paper and could not *think* because Laura was dead and Chris was dead.

Without them he had nothing.

You can get them back, he told himself. Damn it, shape up. You can stop it before it happens.

He bent himself to the task, working for nearly an hour. He knew that no one was likely to come to the institute so late at night and discover him, but he repeatedly imagined that he heard footsteps in the ground-floor hall, the *click-click-click* of SS boots. Twice he looked toward the gate, half convinced he had heard the five dead men returning from A.D. 6,000,000,000, somehow revitalized and in search of him.

When he had the numbers and doubled-checked them, he entered them in the board. Carrying the submachine gun in one hand and the pistol in the other, he climbed into the gate and passed through the point of transmission—

—and returned to the institute.

He stood for a moment in the gate, surprised, confused. Then he stepped through the energy field again—

—and returned to the institute.

The explanation hit him with such force that he bent forward as if he actually had been punched in the stomach. He could *not* go back earlier now, for he had already showed up at that place five minutes after leaving it; if he went back now he would be creating a situation in which he would surely be there to see himself arrive the first time. Paradox! The mechanism of the cosmos would not permit a time traveler to encounter himself anywhere along the time stream; when such a jaunt was attempted, it invariably failed. Nature despised a paradox.

In memory he could hear Chris in the sleazy motel room where they had first discussed time travel: "Paradox! Isn't this wild stuff, Mom? Isn't this wild? Isn't this great?" And the charming, excited, boyish laughter.

But there had to be a way.

He returned to the programming board, dropped the guns on the work desk, and sat down.

Sweat was pouring off his brow. He blotted his face on his shirt-sleeves.

Think.

He stared at the Uzi and wondered if he could send *that* back to her at least. Probably not. He had been carrying the machine gun and the pistol when he had returned to her the first time, so if he sent either of the guns back four minutes and fifty seconds earlier, they would exist twice in the same place when he showed up just four minutes and fifty seconds later. Paradox.

But maybe he could send her something else, something that came from this room, something he had not been carrying with him and that would not, therefore, create a paradox.

He pushed the guns aside, picked up a pencil, and wrote a brief message on a sheet of tablet paper: THE SS WILL KILL YOU AND CHRIS IF YOU STAY AT THE CAR. GET AWAY. HIDE. He paused, thinking. Where could they hide on that flat desert plain? He wrote: MAYBE IN THE ARROYO. He tore the sheet of paper from the tablet. Then as an afterthought he hastily added: THE SECOND CANISTER OF VEXXON. IT'S A WEAPON TOO.

He searched the drawers of the lab bench for a glass beaker with a narrow top, but there were no such vessels in that lab, where all of the research had been related to electromagnetism rather than to chemistry. He went down the hall, searching through other labs, until he found what he needed.

Back in the main lab, carrying the beaker with the note inside it, he entered the gate and approached the point of transmission. He threw the object through the energy field as if he were a man stranded on an island, throwing a bottled message into the sea.

It did not bounce back to him.

—but the brief vacuum was followed by a blustery inrush of hot wind tainted by the faintly alkaline smell of the desert.

Standing close at her side, holding fast to her, delighted by Stefan's magical departure, Chris said, "Wow! Wasn't that something, Mom, wasn't that great?"

She did not answer because she noticed a white car driving off state route 111, onto the desert floor.

Lightning flared, thunder shook the day, startling her, and a glass bottle appeared in midair, fell at her feet, shattering on the shale, and she saw that there had been a paper inside.

Chris snatched the paper from among the shards of glass. With his usual aplomb in these matters, he said, "It must be from Stefan!"

She took it from him, read the words, aware that the white car had turned toward them. She did not understand how and why this message had been sent, but she believed it implicitly. Even as she finished reading, with the lightning and thunder still flickering and rumbling through the sky, she heard the engine of the white car roar.

She looked up and saw the vehicle leap toward them as its driver accelerated. They were almost three hundred yards away, but were closing as fast as the rough desert terrain permitted.

"Chris, get both Uzis from the car and meet me at the edge of the arroyo. Hurry!"

As the boy sprinted to the open door of the nearby Buick, Laura raced to the open trunk. She grabbed the canister of Vexxon, lifted it out, and caught up with Chris before he had reached the brink of the deep, naturally carved water channel, which was a raging river during a flash flood but dry now.

The white car was less than a hundred and fifty yards away.

"Come on," she said, leading him eastward along the brink, "we've got to find a way down into the arroyo."

The walls of the channel sloped slightly to the bottom thirty feet below, but only slightly. They were carved by erosion, filled with miniature vertical channels leading down to the main channel, some as narrow as a few inches, some as wide as three and four feet; during a rainstorm, water poured off the surface of the desert, down those gulleys to the floor of the arroyo, where it was carried away in great, surging torrents. In some of the downsloping drains the soil had washed away to reveal rocks here and there that would impede a swift descent, while others were partially blocked by hardy mesquite bushes that had taken root in the very wall of the arroyo.

Little more than a hundred yards away, the car strayed off the shale into sand that pulled at the tires and slowed it down.

When Laura had gone only twenty yards along the edge of the arroyo, she discovered a wide channel leading straight down to the floor of that dry river, unobstructed by rocks or mesquite. What lay before her was essentially a four-foot-wide, thirty-foot-long, water-smoothed, dirt slide.

She dropped the canister of Vexxon into that natural run, and it slipped down halfway before halting.

She took one of the Uzis from Chris, turned to the approaching car, which was now about seventy-five yards away, and opened fire. She saw bullets punch at least two holes in the windshield. The rest of the tempered glass instantly crazed.

The car—she could see now that it was a Toyota—spun out, turning a full three hundred and sixty degrees, then ninety degrees more, throwing up clouds of dust, tearing through a couple of still green tumbleweeds. It came to rest about forty yards from the Buick, sixty yards from her and Chris, the front end pointed north. Doors flew open on the far side. Laura knew the occupants were scrambling out of the car where she would not see them, staying low.

She took the other Uzi from Chris and said, "Into the slide, kiddo. When you reach the canister of gas, push it ahead of you all the way to the bottom."

He went down the wall of the arroyo, pulled most of the way by the force of gravity but having to scoot along a couple of times when friction stopped him. It was exactly the kind of daredevil stunt that would have raised a mother's ire under other circumstances, but now she cheered him on.

She pumped at least a hundred rounds into the Toyota, hoping to pierce the fuel tank and set off the gasoline with a bullet-made spark, roasting the bastards as they huddled against the far side. But she emptied the magazine without the desired result.

When she stopped shooting, they took a crack at her. She did not stay long enough to give them a target. With the second Uzi held before her in both hands, she sat on the edge of the arroyo and shoved off into the slide that Chris had already used. In seconds she was at the bottom.

Dry tumbleweeds had blown down to the floor of the gulch from the desert above. Gnarled driftwood, some time-grayed lumber washed from the distant ruins of an old desert shack, and a few stones littered the powder-soft soil that formed the bed of the arroyo.

None of those things offered a place to hide or protection from the gunfire that would soon be directed down at them.

"Mom?" Chris said, Meaning: What now?

The arroyo would have scores of tributaries spread out across the desert, and many of those tributaries would have tributaries of their own. The drainage network was like a maze. They could not hide in it forever, but perhaps by putting a few branches of the system between themselves and their pursuers, they would gain time to plan an ambush.

She said, "Run, baby. Follow the main arroyo, take the first right-hand branch you come to, and wait there for me."

"What're you going to do?"

"I'll wait for them to look over the edge up there," she said, pointing to the top of the palisades, "then pick them off if I can. Now go, *go*."

He ran.

Leaving the canister of Vexxon in plain sight, Laura returned to the wall of the arroyo down which they'd slid. She went to a different vertical channel, however, one that was carved deeper into the wall, had less of a slope, and was half-blocked at its midpoint by a mesquite bush. She stood in the bottom of that deep hollow, confident that the bush overhead blocked their view of her from the desert above.

To the east, Chris vanished around a turn into a tributary of the main channel.

A moment later she heard voices. She waited, waited, giving them time to feel confident that both she and Chris were gone. Then she stepped out from the erosion channel in the arroyo wall, turned, and swept the top of the cliff with bullets.

Four men were there, peering down, and she killed the first two, but the third and fourth leaped backward, out of sight before the arc of fire reached them. One of the bodies lay at the top of the arroyo wall, one arm and leg over the brink. The other fell all the way to the floor of the channel, losing his sunglasses on the way.

March 16, 1944. The institute.

When the bottle with the message did not bounce back to him, Stefan was reasonably confident that it had reached Laura before she had been killed, only seconds after he had first departed for 1944.

Now he returned to the programmer's desk and set to work on

the calculations that would return him to the desert a few minutes *after* his previous arrival there. He could make that trip because he would be arriving subsequent to his previous hasty departure, and there would be no possibility of encountering himself, no paradox.

Again the calculations were not terribly difficult because he needed only to work forward from the numbers that the IBM PC had provided him. Though he knew that the time he spent here was not passing in equal measure in the desert of 1989, he was eager to rejoin Laura nevertheless. Even if she had taken the advice of the message in the bottle, even if the future he had seen had been changed and she was still alive, she would have to deal with those SS gunmen, and she would need help.

In forty minutes he had the numbers that he required, and he reprogrammed the gate.

Again he opened the panel on the jaunt recorder and tore the evidence off that spool of paper.

Carrying the Uzi and the pistol, gritting his teeth as the dull throbbing in his half-healed shoulder grew worse, he entered the gate.

Lugging both the Vexxon canister and the Uzi, Laura joined Chris in the narrower tributary off the main channel, about sixty feet from the point at which they had descended into the system. Crouching at the corner formed by the two earth walls, she looked back into the primary arroyo from which she had come.

On the desert above, one of the surviving assassins shoved the dangling corpse off the brink, into the deep gulch, apparently to see if she was still immediately below them and if she would be tricked into opening fire. When there was no fire, the two survivors became bolder. One lay at the brink with a submachine gun, covering the other man while he slid down. Then the first gunman covered the second's descent.

When the second man joined the first, Laura stepped boldly around the corner and squeezed off a two-second burst. Both of her pursuers were so startled by her aggressiveness that they did not return fire but threw themselves toward the deep, vertical erosion channels in the arroyo wall, seeking shelter there as she had sheltered while waiting for the opportunity to shoot them off the top of the cliff. Only one of them made it to cover. She blew the other one away.

She stepped back around the corner, picked up the cylinder of nerve gas, and said to Chris, "Come on. Let's hustle."

As they ran along the tributary, seeking yet another branch in the maze, lightning and thunder split the blue sky above.

"Mr. Krieger!" Chris said.

He returned to the desert seven minutes after he had originally departed for his meetings with Churchill and Hitler in 1944, just *two* minutes after his initial return when he had seen Laura and Chris dead at the hands of SS gunmen. There were no bodies this time, just the Buick—and the bullet-riddled Toyota in a different position.

Daring to hope that his scheme had worked, Stefan hurried to the arroyo and ran along the brink, searching for someone, anyone, friend or foe. Before long he saw the three dead men on the floor of the channel, thirty feet below.

There would be a fourth. No SS squad would have been composed of only three men. Somewhere in the network of zigzagging arroyos that crossed the desert like a chain of jagged lightning bolts, Laura was still on the run from the last man.

In the arroyo wall Stefan found a vertical channel that appeared to have been used already; he stripped off his book-filled rucksack, slid to the bottom. On the way down, his back scraped against the earth, and hot pain flared in the partly healed exit wound. At the end of the slope, when he stood up, a wave of dizziness washed through him, and bile rose in his throat.

Somewhere in the maze to the east, automatic weapons chattered.

She halted just inside the mouth of a new tributary and signaled Chris to be quiet.

Breathing through her open mouth, she waited for the last killer to turn the corner into the channel that she had just left. Even in the soft soil, his running footsteps were audible.

She leaned out to gun him down. But he was extremely cautious now; he entered low and at a dead run. When her gunfire alerted him to her position, he crossed the channel and hid against the same wall off which her new tributary opened, so she could get a clear shot at him only if she stepped out into the arroyo where he waited.

In fact she tried that, risking his fire, but when she squeezed off a two-second burst, it ended in less than a second. The Uzi spat out its last ten or twelve rounds, then failed her.

Klietmann heard her Uzi go empty. He looked out from the crevice in the arroyo wall where he was sheltering and saw her throw the gun down. She disappeared into the mouth of the tributary where she had been laying for him.

He considered what he had seen in the Buick, up on the desert: a .38 revolver lying on the driver's seat. He assumed that she had not had time to grab it or, in her haste to get that curious canister from the trunk, had forgotten about the handgun.

She'd had two Uzis, both discarded now. Could she have had two handguns—and left only one in the car?

He thought not. Two automatic carbines made sense because they were useful at a distance and in a variety of circumstances. But unless she was an expert marksman, a handgun would be of little use except at close range, where six shots was about all she would need before she either dealt with her assailant or died at his hands. A second revolver would be superfluous.

Which meant that for self-defense she had—what? That canister? It had looked like nothing more than a chemical fire extinguisher.

He went after her.

The new tributary was narrower than the one before it, just as that one had been narrower than the main channel. It was twenty-five feet deep and only ten feet wide at the mouth, growing shallower and half that narrow as it cut a crooked path through the desert floor. In a hundred yards, it funneled to an end.

At the terminus, she looked for a way out. On two sides the cliffs were too steep, soft, and crumbly to be easily climbed, but the wall behind her sloped at a scalable angle and was studded with mesquite that offered handholds. She knew, however, that they would be only halfway up the slope when their pursuer found them; suspended on that high ground, they would make easy targets.

This was where she would have to make her last stand.

Cornered at the bottom of this big, natural ditch, she looked up at the rectangular patch of blue sky and thought they might have been at the bottom of an enormous grave in a cemetery where only giants were buried.

Destiny struggles to reassert the pattern that was meant to be.

She pushed Chris behind her, into the point of the dead-end arroyo.

Ahead of her, she could see forty feet back the way they had come, along the five-foot-wide channel, to the point where it angled to the left. He would appear at that turn within a minute or two.

She dropped to her knees with the canister of Vexxon, intending to strip the safety wire off the manual trigger. But the wire was not merely looped and braided through the trigger; it was repeatedly wound and then sealed with solder. It could not be unwound; it had to be cut, and she had nothing with which to cut it.

Maybe a stone. A sharp-edged stone might wear through the wire if scraped across it often enough.

"Get me a stone," she said urgently to the boy behind her. "One with a rough, sharp edge."

As he searched the soft, flood-carried soil that had washed down from the desert floor, looking for a suitable scrap of slate, she examined the automatic timer on the canister, which provided a second means of releasing the gas. It was a simple device: a rotating dial was calibrated in minutes; if you wanted to set the timer for twenty minutes, you twisted the dial until the 20 was lined up with the red mark on the dial frame; when you pushed the button in the center, the countdown began.

The problem was that the dial could be set for no fewer than five minutes. The gunman would reach them sooner than that.

Nevertheless she twisted the dial to 5 and pushed the button that started it ticking.

"Here, Mom," Chris said, presenting her with a blade of slate that just might do the job.

Though the timer was ticking, she set to work, frantically sawing at the strong, twined wire that prevented manual release. Every few seconds she looked up to see if the assassin had found them, but the narrow arroyo ahead of them remained deserted.

Stefan followed the footprints in the soft soil that formed the bed of the arroyo. He had no idea how far behind them he might be. They had only a few minutes' head start, but they were probably moving faster than he was because the pain in his shoulder, exhaustion, and dizziness slowed him.

He had unscrewed the silencer from the pistol, thrown it away, and tucked the handgun under his belt. He carried the Uzi in both hands, at the ready.

Klietmann had thrown away his Ray-Bans because the floor of the arroyo network was shadow-swaddled in many places, especially as they moved into narrower tributaries, where the walls closed in and left less of an opening above for sunlight to enter.

His Bally loafers filled with sand and provided no surer footing here than on the slate of the desert above. Finally he paused, kicked off the shoes, stripped off the socks, and proceeded barefoot, which was a great improvement.

He was not tracking the woman and the boy as swiftly as he would have liked, partly because of the shoes that he had discarded, but mainly because he kept a watch on his backside every step of the way. He had heard and seen the recent display of thunder and lightning; he knew Krieger must have returned. Most likely, as Klietmann stalked the woman and boy, Krieger was stalking him. He did not intend to be meat for *that* tiger.

On the timer two minutes had ticked off.

Laura had sawed almost as long at the wire, initially with the blade of slate that Chris had found, then with a second that he turned up when the first piece crumbled in her fingers. The government could not make a postage stamp that could be trusted to stay on an envelope, could not build a battle tank that was capable of crossing a river on every attempt, could not protect the environment or eliminate poverty, but it sure as hell knew how to procure indestructible wire; this stuff must be some wonder material which they had developed for the space shuttle and for which they'd eventually found more mundane uses; it was the wire God would use to guy the tilting pillars that held up the world.

Her fingers were raw, the second chip of slate was slick with her blood, and only half the strands of wire were cut when the barefoot man in black slacks and a white shirt rounded the bend in the narrow arroyo, forty feet away.

Klietmann edged forward warily, wondering why the hell she was struggling so frantically with the fire extinguisher. Did she really think a blast of chemical fog would disorient him and protect her from submachine-gun fire?

Or was the extinguisher not what it appeared to be? Since arriving in Palm Springs less than two hours ago, he had encountered several things that were not what they appeared to be. A red curb, for instance, did not mean EMERGENCY PARKING, as he had thought, but NO PARKING AT ANY TIME. Who could know? And who could know for sure about this canister with which she was struggling?

She looked up at him, then went right back to work on the handle of the extinguisher.

Klietmann edged along the narrow arroyo, which was now not even wide enough for two men to walk abreast. He would not have gone any closer to her except that he could not see the boy. If she had tucked the boy in some crevice along the way, he would have to force her to reveal the child's whereabouts, for his orders were to kill them all—Krieger and the woman and the boy. He did not think the boy could be a danger to the Reich, but he was not one to question orders.

Stefan found a discarded pair of shoes and a tangled pair of black socks caked with sand. Earlier he had found a pair of sunglasses.

He had never before pursued a man who had undressed during a chase, and at first there seemed to be something funny about it. But then he thought of the world portrayed in the novels of Laura Shane, a world in which comedy and terror were intermingled, a world in which tragedy frequently struck in the middle of a laugh, and suddenly the discarded shoes and socks scared him *because* they were funny; he had the crazy idea that if he laughed, that would be the catalyst of Laura and Chris's deaths.

And if they died this time, he would not be able to save them by going back in time and sending them another message sooner than the one he had sent in the bottle, for the remaining window for such a feat was only five seconds. Even with an IBM PC, he could not split a hair that fine.

In the silt, the prints of the barefoot man led away to the mouth of a tributary. Although the pain in Stefan's half-healed shoulder had wrung sweat from him and left him dizzy, he followed that trail as Robinson Crusoe had followed Friday but with more dread.

With growing despair Laura watched the Nazi assassin approach through the shadows along the earthen corridor. His Uzi was trained on her, but for some reason he did not immediately blow her away. She used that inexplicable period of grace to saw relentlessly at the safety wires on the trigger of the Vexxon canister.

Even in those circumstances she held on to hope, largely because of a line from one of her own novels that had come back to her just a moment ago: *In tragedy and despair, when an endless night seems to have fallen, hope can be found in the realization that the companion of night is not another night, that the companion of night is day, that darkness always gives way to light, and that death rules only half of creation, life the other half.*

Only twenty feet away now, the killer said, "Where is the boy? The boy. Where is the boy?"

She felt Chris against her back, curled in the shadows between her and the wall of the cul-de-sac. She wondered if her body would protect him from the bullets and that if, after killing her, this man would leave without realizing that Chris lived in the dark niche at her back.

The timer on the cylinder clicked. Nerve gas erupted from the nozzle with the rich odor of apricots and the disgusting taste of lemon juice mixed with sour milk.

Klietmann could see nothing escaping the canister, but he could hear it: like a hissing score of serpents.

An instant later he felt as if someone had shoved a hand through his midsection, had seized his stomach in a viselike grip, and had torn that organ loose of him. He doubled over, vomiting explosively on the ground and on his bare feet. With a painful flash that seared the *backs* of his eyes, something seemed to burst in his sinuses, and blood gushed from his nose. As he fell to the floor of the arroyo, he reflexively triggered the Uzi; aware that he was dying and losing all control of himself in the process, he tried as a last effort of will to fall on his side, facing the woman, so the final burst from the submachine gun would take her with him.

Soon after Stefan entered the narrowest of all the tributaries, where the walls seemed to tilt in above him instead of sloping away toward the sky, as they had in the other channels, he heard a long rattle of submachine-gun fire, very near, and he hurried forward. He stumbled a lot and bounced off the earthen walls, but he followed the crooked corridor into the cul-de-sac, where he saw the SS officer dead of Vexxon poisoning.

Beyond that corpse, Laura sat splay-legged, with the canister of nerve gas between her thighs, her bloodied hands hooked around it. Her head hung down, her chin on her breast; she looked as limp and lifeless as a doll made of rags.

"Laura, no," he said in a voice that he hardly recognized as his own. "No, no."

She raised her head and blinked at him, shuddered, and finally smiled weakly. Alive.

"Chris," he said, stepping over the dead man. "Where's Chris?"

She pushed the still hissing canister of nerve gas away from her and moved to one side.

Chris looked out from the dark niche behind her and said, "Mr. Krieger, are you all right? You look like shit. Sorry, Mom, but he really does."

For the first time in more than twenty years—or for the first time in more than *sixty-five* years if you wanted to count those over which he had jumped when he had come to live with Laura in her time—Stefan Krieger wept. He was surprised by his own tears, for he thought that his life under the Third Reich had left him incapable of weeping for anyone or anything ever again. More surprising still—these first tears in decades were tears of joy.

Seven

EVER AFTER

·1·

More than an hour later, when the police moved north from the site of the machine-gun attack on the CHP patrolman along route 111, when they found the bullet-riddled Toyota and saw blood on the sand and shale near the brink of the arroyo, when they saw the discarded Uzi, and when they saw Laura and Chris struggling out of the channel near the Buick with the Nissan plates, they expected to find the immediate area littered with bodies, and they were not disappointed. The first three were at the bottom of the nearby gulch, and the fourth was in a distant tributary to which the exhausted woman directed them.

In the days that followed she appeared to cooperate fully with local, state, and federal authorities—yet none of them was satisfied that she was telling the whole truth. The drug dealers who had killed her husband a year ago had finally sent hired killers after her, she said, for they had evidently been afraid that she would identify them. They had attacked with such force at her house near Big Bear and had been so relentless that she'd had to run, and she'd not gone to the police because she did not believe that the authorities could protect her and her son adequately. She had been on the move for seventeen days, ever since that submachine-gun assault on the night of January 10, the first anniversary of her husband's murder; in spite of every precaution she had taken, hitmen found her in Palm Springs, pursued her on route 111, forced her off the highway into the desert, and chased her on foot into the arroyos where she finally got the best of them.

That story—one woman wiping out four experienced hitmen, plus at least the one additional whose head had been found in the alley behind Brenkshaw's house—would have been unbelievable if she had not proved to be a superb marksman, the beneficiary of considerable martial-arts training, and the owner of an illegal arsenal the envy of some third-world countries. During interrogation to determine how she had obtained illegally modified Uzis and a nerve gas kept under lock and key by the army, she had said, "I write novels. It's part of my job to do a lot of research. I've learned how to find out anything I want to know, how to obtain anything I need." Then she gave them Fat Jack, and the raid on his Pizza Party Palace turned up everything she had said it would.

"I don't hold it against her," Fat Jack told the press at his arraignment. "She owes me nothing. None of us owes anybody nothing that we don't *want* to owe them. I'm an anarchist, I love broads like her. Besides, I won't go to prison. I'm too fat, I'd die, it'd be cruel and unusual punishment."

She would not tell them the name of the man she had brought to Carter Brenkshaw's house in the early morning hours of January 11, the man whose bullet wounds the physician had treated. She would only say that he was a good friend who had been staying with her at the house near Big Bear when the hitmen had struck. He was, she insisted, an innocent bystander whose life would be wrecked if she involved him in this sordid affair, and she implied that he was a married man with whom she had been having an affair. He was recovering from the bullet wound quite well, and he had suffered enough.

The authorities pressed her hard on the issue of this nameless lover, but she would not budge, and they were limited in the pressures that they could apply to her, especially since she could afford the finest legal counsel in the country. They never believed the claim that the mystery man was her lover. Little investigation was required to learn that her husband, only one year deceased, had been unusually close to her and that she had not recovered from the loss of him sufficiently to convince anyone that she was able to conduct an affair in the shadow of Danny Packard's memory.

No, she could not explain why none of the dead hitmen carried identification or why they were all dressed identically, or why they had been without their own car and had been forced to steal one from two women at a church, or why they had panicked in downtown Palm Springs and killed a policeman there. The abdominal flesh on two of the bodies had borne the marks of what appeared to be tightly fitted trusses of some kind, yet neither had been wearing such a device, and she knew nothing of that, either. Who knew, she asked, what reasons men like that had for their antisocial actions? That was a mystery that the finest criminologists and sociologists could not adequately explain. And if all those experts could not begin to shed light on the deepest and truest reasons for such sociopathic behavior, how could she be expected to provide an answer to the more mundane but also more bizarre mystery of the disappearing trusses? Confronted by the woman whose Toyota had been stolen and who claimed that the hitmen had been angels, Laura Shane listened with evident interest, even fascination, but subsequently inquired of the police if they were going to subject her to the cuckoo fantasies of every nut who took an interest in her case.

She was granite.

She was iron.

She was steel.

She could not be broken. The authorities hammered at her as relentlessly and with as much force as the god Thor had wielded his hammer Mjollnir but with no effect. After several days they were angry with her. After several weeks they were furious. After three months they loathed her and wanted to punish her for not shivering in awe of their power. In six months they were weary. In ten months they were bored. In a year they forced themselves to forget her.

In the meantime, of course, they had seen her son, Chris, as the weak link. They had not pounded at him as they had at her, choosing instead to use false affection, guile, trickery, and deceit to lure the boy into making the revelations that his mother refused to make. But when they questioned him about the missing, wounded man, he told them all about Indiana Jones and Luke Skywalker and Han Solo instead. When they tried to pry from him a few details about the events in the arroyos, he told them all about Sir Tommy Toad, servant of the queen, who rented quarters in his house. When they sought to elicit at least a hint of where his mother and he had hidden out—and what they had done—in the sixteen days between January 10 and 27, the boy said, "I slept through it all, I was in a coma, I think I had malaria or maybe even Mars fever, see, and now I got amnesia like Wily Coyote got that one time when the Road Runner tricked him into dropping a boulder on his own head." Eventually, frustrated with their inability to get the point, he said,

"This is *family* stuff, see. Don't you know about family stuff? I can only talk with my mom about this stuff, and it's nobody else's business. If you start talking family stuff with strangers, pretty soon where do you go when you want to go home?"

To complicate matters for the authorities, Laura Shane publicly apologized to everyone whose property she had appropriated or damaged during the course of her attempts to escape from the hired killers who had been sent after her. To the family whose Buick she had stolen, she gave a new Cadillac. To the man whose Nissan plates she had taken, she gave a new *Nissan*. In every case she made restitution to excess and won friends at every hand.

Her old books went back to press repeatedly, and some of them reappeared on paperback bestseller lists now, years after their original successes. Major film studios bid competitively for the few movie rights to her books that had remained unsold. Rumors, perhaps encouraged by her own agent but very likely true, circulated to the effect that publishers were standing six deep for a chance to pay her a record advance for her next novel.

·2·

During that year Stefan Krieger missed Laura and Chris terribly, but life at the Gaines's mansion in Beverly Hills was not a hardship. The accommodations were superb; the food was delicious; Jason enjoyed teaching him how film could be manipulated in his home editing studio; and Thelma was unfailingly amusing.

"Listen, Krieger," she said one summer day by the pool. "Maybe you would rather be with them, maybe you're getting tired of hiding here, but consider the alternative. You could be stuck back there in your own age, when there weren't plastic garbage bags, Pop Tarts, Day-Glo underwear, Thelma Ackerson movies, or reruns of *Gilligan's Island*. Count your blessings, that you should find yourself in this enlightened era."

"It's just that . . ." He stared for a while at the spangles of sunlight on the chlorine-scented water. "Well, I'm afraid that during this year of separation, I'm losing any slim chance I might have had to win her."

"You can't win her, anyway, *Herr* Krieger. She's not a set of cereal containers raffled off at a Tupperware party. A woman like Laura can't be won. She decides when she wants to *give* herself, and that's that."

"You're not very encouraging."

"Being encouraging is not my job—"

"I know—"

"—my job—"

"—yes, yes—"

"—is comedy. Although with my devastating looks, I'd probably be just as successful as a traveling slut—at least in really remote logging camps."

At Christmas Laura and Chris came to stay at the Gaines's house, and her gift to Stefan was a new identity. Although rather closely monitored by various authorities for the better part of the year, she had managed through surrogates to obtain a driver's license, social security card, credit cards, and a passport in the name of Steven Krieger.

She presented them to him on Christmas morning, wrapped in a box from Neiman-Marcus. "All the documents are valid. In *Endless River,* two of my characters are on the run, in need of new identities—"

"Yes," Stefan said, "I read it. Three times."

"The same book three times?" Jason said. They were all sitting around the Christmas tree, eating junk food and drinking cocoa, and Jason was in his cheeriest mood of the year. "Laura, beware this man. He sounds like an obsessive-compulsive to me."

"Well, of course," Thelma said, "to you Hollywood types, anyone who reads *any* book, even once, is viewed either as an intellectual giant or a psychopath. Now, Laura, how *did* you come up with all these convincing-looking, phony papers?"

"They're not phony," Chris said. "They're *real.*"

"That's right," Laura said. "The driver's license and everything else is supported by government files. In researching *Endless River,* I had to find out how you go about obtaining a new identity of high quality, and I found this interesting man in San Francisco who runs a veritable document industry from the basement beneath a topless nightclub—"

"It doesn't have a roof?" Chris asked.

Laura ruffled the boy's hair and said, "Anyway, Stefan, if you look deeper into that box, you'll find a couple of bank books as well. I've opened accounts for you under your new identity at Security Pacific Bank and Great Western Savings."

He was startled. "I can't take money from you. I can't—"

"You save me from a wheelchair, repeatedly save my life, and I can't give you money if I feel like it? Thelma, what's wrong with him?"

"He's a man," Thelma said.

"I guess that explains it."

"Hairy, Neanderthalic," Thelma said, "perpetually half-crazed from excessive levels of testosterone, plagued by racial memories of the lost glory of mammoth-hunting expeditions—they're all alike."

"Men," Laura said.

"Men," Thelma said.

To his surprise and almost against his will, Stefan Krieger felt some of the darkness fading from within him, and light began to find a pane through which to shine into his heart.

In late February of the next year, thirteen months after the events in the desert outside Palm Springs, Laura suggested that he come to stay with her and Chris at the house near Big Bear. He went the next day, driving there in the sleek new Russian sports car that he had bought with some of the money she had given him.

For the next seven months he slept in the guest room. Every night. He needed nothing more. Just being with them, day after day, being accepted by them, being included, was all the love he could handle for a while.

In mid-September, twenty months after he had appeared on her doorstep with a bullet hole in his chest, she asked him into her bed. Three nights later he found the courage to go.

·3·

The year that Chris was twelve, Jason and Thelma bought a getaway house in Monterey, overlooking the most beautiful coastline in the world, and they insisted that Laura, Stefan, and Chris visit them for the month of August, when they were both between film projects. The mornings on the Monterey peninsula were cool and foggy, the days warm and clear, the nights downright chilly in spite of the season, and that daily pattern of weather was invigorating.

On the second Friday of the month, Stefan and Chris went for a beach walk with Jason. On the rocks not far from shore, sea lions were sunning themselves and barking noisily. Tourists were parked bumper to bumper along the road that served the beach; they ventured onto the sand to take photographs of the sun-worshiping "seals," as they called them.

"Year by year," Jason said, "there're more foreign tourists. It's a regular invasion. And you notice—they're mostly either Japanese, Germans, or Russians. Less than half a century ago, we fought the greatest war in history against all three of them, and now they're all more prosperous than we are. Japanese electronics and cars, Russian cars and computers, German cars and quality machinery of all kinds. . . . Honest to God, Stefan, I think Americans frequently treat old enemies better than they do old friends."

Stefan paused to watch the sea lions that had drawn the interest of the tourists, and he thought of the mistake that he had made in his meeting with Winston Churchill.

But tell me at least one thing. Curiosity's killing me. Let's see . . . well, for instance, what of the Soviets after the war?

The old fox had spoken so casually, as if the question was one that had occurred to him by chance, as if he might as likely have asked whether the cut of men's suits would change in the future, when in fact his query had been calculated and the answer of intense interest to him. Operating on what Stefan had told him, Churchill had rallied the Western Allies to continue fighting in Europe after the Germans were defeated. Using the Soviets' land grab of Eastern Europe as an excuse to turn against them, the other Allies had fought the Russians, driving them back into their motherland and ultimately defeating them entirely; in fact, throughout the war with Germany, the Soviets had been propped up with weapons and supplies from the United States, and when that support was withdrawn they collapsed in a matter of months. After all, they had been exhausted after the war with their old ally, Hitler. Now the modern world was far different from what destiny had intended, and all because Stefan had answered Churchill's one question.

Unlike Jason or Thelma or Laura or Chris, Stefan was a man out of time, a man for whom this era was not his destined home; the years since the Great Wars were his future, while those same years were in these people's past; therefore he recalled both the future that had once been and the future that had now come to pass in place of the old. They, however, could remember no different world but this one in which no great world powers were hostile toward one another, in which no huge nuclear arsenals awaited launch, in which democracy flourished even in Russia, in which there were plenty and peace.

Destiny struggles to reassert the pattern that was meant to be. But sometimes, happily, it fails.

Laura and Thelma remained in rocking chairs on the porch, watching their menfolk walk down to the sea and then north along the beach, out of sight.

"Are you happy with him, Shane?"

"He's a melancholy man."

"But lovely."

"He'll never be Danny."

"But Danny is gone."

Laura nodded. They rocked.

"He says I redeemed him," Laura said.

"Like grocery coupons, you mean?"

Finally Laura said, "I love him."

"I know," Thelma said.

"I never thought I would . . . again. I mean, love a man that way."

"What way is that, Shane? Are you talking about some kinky new position? You're heading toward middle age, Shane; you'll be forty before too many moons, so isn't it time you reformed your libidinous ways?"

"You're incorrigible."

"I try to be."

"How about you, Thelma? Are you happy?"

Thelma patted her large belly. She was seven months pregnant. "Very happy, Shane. Did I tell you—maybe twins?"

"You told me."

"Twins," Thelma said, as if the prospect awed her. "Think how pleased Ruthie would be for me."

Twins.

Destiny struggles to reassert the pattern that was meant to be, Laura thought. And sometimes, happily, it succeeds.

They sat for a while in companionable silence, breathing the healthful sea air, listening to the wind sough softly in the Monterey pines and cypress.

After a while Thelma said, "Remember that day I came to your house in the mountains, and you were taking target practice in the backyard?"

"I remember."

"Blasting away at those human silhouettes. Snarling, daring the world to tackle you, guns hidden everywhere. That day you told me you'd spent your life enduring what fate threw at you, but you were not just going to endure any more—you were going to fight to protect your own. You were very angry that day, Shane, and very bitter."

"Yes."

"Now, I know you're still an endurer. And I know you're still a fighter. The world is still full of death and tragedy. In spite of all that, somehow you just aren't bitter any more."

"No."

"Share the secret?"

"I've learned the third great lesson, that's all. As a kid I learned to endure. After Danny was killed, I learned to fight. Now I'm still an endurer and a fighter—but I've also learned to accept. Fate *is*."

"Sounds very Eastern-mystic-transcendental-bullshit, Shane. Jeez. 'Fate *is*.' Next you'll be telling me to chant a mantra and contemplate my navel."

"Stuffed with twins, as you are," Laura said, "you can't even see your navel."

"Oh, yes, I can—with just the right arrangement of mirrors."

Laura laughed. "I love you, Thelma."

"I love you, Sis."

They rocked and rocked.

Down on the shore, the tide was coming in.